MEMORIES, LIES, AND OTHER BINDS

KATY FORAKER

PRELUDE

Elizabeth Abbott was named for the Queen. A bit ambitious of her parents in retrospect. They could never have thought she would end up working as a maid at the secretive research institute for the elite —RIDER.

ONE

Gloucestershire, England, 1781
The Longford Correctional House

Bess breathed heavily as she brought one heavy trunk after another into the dank building that reeked of close confinement, a vile mix of copper and decay—a prison. Even with the sweat beading across her forehead, her dark brunette hair remained piled up underneath her white maid's bonnet. Anne, the other assisting maid who rushed in behind her, was not so lucky, with several mouse-brown curls fallen loose. Though Mr. Sims never seemed to care about those things.

At the last load, Bess's excited blue eyes swept the haul, counting with a finger to make sure it was all there.

"Did you bring everything in?" Mr. Sims asked, hurrying in. He had to yell over the thundering crescendo of screams, shouts, and threats that reverberated off the stone walls.

He was a tall, lean man with dirty blonde hair, and permanently flushed cheeks with a prominent, hook shaped nose crammed in between. Removing his gloves, he counted the trunks himself, even though Bess had confirmed with an obedient nod.

Mr. Sims dismissed the prison's night guards, something the warden allowed after Mr. Sims explained that the revolutionary inmate reform technique he was there to implement was sensitive to interruption. With no reason to question a notable philanthropist and member of London's elite RIDER institution, the warden tipped his hat, bidding him good night as he left.

"Unload the trunks!" Mr. Sims shouted with the wave of his hand. Bess and Anne quickly got to work. "Use the salt to create two circles here and here. Place the contents of the sacks in each circle."

The two women moved around, obeying his instructions but exchanging questioning glances as they unpacked the trunks to reveal their unconventional contents. Chicken feet, old stone runes, and what looked to be a variety of crushed herbs and bottled liquids were all intricately placed according to Mr. Sim's orders.

He then directed both women to kneel inside each circle. Grabbing rope from one of the nearby trunks, he tied their hands behind their backs.

Bess's eyes went wide, uncertain. But ultimately she allowed Mr. Sims to finish tying the knot. RIDER had treated her well during the six months she had worked there, and it was considered an honor for a member of the service staff to be chosen to assist with a research expedition. Why should now be any different?

"What are you doing?" Anne asked, alarmed as Mr. Sims wove the rope around her wrists.

Anne was a sturdy woman known for her red-hot temper that would leave any offender walking around RIDER's London residence with a black eye for days afterward.

"Don't worry; this is just for your protection. I'll remove them once we're finished," Mr. Sims assured, tightening the restraints. He then stood and smiled, appearing deaf to the surrounding noise. "I think we're finally ready to begin."

Out of one trunk, he pulled out a text and a lavender crystal.

Holding it out in front of him with one hand, he read aloud from the pages which were written in Latin, although his pronunciation was terrible. The words spewed from his mouth in short bursts of slurred grunts.

A gust of wind blasted through, blowing out the candles and lanterns that illuminated the area. Electricity and static sizzled through the air.

Bess's hair lifted, and she gasped, looking around the darkened space, waiting for her sight to adjust.

Something was wrong.

As he continued to speak, Mr. Sim's voice bled out of earshot, becoming a mild, garbled hum.

"Go back. I can't hear what he's saying," Dr. Kelley said to me, pulling me out of the memory with so much force it nearly made me sick.

My memory of the Longford Correctional House dissolved in an instant, and I was once again sitting on the gray tweed couch in Dr. Kelley's office. Everything was just as it was before—the matching gray chair in front of me and the glass coffee table to my side. The familiar large bookcase filled to the brim with large leather-bound texts, no doubt containing an ancient prophecy or two, spanned the opposite wall. Having spent over a century at RIDER's New York City office, I had been in this same room dozens—hundreds of times with its previous owners. Yet, it was only until its current owner took residence that it felt foreign. Uncomfortable.

Sitting behind the office desk was my therapist, Dr. Jack Kelley, writing furiously in the thick journal before him. "I really need you to focus. I know the memory is old, but I can feel you resisting me," he said without looking up.

It was literally my job to study all things strange and terrifying at RIDER—the Research Institute of Demonic Entities and Rarities (because we all love a good acronym here), to keep the human world safe and naïve of the supernatural's existence. But my sessions with Dr. Kelley were far worse than anything I'd encountered.

I despised them.

"I'm trying," I insisted, wiping the sweat off my forehead.

"I think we both know you can try a little harder." Finishing his thought in his journal, he closed it with a dull thud and then checked his mobile before shoving it into the front pocket of his dark trousers.

Dr. Kelley had come to RIDER six months ago with the primary responsibility of leading me in hypnotherapy sessions so that I could remember what happened. How I came to be me. Well, immortal me.

No one was sure how or why I stopped aging at twenty-two years old—or if one day the effect would wear off and I'd just crumble into a pile of dust and old bones on the floor.

I just wanted to know if there were others out there with a similar condition. In my long tenure, I'd never come across anyone, or any "thing" for that matter, quite like me.

"Alright Zoey, are you ready to try again?" he asked. Sliding back into the chair across from me, he ran a hand through his dark hair, salt and peppered at the sides, then gave his left arm a good shake to settle the large watch on his wrist back into place.

I hated how he called me by my first name. It wasn't my given name, but it unnerved me just the same. He said it so easily, like we were friends or close colleagues—which we were definitely not. But instead of correcting him, I bit the bottom of my lip and smoothed out the front of my skirt.

"Come on. No need to be shy. You're safe here. Remember, nothing can hurt you during our time together. We aren't even leaving this room. And our sessions are working, aren't they?" he pressed, holding out both of his hands, palms facing up.

Every fiber of my mind screamed to not take those hands as I stared at the fleshy pads, folds, and lines that decorated his inviting palms. It was true, we *were* making progress in finding out exactly what happened. But I still wasn't sure if the side effects were worth it.

Shaking the negative thoughts from my mind, I straightened and raised my hands above his. Maybe this time would be different.

Then, just like stepping off the edge of a cliff, I took a deep breath, lowered my hands, and looked up into his eyes.

Here goes nothing.

Dr. Kelley's eyes were unlike any human's I'd ever seen. Dark gray with an orange sunflower detail around the pupil. A chill always rippled down my spine whenever I looked at them.

The tendrils of orange in his eyes moved, flickering like flames licking the air. I closed my eyes and my consciousness lifted. It was a euphoric, floating sensation. As if my mind were being massaged and I was floating on the lightest cloud without a care in the world. This part I liked, and I let out an audible sigh, feeling content.

When I opened my eyes, Dr. Kelley's office was gone and we were standing in a large, cavernous library. Wooden shelves full of books sat neatly in their rows, lining walls that stretched skyward toward a nonexistent ceiling. Our feet were planted on a thick, dark red carpet that squished comfortably beneath my heels. Behind us, a familiar welcoming pathway cut through the center of the shelving. Bridging the top were large, squat arches engraved with flowers, vines, and flourishes.

Dr. Kelley was Gifted. He could Memory Walk, or enter the minds of others. Not just human minds either, as I'd learned from the overstuffed folders of his dossier and RIDER gossip.

"Come now, let's head to the back. We haven't got much time," Dr. Kelley said.

"Of course."

I spun around on my heel so he couldn't see the forlorn look on my face. Then, trudging forward for the second time in one session, we made our way through the arched path, deeper into the stacks.

Everyone's Mind Warehouse was different. Some were childhood bedrooms. Others were forests, and some were an actual warehouse or a series of storage units. They all served the same purpose: a place to store one's knowledge and memories.

And mine was an enormous, beautiful, ornate library. It even had that slight musty old book smell I loved so much.

Nearing the next arch, I stopped and looked to my right.

"It's down here," I said, pointing to the row. It was darker than the others.

Moving through the row, the books lining both sides became oppressively close. Most of the books in my mind library were bright shades of red, blue, green, and yellow. But the books in this section were different. They held my most painful memories, and that pain reflected in the colors of their covers. All dark moody hues of black, navy, and purple.

When my sessions with Dr. Kelley first started, these texts were hidden behind a smoke-colored glass case with a large metal padlock on the front. But session after session, the books became more easily available. Now they were just at my fingertips.

That didn't mean I wanted to touch them.

Stooping low, I reached for a book at the end of the row. A deep purple text that sat next to a dull brown one.

"I believe we left off here."

Cracking it open, I slid my index and middle fingers down its crease from top to bottom. Then, clearing my throat, I read from the book.

The library faded away and I returned to the cold, clammy environment of the Longford Correctional House from centuries ago. Dr. Kelley and I watched from the sidelines as the memory unfolded like an immersive movie. I saw myself as Bess, kneeling in the salt circle as Mr. Sims read from his text. This time, I concentrated on the sound of Mr. Sim's voice during the playback. It was louder, but the words still weren't distinct.

"Again. I can't make out the words."

Taking in a deep breath, I played the memory back a third time.

This had been the problem. The memory was so old and had been kept closed in my mind for so long that it had degraded. Tiny details like the brocade pattern on Mr. Sims's coat and bits of audio had faded into obscurity. With each replay, the memory became stronger and stronger. But the process was exhausting.

"Animarium... viventium. We just need the last few lines. Concentrate harder!" Dr. Kelley said through gritted teeth.

My mind clouded with fatigued from the focus required to replay the memory with the clarity that Dr. Kelley wanted. I tried again, but it was like trying to burst through a solid brick wall.

"I-I can't. I can't do it." I gasped out of breath.

"Fine then, I'll do it myself." Dr. Kelley reached toward me with both hands.

"No—" I pulled my arms and the book close, recoiling from his touch.

In our session, Dr. Kelley had the power to pull the levers and push the buttons if he wanted. Until now, he had provided me with the courtesy of being in the driver's seat.

He grabbed my left forearm, taking control, and a sharp pain exploded in my mind. It was like a long thick needle slowly pushing between my eyes.

The memory slowed to a frame-by-frame rate. Mr. Sim's mouth opened and closed in exaggerated slow-mo, but it was still difficult to hear the words he read.

"... Ambulare... in terra in aeternum," Dr. Kelley repeated, picking out some words through the feedback.

I couldn't handle the pain anymore. But despite how much I screamed and cried, the doctor ignored me, clenching my arm in a death grip. I thought I was going to pass out.

Gathering what mental strength I had left, I swallowed hard and jerked away, breaking free from his hold.

The memory in front of us snapped out of slow motion and

replayed at a normal pace. Mr. Sims read the last line of the incantation, and white orbs of light appeared out of the crystal he held and whipped around the room.

The prisoners in their cells screamed in agony and fell to the floor, withering in an unseen pain. The orbs raced around the room and knocked into both Bess and Anne, causing both women to gasp and fall forward. Strands of light extended from each woman until it tethered to the crystal in Mr. Sim's hands, which now glowed a pulsing white. As Bess knelt on the floor, I remembered feeling as if my soul were being ripped right out of me.

A sound of rage ripped through the air. It wasn't a scream or a war cry, but something in between. Anne somehow had gotten to her feet and was running full speed at Mr. Sims. She knocked into him with a surprising force that sent him flying in Bess's direction.

Mr. Sims slammed into Bess, knocking her out of the circle. She skidded on her side, feeling for the loose ends of the ropes and quickly wriggling her hands out of them.

The crystal Mr. Sims was holding laid in front of her and she reached for it, intending to toss it further away. But when she grabbed onto it, it glowed even brighter and a small tether of light extended from Mr. Sims, who laid unmoving in the circle.

I remember the sensation had been overwhelming. Like my entire body was humming.

The ground shook and quaked. Bess instinctively clutched the crystal with both hands and curled into a fetal position on the floor.

When the shaking stopped, a pulse of energy cracked loudly around the space, and the memory faded.

With a jolt and sharp inhale, I was back on the gray couch in Dr. Kelley's office. Drenched in cold sweat, the familiar wave of nausea washed over me, signaling the end of another session. I started gagging.

Dr. Kelley, who still sat across from me, grabbed a trash bin that had been by his side and placed it in front of me. Grasping the bin with both hands, I vomited into it, then panted as I slowly came to my senses.

Dr. Kelley jumped out of his chair and raced behind his desk. He flipped open his journal and scribbled in it wildly.

"Ambulare in terra in aeternum. Now we just need to figure out the possessing term," he said to himself.

To walk on the earth forever. Definitely immortality-related, but what did it mean for me? If Earth were destroyed and I was on some distant planet, would I also perish?

I sniffed and swallowed, trying to clean up the gross stringy bits that dangled from my nose and mouth as I hovered over the bin.

"Oh, here you go."

Dr. Kelley was by my side again, waving a single tissue in front of me. I flinched, startled by his presence, but ultimately accepted the tissue and cleaned myself up.

"Do you know where you are? Do you know when you are?" he asked absently, back at his desk.

"I'm at RIDER, the New York City office. It is 2021... September 15th, 2021," I answered evenly. These were the typical post-therapy questions to help bring me back to reality.

"Very good," Dr. Kelley said airily, scribbling more notes.

I looked at my watch. It seemed like hours had elapsed, but it had only been fifty-five minutes. Unbelievable. I still hadn't gotten used to that part.

Placing a shaky hand on the arm of the couch, I used it to push myself to standing. I had to keep my knees bent to steady myself.

"So we're finished, then?" I asked, hoping the question was rhetorical.

"Oh, yes," Dr. Kelley said, looking up. "That'll be all. Good work. I'm hoping next time we can really focus on that last part. Remember, this is for your own good. We can't help you unless we know exactly how this happened. See you again next month!"

"See you next month," I repeated quietly. Our sessions were

monthly, as it took a while for the after-effects of each Memory Walk to subside.

I opened the door and stepped into the hallway, where cool air brushed my flushed cheeks, and I closed my eyes for a moment of silent relief. The doctor's words lingered in the air around me: *this is for your own good.* They echoed the words of Mr. Sims from over two centuries ago when he bound my hands together with the intent to suck the literal life out of me.

TWO

Staggering into the elevator, I smacked the top button and leaned back into a corner of the car, letting out a long sigh of relief. The car slowly made its ascent, issuing a pleasant beep as we passed each floor.

Seeing myself as Bess Abbott always reminded me of how much had changed. How much I had changed. Time wore away most things, including my accent. Over the years, and after transferring to RIDER's North American Headquarters, it had eroded away to be replaced with the twangy, harsh tones of an American one.

I was the only survivor of the events at The Longford House. When I finally made my way back to the London office, there were a lot of questions and eye rolls when I explained that Mr. Sims appeared to cause his own demise. A cover-up report issued afterward mentioned a freak earthquake.

No one paid much attention to me until I turned fifty. At that point, my youthful appearance could no longer be dismissed as good genetics. The event—whatever it was—had left me altered.

The elevator paused and sang a short, melodic tune when it

reached the top floor. I shuffled out of it, holding onto the door sides for support. My movements were tired and jerky as I moved down the hallway.

Fumbling for the ornate skeleton key in my bag, I unlocked the door at the end and nearly fell into the foyer when it pushed open.

In my cozy, one-bedroom apartment on the top floor, glass skylights curved down into large windows on the south side, showcasing the fading afternoon light. RIDER was housed in a large, city-block encompassing building on the Upper West Side that looked like an upscale apartment complex to passersby. And although Dr. Kelley's office was only a few floors below, the elevator ride felt like it had taken days. It always took a few hours after each session for time to feel like it moved normally again. At least now I was safe at home.

I dropped my bag and keys on the entry table and breezed through the dining room, into the nook of a kitchen for a much-needed drink. My heels clicked pleasantly on the herringbone wood floor.

A knock at the door whirled me around, and I let out an exhausted groan. Days with Dr. Kelley's sessions made everything —even just answering the door—all the more challenging.

When I opened the door, my new intern, Ellie, was standing in the hallway with her large designer work tote over her shoulder, and a stack of folders clutched to her chest.

"So sorry to bother you, Miss Prescott," she said, her dark eyes were bright and eager as she tucked a dark springing curl behind her ear. "But I wanted to bring by the new Vampire Top Ten Chart for your review. Mrs. Brooks said she needed the final tonight."

Of course Diana did. I was still on our department director's Top Ten Shit List for delivering an updated slide deck just minutes before her presentation the other day.

"Oh, right. Come in," I said with an exhausted breath. My head was pounding and my thoughts were a foggy mess.

"Hold that door!" a man shouted down the hallway.

A man in his mid-thirties, with carefully styled dark hair, dressed in a well-fitting navy suit and expensive camel-colored shoes, jogged into view.

"Mr. Campbell!" Ellie gasped. "What a surprise! I never thought—I mean, I didn't expect you to come all the way up here. How-how are you?" Her face flushed a deep beet color against her dark skin and her eyes glazed over a bit.

It didn't surprise me. Most of the young women at RIDER reacted similarly to the sight of Tristan Campbell. I rolled my eyes.

"Are you kidding me? This is Zoey's Fortress of Solitude. You know, when she's not spending hours upon hours in the Lost Cities section of the library," he said with enough slyness to make a fox faint, which looked to be exactly what Ellie was about to do.

Tristan had started his career as my assistant, but quickly climbed the ranks to become the youngest person in RIDER history to be promoted to director. He now led the Department of External Affairs, which seemed like a good fit considering his politician-like charm. All those hours sitting across from one another in the Lost Cities section during his formative years must have made an impact, because despite working in a different department and a different role, we still saw each other just as much. Even if it was mostly just to gossip about which demon clan leaders were paying a diplomatic visit to the New York office that day.

"So what honor brings you to my floor, Mr. Campbell?" I said in a slightly mocking tone, ushering them both inside. RIDER was an organization that operated on a strict hierarchy, but my apartment was not a place it could be enforced.

"Oh, you know, just checking up on my two favorite ladies of the Demonic Infectious Diseases department on this beautiful Wednesday afternoon," he said, plopping down in a chair at the dining table.

My transition from service staff to researcher had been an easy one when I found my calling in the Demonic Infectious Diseases department. In DIDs, we studied anything demonic that could 'infect' humans. Vampires, zombies, werewolves, and (intentional or not) demonic possessions; they all fell within our jurisdiction. My work focused on studying trends, behaviors, and Creatures of Interest—COIs. Those were the particularly nasty individuals who liked to cause a lot of noise and bloodshed.

"Ugh. What a day," Tristan continued, leisurely stretching out and thumbing through his mobile. I often wondered if he'd had someone bewitch the device to his palm. "This morning I sat in a Witchcraft Relations briefing on Familiar rights in the US versus Europe. Then, after beta testing the new database to catalog the Gifted and their abilities, I was on the phone for hours with California legislators, discussing the best way to handle their latest chupacabra infestation. Apparently, the buggers procreate faster than rabbits. Anyway—I needed to blow some time before I pick Sadie up for dinner and The Lounge isn't open for another hour."

Out of the corner of my eye, Ellie, who sat across the table, seemed to deflate like a sad balloon at the name of Tristan's current fling—I mean, girlfriend. I had heard about her for the past eight months, so I guess I should give him the benefit of the doubt.

"Have you told Sadie exactly where you work yet? Or does she still think you're some finance bro who can give her a private tour of your office in Freedom Tower One?" I asked, trying to conceal the mischievous grin growing on my lips. Ellie had introduced me to the term 'Finance Bro' (along with many others, so I didn't appear as tragically ancient as I was), and I loved using the phrase wherever possible.

"Not... yet," he admitted. "But I think she might actually be the one who could handle it. She's cool like that. I'll tell her in time. You, of all people, should know that patience is a virtue," he said with a playful wink.

"Whatever." I shook my head and let out a light laugh at his lame comment. "Oh, let me get this out of the way," I said, noticing the stacks of research materials splayed out on the table in front of him. I had told the rest of the DIDs office I was working from my apartment to be more productive—which was true—but the real reason was to avoid my director's disapproving glare.

"Are you okay? You seem... out of it. You haven't been daydreaming again, have you?" Tristan asked as I carefully placed my notes and texts on the nearby banquet.

For a new article, I had been researching an odd regional group of fangless vampires in the Pacific Northwest whose skin shimmered in the sun instead of burned. I was certain they were actually blood-drinking faeries with a serious identity crisis.

"No," I said tartly with a frown. While I had spent the past hour in the depths of my mind, it was certainly no dream. "I'm fine. Just tired."

My mind still felt scrambled from Dr. Kelley's psychic lobotomy, but I didn't want to speak ill of another colleague in the presence of an intern. I would tell him about it later.

"Alright Ellie, let's see what you've got." I held out my hand and she handed over a thin manilla folder.

Inside was a draft of the current Vampire Top Ten Chart with a list of familiar names on the left. Some were given names, but many were over-the-top nicknames like Henry the Harbinger of Pain. Vampires were known to be over-dramatic.

I studied the faces to the right. Again, all the usual suspects. As a lead researcher, it had been my job to approve said list for the better part of the last century. The vampires depicted on the pages in my hands had terrorized North America for decades. These were the baddest of the bad.

Most were drawings. It wasn't until the invention of digital mirrorless photography and video that vampires could have their image captured.

Two faces accompanied each listing: a human-looking one and their real face. Vampires could appear human when they wanted to, but shifted into their Other Face for feeding, when they were overcome by emotion, or at will.

Their Other Faces were feral. With sharp, serrated teeth and elongated upper canine fangs, amber-colored irises, and unique protruding skin folds on the top bridge of the nose and underneath their eyes, all features of the demon that lurked beneath the human-looking surface. Their ability to blend in amongst humans made them especially dangerous.

The recent serial killer murders out in Louisiana? A cover up for Number Four, aka Blue-Eyed Bill. A ruthless vampire whose encounter with a witch who refused to be Bill's dinner left him with a sizable scar and an eerie light-blue eye on the left side of his face. The blue eye remained no matter which face he wore.

I flipped through the pages until I found Number Seven.

He had dropped a few spots over the past few decades from inactivity, and many of my colleagues thought he was dead. Not like vampire undead. But like dead-dead.

Despite their ferocious nature, it only took a wooden stake to the heart, fire, or decapitation to reduce a vampire to nothing more than a pile of greasy, smoking ash. Holy water and crucifixes also worked, but were less lethal, like demonic Bear Spray.

The sketch of Number Seven was relatively accurate. Square face, triangular blocky nose with longish, unkempt dark brown hair and eyes. The sketch was based on a sighting from the 1980s.

"Any more intel on lucky Number Seven?" I asked Ellie, thumbing through the notes on his ranking.

"Nope, sorry. Theo's trail has been cold for a while."

"Hmm." I snorted, pursing my lips to the side. We'd need to look harder—maybe even reach out to the South American headquarters again to see if anything had crossed their desks.

I sighed, closing the folder and handing it back to Ellie. "The list looks good to me. Nice job." While the lack of information on

Theo's whereabouts annoyed me, I wasn't about to let it deter me. And as Tristan had noted, time was something I had a lot of.

"Oh, and before I forget, can you email Mark and tell him I analyzed the photos he sent over on the mauling victim from Vermont? It's not a vampire with fang deformities, but a wendigo. He'll know the protocol," I added. I could already envision our North American indigenous folklore specialist doing cartwheels around the office when he received the email. Wendigos were rare.

"Got it," Ellie said. She pulled out her mobile and tapped on the screen before glancing back up at me. "A wendigo, really? At first, I thought it might be a werewolf. But since there were no claw marks or fur fibers, I was sure it was a vampire who needed braces. How are you so good at this?"

"The bite was too deep to have been made by a vampire. Plus, the incident happened just outside the Appalachian Trail. Wendigo territory. But to answer your question: practice. I've been doing this for a very long time," I replied with a smirk.

"Did Marcy stop by? She bring anything I can munch on? I love those little canapés she makes," Tristan asked. While I was working, he had weaseled his way into my kitchen. Typical.

"No canapés, but there's a container of chips and guac. Just don't touch the croque monsieur." I called back. Along with my housing, RIDER provided a private chef to cook all of my meals. Marcy's French dishes seemed to contain a magic of their own. Her croque monsieur alone could raise my spirits and bring me to my knees in a single bite.

"Miss Prescott, there's something I've been wanting to ask you," Ellie said, a bit confused. I gave her a look to proceed. "Why are you still just a researcher? I mean, you're really good at this. I think you'd do a great job as department director."

I took in a deep breath. Interestingly enough, no one had flat out asked me before.

"Well, as you know, creatures—certain creatures—and the Gifted, are allowed to work at RIDER. But only humans can hold senior positions. Something to do about balancing power. Since they're still trying to figure out exactly what I am, or what gives me my longevity, I'm currently ineligible from holding such positions." I hated to have to say it out loud, because I was very much still human. But it was the truth and Ellie would find out eventually. I'd rather it be from me than the RIDER gossip channels.

"Oh," Ellie replied, uncertain. It was obvious she hadn't been exposed to RIDER's complex politics yet.

An abrupt vibration on my left arm startled me.

I glanced down at the buzzing gadget on my arm. A bubble expanded to fill the screen.

Therapy Session—Dr. Kelley—Office 203

Ugh, these things could be so finicky. I had been able to silence it for the last hour, but it still continued to go off. Somehow, the annoying (and demonically possessed, I've always said) piece of technology always seemed to impress the new hires.

"Tris! Help, please," I said, sticking my arm in front of Tristan's face when he wandered out of the kitchen, wiping green from his fingers onto a paper towel.

He looked bewildered for a moment before carefully lowering my arm with both hands. With fingers that looked like they were playing a musical instrument, he tapped and swiped until the noise and vibrations dissipated, reverting the device back to its quiet, time-keeping form.

"So I see you had a hot date with Dr. Kelley earlier, huh?" he asked.

"Don't remind me," I said, jerking my arm back protectively. While I didn't want to badmouth the doctor, the reason behind the sessions was fair game. "Can you please tell senior leadership to stop them? There have been no new clues to my immortality—or whatever. And the only thing the lab tests have concluded is that aside from my hair and nails growing, not a single molecule of myself has changed—not even my weight."

Tristan held up his hands. "Hey, if I could, I would. You know that. Unfortunately, I am but a humble bee in the hive that we call RIDER."

I sighed and looked at Ellie, who offered a cheerful smile as she stood to gather her files.

"I can drop these off at Mrs. Brooks' office before she leaves for the day, unless you'd like to," she offered, moving toward the foyer.

I sucked on my lip. "Is she still mad about The Quarterly Update slides?"

Ellie grimaced. That was a yes. Thirty minutes before our department's presentation at the Quarterly Update, we received new data that changed *everything;* the heat maps, the population charts, newly identified COIs. Unfortunately, Diana Brooks did not share my enthusiasm for perfectionism.

"You better drop them off, then."

Ellie nodded, then stood up straight. "Oh! By the way, I know it's a little unconventional since you're technically my boss and all, but some friends and I are going to a new bar in SoHo. Wanna come? It's supposed to be a 'Haunted Speakeasy.' So if we slip up talking about work, no one will notice!"

"Oh, thanks, but I can't go. I have to... finish my article," I replied with a forced smile, not ready to divulge the real reason.

"Come on," Ellie pleaded mischievously. "You've been working on that thing for months! One night of fun won't ruin it."

My smile faded. Okay, divulging it was.

"I can't go. I'm not allowed to leave the campus. It's one of the conditions of my employment."

While living and working at RIDER came with many benefits, there were also rules. Many of them. Most employees lived off-campus, and creatures were free to do as they pleased within the laws governed by their kind. But as the only-known immortal human, I didn't have a 'kind'. So RIDER made the rules for me.

Rule Number One? No venturing off campus. Why would I need to when anything I wanted could be procured at whim? If the temptation to leave the grounds became too great, a full security detail was required to escort me, and I doubted Ellie wanted that kind of chaperone on a night out with her friends.

Ellie scrunched her face. "Wait. What do you mean? Like ever?"

"Yeah." I nodded.

A few years ago, there was an incident involving a Cronut where my curiosity got the best of me. As punishment, it seemed like I always had some pair of eyes watching me.

Tristan put an arm around Ellie's shoulders and her entire face flushed purple. I wasn't sure if she was about to scream, cry, or shit herself. If she were more than human, she definitely would have melted into a puddle on the floor.

"Oh, come on, Ellie. It's not ideal, but if some tourist takes even a photo with Zo, it would just create a bunch of unnecessary questions decades later. You ever watch Wonder Woman? Also, could you imagine what she'd do if she saw an electronic billboard?"

I shot Tristan a dirty look. While centuries old, I still owned and used a TV. I knew what electronic billboards looked like, among many other newfangled technology thingies.

"Oh," Ellie said as Tristan unhooked his arm and they both headed to the door. "We'll definitely have a drink in your honor," she added, optimistic.

Bidding them both goodbye, I closed the door and locked the deadbolt.

Conversations like that were always awkward and hard. I had to remind myself that all the precautions were to keep me safe. With my condition, the alternative to living and working at RIDER would be to constantly move around, living on the outskirts of society so I wouldn't draw attention. The human world fears what it does not understand. I'd be living like the creatures I studied. Worse even.

With my current arrangement, yes, I had rules. But I also had friends and colleagues and purpose. And an article I needed to finish for my department's contribution to RIDER's scientific journal: *Supernatural Today*.

In the kitchen, I pulled down a cocktail glass from one of the navy-blue cabinets and set it on the stone island in an exhausted huff. What a day.

Two ice cubes and a heavy pour of scotch joined the party before bringing the concoction to my lips. Warmth and ease spread throughout my tired body.

Between "therapy" and the impromptu work session, I had no appetite—not even for Marcy's croque monsieur. And no coherent thoughts left either.

I took another sip, rolling the spicy liquid around in my mouth before swallowing.

Taking the glass with me, I walked out of the kitchen, where I unceremoniously kicked off my heels and padded to the balcony.

Sitting at the small bistro set there, I surveyed the courtyard below. It was still and calm compared to the bustling and chattering colleagues that filled it during the day. And beyond the building's thick walls, I knew the city that never slept was buzzing with its bright lights and urban clamor. But tonight, my view was private and peaceful.

I swirled the tip of my finger on the lip of the glass. The rhythmic motion was comforting, but I still craved the long draw of a cigarette. Preferably Sobranies.

I frowned, remembering I had quit over three decades ago at the urging of the clinic's physicians. Apparently, they didn't think immortality made one any less susceptible to environmentally triggered disease. But nights after Dr. Kelley's sessions always made me reconsider.

Swirling and sipping on my dinner of alcohol and thoughts, I hoped it would ease me into a dreamless sleep. Dr. Kelley was close to finding what he was looking for in my memories. And as much as I wanted to understand what happened and how the event had reshaped my DNA, an unsettling feeling in the back of my mind begged he would never find it.

THREE

I woke with a start to the sound of pounding at my front door.

I moaned. And still lying in bed, I hoped it had been a dream. But in the unmoving silence of my darkened apartment, the rapping continued. Urgent and unrelenting. Ugh, what now?

Emergencies in the middle of the night were not uncommon. After all, most of the creatures I studied were nocturnal. And every once in a while, a big bad COI would have the audacity to muster up some especially nasty carnage, typically of the world domination kind.

To my left, the red digital lights of my alarm clock glowed 4:12 AM. This morning's wake up call.

I stretched and tasted the gross, heady, stale scotch still thick in my mouth. Treading out of the bedroom, I grabbed a robe that hung on the back of the door and slipped it on, tying the waist belt as I neared the front door.

Flicking the deadbolt, I swung the door open amid covering my mouth to stifle a yawn.

I expected to see a hungover Ellie, another intern, or even another researcher standing in the doorway, hand outstretched with the most up-to-date dossier to acquaint myself with the upcoming apocalypse or demonic murder spree.

That's why I was so perplexed to see Tristan standing on the other side of the threshold.

Dressed in the same navy business suit from the previous day, his mobile was clutched in one hand, which vibrated and flashed angrily for attention. His normally pristine combed hair was flat and out of place, the result of him running his hands through it too many times. His expression was grim and haggard.

"Let me guess, you told Sadie that you work for a global demonic research organization?" I asked casually, leaning against the door.

I was about to usher him in for some hot tea or something stronger, but he shook his head.

"No. You need to come to the lab—you're gonna want to see this."

———

A quick change into something more presentable, and we were on our way to the basement. The expansive, windowless lab was filled with all the latest technology gadgets and gizmos for analyzing supernatural phenomenon from banshees to Sincer demons and everything in between.

We passed by an array of whirling machines and large flashing monitors that made my smart watch look like a sundial. I kept my hands close, fearing I might accidentally set off one of the sensitive devices.

Tristan routinely worked across departments (less because it was his job, and more because he was nosey), but when we reached one of the larger glass conference rooms that lined the walls, I was surprised to see a collection of colleagues from other departments, not just from DIDs.

Unease rushed over me, and the last bits of sleepiness fell away in an instant.

It meant something especially big, bad, and nefarious was going on. Perhaps I should have eaten something more solid for dinner after all.

A man with brown hair, now turning a gray-white at the sides stood in a corner with tired eyes and a hot, steaming cup of coffee in one hand. When our eyes met, he smiled warmly and raised his hand to wave a discrete greeting.

There was a light tug in my chest.

It was Augustine Hughes. This past year, he was promoted to the senior executive leadership team. A prestigious role he had worked toward his entire career.

I took a deep breath before returning his silent greeting with a half-smile. He nodded and sipped his coffee.

To his right was Matt Riley, the director of Witchcraft Relations. His attention was laser focused on the monitor ahead, which replayed jerky CCTV footage.

Sitting at the laptop's helm was Mirza Ahmani, the sharp young lab analyst I worked with for all of my demonic statistical needs and COI tissue samples. While his lab coat looked clean and pressed, his unruly mop of thick wavy dark hair and sallow olive skin suggested it was a facade for long hours in the lab.

Despite his tired appearance, there was still an unnatural glow behind his light green eyes. When I first met him, I assumed he was part creature or Gifted, but he was one hundred percent human with an infatuation for the supernatural.

Next to Mirza sat Astrid Scott, clicking away at her own impressive laptop set up. Her quarter-leprechaun genetics made her very petite, but still passing by human standards. With her strawberry-blonde hair pulled back into a ponytail, she readjusted the glasses over her almost cartoonishly large round brown eyes and nervously fiddled with the many layered gold necklaces she wore. She was new at RIDER, but I had already heard the rumors that she was heavily into Bitcoin.

Her gaze ticked around her many monitors with a worried expression. Last night was probably her first midnight oil-burning emergency. I couldn't relate.

Someone was missing from the room.

"Where's Diana?" I asked with a little alarm. We couldn't start without my department director, and time was precious in these situations.

"Well, and hello to you too, Zoey," Mirza drawled sarcastically. His fingers fluttered along the keyboard, and he pointed to something on his screen that made Matt lean in for a closer look.

"Diana's been briefed, and she's on her way. But we wanted to bring you in right away," Augustine said. His expression and tone were just as foreboding as Tristan's.

My anxiety spiked. "What's going on?"

Matt let out a long sigh before looking up from Mirza's laptop. "Over the past year, there have been a string of witch slayings across the country. About six in total, both male and female. Typically high-ranking, powerful spell casters in major cities. Each had been systematically hunted and had their magic taken from them before being brutally murdered."

As Matt explained, Mirza flashed the faces and profiles of the slain witches across the large monitor.

"I don't understand," I said, shaking my head. "Witchcraft Relations is completely out of my wheelhouse. What does this have to do with demonic disease variants?"

Matt pursed his lips together and motioned to Mirza, who spoke at a rapid, caffeine-fueled pace.

"Okay, so last night there was another attack, this time in Philly. When the investigative unit arrived at the victim's apartment, we found one of those in-home video security systems. We think he knew he was going to be targeted. But that's not why we asked you to come down here. I mean, obviously witch stuff—not your thing." Mirza paused, punching and clicking on his keyboard. "We were able to recover the SIM card. Unfortunately, video from the actual time of the murder was corrupted, but we found this."

Pixelated, jerky video footage splashed on the screen. When Mirza hit the play button, a body was lying face down in a pool of blood in the center of the screen in what looked like a living room.

A figure in a dark, long coat entered the frame. It stooped down to the victim and dipped two fingers into the blood before putting them into its mouth.

I crossed my arms and pressed the knuckle of my forefinger to my lips.

This was definitely trending toward the demonic or possibly deranged human. There were actually more voluntary blood-drinking humans in the world than I liked to think.

The figure on the screen sat crouched for a few moments before it looked up and noticed the security camera. He cursed loudly and moved toward the device with an angry gait, one hand outstretched.

Mirza paused the video and then zoomed in on the figure's face, tenfold. But it was unnecessary.

Although his hair had been trimmed to a more modern day cut, his face remained the same. Same square face and blocky nose. It was the evidence I had been waiting to see for over two centuries.

Through the monitor, Theo stared at me with his cold, dark eyes.

As I gazed at the frozen image, I always wondered how many similarities we shared. A similar nose perhaps, and most definitely the same oversized eyebrows and dark brunette hair. Those traits ran in the family.

Theo, Number Seven on the Vampire Top Ten Chart was my brother. Older brother by three years, to be exact.

FOUR

"I'm coming—I have to." I panted between strides.

Tristan and I were in the RIDER gym, an all-glass annex structure that formerly housed the building's greenhouse. With each pace on the treadmill, I tried to shake the image of the dead witch from my mind. His vacant eyes wide and face permanently twisted in terror as Theo loomed over him with his sinister glare.

While most of my colleagues knew I was aging challenged, only a handful knew about my family. That I was the daughter of a successful spice merchant in the English port town where I grew up, and I had enjoyed all the privileges that came with being born into a wealthy family in the eighteenth century. My entire childhood—from etiquette classes to mingling with lower levels of the monarchy at elaborate balls—had centered around becoming the proud wife of a notable husband in my very planned life.

Then my brother became a vampire, and my life turned to shit.

Pure luck had me traveling with my soon-to-be in-laws when it happened. While I naively scoped out their many summer estates to choose one to inherit to start my new life, Theo ruthlessly murdered everyone in our family's manor house. Not just our

parents, but the staff, our visiting uncle, and even our father's business partner, who had come over that night for a nightcap.

Theo wasn't a kind person when he was human, which meant
that he was especially evil when he became a vampire. At RIDER,
we debated on the influence a person's mind and personality had
on how they behaved when they became a vampire. But at the
most basic level, a demon enters and takes possession of a human
body. No matter how much the vampire might remember their
human life, the person they were had died. They were never
coming back.

By the time I returned to our family's home, Theo had worked
his way through our family's network of relatives and family
friends. The press claimed it was a fresh wave of plague moving
through the neighboring towns and villages, but I just thought
Theo had lost his mind. Eventually, not even my fiancé and his
family could escape.

With few places to hide, I ran as far as I could from anything
that tied me to our family, anywhere where Theo might find me.
And I've been at RIDER ever since.

But if I was going to take down my witch-killing vampire
brother, I needed to be in peak physical condition.

Popping off the treadmill, I grabbed two training quarter-staffs
and tossed one over to Tristan, who caught it in the air with one
hand. I stepped onto one of the training mats and settled into a
fighting stance.

RIDER was foremost a research facility, but it had a heavily
trained enforcement arm when it was necessary. For the many
comings of the apocalypse and capturing the deadlier COIs, of
course. Regardless of role or level, all RIDER employees had to
complete the mandatory annual combat course. I liked to think it
was to allow even the most bookish of staff (like myself) a fighting
chance if they found themselves face-to-face with the same nasty
they had been studying.

"So, what's your plan? You're just going to roll in there like

Van Helsing dressed to the nines in garlic, crosses, and holy water and expect to drive a stake right through your dear brother's heart?" Tristan asked.

I lashed out toward Tristan in a series of offensive moves, striking and swinging the staff in precise movements. All mostly muscle memory. I had taken the combat course dozens of times at this point.

"No," I said curtly, dealing out a few more strikes with the staff. "With the help of the enforcement team, I'm going to track him, corner him, and have someone hold him down for me long enough to drive said stake through his chest. And you should know that garlic does nothing to vampires. They just find the smell annoying."

"Don't be delusional," Tristan said tiredly, effectively blocking each move. "Diana will never allow it. Actually, I think she'd be more likely to have a drunken make-out session with a Basilisk at the next holiday party than give you sign-off on being part of the mission team. I mean, we all remember what happened with the Cronut."

Ugh, I swear I'll be five hundred by the time I live that story down.

But he was right about Diana. She was a stickler for rules and the most difficult of directors I've ever reported to. Her mood could sour for the rest of the day if the first-floor café so much as got her latte order wrong.

"This is my brother we're talking about, not some trendy pastry," I replied through gritted teeth, blocking his return strikes.

Before falling off RIDER's radar, Theo wrought havoc over both Europe and North America, eating his way from town to town and threatening to expose his kind to the human world. Oh, and of course there was that one time he tried to take over the world by releasing Hell on Earth.

Now, as Mirza and Matt explained, Theo was methodically murdering high-profile witches. Their intel suggested he was headed to Washington, DC, where his next likely target was a witch from a prominent family who had recently moved there after graduating from UCLA to head one of RIDER's affiliate sites.

A cross-functional team between Witchcraft Relations, DIDs, and External Affairs was being assembled to safeguard the witch and apprehend Theo. I was currently part of the remote mission team. So unless something drastic happened, I was going to watch the team take Theo down from the wall of monitors in the command center in New York. And after everything Theo had done, I couldn't let that happen.

But something odd about the whole thing kept eating at me. Vampires rarely messed with witches. Mostly because witches could hold their own. Blue-Eyed Bill was enough proof of that.

"Was there anyone else on the tape? Any strands of red hair found at the crime scene?" I asked.

"What are you thinking? Daisy?"

"Of course I'm thinking Daisy—who else?"

Daisy was Number Six on the Top Ten Chart and had been Theo's accomplice at one time. Despite her delicate-sounding name and affinity for wildly feminine, ostentatious dresses (downright gaudy, if you asked me), Daisy was about as deadly as vampires came.

Daisy wasn't Theo's maker, an unsolved mystery of its own, but they had met sometime at the end of the eighteenth century. The last time anyone had seen or heard of her was seven years ago in Las Vegas, where she had become the ring-leader of an all-vampire burlesque troupe who fed on unsuspecting tourists. But by the time the RIDER extermination team arrived, Daisy had vanished.

I tried not to think what mayhem the two could cause in modern-day Washington, DC.

"No," Tristan replied, ducking a swing to his upper body. "The team searched the entire apartment, top to bottom. No sign of her. But that doesn't mean she's not involved. From what you've said, it sounds like her and Theo were like the undead version of Bonnie and Clyde."

I frowned, unsure if it was a good thing or not to simultaneously apprehend two dangerous vampires, or if it would stretch RIDER's resources to the breaking point.

And stealing a witch's magic—that was especially strange. Vampires could invoke certain incantations and charms, just like humans. But they could not possess magic themselves. They were likely working with a witch partner.

Perhaps they were collecting magic to sell on the black market.

I shivered at the thought. From what Matt had told me, witches regarded their magic as humans regarded their soul.

And it was at that shiver that Tristan blocked another blow before pummeling me with three whip-like strikes in a row that landed me flat on the mat on my back. Ouch.

He hovered over me with a weary grin before offering a hand.

"You know all the moves, but there's no passion—no force behind them. Research, that's where your passion lies. With combat, something's holding you back. Maybe you should just let—"

"I'll have all the force I'll need when I'm face-to-face with my brother," I retorted, cutting him off. Grabbing onto his hand for support, I came to my feet. "All it takes is just one splinter of wood in his heart and then 'poof'—he'll be gone for good."

"Is 'poof' the official sound of vampire self-incineration?"

Knowing that Tristan spent most of his time in the high-ranking offices of government agencies, he had probably never seen one slain. I had only personally seen two vampires up-close myself before they met their demise.

"I always thought it would be like a scream that fades into the ether," he mused.

I came at Tristan again, this time thinking of the bloodied entrails of our parents Theo had left strewn across the floor and walls that had me running screaming out of the manor house on that summer morning.

"Tris, this is something I have to do—to be a part of. It's, you know, just all I've thought about for the past two hundred years," I said, delivering two more offensive strikes and a front kick.

He didn't see the kick coming, and it knocked him back a few steps.

He smiled. "Tell you what, if Diana says no, I'll buy you a pack of those fancy donut things and let you press the red button in the command center when I find him."

———

I spent the rest of the morning mentally preparing for the next thirty minutes. Ellie helped craft the meeting invite, which was accepted on the spot. And in the shower after the gym, I rehearsed what I would say in every probable scenario.

Now, more determined than ever, I knocked on Diana Brooks' office door.

"Come in!" My director's voice rang from the other side.

Entering Diana's office was always a perplexing experience. As department director, she had one of the larger offices with a large bay window that overlooked a charming street view of brownstones and mature oak and ginkgo trees that were tie-dyed yellow and brown with the coming autumn.

Tristan called RIDER's neighborhood "Film-Set New York." Its picturesque, urban landscape often drew TV and movie crews to set up shop up and down the street. I always loved to watch the actors retake scene after scene from different viewpoints within the building.

Diana sat behind her desk, a large blocky edifice similar to Dr. Kelley's, except hers had wispy, hand-carved vines decorating the sides and legs. Her body held perfect posture and equally perfect coiffed blonde hair that had now turned mostly white. In her elegant navy sheath dress and fine jewelry, she looked more ready to have tea with the Queen than to be sending out emails about the latest zombie outbreak in rural Alaska.

In stark contrast, the rest of her office was a total fucking mess.

I made my way through the short maze of stacked papers and folders, clutching my black Moleskine journal close to my chest for fear of tripping over one of the tiny pillars and falling flat on my face.

There was no method to the madness. I glimpsed a vampire report from 1992 in a folder labeled 'Werewolf COIs 2002', and a map of the trail left by a demonic body-jumper in Denver from 2010 at the top of one stack. Between the piles were scrunched up paper balls. Missed throws to a trashcan that was overflowing so much it looked like a mini volcano that erupted office supplies instead of lava.

The far two corners of her office were small graveyards of dead flora, dried and twisted in their last moments of life in their rock-hard pots. And on top of Diana's desk was a small cactus that resembled a greenish-brown deflated balloon.

"Oh, Zoey. Please, take a seat." Diana gestured to one of the two guest chairs submerged in papers.

Gingerly moving the stack of documents and rumpled legal notepads filled with writing to the floor, I lowered myself into the chair.

"Mrs. Brooks." I paused, casting a sweeping gaze around the minefield that was her office. "You know housekeeping can clean this up for you?"

"Bah." Diana snorted. "They've tried that before and I couldn't find anything for months. Anyway, what's this 'High Priority' meeting about? Please tell me you've found the cure for vampirism or something?" she asked dryly.

Popping a mint into her mouth, she massaged her right temple with her fingers as if she had a headache.

I inhaled deeply and fidgeted with the hem of my dress.

"No, I haven't. I-I want to talk about my brother. Theo. I'm sure you've read the briefing from this morning?"

"Oh yes, Theo. COI Number 86. What a dreadful vampire. We hadn't heard from him in so long that I hoped he might have tripped and impaled himself on something sharp and wooden," Diana said, sounding uninterested.

"Yes, so." I had gotten this far, there was no use in holding back now. "I'd like to volunteer as part of the core investigative mission team," I said in a quick stream, staring down at my Moleskine before carefully looking back up at my supervisor. It was like ripping off a band aid.

Diana's eyes bulged, and she choked on her mint.

"You're joking, right?" she asked between coughs.

"I'm serious. I'm formally requesting sign-off to accompany the team to Washington to oversee the extraction and elimination of COI number 86," I stated firmly. Although I was shaking inside, my tone held steady.

Behind her eyes was an explosion of emotion that made me worry she was about to have a coronary. But the stately woman inhaled and blinked slowly to collect herself.

"Miss Prescott." Switching from the informal to formal was not a good sign. One scenario I didn't account for.

"While I understand—and appreciate—the... personal connection you have to this investigative mission, you know the rules as much as I do. Wandering around New York City is dangerous enough. We both remember what happened a couple of years ago, right?"

Ugh, how could I forget? I pursed my lips and looked down at my lap.

"Traveling outside of New York, especially to another major metropolitan area like Washington, DC, is completely out of the question. It's too dangerous for someone like you."

My eyes watered from a combination of anger and devastation, and I quickly swiped my hand across my face.

"I've spent the last two hundred years researching how to avenge my family's death. This is the closest we've come to finding Theo in decades. I have to see this through. In person. Not on some monitor. Who knows when the next time will be—or-or if there even will be a next time!" I pleaded.

Diana closed her eyes for a long moment. When she opened them, her hazel eyes softened, but only slightly.

"Zoey, you are one of our most trusted historians at RIDER. Not just in New York, but all of RIDER. We still don't know the limitations or fragility that come with your perceived immortality. That's why we have the rules. To keep you—"

"To keep me safe. Everything is to keep me safe," I interrupted in a mocking tone. I couldn't handle it anymore. The rules were too much. They were like an oppressive fortress, keeping me locked inside RIDER's already enormous, gated walls.

"What about the witch in DC? The one who's Theo's next target? If she's as powerful and important as I've read in the report, and in need of the almost laughable extensive security detail we're about to deploy with the mission team, then why? Why isn't that good enough for me, too?" I asked. My voice cracked as it raised another octave.

Diana sighed deeply and her body fell inward, resembling the half-dead cactus on her desk.

"Zoey, you have to understand—"

I surprised myself when I stood up from the chair, fists clenched at both sides. "But that's the thing. I don't understand! I'm two hundred sixty-two years old—I'm not some child! And Theo—if Theo never became a vampire, I wouldn't be standing here, in your office in twenty-first century New York. He took my entire family, my whole life, away from me. As long as I'm still here, I have to be a part of this!"

Diana was silent as she appeared to search for words that evaded her.

"Diana," I said slowly, looking her square in the eye. "I *need* this."

Diana bit her lip before straightening and returning my gaze with a sincere look of authority.

"*If* I provide sign-off on this—I can't believe I'm saying this. On this... excursion of yours," she said. "You will have a full security detail and a dedicated security handler at all times. No exceptions. You are also only permitted to go to RIDER-only facilities. That means no time in the field. Period. The team already has instructions to locate and extract COI 86 and bring him to the closest RIDER facility in the area. They will then escort you there to oversee the elimination. Once the COI has been eliminated, you will return here to the New York office at once for a full debrief, followed by physical and mental exams. It's been a while since you've been out in the real world. We want to make sure you're okay."

Great, another session with Dr. Kelley in less than a month. But it was a small price to pay to see the look in Theo's eyes when that stake landed in his chest. Or, who knows, maybe we'd spice it up and choose decapitation instead. That was a memory I'd look forward to having Dr. Kelley replay over and over.

"Absolutely," I said with a stern nod, trying to contain my excitement. Preparing to leave, I picked up my Moleskine and stood.

"I'm sending over the approvals now. You'll leave first thing tomorrow morning." Diana said, furiously typing at her computer. "Oh, and one more thing."

Anything. "Yes?"

She paused and locked eyes with me. "This is a RIDER-sanctioned mission. There is no room for mistakes. Your role will be to lie low and assist the teams in locating him. Unlike the Quarterly Update, you won't have a chance to resubmit slides at the eleventh hour. Any miscalculations could cost someone on the team their life. Keep that in mind."

I had hoped that Theo's resurfacing would have helped her

forget all about the Quarterly Update. No such luck.

"Of course," I said hastily. "I won't let you down."

"More like don't embarrass me," Diana corrected. She gave me a stern look over her glasses that balanced on the tip of her nose and my blood ran cold.

I gulped and nodded firmly, like a soldier, before retracing my steps through the labyrinth of papers to the door.

Out in the hallway, I wanted to scream with joy but settled for bouncing on the tips of my toes in a little dance.

A few office doors down the hall, a man in a suit I did not recognize exited and walked in my direction. Slipping a hand in the pocket of his waistcoat to pull out a gold pocket watch, he flicked open the cover with his thumb and checked the time.

I suddenly found myself mesmerized by the piece. Delicately carved Laurel branches decorated the circumference, and a blue enamel plate adorned the center with a white star in the middle. My father had one just like it.

I turned to look in the opposite direction and the RIDER hallway blurred, becoming hazy. When it snapped back into focus, I found myself walking down the grand, curving staircase in my family's manor house. Descending each step slowly, I kept one hand on the railing to maintain my balance as my layers of skirts swayed from side-to-side. I tried not to pull at the navy silk and gold embroidered gown on top.

The sounds of a string quartet grew louder as I approached the bottom, where my father waited. Dressed in formal wear, with a similar blue silk jacket and breeches and his best wig, his focus cast down on the gold pocket watch in his palm. Closing his hand and the watch within it, he deposited it back in his pocket and looked up to meet my gaze.

"Ah, Bess," he said as I stepped off the last step. A wide smile took up the width of his face and his brown eyes shined with gloss before he blinked it away. "Come, everyone is waiting in the drawing room."

"How does my hair look? Mother said I should try something new," I asked, not able to conceal the anxiety in my tone. I gently touched at my hair that had been woven with ribbons and piled on top of my head, overtop bundles of perfumed hemp wool and horsehair to add an unnatural amount of volume. The women in Paris pulled off the look flawlessly, but I wasn't sure I could do the same.

Father offered his arm, and I looped my own through it as we made our way toward the music. "You look lovely as always. I can tell you're going to make our family so proud," he said, patting my hand.

In the drawing room, rich carpets in reds and blues covered the floor while chandeliers filled with flickering candles and dripping in crystals dotted the ceiling. A white stone fireplace on the right roared with warmth, throwing its light onto the many guests seated in meticulously arranged chairs and settees as our servants flitted around them refilling their drinks. Extravagant parties were my favorite, and my parents always threw the best.

My father directed me to an empty chair next to where a blonde man in his twenties sat with a gin flute in his hand.

"Mr. Ballard?" The man whipped around, seemingly startled by our presence. My father continued, "May I present my daughter, Elizabeth? I'm sure the two of you will have much to discuss."

As I took my seat, my father winked at me before turning away to join my mother, who was chatting away at the small crowd that surrounded her.

"He-hello, Elizabeth," Mr. Ballard blinked rapidly, rubbing his hands. "S-sorry, I'm a bit nervous about this is all."

I had butterflies in my gut as well, but they flapped with excitement, not fear.

I leaned toward the man and smiled, feeling subtle heat flush my cheeks. "As am I. Please, call me Bess."

A loud crash sounded out in the hall, followed by a string of angry shouts and an all-too familiar voice shouting back. My smile suddenly dropped to a frown and a pang of dread in my abdomen sent my butterflies flying away.

My parents exchanged a pained look between them, just for a moment, before continuing their respective conversations.

"I apologize, I must excuse myself." I said quickly, standing and moving toward the exit. I didn't give Mr. Ballard a chance to respond.

Out in the hall, Theo was stumbling around. One of our servants was a few feet behind him, cleaning up broken china and glass onto a silver tray that had been the source of the crash. Theo tripped, but the nearby wall caught him and he grabbed onto it tightly. Finding his footing, he stood up and smoothed the front of his waistcoat and jacket. But Theo being Theo, his wig was now barely hanging onto his head, revealing his brunette hair underneath.

I strode toward him, lips drawn tight as I tried best to keep my composure.

"You promised," I hissed through clenched teeth when I reached him. "You promised you wouldn't embarrass me tonight." The last thing I needed was my befuddled brother staggering about in front of our town's most notable families. Especially since he refused to take part in our father's business, or marry himself—it left me to continue our family's legacy.

"Wouldn't dream of it," he said airily. "I'm just enjoying the evening's entertainment, little sister." He reached out with a hand to give my cheek a painful pinch, as he always did when he was being a facetious asshole.

I swatted away his hand and recoiled at the scent of gin that soiled the air each time he spoke.

"I am most serious, Theo. This is important to me."

"Important? What, having mother and father parade you around like the good-stock horse you are?" His face twisted into what I think was meant to be a deprecating glare, but the alcohol in his blood turned it into a clownish half-smile.

I opened my mouth, retort ready, but the sound of nearby footsteps gave me pause.

"Theo! We've been looking for you all evening. Is this where you've been hiding?"

I looked over my shoulder to see the twin Gilbert sisters with their matching auburn hair and green gowns wave and bat their eyes at my brother. I rolled my own at Theo.

"Time for my favorite two parts of the party," he smirked. Then, leaning in, he spewed his hot, rancid breath into my ear, making me want to gag. "Good luck finding a man to court you with your hair looking more suited as a home for sparrows, and reeking like days-old rubbish."

Before I could reply, Theo pushed me aside, so forcefully that I stumbled, and toward the twins, greeting them with his recycled lines of their beauty he said to every woman who struck his fancy, and an arm for each to take.

"Miss?"

I turned to my left to see the man in the twenty-first century suit.

"Miss?" He repeated, his brow furrowing. "Are you lost?"

I blinked and my childhood home from centuries ago disappeared in an instant, leaving me standing in the hallway outside my boss's office in New York City, my Moleskine journal still clutched in my arms.

I took in a sharp inhale and shook off the last bits of the memory. "No, I'm not lost. Thank you."

Daydreaming happened sometimes, with a life as long as mine. A smell, a glimpse, a sound, and suddenly I was back there, reliving the moments of the past. That memory had taken place just a year before Theo was turned.

"Alright. Have a good day then," the man replied with a puzzled, but amused look.

For all he knew, I was an intern on her first day at RIDER who had strayed from the orientation group.

FIVE

As soon as I returned from my meeting with Diana, I excitedly began to pack for Washington. Warm light from the cloudless day shone through the floor-to-ceiling glass windows, illuminating the absolute mess I had made.

Notebooks and papers haphazardly covered the desk, coffee table, and dining table. Not even the green velvet sofa in the living room could escape.

And then there were the clothes.

It was as if my closet had projectile-vomited garments of every type and every season all over my rooms.

The closet was where I continued to dig, teetering on the tiptoes of one foot on a small step-stool. My hands blindly searched the top shelf for the telltale touch of smooth leather. Amongst the plastic bins and banker's boxes yellowed with age, I was certain there was an avocado green suitcase I had won in a Christmas gifting game during the 1970s wedged somewhere in between. Not having traveled for almost half a century, I was eager to use it.

If I could find it.

Unfortunately, my walk-in closet didn't share the same well-ordered organization my memories did in my library Mind Warehouse.

A solid knock at the door threw off my concentration. Losing my balance, I fell off the stool to the floor, taking down a dust-covered folder in the process. As the folder fell, its covers flew open like a pair of wings, fluttering its yellowed paper contents to the floor around me.

I cursed under my breath as I picked up the papers, quickly stashing them back where they belonged. Eying one page, I noticed it was a draft of an article I had written on vampire child-sire bonds. I had found evidence that strongly-worded commands delivered by sires had a mind-control-like effect on their children. Apparently, it was used to control the most unruly of the undead, a fact I had verified from a rare personal diary of a vampire from the sixteenth century.

With another knock at the door, I rose and shoved the folder back into its nook with a frustrated grunt.

"Coming!"

The sound from the door was deliberate, yet patient. A stark contrast to Tristan's frantic rapping.

When I glanced through the peephole, I gasped.

Whirling around, I pressed my back up against the front door and sucked the bottom of my lip. It had to have been a mirage.

After a moment to muster enough courage, I carefully looked again.

The second sighting confirmed it. Augustine Hughes was standing outside my apartment door.

Now in his forties, he looked most like his mother, who was originally from Kerala, with his brown skin and smooth facial features. His father, who hailed from Wales, was a RIDER alum who I had worked with during the 1960s. From him, Augustine had inherited his tall height and slim build.

I routinely saw Augustine at RIDER all-hands and cross-departmental meetings, but it had been twenty years since I last saw him outside my apartment door. He stood there on the red Berber carpet, relaxed and studious.

I analyzed my reflection in the foyer mirror. Always preferring what Ellie called 'vintage' styles, I wore a white silk blouse, a blue a-line skirt with a grey argyle pattern, and heels. Dresses were infinitely more flattering on me, but it was too late to change.

Instead, I ran a hand through my dark brunette hair, fluffing it to add volume before smoothing down the frizz on top. I needed to look good, but not like I was trying or anything.

Swinging the door open, I popped my hip to the side in a forced, casual stance. My heart pounded so intensely, I could feel it in my throat.

I could see that the last couple of decades, not to mention the stress from working at a place like RIDER, had brought lines across his forehead and around his eyes. They weren't deep, but frayed gently at the outer corners. He had also filled out a bit in width, as men do when they age.

In a strange way, the age suited him. Now part of senior leadership as a generalist, his years of knowledge and wisdom were appropriately represented in his physicality.

The only thing that hadn't changed were his eyes. They held the same calm kindness I had seen when we had first met.

He looked back at me with a sparkling curiosity before blinking back to focus.

"Auggie! What, um, what brings you to my floor?" I asked, trying best to keep my cool. Inside, I felt panicked and a little excited. Years ago, Augustine regularly came to my apartment before and after work. But that was then, a previous life almost. Why was he here now?

"It's nice to see you too, Zoey," he replied with a smile. "I wanted to talk to you about the mission to DC."

My brow knitted and I tilted my head to the side. Why did he need to speak in person? He could have just sent an email.

But then I saw that smile. The way it creased at the outer

corners of his lips and eyes, folding in the same worn pathways they always did. A shiver ran down my spine.

There was a still silence between us as we stood a foot apart from one another. We might as well have been worlds apart.

"Can I... come in?" Augustine prompted, lifting his brow to note the odd pause.

"Oh yes, yes. Of course. Where are my manners? Please, come in," I said, flustered.

I tucked some hair behind my ear and turned to the side to beckon him inside the apartment.

"Can I get you some tea? Or coffee? I still have some Turkish coffee Angela brought back from the United Arab Emirates when she was researching the were-hyena there." Turkish coffee was always his favorite.

"I'm fine, thank you," he replied, striding in. His eyes widened as he took in the mess in the apartment. "So I'm guessing it's a good thing I came to bring you this."

Augustine held up a large chestnut-brown leather weekender he had been carrying. It looked new with its rich color, oily sheen, and smooth exterior. The gold zippers that adorned the top and sides shined in the sunlight.

"Oh, yes. That's perfect. Thank you. It's been a long time since I've gone on a trip. Any luggage I have is probably half dust by now," I said with a light laugh. It was honestly probably the reason I hadn't been able to find the avocado green suitcase.

Accepting the bag with both hands, I placed it on the dining table after shoving a swath of clothing and books to the side to make room for it.

When I turned around, Augustine was right behind me, his chest just inches from my face.

Almonds had always been his favorite snack, and he constantly carried around a small bag to munch on throughout the day. Like when we used to discuss the origins of demons in the courtyard on warm mornings. The light, nutty scent rolled off him along with the rose water and woodsy-smelling cologne he always wore.

The scents intertwined in my nose, giving me pause. What had we been talking about?

Suddenly Augustine was kissing me.

Slow and passionate on my lips. The stubble below his nose and on his cheeks scratched my face as he pushed me up against the dining room wall.

I gasped, surprised and delighted as he worked his way down my face to my neck, his lips marking a trail on my skin as he went.

Augustine ran a hand down my body, from my waist to my hips, until pausing on my thigh. Then up my skirt, his fingers carefully pulled down the waistband of my hose, searching until they found their target in the depths of my clef. I gently raised a knee and wrapped my leg around him to provide more access.

His fingers pulsed. Slow, deliberate, and gentle, knowing all the right spots to relieve the pressure that had been building there since I first spied him through the peephole.

I sighed with pleasure and whispered his name in his ear.

Then, in a single motion, he lifted me up and onto the dining table. I always felt so delicate in his arms.

He was kissing my lips with more intensity and quickly brushed away the remaining papers and clothing that laid haphazardly on the table. The weekender too, now in the way, toppled off the side and onto the hardwood below with an indignant slap.

Augustine leaned me back slowly on the table, pushing up my skirt to peel the hose off my legs.

I had been yearning for so long what was about to happen with Augustine on the table. And on the couch. And eventually in the bedroom.

"Zoey?" he asked. His voice suddenly sounded muffled. Distant and dreamlike.

"Mmhm?" I moaned, not wanting him to stop.

"Zoey? Zoey, are you listening?"

A firm hand gripped my shoulder.

Augustine was looking at me with a curious but concerned expression. We were standing in the dining room, where I was still very much clothed with a hand on the weekender that still sat studiously on top of the dining table.

Heat rushed to my cheeks.

I had been daydreaming again. It had been happening more frequently since I started the sessions with Dr. Kelley, but this was the first time that parts of the present mixed with the past.

"I was just telling you the good news," Augustine continued. "Daphne just accepted her internship at RIDER for next semester."

My stomach flip-flopped and I suddenly felt ill.

Daphne was Augustine's daughter who just finished her freshman year at college, making us closer in physical age than I felt comfortable with. I gulped.

"That's—that's wonderful news. Another generation carrying on the family legacy. You must be so proud." I literally had to force the words out of my mouth and silently prayed that Daphne would not be placed in my department.

"I am," he replied with a nod, beaming.

Once upon a time, Augustine Hughes made me feel like I was the luckiest girl in the world. But on a beautiful, small-puffy-clouds-over-a-deep-blue-sky kind of day in the spring of 1993, it ended.

We ended.

Just like every Sunday afternoon when we were together, we were enjoying the lazy day under the big oak tree in the RIDER courtyard. I laid with my head in his lap, scribbling in and crossing out wrong answers in the New York Times' crossword. Augustine sat propped up against the old tree, reading the rest of the newspaper.

But on that day, he stroked my hair with his strong, but gentle hand. Then folding the paper in half, he said, "Listen, there's something I've been wanting to talk to you about."

I thought he was going to ask me to marry him. That's how I'd imagined it would happen. Simple, casual, intimate. Proposals that were all big bands in public places were too showy for either of us.

Augustine broke things off that day because even though I wanted to give him the world, there was one thing I couldn't give him.

Someone to grow old with.

That's what he said he wanted. The mortal fantasy of grey hair and wrinkled faces, holding spotted, bony hands in rocking chairs on a porch as the sunset before them. What was so great about that, anyway? The whole idea seemed overrated.

Well, that and a child. Another thing I could not give to him. Because for better or worse, related to my inability to age or not, I had never been pregnant.

Sometimes, when the pangs of grief and bitterness bubbled up out of nowhere, I liked to think he was just being selfish. I couldn't help my condition and Augustine had punished me for it.

Three months after ending our relationship, Augustine met a woman at a friend's book club. Six months later, they got married. And after traveling the world, and buying the perfect brownstone in Brooklyn together, they had a daughter.

A daughter who would soon walk the same halls and attend the same meetings I did.

Fantastic.

It would be a daily reminder of the life I couldn't have. I still haven't been able to look at a work by John Grisham the same way.

I, on the other hand, remained stationary. Always moving but never changing.

"Well, that's wonderful," I repeated in a slightly deadpanned tone. "And thank you for the luggage. As you can see, I have a lot of packing to do before tomorrow."

Encounters with Augustine always left me with a whirlwind of mixed emotions that usually required a strong scotch on the rocks to process. The sooner he left, the better.

But he stood still and put his hands in the pockets of his trousers. There was more to this visit than just a weekender.

"That's what I also wanted to discuss with you. I know how important this mission is to you. To find and apprehend your brother. Diana mentioned you're to have a handler. For security purposes, of course. Matt Riley volunteered, but something's come up in Salem that he needs to attend to. He won't be able to come to Washington until later in the week. In his absence, they asked me to fill in."

I blinked. It was the only reaction I could make without my jaw dropping to the floor.

"You?" I asked. "You're going to be my handler? On the mission?" Hard as I tried, I couldn't keep my voice from cracking.

Seeing Augustine in meetings and being CC'd on the same email chains was hard enough. But the thought of having my ex constantly by my side made my head spin.

"Well, just until Matt makes it back. It should only be a few days. But I wanted you to hear it from me first," he said.

Speechless, I looked out the large windows and across the way to a balcony opposite the building. It was off one of the two large cafes in the building and a warm September afternoon, so a handful of colleagues leisurely sat out on the terrace enjoying their coffee. I desperately wished to be one of them instead of being stuck in my messy apartment with my ex-boyfriend.

"Listen, I respect that you can take care of yourself," Augustine continued. "You have been here far longer than I've been around. I won't smother you with the laundry list of precautions, and check-ins like RIDER wants. But they chose me and I agreed. I still care for you, even though we aren't... you know, anymore. I always have."

A dangerous mix of emotions swirled within my chest, weighing it down.

"Augustine. Don't," I warned, turning to look at him with glossy eyes.

My heart was breaking all over again. It was like smashing a mirror. Shattering on impact at first, then bit by bit, the pieces fell off and rained down slowly.

But I didn't want to unravel our history in my dining room on a weekday afternoon. I didn't want to hear him tell me all over again and in so many ways that while he still cared for me, that the 'timing's not right.'

The timing was never right because time hated me.

Like most pain, it was easier to bury it all six feet deep and walk away. Never to revisit again. Eventually, time would heal it. It always did, and I've got plenty of it.

"Zoey, I'm sorry. Look, I didn't mean to upset you. I just wanted to be the one to tell you. And also let you know that I won't get in your way. You have Diana for that," he said with a dry laugh, trying to lighten the dense mood that had settled around us.

"Well, good. I'll be busy trying to locate my vampire brother before he feeds on the entire capital, so the fewer distractions, the better," I said, sniffing back tears, trying to compose myself.

"Okay, well, um. I should get going," Augustine said, flustered. I was thankful he realized he'd overstayed his welcome while I still had some dignity left.

He moved to the front door, where I followed him.

"Thanks for the bag, and for the visit. Tell Marie I said 'hello,'" I said with a forced smile and in my best, albeit robotic, hostess voice.

"I will. By the way, you look lovely. You know, sometimes when I look at you, it takes me back to my first days at RIDER. And then I blink and suddenly I'm back in the present and here you are, looking exactly the same. Radiant as ever. As if the time hadn't even elapsed. I have to catch myself sometimes," Augustine said in a bit of awe.

How was I even supposed to respond to a statement like that?

In lieu of words, I looked downward, bit the bottom of my lip, and played with the door handle to fill the silence.

After a moment, Augustine chuckled to himself.

"Oh, listen to me. The ramblings of an old man. I'll send Marie your regards. See you tomorrow, Miss Prescott," he said with a sincere smile, bowing his head farewell. We were officially back on formal RIDER terms now.

I seriously doubted his claim to tell his wife about any aspect of our interaction, let alone my warm regards.

Closing the door, I thoughtfully latched the deadbolt and chain. Then, leaning my back against the wood surface, I let out the loudest sigh in all of my two hundred sixty-two years.

In the kitchen, I pulled down my favorite glass. A cocktail glass with a gold rim and an art déco-styled pink and white fleur-de-lis pattern that tessellated around the circumference. I filled it with a handful of ice and healthy glugs of scotch.

Although I'd had suitors and relationships before and after our time together, none of them could compare to that of Augustine Hughes.

SIX

Friday morning brought a dense fall fog that blanketed the entire RIDER campus. It hung there, suspended only a few feet from the ground, encircling the courtyard's trees and benches. Even the large fountain in the middle appeared to erupt water from a thick cloud.

It was the type of weather I loved most during Fall. The fiery red and yellow leaves poked through the gray, and the cool, wet air created an overall feeling of cozy leisure. The perfect weather (and excuse) for curling up with a blanket, warm drink, and a good book or research article—depending upon how productive I needed to be that day.

But not today. Today would be different.

Today, I was leaving RIDER and New York for the first time in, well, ever. To accompany the mission team. To finally find Theo. To remove one more monster from the shadows.

Bursting through the shining brass lobby doors, weekender in hand, I found Augustine and Tristan waiting in the main entrance's driveway.

They stood underneath the gothic-styled iron wall lanterns that glowed a bright yellow-white through the thick fog. Above those, the large American and RIDER flags flapped in the gentle breeze, slapping against their poles with a rhythmic metal clanking.

A new model silver Mercedes SUV idled in the cobblestone driveway next to them, which I immediately recognized as Tristan's.

RIDER service staff in their sleek black uniforms and matching gloves with an 'R' in a flourishing serif font embroidered on their left chest made hurried trips from the lobby to the car, packing away the luggage in the back trunk like a live game of Tetris.

"I thought we were taking one of the RIDER black cars?" I asked.

"And miss taking this baby on her first trip to the South? Absolutely not! Plus, the suspension can't even compare to the ancient dinosaur black cars," Tristan replied, one hand scrolling through the news on his mobile while the other mindlessly twirled his car keys around his fingers.

I'm pretty sure the RIDER black car fleet operated on a two-year lease, but Tristan had strong feelings about seemingly insignificant things. Like simple transportation or the specific font and size of a press briefing.

"Good morning. I hope you're ready for four hours of unhinged driving," Augustine quipped to me, smirking at Tristan. The comment earned him a loose eye roll and nod from the director of External Relations, taking the remark in jest.

It was a relief to see that Augustine was taking the initiative in making things less awkward than they had been in my apartment.

"Can't wait," I said, enthused. Whether it would be a four-hour roller coaster ride or like riding in a cloud, I couldn't wait to see what life was like beyond American TV and RIDER's black gates.

I handed my weekender off to a service team member and motioned toward the SUV. "I'll wait in the car."

I found Mirza on the back passenger bench on his phone. He

smiled and held his hand up in greeting as I slid my work tote off my shoulder and scooted into the far side seat.

"Okay, okay. And oh, one last thing. If Mango creates any portals, which he probably will since it's the night before the full moon—there's an incantation on top of the refrigerator to close them. Just say the words... no, you don't even need to be good at Latin. It literally works like a charm. Well, technically, it *is* a charm. That's what the witch said who gave it to me... From who? Beatrice in accounting... yeah, I know, I had no idea either. Apparently, she used to be the high priestess in her coven. Crazy, right? She's so quiet. But listen, if you ever need a Mercury in retrograde protection charm, Bea is your girl. She'll give you a good price too."

A year ago, Mirza rescued two cats, Mango and Salsa. Technically, they were goblins who preferred to shape-shift as cats that Mirza had found in an alley on his way home from the lab one night after they came through a portal from their home dimension. They preferred his West Village studio apartment to wherever they had come from, but Mirza complained that Mango still had a penchant for opening small portals in the living room.

What was that saying? A goblin will do as a goblin does.

While Mirza chatted, I pulled out my Moleskine journal from my workbag and started jotting down the day's lengthy To-Do list.

Diana had sent a novel of an email detailing the around-the-clock reports and progress check-ins she expected. Although I would be physically outside of RIDER HQ, the strings were still very much attached. And taut.

Bidding a quick goodbye, Mirza hung up the phone and let out a long sigh.

"Is Jason watching Mango and Salsa?" I asked.

Mirza's boyfriend was not immersed in the supernatural world but, as an avid animal lover, had taken a liking to the inter-dimensional cat-goblins.

"No, Jason's out of town this week, visiting his sister. Astrid's watching them."

The trunk slammed with a thud, and Tristan and Augustine slid into the driver's and front passenger seats. Rumbling over the cobblestone driveway, we ambled out of the front entrance and onto the street. Towering buildings flanked either side as the spunky car raced ahead, picking up speed.

I gazed out the window, noting the familiar townhomes and buildings of the Upper West Side as they passed by in a blur. As we moved further away from RIDER, we turned down streets that were less familiar, and therefore all the more exciting.

"So, the witch we're safeguarding? She's not a RIDER employee, but she works with us?" I asked. This was number three on my To-Do list. An internal memorandum documenting the witch along with her background and relationship to RIDER.

"Her name is Charlotte Tennet," Augustine said from the front passenger seat. "She comes from a very well-known and powerful family of spell casters. They go back centuries. She inherited a house that RIDER has identified as a location of interest, meaning that we provide an allowance—and a substantial one at that—for RIDER to use the property as needed, and for her time serving as the head coven liaison to the Witchcraft Relations department."

I jotted down some notes, but paused when the car descended into The Lincoln Tunnel. Daylight quickly clipped away and the car's interior lights brightened as if it were night.

This was it.

I was leaving behind the bubble of Manhattan and soon would emerge into the rest of the world.

———

I must have fallen asleep at some point because I awoke to the car swaying back and forth as it lumbered along a cobblestone road. Poking my head up, I realized we were moving through an alley better suited for a horse-drawn carriage than a modern-day SUV.

The brick buildings that lined the alley were oppressively close, yet to my (and Tristan's) thankful surprise, we continued to just barely sail through unscathed.

Unsurprisingly, Tristan and Augustine were bickering in the front. It was like being in the Monday morning all-hands meeting all over again.

"We are on the complete opposite side of M Street from where we need to be!" Augustine shouted.

"I would be on the right side if it weren't for all these one-way streets!" Tristan replied. "Every time we pass it, I have to go all the way back around! Did you read the directions right?"

"Of course I've read the directions correctly. She said we all need to think hard about the address when we approach the intersection of O Street and Twenty-Ninth. Whatever that means," Augustine said tiredly.

He flashed the screen of his mobile toward Tristan, who squinted at it before rolling his eyes.

"We've been up and down Twenty-Ninth Street ten times already! Are you sure you can't reach her on her cell? Asshole! This might be worse than driving in Manhattan," Tristan said, slamming his hand on the horn as someone cut him off.

The car was finally back on black pavement and we skirted up a hill and across a busy street where I caught glimpses of storefronts that were a mix of original and modern builds. The area reminded me of shorter versions of the buildings in SoHo.

As the car zoomed up the incline, we entered a neighborhood just above the shopping district. Here, we passed by townhouses from an array of time periods. Some made me think of photos of modern-day London that my colleagues from Motherland HQ sent me, while others looked distinctly American Federalist, with a mix of early twentieth century designs inbetween.

The city noise quieted as we ventured farther from the bustling main street. Then, slowing, Augustine and Tristan leaned forward, craning their necks to scan each house we passed through the dashboard window.

The streets were beautiful. Lined with lofty, mature trees bright with color from early fall in an array of green, red, orange, and yellow leaves. The vibrant colors starkly contrasted the neutral hues of the houses behind them.

As the Mercedes treaded through, its tires whipped up the yellow leaves that covered the streets, whirling them in the air. It was like living in a watercolor painting where the canvas expanded on indefinitely.

When we hit a small pothole, Mirza, who had also fallen asleep, woke with a gasp followed by a disgusted "Oh, ew" when he noticed and wiped the saliva that had dripped from his mouth onto his shoulder. He yawned, noisily slapping his tongue in his mouth before turning his tired eyes toward the window to admire the view.

Tristan repeated the address, and we slowed to a snail's pace.

"If we don't find it this time, I swear the neighbors are going to call the cops on us," Augustine said.

I joined the search, rolling the numbers in my mind as I examined each house from my backseat view. Tristan mumbled off the digits under his breath and the entire car fell silent as we entered the intersection of O and Twenty-Ninth Streets.

To the left, the air shimmered. A quick, subtle flash of holographic light bent and pulled back like a stage curtain. In a space that previously held a cluster of smaller townhouses, a single house took its place.

The entire car gasped. The sight even earned a "Damn" from Mirza, as the house came into view.

It was a massive, whitewashed, red brick residence that took up the corner block. A large turret donned the left side, and a glass-covered walkway connected to the right, adding to its castle-like appearance.

Perfectly rectangular Federalist-styled windows with matte

black shutters dotted the entire facade. Below each one, coordinating flower boxes overflowed with boughs of blossoms. A tall iron gate wrapped itself around the entire property.

As the car approached the side gate, it creaked open to reveal a pebbled mosaic driveway in a circular pattern of flourishes with a decorative pentagram in the middle.

The house was absolutely stunning, and in my long life, I had seen nothing like it.

"Finally," Tristan said with a relieved laugh as he and Augustine high-fived. "That was harder than getting ectoplasm out of my suit."

The house's red front door popped open and a woman in her twenties bounded down the steps to the driveway.

Her thick dark hair with caramel-colored highlights fell below her shoulders and bounced around her oval face and high cheekbones as she moved. She wore a silk navy blazer with matching trousers and a loose white camisole underneath. Black-and-white tall striped heels that didn't seem to hinder her graceful descent were strapped to her feet. She had the sleeves of her blazer scrunched to her elbows, revealing tanned, olive skin with deep caramel undertones and multiple gold bracelets and rings that donned her hands. Laid-back, California cool oozed from her entire being.

"Took you guys long enough! Another hour and I would have given up!" she teased through a wide and warm smile.

All four doors of the car released in a chorus of dull pops as we exited the car. Mirza was the first to the rear hatch and dutifully unpacked its contents, handing over my leather weekender. I grasped the handles with both hands and surveyed the driveway in awe. It was beyond exciting to be out in the modern world, and the tingle in the pit of my gut agreed. What I didn't expect was to feel vulnerable. Everything was shiny and new, but nothing had that favorite, broken-in-shoes habitual comfort.

"Tristan Campbell," Tristan said, and his voice sent my

thoughts flying away. I turned to see him introduce himself to the woman with a firm handshake. "You have no idea how hard it was to find this place."

"Nice to finally meet you. I'm Charlotte—Charlotte Tennet. And I know, the wards are pretty good, huh? I set them myself," she said, looking proud.

"Too good." Tristan laughed. He motioned to us at the car. "These are my colleagues: Augustine Hughes—he's standing in for Matt Riley until he's able to get here later in the week. That's Mirza Ahmani, our top lab tech, and Zoey Prescott, our Demonic Infectious Diseases expert."

I half smiled and waved at my introduction. Charlotte returned it with a nod.

Charlotte looked around for a moment, confused.

"So, where's the rest of you? I thought there was some big fancy SWAT team or something. You guys look more like a bunch of adjunct professors than someone who can take on a witch-hunting vampire. No offense, of course."

"None taken. They'll be here shortly. They're staying at a hotel nearby but will take watch rotations in the house soon. And don't let the suit fool you—I'm full of surprises when it comes to battling the forces of evil," Tristan said with a foxy expression.

I did my best to cover my rolling eyes. Tristan's flirtatious prowess was laughable but not as laughable as the thought of someone who spends most of their time in board rooms trying to take on a legendary vampire.

"Well, we can get settled and catch up on everything until they get here," Charlotte said, bounding back up the front steps.

We followed her but stopped at the top when Charlotte became fixated on a flower box from the right second story. A tendril of green vine grew down and toward her, like a thin bony hand extending itself for a handshake. When it reached eye level with Charlotte, the vine paused before it bloomed into a cluster of bright pink flowers. Okay, so this witch liked to show off.

"Aw, look at you. Putting on your Sunday best for our guests," Charlotte crooned at the vine before plucking the cluster of flowers and sliding it into her hair behind her ear.

She looked over her shoulder to catch me staring at the spectacle, returning my shocked and devoid-of-thought gaze with a wide smile and a wink from one of her almond-shaped blue eyes.

We crossed through an elaborately decorated vestibule tiled in a pattern of terracotta stars and white marble circles. Inside the main foyer, the interior dripped with rich Victorian-styled fabrics and dark woods. It was the opposite of Charlotte's laid back, sunny persona, but it instantly felt like home to me.

But there was something about the house that seemed off. I couldn't put my finger on it, but even the air inside moved strangely. It ebbed and flowed, as if someone—or something—was breathing.

I scanned the parlor rooms, elegant wood staircase, and circular hallway of balconies above for answers, and frowned when none came.

A large gust of wind blew from the back of the house and into the foyer. Goosebumps broke out on my arms and legs as the air whipped around my body.

Then the air sighed. A warm, comforting tone and two hands rested on the back of my shoulders in a calm embrace.

I gasped in alarm and froze until the hands lifted. The air stirred before the presence sailed upward, dissipating above.

Maybe staying home at RIDER wasn't such a bad idea after all.

"Oh, it likes you, Zoey," Charlotte said in a cheeky tone. As if telling me a boy had a schoolyard crush.

"Is the house haunted?" I asked wide-eyed, expecting to see a transparent apparition close by.

Vampires, witches, and the occasional werewolf—I could handle. But ghosts were unfamiliar territory, usually handled by the Departed Human Affairs department. I'd heard poltergeists were handsy, and was not the least bit eager to find out for myself.

"Oh, don't be ridiculous." Charlotte dismissed with a wave of her hand. "It's not haunted. It's bewitched." She looked at us with unblinking eyes, as if telling us the sky was blue. How could we not know?

My colleagues and I exchanged confused glances. We had all heard that the house was of interest to RIDER, but without someone from Witchcraft Relations in the room, we were all still pretty clueless.

Footsteps and the murmurs of conversation floated our way before two people, a man and a woman, emerged from the back of the main hallway.

The man was tall with an athletic build, like an American football player. There was a ruggedness to him, with his flannel shirt and jeans, floppy brown hair that cascaded down the nape of his neck and a close-shaven beard.

The woman who kept in pace with his long strides had bubblegum pink hair, alabaster skin, a heart-shaped face, and brown, almond-shaped eyes. Her style was punky compared to the man's Midwest Americana. She wore a black sweatshirt over a black skirt, fishnets, and combat boots with a chunky rubber tread. Around her neck was a gold necklace of circular slivers, with a full circle in the middle. She fiddled with it, running her fingers through the charms and chain as she moved.

Her delicate build made her look like she could have a promising career as a professional ballerina, if she wasn't one already. But there was something about her—maybe her walk? Or just the way she carried herself. That made her seem more formidable than her stature led on.

"Hey! We came in from the back," the man said, gesturing to the brown paper bag he carried. "Got some big steaks from Whole Foods to grill up tonight before the big—"

"Big game!" Charlotte said quickly. "Of course! I can't believe

I forgot that was tonight. Everyone, this is my cousin Luke Weston and his girlfriend Olivia Saito. They're in grad school at Georgetown for some crazy engineering stuff. And they've been helping me with the whole witch-hunting-vampire thing, too. Luke and Liv, this is that supernatural research team from New York I was telling you about."

Luke and Olivia exchanged confused glances before returning tight-lipped nods our way. Something was clearly off in Charlotte's introduction. But whether or not it was supernatural related, I couldn't tell.

Tristan pulled out his leather folio and flipped through a few pages.

"Cousin?" he asked, scanning some seal-stamped papers. "I know you come from a big family, most of which are affiliated with RIDER. But um, we have copies of their NDAs, right?"

"Oh yeah, totally," Charlotte said. Tristan gave her a skeptical look, so she continued. "You government types and all your red tape. Don't worry, our family's lawyers took care of all that stuff."

"RIDER isn't part of the federal government. It's a common misconception. RIDER is a private, faux-governmental research organization," I clarified. It was a personal pet peeve of mine, and I couldn't help but to speak up.

All eyes fell on me, and I felt uneasy. I hated being the center of attention, and could already feel the rush of overwhelming anxiety that came with it.

"But with gobs of paperwork. Noted," Charlotte said to Tristan.

"So the house," Mirza said, changing the subject (for which I was eternally grateful). He cast nervous glances around the house. "Is it going to like attack me in my sleep or something?"

"Not unless you give it a reason to," Charlotte warned in a deadpanned tone to match the serious expression on her face.

Her body language instantly softened as she motioned to the surrounding space.

"My ancestors built The House like a hundred million years ago. My heritage is Nacotchtank—on my mom's side. All the materials came from some super-sacred ground or whatever. And they charmed everything from the foundation to the roof. The charms give this place a unique power source for magic, like a conduit. But someone from my ancestral line has to take residence in the house or else the magic becomes dormant. When it does that, it goes into like a hibernation mode and basically looks abandoned. Peeling paint, shoddy roof, shattered glass in the windows, the whole nine yards. I'm even told it makes a very convincing 'Keep Out' sign. Anyway, my uncle used to be the house resident, but he decided to retire early and moved to Boca. Something about the warm weather doing wonders for his incantations."

"And so now you're the current resident," Tristan said.

"Yes. Technically, I also have a condo on the Waterfront. The house... let's just say sometimes we agree to disagree about those I choose to fraternize with—even though I'm a grown woman!" She shouted the last bit upwards as if speaking to someone upstairs. "Also, the closet space in here is terrible. I can barely fit a season's worth of clothes."

At Charlotte's last comment, all the doors upstairs slammed shut angrily, shaking the surrounding walls. Charlotte rolled her eyes before shouting upward again.

"We talked about this—you know it's true! I'm just stating the facts!"

The witch shook her head. "The House gets pissy when you point out its shortcomings. It's sensitive like that. Anyway, yes, I've been appointed the current caretaker and lead witchcraft liaison on coven matters to RIDER."

"Nepotism at its finest," Luke said with a grin.

Charlotte narrowed her eyes into thin slits. "Or, it could be because I'm highly skilled and, you know, like, really good at my job. My cousin Paige wanted this gig, but she's been on probation since she got caught using black magic last year."

"Yeah, okay Sparky," Luke replied under his breath with a puff of laughter.

I could see the wheels in Charlotte's mind click. She was making a mental note to get back at him later at what I could only assume was an inside joke.

"Anyway, you've got bags, and I've got rooms—let's see to it."

SEVEN

Charlotte directed me to a room on the second floor with a view of the backyard lined with colorful hydrangeas and a towering magnolia tree. Detailed pink floral print that reminded me of a Laura Ashley catalog lined the walls, curtains, bed comforter, and shams. I was shocked that the rugs weren't in a similar print. Instead, they were a light shade of agreeable gray.

I plopped the weekender on the bed and asked if there were any service staff to help with the unpacking. Charlotte laughed until she caught herself with an, "Oh my goddess, you're serious? No, it's just me."

I guess being a RIDER affiliate site meant it didn't come with all the perks of a head office.

After settling in, I headed downstairs to find that the security detail had arrived. Unfortunately, they appeared to be experiencing some technical difficulties.

From my view on the staircase, four men and two women dressed in all black with handguns holstered to their sides, shielded themselves from a constant pummeling of living room pillows thrown at them from an invisible force.

"Stop it right now, House! I mean it! This is *not* how we treat our guests!" Charlotte shouted, trying to stop the barrage of cushions flying across the room.

She stepped forward and flicked her wrists open at her sides, curving her fingers as if holding two large balls. White flames ignited in each palm and flickered there as she sent a smoldering glare to the side of the room from which the ammo of upholstery came.

The pillows dropped out of the air in mid-flight, just short of their targets.

Everything was eerily silent for a tense moment. Then, a single sham picked itself up from the ground and launched itself at the nearest guard, hitting him square in the nose.

Unprepared, the man winced and gave an audible 'Ah!' before massaging his face.

Everything fell still again.

Charlotte swept a dirty look across the room, looking for the tiniest of suspicious movements from any of the inanimate objects in the living room. Satisfied that The House had silently agreed to a truce, or at least a ceasefire, she closed both hands into fists, extinguishing the flames.

"That's better," she said with the assertiveness of a schoolteacher reprimanding an unruly classroom.

Noticing my presence, her composure softened as if the last thirty seconds hadn't happened. "Oh, hey! Dinner's been set up in the dining room. Let's eat!"

I followed Charlotte past the security team, who were still collecting themselves and exchanging dubious looks, no doubt questioning what kind of mission they had signed onto.

In the kitchen, Charlotte let out a sigh and pulled out two wine glasses onto the counter, where a bottle of light pink rosé sat chilled in a stainless steel bucket of ice.

"I swear," she said tiredly, pouring two glasses. "Not even

Martha Stewart could host guests without The House getting upset."

"What upset The House?" I asked, a little confused. It hadn't reacted like that when we arrived.

Whirling around with a smile, she handed me a glass and clinked it against mine.

"Oh, you know: the weather, my outfit, the music playlist. But this time I think it was the guns. The House doesn't seem to like automatic weapons. Powerful witches? Fine. A succubus or two? No problem. But guns seem to set it off. My ancestors had problems with men coming in with guns, so I think it comes from that. The House tends to hold a grudge. Anyhoo—cheers!" she said before taking a long drink.

She and The House seemed to have a complicated and tumultuous relationship. I was suddenly thankful that the RIDER building lacked any sort of sentience. If it did, I think I would have lost my marbles decades ago.

Charlotte led me to the formal dining room where catering had dropped a selection of Greek dishes. The table was a landscape of chicken souvlaki, marinated olives, pitas, and an array of hummus and tzatziki dips. One item I didn't recognize was a block of baked feta wrapped in filo dough and drizzled with honey.

"Oh, my god. This is delicious!" I said between bites as I shoveled forkfuls of feta and pastry into my mouth. Honey dripped down my chin, and I quickly mopped it up with a finger.

Sweet, salty, rich, and creamy. It had been a long time since I'd eaten anything not prepared by Marcy or the RIDER cafeteria. And the new, inviting flavors exploded on my tastebuds. I closed my eyes to savor the last bite when I realized I had eaten the entire dish myself. Oops.

"I guess you need to get out more, huh, Z?" Mirza asked from across the table.

He wasn't wrong. I shrugged, in passive acknowledgement, too enthralled in my dinner to respond verbally.

Luke and Olivia grilled their steaks in the backyard before joining the table. What I thought for sure would have resulted in leftovers for days had been hungrily scarfed down between the pair. Despite Olivia's petite frame, she impressively piled up rib and porterhouse bones high on her plate until it loosely resembled a game of Jenga.

"So Zoey—I mean, Miss Prescott, sorry. I'm not used to all this super-formal stuff," Charlotte said with a sheepish look.

"Oh, you can call me Zoey. RIDER's obsession with formality can be a bit excessive. And technically, we're outside HQ," I said with a laugh, now three glasses of rosé in.

"Cool. So, like, what's your story? RIDER sent over your file when they said you all would be coming. It's no secret you're a lot older than you look. How did you come to RIDER? Are you Gifted?"

Typically, there was one of three ways a person came to RIDER. Through a lineage of family alumni, Gifted humans who were easily identified once they'd reached puberty, or through RIDER's strategic program to recruit the best and brightest.

"No, I'm not Gifted. Something... happened to me. But it was after I started working at RIDER," I said, keeping the explanation brief. It was a long story.

"Zoey came to RIDER as a member of the service staff. A maid, if I remember correctly. Ain't that right, Zo?" Tristan said with a cocky smirk, sloshing pale pink liquid in his wineglass before taking a sip.

Charlotte, Olivia, and Luke turned to look at me with the same curious glance, waiting for me to confirm the accusation.

"Yes," I said slowly, shooting Tristan a piercing warning glare. I slowly traced the lip of my wineglass with a finger to mask my rising anxiety. "But that was a very, very, long time ago."

It wasn't that I was embarrassed about my early days at RIDER. The service staff were vital in keeping order amongst the day-to-day chaos of a demonic research facility. But the way Tristan said it—like he was outing me—struck a nerve. I was a different person back then. I wasn't Zoey Prescott, the researcher. Not yet anyway.

"Well, talk about climbing the corporate ladder," Charlotte said brightly, breaking up the tension. "I've also been wondering, you've been around for centuries at this point—what's that even like?"

Colleagues often asked me that. What it feels like to see generations of people come and go, while I remained exactly the same.

These questions were usually asked at a cocktail reception or holiday party when they'd had too much to drink. Always spoken in a hushed whisper, coming out all at once. Eyes bulging with a mix of curiosity and awe. Just like Charlotte had.

The answer? Mortal lives were so short, that it happened with a rhythmic regularity. It was never easy, but never truly hard, either.

Bosses and colleagues grew old and retired. I might see them every few years when they came to visit the New York Office when they would come in, wobbling along, unsteady on canes and the occasional oxygen tank. And a few years after that, they would pass onto their next life that I would read as a single sentence in the RIDER Dispatch. Then the cycle would repeat itself. It always did.

But a Mediterranean-themed dinner was no place for my existential melodrama. So instead of telling the raw truth, I took a long drink of rosé, swirling the wine around in my mouth before settling on what I always said.

"It's like coasting along on a train ride with no destination. But you acknowledge the rolling plains, mountains, and lakes as they pass by."

I panned the table, anxious about how my response would be received. Tristan, engrossed in his mobile, seemed not to have heard. Augustine avoided my gaze, while Mirza nodded and Luke and Olivia appeared too pre-occupied in the last bites of their own meals to notice.

"Very... poetic! But I guess you've been around so long to have rubbed elbows with all the great writers and poets, huh?" Charlotte replied positively, searching the eerily quiet table for unity. When she saw none, she shifted uncomfortably in her chair and directed her gaze at Luke. "Luke! Why don't you tell us the story of how you and Olivia met? I always love hearing it."

"Actually, I think it's time for us to go," Luke said, calmly putting a hand over Olivia's.

Olivia looked at Luke and he shifted his eyes toward the large dining-room windows that showed the setting sun over the horizon of the backyard.

Following his gaze, a shadow crossed Olivia's face, and she cursed under her breath when she saw the view.

"Oh yeah, we really need to get going. Nice meeting you!" Olivia said, standing up and dropping her cloth napkin on the table.

Without a word, the pair headed down the hallway, opened a door, and descended into what I could only assume was the basement.

Charlotte also quietly excused herself, muttering, "Oh, the football game. You know how Hoyas can be." She followed their path to the basement.

Tristan looked confused for a moment before shaking it off. "I couldn't imagine still being in school. I could not wait to start my career," he said, reaching forward to grab another pita wedge before smothering it with hummus.

"And what career is that? A career in bullshitting?" Augustine mused.

After another round of wine and the sun had sunk below the horizon, Mirza and I sat out on the back veranda with steaming cups of chamomile, enjoying the cool evening weather. From our view, we watched Charlotte in the backyard hone her more deadly skills to prepare for potential run-ins with dangerous, magic-siphoning vampires.

Augustine stood behind her, offering moral support and critique. But mostly critique.

"I keep veering to the right no matter how straight I try to aim," Charlotte said.

"Mmhm. And you've cleared your chakras? Negative energy can cloud spell casting," Augustine said.

"Yes. I've done all that. Nothing seems to work. I've even been walking around with this stupid rock in my pocket to absorb bad juju or whatever."

Charlotte dug into her pants and pulled out a small black stone. Most likely black tourmaline. In my crash course on all things witchcraft for the trip, I had learned that black tourmaline was one of the most popular crystals used by witches to keep their energy flowing unobstructed.

Depositing the crystal back in her pocket, she flicked her right wrist, igniting a palm-sized white flame. Concentrating, she lifted the fire out of her hand and into the air at eye level, where it shaped itself into a ball and flickered intensely. Then, with the slightest motion of her right fingers, the ball sailed across the backyard toward an aluminum bucket filled with water.

A few feet from the bucket, the flame banked a hard right and landed in a bush of blue hydrangeas. The bush ignited in an instant, becoming engulfed in flames.

Charlotte calmly turned around and looked at Augustine, who had his lips pressed firmly together and slowly nodded his head, now understanding the full extent of the situation.

"Well, I guess you could always just pivot to the left to accommodate the, um, that issue. That's what's recommended to correct this problem in golf," Augustine suggested brightly. He swiveled his upper body to the left to illustrate what he meant.

Charlotte, on the other hand, did not look hopeful.

She sighed heavily, her body wilting with defeat. Then, raising both arms toward the bucket, water snaked out of it as if siphoned from an invisible hose. She directed the water onto the small, smoking brushfire. The fire hissed in an angry defiance as it extinguished.

"Okay, so I guess from now on, I'll only be standing on Charlotte's left side then," Mirza said with a weary smile.

EIGHT

My boots crunched on brown stone gravel as I strolled along the path. Reaching out with my fingertips, I grazed the tall, flowered tops of baby's-breath that lined the edges, swaying in the breeze.

"I do love this time of year," my mother said, walking next to me. "Everything is just coming into bloom."

She wore her typical gardening costume—a white linen dress with a baby blue ribbon around the middle that tied into a bow in the back. Her normally pinned up blonde hair was worn down, encircling her shoulders underneath the wide brim of a straw sunhat bursting with flowers and feathers on the side.

We turned right at a fork and came to a plot of flowering bushes. Bees and other flying insects hovered over the blooms, diving into each one before emerging and seeking out the next.

"Can you tell me about these flowers?" Mother asked, pointing to a bush on the left.

"Yes," I said, clasping my hands in front of my white eyelet dress. This was an easy one. "Those are roses. You may pick the blooms now for arrangements, dry the petals to make rose water, or leave them be until they produce hips that can be used to make tea or jam."

My mother's dainty features stretched into a smile. "Very good. You've been studying."

Producing a pair of shears, she clipped off two stems and motioned behind her. Our servant, who had been waiting off to the side with a shallow wicker basket, stepped forward for my mother to carefully lay the stems inside.

"But I don't think you've seen this," she said, moving toward the stone wall perimeter of the garden covered in ivy and small white blossoms.

When I followed her there, she plucked a blossom and pulled the stamen away from the petals.

"Taste it."

Pinched between my fingers, it had a tiny drop of nectar gleaming on top. I put it in my mouth and licked it.

My eyes went wide. "It's sweet!"

Mother nodded and smiled, and then we both made our way toward another plot, this one bursting with peonies, my favorite. Mother handed me the shears, and I cut off one stem, then held the bloom to my nose, smelling its sweet, perfumed scent.

I held it out for my mother to smell, but as it hung there in the space between us, a single drop of crimson fell on an outer white petal.

"Mother?" My gaze slowly drifted up to meet hers, and when it did, I screamed. The flower dropped from my hand.

Her throat was ripped open. A large, deep gash in her jugular. Blood dripped down her neck, staining the front of her dress and falling to the gravel in streams.

"I hope you're ready," she gurgled, her face twisted with worry as blood poured from her mouth. "Theo will be."

My eyes shot open, and I gasped, heart pounding in my chest like a sledgehammer. Something grabbed my wrist and I flinched, but when I held up my arm, it was nothing more than my vibrating smart watch.

Good Morning! Filled the screen before it disappeared and displayed the day's forecast. Seventy-two degrees and sunny.

I cursed and sat up in bed.

"It was just a dream," I said, massaging my face with both hands and brushing away the sweat. A horrible, terrible dream that played on the insecurities in my subconscious, but a dream nonetheless. It was not real.

But Theo was.

That was all the motivation I needed to get out of bed.

Slipping out of the marshmallow-like bed covers, a calm cooing from a pair of mourning doves on the windowsill caught my attention, and I padded over to investigate.

Morning dew clung to the backyard grass, giving it a frosted look. In the sill below, one dove sat in a half-made nest, while the other meticulously repositioned twigs around it. The House seemed to approve of its new residents; the sill on the side of the nest jutted out unevenly to accommodate the structure. Last night, I was positive that the sides were of equal depth. Interesting. The House seemed divided in its need to be both nurturing and ferocious.

Leaving the doves to their nest building, I dressed for work and headed downstairs, hoping that each step would put more distance between me and my nightmare.

In the kitchen, a breakfast buffet had been set up on the marble island. Assorted bagels and toast were neatly arranged on white trays next to small bowls of jams and cream cheeses. A large bowl held brightly colored cut fruit, and next to that was a collection of carafes filled with juices in various shades and clarity set beside stacked cups and mugs.

Tristan was there with a piece of jam-slathered toast crammed in his mouth as he held a travel mug under a complicated machine that somehow dispensed coffee. He was wearing his EarPods and nodded intermittently, listening intently on a call as his other hand cradled his mobile.

"Good morning." I smiled, grabbing and splitting a sesame bagel before popping it in the toaster.

It was sacrilege to toast bagels in New York, but I could tell these lacked the girth and chewiness needed to properly support a healthy swath of cream cheese. They required a toasty foundation.

Tristan returned my greeting with a friendly wave of his brow as he chomped through another row in his toast.

"Mirza and I are going to set up in one of the third-floor rooms in the south wing. I have some good leads on where Theo might be hiding out during the day," I said. My tone was full of hope for a productive day ahead.

Tristan swallowed his last bite, took a swig from his coffee, and muted himself on his phone. All within a fraction of a second.

"Oh, I'm not coming. I've got a ton of meetings, so I'm going into a nearby RIDER satellite office for the day."

Grabbing a mug from the island, I slid into the space where Tristan had been moments before and placed it on the cup-sized ledge of the machine. The machine issued a friendly beep, registering the cup, and the screen above flickered to life. It was a touch screen. I think. And it started to display a multitude of rotating beverage options. Too many options. Panic set in.

Reluctantly raising my finger up toward the screen, I bit my bottom lip. I just wanted a hot drink. Why did technology have to make it so complicated?

"Here—Dirty London Fog, right?" Tristan asked, leaning over to the machine.

I nodded. It was my go-to order.

A hand swipe and several finger dashes across the screen and suddenly liquid began pouring out into the cup. Looking up at the screen, the words 'Earl Grey Latte with Espresso' marched above an animated progress bar and a dancing anthropomorphic mug. It dinged proudly when it was done.

Picking up the steaming mug, it was the perfect shade of gray-brown.

"Where would you be without me?" Tristan asked, flashing a smile.

I laughed. "Uncaffeinated and miserable, obviously."

Charlotte was sitting outside at the table on the back veranda in a thick white sweater and matching skirt with chunky gold jewelry around her neck and fingers. She looked more suited to be on the cover of Vogue than to be enjoying breakfast in her backyard. With one hand grasping her steaming mug, her contemplative gaze looked out over the lawn as she gently twirled a stem of leaves with the other.

The leaves were oval-shaped and formed the shape of a rosette. A mandrake. I had seen illustrations in books before, but never one in person.

"Oh, hey," Charlotte gasped, a little startled when the door helpfully opened and closed itself when I walked out onto the veranda with full hands.

"Mind if I join?"

"Please, come," she replied, moving the items on the table to make room.

I took a sip of my latte and smiled as the liquid warmed itself through my chest. It was especially refreshing given the morning chill in the air.

"What's that?" I asked, shooting a glance toward her hand.

"This," she said with a long exhale, twirling the leaves in front of her. "Is a mandrake leaf. I've been sent a message."

I took a bite of bagel and chewed through it. Definitely not one from New York, but not absolutely terrible. I scrunched my face in a way that said, '*go on.*'

"I have a contact who's been tracking the witch homicides. And the info they've had has been solid. They mentioned they thought the next victim was going to be in Philly two days before it happened. They go by the name Mandrake. Get it?" She held up the leaves in front of her. "So this is obviously from them. They're very skittish and had been sending messages through burner phones and untraceable Telegram messages. But they're here now since I'm thought to be the next target. I found this on the porch this morning," Charlotte explained, eying the cluster of leaves. Her tone was heavy and emotionless compared to her bubbly demeanor yesterday.

"What does it say?" I asked, half-expecting the mandrake to talk or write something in the air with its many leafed arms.

Charlotte turned the palm around and held up the back of one of the leaves. Written there in black marker read:

AT-DO
WH

I was a bit disappointed to see Mandrake had sent her a literal message and not something with magical properties.

"AT-DO WH. What does that mean?" I asked. No familiar acronyms came to mind.

"It's code. I performed a locator spell on where the plant had been growing. Nearby in a park, actually. Dumbarton Oaks— that's what the 'DO' stands for. 'AT' refers to the Arbor Terrace within Dumbarton Oaks. 'WH' is pretty standard amongst us spell casters. It stands for Witching Hour. Mandrake wants to meet in person at three AM," Charlotte said, so unenthused she seemed bored.

I didn't understand.

"Well, aren't you excited to meet this person? Mandrake? Seems like we can get some actual information on Theo if this person is tracking him."

"Yeah, I totally agree," Charlotte said. Then, frowning, she added, "But when I say Mandrake is skittish, I mean very. They have taken every precaution to conceal their identity. The only way to leave this house is with the enforcement team. That for sure will spook them. Then it's goodbye to any good intel. It's so frustrating. I really need to know what they found."

"Hmm," I mulled over the issue. Considering that we only had a handful of good information, this Mandrake person could lead us right to Theo.

"Well, Mandrake must have touched this leaf. Can you do some kind of reverse look-up spell on who they might be?"

"I'm a witch, not a freaking goddess," Charlotte retorted, rolling her eyes. Then, with a smirk added, "Even if the new guy I've been seeing might say otherwise."

Charlotte sucked down the rest of her coffee and stood, picking up her things off the table. A smart tablet she had been reading tipped forward, and I caught a familiar black title bar flash across the screen.

"Wait—what is this?" I asked, sliding the tablet around to view its contents.

It was an article that looked very much in the same format as Page Six, a gossip page that Ellie always seemed to have up on her laptop screen between zombie cluster maps and werewolf incident reports.

Except the website on Charlotte's tablet was called *Page SixSixSix* and the article she had been reading was entitled, HUMAN CELEBRITY PASSING PISHACHA GOES INTO HIDING AFTER CAUGHT EATING HUMAN FLESH—HOLLYWOOD CAREER OVER. Next to the headline was a photo of a human-looking celebrity I recognized from the movies. I think he had even won an Oscar.

"Oh, that's right, I guess you more human RIDER folks don't get *Page SixSixSix*. They have the juiciest demon and witch celebrity gossip. Can't start my morning without it."

———

With the help of a handful of field agents, we turned what had been a rarely-used sitting room on the third floor into a fully functional, albeit makeshift, command center.

Partially nestled within the turret of The House, it provided a row of curved windows that looked south over the rest of the Georgetown neighborhood and parts of its main street. I could see a gold shining dome sprouting up above its more Federalist styled neighbors. Charlotte said it was the top of Riggs Bank.

The Victorian-styled seating was removed and a long conference table took its place in the center. Along with it, an array of computer monitors, displaying the now recognizable faces of the slain witches and detailed maps. A large flatscreen TV was mounted on one side of the room. In the middle of the table sat a conference phone, legal pads, highlighters, and pens neatly stacked and ready to be used.

Pleasantly caffeinated and full, I buzzed along with the number one item on the day's To-Do list: identify Theo's likely day hideouts.

Astrid had emailed over a list of potential hot spots, and it was my job to mine through them and shorten the list. Theo preferred places with a view and historic notoriety. He was also partial to the dramatic and ostentatious, as vampires were generally drawn toward.

Vacant, on the market, former diplomat residences off of Embassy Row in the Kalorama and Woodley Park neighborhoods made the short list. Especially those situated on hills with a view of downtown and the Washington Monument. The Great Recession triggered a trend amongst vampires to squat in foreclosed mansions. Aside from living in grand, perfectly staged residences, they could feed on real estate agents, buyers, and the weekly cleaning staff as if they'd ordered delivery. I wouldn't put it past Theo to do the same.

Other probable locations included The Hay Adams Hotel for its proximity to The White House and reputation for privacy, along with The Watergate Hotel for its scandalous history and riverfront views.

It was midday by the time I submitted the list to Augustine

and Diana, where it was quickly approved and then sent to the enforcement team, who would map out and strategically scout each location while there was still daylight.

Lunch was served on the roof deck because the weather was warm and dry. Underneath the delicate glass overhang that connected The House's wings, the rest of the roof deck extended outward in whitewashed brick that matched the exterior.

Admiring the view from the edge, Augustine pointed out Arlington, the city on the other bank of the river, the Watergate building from my research, and the notable Georgetown University steeple.

Having worked up a hearty appetite (my metabolism was something Tristan always teased me about as his waned), I was famished and piled up food from the buffet, sandwiches and salad this time, high on my plate.

This was also the first and only time that Luke and Olivia made an appearance. They hobbled up the brick steps, slow and steady. Luke held an ice pack to his side. A heating pad, the kind that sticks to the skin like a sticker, was visible underneath Olivia's camisole on the back of her left shoulder.

Hungrily grabbing portions of the Italian sandwich with five different types of meat, they seemed to inhale their meals, gobbling the sandwiches up in what seemed like a single bite.

Olivia leaned back against a nearby brick wall and let out an exhaustive 'Ooof.' Luke reached out with both hands to massage her back. She closed her eyes in peace for a moment before they shot open again.

"Ow! Babe, stop! It's too tender," she said with a sharp inhale. She gave him a dirty look and moved away from his touch.

"Did the muscle relaxing tea and energy bath not help?" Charlotte asked the couple, a little alarmed.

Luke frowned and took Olivia's hand, lightly patting it to comfort her. "No. It was a long night last night with the... game and all. We should get back to campus. We both have group projects we need to meet with this afternoon. We'll be back later, of course."

At that last remark, Luke and Olivia shuffled back downstairs, grabbing the railing for extra support as they descended out of sight.

————

"So, are you in, Mirza? Come on, who doesn't like the sound of espionage at three AM?" Charlotte asked coyly, shaking the mandrake stem in his face. The green leaves made a soft, rustling noise as they swayed back and forth.

After lunch, Charlotte joined Mirza and me in the command center, noting it as an opportune time to devise a plan to meet the mysterious Mandrake with somehow no security detail. I had a feeling we would need more than just witchcraft to pull it off.

The lab tech politely pushed the witch's arm away from obscuring the view of his laptop.

"No, no, no. There's a reason I spend most of my time analyzing samples in a basement. Field work is not for me. Too much creep factor. And this field trip of yours—most definitely dripping in creep. The only place you'll find me at three AM is at the club under the strobe lights with a strong vodka soda."

"Ugh, lame." Charlotte sighed and turned to me, shaking the leaves in my direction. "Zoey? Come on, I can't go by myself," she pleaded with puppy dog eyes.

It wasn't that I didn't want to go. Being outside of RIDER HQ was fun and exciting, with an endless amount of fresh sights, smells, and tastes. I was very much enjoying the ride.

"I would go—I mean, I want to go. But I'm kind of under lock and key. If RIDER found out, I'd be shipped back to New York and never let out of my apartment ever again."

Mirza laughed. "Yeah, apparently there was a thing a few years ago about a—"

I knew where he was going and shot him a deadly look across the table that silenced him.

"Can't you ask your cousin, Luke? He's a witch too, right?" I asked. At least she would have some literal back-up fire power.

Charlotte's face fell into a frown. "Luke's tied up tonight. Also, I'm the only spell caster here. He's... non-practicing. Personal life choice. That's why I need you, Zo—and you *want* to go, right?"

Augustine hurried into the room a little flustered. Taking his seat at the head of the table, he turned his mobile on silent before slipping it into his shirt pocket, muttering something about Fresno nightcrawlers under his breath.

Charlotte's face brightened the second he entered the room.

"Oh, Augustine—perfect! Zoey wants to go meet up with Mandrake to see what they know about her brother. Which— Mirza, you were talking about creep factor? This Theo guy gives off total creeper vibes. Anyway, I think Mandrake knows exactly where Theo's been keeping his coffin or whatever. They haven't fed me any bad intel yet."

"Charlotte, I didn't—" I said, trying to correct her on more than one front. She was right about Theo being a creep, but modern vampires rarely slept in coffins, much preferring beds. Crypts, on the other hand, were a totally different story.

"Oh, don't be shy, Zo. Anyway, she can't leave the house without you. And I also need you to come since you're like a big-wig or whatever. And who knows, this person—or creature— might be useful as an informant to RIDER too. Just think of the possibilities," Charlotte said, returning my gaze with a smirk that said *trust the process.*

Augustine took a deep breath and scoured his work area for a sense of direction. He seemed distracted, as if this plan of Charlotte's was the least of his worries.

"This Mandrake, refresh my memory. They're the contact who gave us the lead in Philadelphia, right?" Augustine finally asked.

"Yup! That's the one," Charlotte said, shaking the mandrake leaves as she enunciated each word.

Augustine rubbed his brow pensively. He turned toward me, cocking his head slightly to give me a thoughtful look. "Well, Miss Prescott, what are your thoughts? Do you think we should go on this adventure that Miss Tennet has, um, brought to our attention?"

This was a pleasant surprise. His tone was not condescending, but refreshingly playful. Augustine was keeping his promise of guardianship without being overbearing.

I didn't know what to say. While I wanted my words to be profound, concise, and meaningful, they ended up just spilling out of my mouth as I stammered, verbally tripping head over heels. "Oh, um, well. Perhap—I mean, um. Yes. Yes-yes. We should."

"Well, Miss Tennet, there's your answer. But I think we'll need to fly under the radar with this one, if you catch my drift. You know, omit the details from any reports that might go back to HQ." Augustine said the last bit with a nod in my direction.

"Awesome!" Charlotte said excitedly. "I mean, I was gonna go anyway, but it's way more fun with company."

"You don't think it'll be too dangerous?" I asked Augustine. It seemed a little suspicious that it had barely taken any convincing to break 'the rules.' "And the security team. What's our plan there?"

Between the agents who were Gifted, and those that were highly skilled, it was difficult for even a fly to get past them. Let alone a witch, a researcher whose face had been plastered on every security briefing, and a high-ranking RIDER official.

"Meetings with informants are typically low risk, quick in-and-out operations. This Mandrake person has proved themselves to be legitimate in the past, and if they are as skittish as Miss Tennet says, they will probably not want to stick around for a second longer than they need to. Now, the security team, that's a different—"

"Leave it to me!" Charlotte said with a satisfied look. "Nothing a little magic can't solve."

A buzzing noise radiated through the room, and Charlotte pulled out her mobile.

"It's Mother. I gotta go. I'll catch up with you later on the deets. Get excited!" she said quickly before answering the phone. "Hi Mom!... Yes, the guests are still here and yes, The House and I have been the perfect hosts."

The rings on her fingers clanked together as she waved goodbye and walked into the hallway, sliding the pocket doors closed so that only a sliver remained open.

"Quite an adventure you're having, huh? And to think, it's only Saturday," Augustine said to me, flashing a warm grin that made me melt inside.

"Well, I guess I've got to milk it for all it's worth before I go back to New York. Just don't tell me there's a pastry shop across the street glamoured to look like a garage. Otherwise, I'll start going rogue," I replied coolly.

This earned me a smile from Augustine before he cracked open his laptop, even though I had wished for something more.

It still felt weird trying to make pleasant small talk after our conversation a few days ago. Our work relationship wasn't usually so direct. When we were at the real command center in New York, we had more than half of the DIDs department separating us.

I also returned to my laptop for any updates on Theo. The enforcement team had been to four of the ten locations I listed. And while they found and disposed of a vampire nest in one of the vacant mansions on Woodland Drive, Theo, unfortunately, had not been among them.

"No, Mom!" Charlotte shouted as she paced back and forth in the hallway. Her mobile was pressed firmly to the side of her face. "I'm so busy, I don't have the luxury of spending all day practicing magic like you and Dad did... Yes, I've asked for help from the RIDER people, but it's still not helping!"

Through the slit in the door, I could see her hunched over in the hallway staring at the blue runner decorated in middle-eastern styled flourishes and flowers. She tapped her foot impatiently, lips pursed together as she listened intently on the phone. Her expression suddenly soured into one of anguish and her free hand flew up in the air. Small sparks erupted from her fingers that she quickly extinguished when she balled her hand into a tight fist.

"Mom! I am not acting like a New Broom! It's just, I'm dealing with a lot right now, OKAY? New job, new city....yes, I know how important Samhain is to the family. I just... I don't know if I'll be ready by then."

Charlotte's gaze drifted toward the room's door, and for a moment, our eyes locked. Then, her gaze ticked away, and she retreated down the stairs to the lower levels of the house.

"Word on the street is that her family is crazy intense," Mirza said in a hushed whisper, his voice tinged with mischief as he slipped the table a sly look. "Apparently, each person is expected to be witchcraft's new best thing. Thank god my family's as boring as Midwest transplants get."

"Are a witch's powers inherited or learned?" I asked. Despite the crash course from Matt Riley, I was still trying to understand all the intricacies of the witchcraft world.

"Both," Augustine replied, gazing up from his laptop. "A person must be born with powers to be a witch. They're mostly inherited from long familial lines. But new lines of witches can spring out of powerless and non-Gifted families. It's why Covens are so vital to the Witchcraft community. They support both legacy and new, fledgling witches. But even someone born with powers still has to build up their skill set. Just like someone could be a natural basketball player, but you still need to practice to become really great at it."

"That's why she took this job and became the house's current resident," Mirza said. Augustine and I gave him the same confused look, and he shrugged. "Based on what I've heard. She was hoping The House and working with RIDER would help expedite the process. But from last night's spontaneous hydrangea bonfire, I think our girl could use *all* the help she can get."

"She'll get there," Augustine said. "She just needs some time to focus. Magic is as much about the spell as it is the caster. Charlotte has the fire—in both the figurative and literal sense. She just needs to improve her control of both to get to the level of mastery she's after."

Even so, I hoped Charlotte had enough mastery to at least get us to our meeting with Mandrake and back with no hiccups. Or in my case, any immediate recalls back to New York before we found Theo.

NINE

After wrapping things up for the day in the command center, Mirza, Augustine, and I met Charlotte and Tristan in one of the parlor rooms for an impromptu happy hour organized by the hostessing witch herself.

Tristan spent the hour going a mile a minute and sloshing the wine in his glass around wildly as he tried to explain the politics around mermaid and siren agreements (or really lack thereof) and how that had been severely impacting US bound cargo ships and the US supply chain. Apparently, the absence of clear hunting territories had led to overfishing of the human sea mariner kind. Now, many crews were too spooked or shorthanded to sail their ships into port on time.

To reciprocate, we briefed him on our plan to meet with Mandrake. Tristan let out a long sigh, and despite my excited pleading that almost turned into full out begging, he would not budge.

"I would love to pick this Mandrake person's brain on how they've been able to track the witch murderer, but I can't. Nine AM call London-time with my counterpart at Global HQ. No way

I'd make it back in time," he said glumly, sipping down the rest of his wine and motioning toward the carafe for a refill.

It had been a full and busy day. Yet as I tried to sneak in a quick nap before our three AM outing, rest did not come. Instead, I flopped around restlessly on the plushy floral pink bed in my room.

Conceding defeat, I threw the comforter and blankets aside, crawled out of bed and slipped into my slippers. If I couldn't sleep until we left, I might as well caffeinate myself.

Padding downstairs, I crossed through the living room. There, a handful of RIDER agents casually stood at their posts. Others were playing a game of poker at the coffee table. One agent, who was obviously Gifted, shuffled the deck and dealt out cards at a speed too fast for human eyes to keep up with.

In the kitchen, I spotted the fancy electronic coffee maker and paused. It glowed back at me with a formidable luminosity.

I eyed it up and down as if it were a wild stallion, determined more than ever to master how to use it. While it was always nice to have Tristan's help with what seemed like my allergy to all things new technology, he had retired to his room hours ago to attend more calls.

I needed to figure this bitch out on my own.

"Okay, machine. Let's see what you can do," I said under my breath, sliding a ceramic white mug into place beneath it. It responded with a short beep, accepting the challenge.

I poked at the screen in a quick jabbing motion as if it were about to come alive and grab onto my hand. Retracing the steps Tristan had walked me through earlier, I finally came to that beloved screen with a button labeled 'London Fog Latte' and clicked to add a shot of espresso.

The loading bar scrolled underneath. The cartoon mug with a face danced.

A moment later, a loud gurgling sound and a stream of hot liquid dispensed into the mug. I grinned with satisfaction. Maybe technology wasn't so terrible after all. I couldn't wait to show Tristan.

Grinning like a fool, I carried the steaming mug through the back of the house toward the staircase, trying to avoid the raucous game of poker in the front living room. I walked through the empty dining room, where I crossed by the long back hallway.

Something moved down the hallway. It was quick. A flicker of movement or the end of a shadow. But it was definitely *something*.

Curious, I pivoted to walk down the hallway instead of passing by it.

As I moved down the hall, my footsteps released a high-pitched creak along the wide, old hardwood planks. This was an area of the house I had yet to explore, and seeing how The House had behaved in the past couple of days, I had no idea what could be lurking around the corners. At this point, it wouldn't surprise me to enter a room where a bunch of formal dinnerware and antiques were in the midst of doing the cha-cha, with the china cabinet applauding in the back.

The door to the mysterious basement where Olivia and Luke kept running back to loomed a few feet ahead. They hadn't made an appearance at the early evening happy hour, and I wondered if they were okay, after the state they were in at lunch.

I grasped the white ceramic knob in my hand, feeling it vibrate as it came into contact with my skin. How odd.

I leaned forward and put my ear to the door to see if I could hear if it was noise. Expecting to hear the murmurings of a large TV or a sub-woofer. I couldn't hear anything distinct, just a rumbling that rolled up from the basement.

Raising my hand to knock, I paused when a gust of wind passed by me and down the hallway.

A dull thwack sounded a few feet away.

I looked to my left to see that a mobile in a light pink leather case encrusted with rhinestones had clattered to the floor.

"House! What did I tell you?! Cell phones are not toys!" Charlotte's frustrated voice called out ahead.

"Charlotte?"

Leaving the secrets that laid beyond the basement door, I cautiously moved toward the fallen mobile.

Charlotte's bangled hand reached out into the hallway and quickly snatched it up before retreating from view.

I found the witch sitting in a recessed nook of the hallway that had been transformed into a sitting area. She sat in a cream-colored tufted love seat behind a cherry wood coffee table that was flanked by two matching armchairs. In her hands, she shuffled a deck of cards that were larger than typical playing cards.

Expecting her usual exuberant, extraverted greeting, it surprised me when she didn't acknowledge me at all. Instead, she intently shuffled the cards with her eyes closed. Her mouth moved quickly, whispering words I couldn't quite catch.

Her eyes snapped open, sudden and alert. Condensing the cards into a single deck in one hand, she thoughtfully peeled off the top card and laid it on the table, right side up.

Tarot cards.

The card on the table depicted a man in armor sitting in a carriage with two sphinxes on either side and the walls of a castle kingdom behind them. From my view, the card was right side up, but downward facing to Charlotte. "The Chariot" was inscribed at the bottom.

Charlotte sighed and cursed under her breath.

"Oh, hey girl!" She beamed, looking up at me as if just now noticing my presence. "What are you doing down here? I thought you were going to get some shuteye before our *super-secret rendezvous*." She said the last three words in a hushed whisper.

"Couldn't sleep. So, now I'm in re-caffeination mode," I said with a small laugh, motioning to the mug in my hand.

My eyes drifted behind her and landed on a chess table and set in the back corner. I moved toward it and picked up the black queen piece, feeling the intricate, wood-carved curves and edges between my fingers and admiring the rich lacquer finish. It felt so familiar, but when I flipped it over, it didn't have my father's initials carved underneath.

"Do you play?"

"No." My voice sounded distant as I placed the queen back in her spot. "But my parents did. They had a set like this one, made of boxwood and lacquer. I've actually been scouting Sotheby's for decades to see if it's turned up somewhere after all this time. Maybe one day." I shrugged and fixed my eyes back on the Chariot card on the coffee table. "What's the card mean?"

Tarot was wildly popular at RIDER, especially amongst staff that were Gifted with the slightest of psychic abilities. However, I never really took any interest in the hobby. I mean, it seemed unlikely that a pile of cards had the power to interpret or steer someone's future.

"Ugh," Charlotte replied, exasperated. "It means I've still got a lot of hard work left to do."

I picked the card up off the table, analyzing its illustration to see if it offered any more context.

"It's the Chariot card. Usually that means that I'm on the right path, overcoming all the obstacles to achieve, you know, my goals. But when it's reversed like that, it means my energy is scattered, and I'm lacking direction to the right path," she explained glumly.

"Is Tarot a—"

"A witch thing? Yeah. Well, kind of. Our powers come from our ancestors who can see all the events time holds. The Tarot cards help us channel our connection with them. And if there's one thing I've learned, it's that the cards never lie."

I gave the card back to Charlotte, who shuffled it in her deck, and took a seat in one of the side chairs.

"My family is totally old school with tradition," she continued. "And at my age, I should have—well, *they* think I should have mastered my powers by now. But I wanted to go to Norm school, you know?"

I definitely didn't know. "Norm school?"

"Wow, you really have been locked up at RIDER for a long time. Norm school—school for Normals? Humans without powers or creature lineage? My family, being the way they are, sent me to the best private schools for witches. But for college, I wanted to go to Norm school. So I could have the real American college experience. I mean, we spend our entire lives living amongst Normals. I wanted to get to know them. See what makes them tick, go to frat parties, drink jungle juice that wasn't bewitched. Although I seriously have doubts when it comes to Everclear."

"Uh-huh," I said, a little skeptical. Charlotte had strong feelings about this topic.

"Anyway, powers don't really manifest until the late teens for female witches. So a traditional witch's college experience is focused on mastering her magic. And now my parents think I'm behind—which I'm not. I just need more time. But everyone knows my family. Sometimes the pressure to be the perfect spell caster can be, you know, overwhelming," Charlotte trailed off, looking down at the red and cream area rug beneath her feet.

Then, as if breaking from a trance, she snapped up to look at me.

"Okay, your turn! It'll take my mind off all this stupid family drama and help practice my craft," she said with an encouraging look, shuffling the cards again.

Why not? If I remembered correctly, there was a justice card that would confirm a successful mission. It would be reassuring to know it was fate. We also still had hours before we needed to meet up with Mandrake, and the idea seemed to restore Charlotte back to her upbeat self.

"Alright."

"Okay, now cut the deck into three piles. However you like," she instructed.

Accepting the deck with both hands, I placed it on the table and then lifted it twice to deposit various sized stacks into three piles. Charlotte gathered the cards back into a single pile and similar to as she did before, she whispered over the cards. Her mouth again moved too quickly for me to pick out the words—if they were even English, as she spoke.

Something different happened this time.

Her eyes, staring blankly ahead, took on a thin, milky glaze. She sat on the love seat completely unmoving except for her mouth.

I leaned forward and reached out my arm toward her. Concerned something had gone wrong, I waved in front of her unblinking eyes. Nothing.

"Char—" I said, but in an instant Charlotte's eyes snapped into focus and the gloss faded.

"Okay, what does Zoey's future hold?" she asked with girlish excitement.

It was as if she didn't realize she had just had some kind of out-of-body experience.

Peeling off the top card of the deck, she laid a single card down in front of me.

The card depicted a circle in the center that looked like the face of a clock with symbols from different cultures. Roman and Hebrew stood out the most. In the four corners were winged animals; a bird, a griffin, a cow, and even an angel, floating on clouds while a sphinx sat at the top of the clock. A snake and a red devil curved around the other sides of the clock, completing the illustration.

"Wheel of Fortune," I read the bottom of the card as it faced me. "So... what's it mean?"

An excited grin stretched across the witch's face.

"It means change is coming for you on the horizon. Something that'll mix things up from the status quo, but definitely something that's part of your destiny," she explained, tapping the card with a perfectly manicured finger.

"Hmm, I've had the same routine for the past two centuries. I wonder what it could be if it's fate," I said, unconvinced.

"Oh! Maybe it means there's a new special love interest in your future!" Charlotte said, blue eyes bulging. "There's only one way to find out." She placed her hand over the remaining stack and closed her eyes to concentrate. "Asking for clarity. What kind of change is in Zoey's future?"

Charlotte drew another card and placed it face up on top of the Wheel of Fortune card.

It was a card I knew despite my lack of Tarot knowledge.

The illustration was of a skeleton slicing at the ground with a large scythe. Buried in the ground were people of all classes: kings, queens, and commoners. All dead and dying, trying to climb their way out as the skeleton kept them at bay. A large sun set in the background.

It was the Death card, also confirmed by the title beneath the drawing.

My mouth opened in surprise. "Death?" I asked Charlotte, obviously concerned.

I had lived for so long that the concept seemed a little strange to me. Why this card now?

"Don't worry." The witch dismissed with a wave of her hand. "In Tarot, the death card isn't literal. It's facing up, so it means there will be an abrupt change. In an end of an era kind of way. It doesn't have to be bad. Let's ask for clarification."

Once again, Charlotte placed her hand over the remaining stack and concentrated.

"Asking again for clarity. This is a symbolic death, a metaphor?"

She breathed out deeply and peeled another card off the top of the stack. Then, carefully placing the card face up on top of the Death and Wheel of Fortune cards, she withdrew her hand.

Charlotte gasped, frightened.

"Oh, no," she moaned, biting her bottom lip.

I didn't get it. The card looked innocent enough. Kind of. It showed a castle tower being struck by lightning, with flames shooting out of the windows. Two figures fell out of the tower into the water below. It didn't look very positive, but definitely not as foreboding as the Death card.

"What is it? What does it mean?" I asked, intrigued.

"This," she said, leaning over the table to look at the card. It was as if she didn't even want to touch it. "Is the Tower card. It represents unforeseen change and danger. And with 'yes' or 'no' questions, it's associated with a clear 'no.'"

That meant that no, the death card did not represent a metaphorical death.

I swallowed hard, trying to remove the knot that had formed there. I knew there was a reason I'd never really been into Tarot.

"Wait, so this means I am going to die? But how—why? How soon?" I asked, my tone quickly becoming frantic.

It seemed strange that a little cardboard card would be able to tell me that after two hundred years, death was in my near future. But it was also scary. Living as long as I have, death seemed unreal. Like the Bogeyman—even though he was kind of real, according to recent reports in the Florida Keys. Over the centuries, I couldn't imagine what no longer being alive would be like. And when I did, the very thought paralyzed me with fear. The cards had to be wrong.

Charlotte shook her head and scooped up the cards in her hands, placing them back in the deck.

"I don't think it means anything. I mean, my magic's wonky anyway, right? Must not be interpreting the cards right. You've lived for what? Over two hundred years at this point without coming close to dying or anything? I'm sure you'll live for another two hundred."

"Sure," I replied, a little uneasy. "I mean, they're just cards, right? Must be some kind of convoluted metaphor. Who knows, maybe it means I'm finally getting a promotion." I tried to replace the fear in my voice with smugness to reassure myself.

"Exactly!" Charlotte agreed, flashing a toothy smile. "Anyway, I should get going. I need to get ready for later and that's some magic I can't screw up."

Although Charlotte dismissed the reading of any bad omens, I could not shake the sinking sensation and the small voice in the back of my mind that urged, *Are you sure?*

After all, a murderous vampire was still on the loose.

TEN

At 1:45 in the morning, we assembled in the sitting area of Charlotte's master suite. My mind was a cluttered mess, apprehensive of what might, or might not happen. But I was also excited and hopeful if Mandrake had more clues on Theo's whereabouts.

Charlotte, Augustine and I stood in the glass-paned portioned room adorned with oversized plush gray sitting chairs and a rounded cozy lounger in front of a small fire that danced in the fireplace.

I wore a robe over my clothes as to not draw suspicion when I passed by and waved to the enforcement agent monitoring the hallway outside my room. For all she knew, I was slinking off to do some insomnia-driven work in one of The House's many unused rooms.

The robe, now discarded in a careless heap on the lounger, revealed the woolen pleated cigarette pants, white T-shirt, and oatmeal-colored cardigan underneath. The fact that the bathrobe could conceal the entire ensemble made me wonder if I possessed some kind of magic myself.

Changing out of my slippers and into a pair of white sneakers I had also smuggled in, Charlotte explained how she intended for us to get by the security detail and out of The House unnoticed.

"I'm going to cast some cloaking charms for us and we'll take the back door on the first floor to be extra safe," she said, pulling on a long hunter-green quilted jacket and gray beanie.

"I like it," Augustine said. "And you've practiced weaving this charm before?"

"It's one of my best spells. How else do you think I evaded the cops when they showed up at frat parties? It wasn't just luck or hiding in the pool house."

"Excellent. And even though you say this Mandrake person has been helpful, we still don't know if they're human or creature. Zoey, you know how to use one of these, right?" Augustine asked, handing me a miniature crossbow and a small quiver of arrows from the messenger bag he carried.

"Of course," I lied.

Well, not completely. To prepare for the mission, I spent more time than I had in the past fifty years at RIDER's shooting range. And while I knew how to operate the device, my aim still wasn't great. But given my recent Tarot card reading, it wouldn't hurt to have something sharp and pointy at my disposal, just in case.

"And Charlotte, remember to turn toward the left in case we need some backup firepower."

"Got it, boss," Charlotte replied with a stern nod.

"What about you?" I asked Augustine. Although well acquainted in all things supernatural, Augustine was still human and not the least bit Gifted.

"Don't worry, I'm packing my own heat," he said with a smirk, pulling his jacket to the side to reveal a handgun. "Loaded with silver bullets, just in case."

Silver affected more creatures than just the various breeds of werewolf. And human bodies did not discriminate between the types of metal they were shot with.

"Alright, are we ready to do this?" Charlotte asked, cracking her knuckles.

I slipped a look at Augustine, who offered a reassuring smile.

Charlotte turned to me, arms raised, and pinched the air as if pulling two strings out of the ether. Then, concentrating, she braided the air while mumbling under her breath.

She kept braiding in a downward motion and when she got to my torso, she stooped down to her knees, continuing the braid down my legs and eventually to my feet.

The air in front of my face shimmered, just like The House when we first broke through the wards. The tiniest bit of weight draped over me like a light blanket.

"There," Charlotte announced proudly, standing upright. "I tried to knit it to give you room to walk, but keep your arms close to your body. Otherwise, you'll bust through the charm and the spell will break."

"Nice work. Beautifully executed," Augustine remarked. He looked in my direction, but instead of meeting my gaze, he seemed to look right through me.

"But we can still hear each other, right?" I asked nervously, hoping I hadn't become a living ghost.

"Loud and clear," Augustine said. "Okay, now let's quickly get you and me taken care of, so we're not late."

Charlotte wove her spell over Augustine. When she tied off the long braided seam at the bottom, Augustine quickly faded into the air. The painted portrait of one of Charlotte's ancestors that hung on the wall behind Augustine was now clearly visible.

Finally, Charlotte quickly wove the spell on herself. With the last stitch near her feet, she also became translucent, fading out of sight.

But another obstacle presented itself. We could not see each other.

"How are we going to know where we all are if we can't see each other?" I asked.

"Oh yeah. The House is going to help us with that part. Well, indirectly. We'll all go in a line. When you leave my bedroom, lightly knock on the wall as you exit so we'll know you've passed through. The last to go will close the back door behind them. Hopefully, the security team has gotten used to ignoring The House's knocking and banging. We'll meet at the corner of Thirtieth and P Streets in front of Morgan's Pharmacy. There's a mail deposit box there. When you get there, wait a minute and then bang on the mailbox three times so we know when each person makes it," Charlotte's voice answered.

"It doesn't sound like this is the first time you've done something like this, Miss Tennet," Augustine said with a sly smugness in his voice.

"No, it's not. But believe me, every time I have, it's been for a good reason. Now let's go."

We filed out the door, waiting for the sound of a soft rap on the plaster wall. After Charlotte communicated she had gone ahead, I moved toward the door, careful not to move too quickly and rip the charm. At the door, I nudged it open and looked around. One agent strolled through the hallway, toward the opposite wing. Otherwise, the coast was clear.

I gave my signal to Augustine, slipped out the door and padded down three levels to the main floor. On my way, I passed two agents in a heated discussion about the current season of the Bachelorette.

Holding my breath as I breezed by, they paused, gazed in my direction before one agent said to the other, "I know this house isn't haunted, but it still gives me the creeps."

"Just wait until you actually go to a haunted house. Makes Ghostbusters look like Sesame Street. And good luck getting the ectoplasm out of your clothes. Shit's worse than blood," the other agent remarked.

Breathing a (quiet) sigh of relief, I continued until I made it to the back entrance where I first crept out, then rushed into the backyard. Cold, dewy morning air filled my lungs.

Walking north on Thirtieth Street toward P Street was a bizarre feeling. Thankfully, it was a full moon (although that carried its own precautions), and I could see well in the dark with its light. But that wasn't enough to comfort me from the reality that I was alone, in a foreign city, without an escort by my side. I felt vulnerable and exposed, but also energized and free.

In the quiet of night, every insect buzz, chirp, and occasional dog bark startled me and I flinched, ticking my attention in the sound's direction to make sure it was nothing more.

And just when I thought something might leap out of the shadows to grab me, I finally saw the decals in the top square window panes of a storefront that spelled out Morgan's. Counting to sixty, I knocked on the nearby blue mailbox. It rang out three dull, metallic reverberations. I made it.

"Hey, Zo—is that you?" Charlotte's voice whispered to my right.

"Yes, it's me."

Another minute ticked by and a tide of anxiety rose in my gut. What if Augustine didn't make it? Maybe he tripped on the enchantment, breaking the spell. He was always clumsy like that. He had tripped on the black and white checkerboard tile in the front lobby at RIDER more times than he'd like to admit. My mind suddenly shifted to thoughts of the worst-case scenario.

If Augustine had been caught, the cloaking spell would incriminate all of us, given that Charlotte was the only spell caster in The House. The enforcement team would immediately scour The House for Charlotte and me. What would happen when they couldn't find us? Would Augustine be fired immediately? Would they call off the mission?

I was finally getting comfortable having just a working relationship with him again. And I enjoyed watching him give Charlotte the encouragement she needed in practicing her magic. I didn't want that taken away from her, either.

Someone was breathing to my left. A moment later, three more metallic bangs rang out.

"Gang?" Augustine's voice asked.

"All here," Charlotte said, a bit of giddiness in her voice.

The witch slowly faded into view, her hands were working to rip up her woven charm as if breaking out of a sheet of fabric.

Searching in my direction, she outstretched her hands, palms up, and moved toward me.

"Okay, each of you grab onto my hands."

I gripped her left hand and saw her right bob in the air as Augustine did the same.

Charlotte closed her eyes, mumbling her incantation. Then, in one swift motion, she grabbed onto the air just above our hands and jerked.

The air shimmered again, a flash of bending gossamer light. The veil lifted, and all three of us stood in front of the quaint neighborhood pharmacy that was the bottom tenant in a cream-painted row house.

"Come on, it's almost three AM," Charlotte said, a sense of urgency in her voice. "Dumbarton Oaks is just a few blocks away."

———

For Charlotte's next trick, she demonstrated why banks and museums should be grateful she pursued the role as RIDER's Coven Liaison instead of a life of crime.

At the entrance of Dumbarton Oaks, tall, red brick walls and an ornate iron gate marked the perimeter. The gate's thick iron bars soared skyward, then crested into two gold painted cornucopia, bursting with curving vines and leaves around a bouquet of wheat in the center.

Beyond the gate was a wide gravel driveway that wound up a

hill, ending at a regal manor house with columns flanking the sides of its grand front entrance.

The three of us crouched over a chain secured with a palm-sized lock that wrapped around the gate's doors.

"Wait till you see this, Auggs," Charlotte said, cracking her knuckles again.

"Please, do not call me Auggs." Even in his youth, Augustine had never been one for nicknames.

Charlotte ignored his comment and shaped her hands into an oval in front of her. Then, making slow, rhythmic pinching motions, she drew her hands slightly apart each time as if she were drawing something out of the air.

She closed her eyes. Then, a few seconds later, she opened them to reveal the same milky glaze I had seen during the Tarot reading.

Small particles, like dust, lit up around her hands. They looked like bioluminescent plankton, tiny little bits of energy.

When enough of the glowing dust accumulated around her hands, it moved into a shape in the air. Long and thin, until it took on the form of a key. Complete with a large, circular bow and a small pentagram carved as a key ward in the bit.

Satisfied with her work, Charlotte blinked to clear her eyes and the key fell out of the air, into her palm. No longer glowing or floating in midair, it was as corporal and unassuming as the key to my apartment.

She fit the key in the padlock with a satisfying click. Then, working quickly, but delicately, she twisted the key in micro adjustments until a heavy pop signaled the padlock's release.

Charlotte pulled the lock off the chain, and Augustine lent a hand to unwrap it from the gate.

"Ta-Da!" Charlotte exclaimed, throwing her hands in the air like a proud magician.

"Nice work again, Miss Tennet. Although I'm getting the

sense that the spells you excel at also have ulterior uses," Augustine said.

He had a point. Between her cloaking spells and lock-picking skills, it made me wonder if her family's wealth came from purely legitimate means.

Charlotte responded in jest, placing a finger in front of her mouth as if to say 'shh' and winking. Then, wrestling the key out of the padlock's mechanics, she tossed it to the side, muttering the phrase, "Propositum servivit." My mind quickly translated the Latin *'Purpose served.'*

The magic key turned to ash as it sailed through the air, blowing away with the next gust of wind before it could touch the ground.

Charlotte opened the gate, and it let out a dry, creaky moan in protest. Slipping through, she motioned for us to follow.

We didn't head toward the house on the hill, but followed a smaller gravel path to the left. Then, crossing through a well-kept grassy lawn, we came to Dumbarton Oaks' Orangery.

From the information Ellie had emailed over earlier in the day, seeing it in person confirmed that it was a structure almost as old as I was. But I still clipped it by a century.

And while it looked and served a similar purpose to a greenhouse, the difference came from the Orangery's brick exterior dotted with tall, long ovals of paned windows and lantern-like glass roof. A large door with a curved transom marked the center.

Vines bursting with late summer flowers trailed down from boughs anchored on the exterior sides and roof. We were far south enough that the weather hadn't hurried them into the next season yet.

"Through here," Charlotte said, pointing to the Orangery's front door.

"Oh, wow," I remarked, carefully crossing over the threshold.

My sneakers squeaked on the hexagon-shaped brick tile that covered the entire interior. Potted trees in terracotta pots filled the space but still provided ample room to move around. A couple of tattered bistro sets were scattered throughout the large room. Their white paint chipped in places to reveal the silver aluminum underneath.

All of that paled compared to the ivy. Majestic vines covered the walls and ceiling in thick strands, like garland.

In the daytime, I imagined it had a sort of farmhouse whimsy to it. But at night, the space was eerie. As if at any moment the ivy might come to life, reaching out of the shadows to grab onto my arms and legs. I wrapped my arms around my chest.

Following Charlotte, we turned right to exit through the Orangery's side door that emptied us into a brick enclosed courtyard with a large mature birch tree in the middle. The birch's roots twisted and knotted the ground so much that I had to be careful not to trip. Charlotte and Augustine powered on the flashlights on their mobiles to survey the surrounding area.

We passed through the courtyard to find we were at the top of a tall brick staircase. From our view, we could see the glittering city lights of an adjacent neighborhood.

"That's Adams Morgan," Charlotte said, pointing to an illuminated cluster in the distance. "The scene's a little bro-y, but I mean, what place in DC isn't? The cocktails at Jack Rose make up for it, though."

"How much farther?" I asked in a hushed whisper. The endless landscape of gardens and nineteenth-century buildings had just as many turns and quirks as the scenery in Alice in Wonderland.

"We're close. Just keep moving," Charlotte replied.

Descending the staircase, we entered the Rose Garden, according to the brass plate affixed to the outside wall. The garden was a beautiful lattice-patterned labyrinth of slate tile and walls of thorny rose bushes in bright white, pink, and red that even towered inches above Augustine's head.

Then finally, as promised, we descended another staircase to the terrace level. This space was filled with stately round balls and swirling cones of topiary and I half expected to see an English cottage nearby. Two large, rectangular pools of water with matching bubbling fountains in the shape of cherubs flanked each side of the garden. The rest of the terrace was covered in thick, freshly clipped grass.

Veering left, we came to a stone plaza cordoned by a fenced wooden retaining wall as the space jutted out of the side of a sloping hill. Below it were even more lofty gardens and pools.

Charlotte stopped abruptly in front of a curved pedestal fountain in the middle.

"Okay, this is it. The Arbor Terrace," she whispered, throwing up her arm in a right-angle shape like you see in military shows. *Stop here.*

Augustine and Charlotte powered off their flashlights. The clear sky and full moon were enough to offer ample light. Around us were potted plants and trees of varying species. I even spied a couple of pear trees bearing their small fruit.

In front of the fountain was the garden's namesake: the arbor. It had been a long time since I heard the term used. People just called them pergolas now.

This one curved at the top like the lid of a chest and was covered in a heavy mop of wisteria. The plants were thick and lush with lavender flowers and green leaves dangling from the boughs. It made the arbor look like a large treetop with trunks carved into posts to create the projecting eave.

"And now we wait?" Augustine asked, looking at the Rolex on his wrist.

I had been sure to conveniently leave my smart watch on my room's night table in exchange for a mechanical one, paranoid that someone might be monitoring my location. Strange enough, I felt naked without its near-constant buzzing.

"Two minutes," Charlotte said brightly, flashing her mobile's clock. 2:58 AM.

Two minutes went by.

Then ten. Then fifteen.

At twenty minutes past the hour and rendezvous time, I let out a sigh.

"Are you sure this is the right place? The right time? Maybe there's another Arbor Terrace nearby."

Charlotte's face twisted into a look of disdain, and she shook her head. "I don't get it. Mandrake is always true to their word. And they use code that they know I'll understand."

"Well, as a voice of experience, I, for one, am happy with this anti-climatic excursion. It's possible that the informant felt compromised and reconsidered tonight's meet up. Anyway, it's well past all of our bedtimes, and we have another long day ahead of us... today, actually. We should start heading back before the agents switch out shift teams," Augustine said, moving toward the adjacent garden where the staircase waited.

Frowning, I looped the holster of the crossbow over my shoulder and followed Augustine's lead.

Expecting to hear the heavy tread of Charlotte's designer combat boots behind me, the lack of which made me look over my shoulder.

Charlotte stood still, unmoving. Her unblinking eyes were transfixed on the shadowy void of the arbor's interior.

I followed her gaze, expecting to see what she saw. But nothing was there. Just darkness. The arbor's wisteria roof too thick for the moonlight to penetrate.

"Charlotte," I said. "Are you comin—"

"Shhh!" she hushed, still not moving any other part of her body except her lips. "We're not alone."

Carefully walking toward her, we both stood on the terrace, waiting and listening. Everything remained still and nothing moved within the depths of the arbor.

Must be an animal rummaging around for the crumbs of a

snack a tourist had left earlier. I reached out to touch Charlotte's shoulder.

"It's gotta be a fox or—"

"It's not a fox," Charlotte said evenly. She suddenly stiffened and her eyes went wide with panic. "Oh my goddess, it's a—"

The witch wasn't able to finish her sentence.

"I thought we were cool, Charlotte," a male voice rumbled out from the arbor's shadows.

The voice was low, and its tone was tinged with annoyance in a way that it sounded like a growl.

"Mandrake? Is that you?" Charlotte called out. Her face was pained as her eyes searched wildly for the source of the voice in the dark.

Silence.

Augustine quietly rejoined us. He drew his pistol and took a cautious step toward the arbor.

"Mandrake? We-we are cool. I don't know what you're talking about," Charlotte continued, standing her ground.

"I think you know exactly what I'm talking about," the voice said.

The voice had an odd sense of familiarity, but the accent was strange. The large Rolodex in my mind's eye flipped wildly through every face, name, and species I knew. But nothing came into view as a match.

"I'm leaving. I don't have time for your stupid mind games. I should have known better than to trust a witch," the voice continued, becoming more irritated each time it spoke.

"No!" Charlotte shouted, taking a step forward.

Augustine threw her a nervous glance and swept his closest arm toward her to brace her from whatever lurked ahead.

"Don't leave! I've been straight with you this whole time. It's time for you to be straight with me," she said bluntly, her own anger beginning to swell.

Charlotte's strategy to further provoke the voice wouldn't have been one that I would have taken. Especially considering we didn't know what kind of creature was on the other end, and if they had automatic weapons of their own. But then again, I could not ignite fire from my palms or make myself invisible. I hoped Charlotte knew what she was doing.

The sound of clapping echoed out of the abyss. Slow and deliberate.

"Congratulations. You figured it out," the voice growled. "You've done your research, too."

The tips of the voice's black boots breached the shadows, illuminated in the moonlight just beyond the arbor's overhang.

Prowling out of the dark, his motions were smooth and precise, like a tiger about to pounce. He took a few steps, slowly at first. Then, in the blink of an eye, he was suddenly standing just a few feet in front of us.

He was young, appearing to be in his mid-twenties. His tall stature, with wide shoulders that clipped down to a trim waist and then into sturdy legs, gave him a towering, almost Frankenstein-like appearance.

The clothes he wore were modern. Black jeans and a simple heathered grey t-shirt underneath a waist-length, smooth black leather jacket. A single pendant necklace hung from his neck and several silver rings dotted his fingers.

The most prominent features were on his face. Square shaped with a defined jaw, his lips were drawn taut with irritation. A blocky, rectangular nose with sharp angles dotted the plane of his face. It flared. But whether in anger, to take in scent, or both, was a question left to be desired.

His dark brown hair was stark against his pale skin. It was cropped close to the nape of his neck and brushed back from his forehead, like how most men wore their hair in this decade.

Below his forehead, his eyebrows were thick and dark. They knitted tightly together to show their displeasure.

Heavy dread washed over me and I broke out in a cold sweat.

My eyes quickly scanned him while his own were transfixed on me. I wanted to scream, but I was paralyzed with fear.

It was like I had been transported back to RIDER, reviewing the Vampire Top Ten Chart.

Except he was standing right in front of me.

And he was angry.

"And now you've bewitched one of your friends to look like my dead sister to screw with me. That, Charlotte, is not what I would call cool," Theo said.

Eleven

Charlotte glanced at me nervously.

There were so many things that I wanted to scream at her. *Stop! Run!* And definitely *Don't piss him off!*

But in that millisecond of time, all I could do was stand there with my mouth open, speechless.

Theo, my brother, Number Seven on the Vampire Top Ten Chart, was standing right in front of us.

And as if that wasn't bad enough, he was pissed off. Pissed off at me.

Icy dread beginning at the crown of my head seeped down into my chest and my mind raced.

Theo is Mandrake? But how? It all had to be part of a larger plan.

And we just walked right into it without back-up. Shit.

"Wait, a second. You're *that* vampire? The one everyone's been talking about? Well, I've got news for you, tall, dark, and fangy: no witch tricks here. Your sister next to me? Oh yeah, she's the real deal, and she's not dead either. She's like immortal or whatever. And we're all about to kill your undead ass. Again!" Charlotte said.

My eyes widened. If I hadn't been so scared, I would have scolded Charlotte for giving a murderous creature all of our cards.

"The Immortal?" Theo repeated softly to himself, his brow knitting with confusion. His gaze moved from Charlotte to me, and an unsettled look crossed his face. Then he shook his head as if to clear his focus and narrowed his eyes at the witch. "You're lucky I'm not the same vampire you've read about. Otherwise, you wouldn't make it two steps from where you're standing." His words were smooth, almost flirtatious, like a cat playing with a mouse.

Not the same vampire you've read about. What was that supposed to mean?

Looking over at Augustine, he had his gun lifted and pointed at Theo's head. I understood his hesitation to fire. Bullets could not kill vampires. Not even silver ones. A bullet to the head usually caused them to pass out. But if Augustine fired his gun too early, even if he struck his target, it could cause Theo to flip. 'Flipping' was a slang term to describe when a vampire became irrationally enraged and incredibly dangerous. Theo could easily rip out all our throats in a millisecond of time—even with a bullet lodged in him. It wasn't worth the risk. Not yet, at least.

"Theo, this ends tonight," I said. I thought of our family: our father's warm, rolling laughter that always filled our house and the way our mother always smelled of honeysuckle and lavender. They suffered a horrible death just to satisfy Theo's voracious appetite.

Thinking of them gave me enough courage to quell my fear and lift the loaded crossbow in front of me. I pointed it directly at his chest, but slightly to the right. Just like I had learned in combat training to precisely aim at his unbeating heart. My finger rested on the trigger.

"I am also not the same person you knew two centuries ago."

The sight of the crossbow, loaded with a deadly wooden arrow, seemed to trigger something in Theo. Feral and animalistic.

He shifted to his Other Face—his true face. The skin over his nose and underneath his eyes crawled into formation, folding and shaping into the demonic visage of a vampire. With a single blink, his brown eyes became a wild amber color. He snarled, revealing rows of sharp, uneven teeth and a long pair of canine fangs.

Theo took a single step forward, toward Charlotte and me.

Augustine fired his gun. He missed. It was unclear whether it was shoddy aim or that Theo had dodged the shot too quickly for my eyes to catch.

The sound of the gun reverberated around us. The loud bang made me flinch, and I pulled the crossbow trigger earlier than I had planned.

The wooden arrow flew through the air, arcing to target the vampire's chest.

Theo caught it in one hand at the shaft before it could make contact. Squeezing his hand, the wood snapped like a twig. He tossed the pieces to the ground and growled.

He took another step forward.

Charlotte and I took a collective step back.

I fumbled to reload the crossbow with another arrow. My hands, suddenly frozen with fear, were stiff and clumsy. The arrow fell out of my hands and clattered to the stone below. I drew another and looked at Charlotte for back-up.

Charlotte was shaking, almost as much as I was. She threw her arms down, palms up, and curled her fingers, ready to ignite fire within them. Theo snarled, but remained in place.

But instead of fire, sparks flew from Charlotte's palms. They rained down from her hands, falling to the cold stone below with a hiss as they extinguished.

"No, no, no," Charlotte cried out. She was hyperventilating, taking in large gasps of air.

The witch flicked her hands again and again, trying to invoke a stable flame. But more sparks erupted. And not only her palms this time, but her fingers too. The sparks took on a life of their own, shooting out in all directions.

I ducked. Augustine pulled his jacket over himself like a shield. One spark landed on Theo's shirt, igniting into a small fire. The vampire hissed and backed up a few steps, swatting to stamp out the flame with his hand.

Augustine was moving. Not toward Theo, but to Charlotte. From behind, he grabbed her arms and thrust them into the fountain in front of her. There was a sizzling sound and a large plume of steam rose into the air as the water extinguished her hands.

Charlotte was still gasping for breath, but it was more controlled. She was panting now, leaning over the fountain for support.

"Theo!" I exclaimed under my breath.

Distracted, I had taken my eyes off of him. Jamming another arrow into the crossbow's flight groove, I pulled it back and pointed the weapon in the spot where my brother stood.

It was empty.

Whipping around wildly in place, with the crossbow in tow, I searched the terrace for him. Every shadow and potted tree where he might be lurking. But he was gone.

We were alone again in the eerie silence before morning twilight.

The only sound that filled the Dumbarton Oak's Arbor Terrace was the labored noise of Charlotte's breathing and Augustine's calm, measured murmuring.

"It's okay, everything's going to be okay," he said, rubbing her upper back and shoulders like a caring parent did when their child fell and scraped a knee.

Augustine's gaze met mine, and we exchanged the same strained, but relieved, look.

We should have died tonight. But somehow we lived to see the approaching dawn.

TWELVE

"You should have told me you were sparking."

We were walking fast through the residential streets of George-town back to Charlotte's house. The first blue rays of morning were barely breaching the night sky. I had never been so thankful to see the sun again. My heart pounded in my chest like a sledge-hammer as I silently digested what had just happened.

Meanwhile, Augustine was interrogating Charlotte.

"I thought I had a handle on it. It only happens when I'm like freaked or anxious," the witch replied.

"You mean *freaked* like one would be when they're face-to-face with a murderous demon? Charlotte, what were you thinking? You were in no condition to think you could take on a vampire," Augustine said, shaking his head.

"Hey!" Charlotte ran up ahead of Augustine and I and walked backward so she could face us. "Witches don't run."

"What?" Augustine asked, as if he hadn't heard her.

"Witches. Don't. Run," she repeated, enunciating each word and looking Augustine straight in the eye. It was the most serious I had seen her.

Augustine rolled his eyes and threw his hands in the air. "Oh no, we are not starting with that," he moaned.

"Witches are not victims. We don't run from what scares us. We run toward the things that are frightening because we are the ones that possess power to help the powerless," she said, gesturing wildly in the air with her arms. I noticed the skin on her palms was chapped and the edges were charred.

"Charlotte, that motivational piece of witch rhetoric is a mantra for witches who have complete control over their powers. Which you haven't mastered yet. You know how in an airplane they say to put your oxygen mask on before you can help others? You can't help others before you've helped yourself. What happened back there—we all could have..." Augustine trailed off, but we knew what he was thinking.

"It's my fault," I blurted out. I couldn't stop thinking about it since we exited the gates of Dumbarton Oaks. "I let my curiosity get the best of me. If I hadn't, we'd all be sleeping soundly in our beds. Instead, we're running for our lives with absolutely no backup."

The whole thing made me sick to my stomach. What was I thinking? Diana and Tristan were right. I had no business thinking I could be in the field. RIDER's rules are in place to keep me safe and I knowingly went against them, which not only put my own life in jeopardy, but also my colleagues'.

Including Augustine.

I crossed my arms tightly around me, feeling more nauseated.

If something had happened to Augustine because of my stupid fantasy of being out in the real world, I didn't think I could live with myself.

"Zo, that's not true. We all agreed to be here tonight," Charlotte said.

"But I had the final say. I encouraged us to go."

"You are not responsible for what happened tonight. Direct meetings with informants who have proved helpful in the past rarely end up like they did tonight. This was supposed to be a simple information exchange. There was no way we could have known Theo was going to be there," Augustine said.

Two blocks from the house, we all abruptly stopped in case a RIDER agent might be patrolling the perimeter.

"The cards," Charlotte said slowly.

I had been thinking about their meaning all night, but didn't understand the connection Charlotte was trying to make.

"Wheel of Fortune, Death, The Tower," she said, counting the reading on her fingers. "It makes total sense! Finding Theo, we faced death but overcame it."

"And it also represents an end to an era. Theo had been flying under the radar, but now we have actual proof that he's still alive. In, you know, the best way a vampire can be," I added.

"Exactly!" Charlotte said, bursting with excitement. "The Tower card must mean that we need to stop Theo from killing anyone else—witch or not."

A dark shadow crossed Augustine's face.

"Who had that reading?" he asked with a stern look, eyes ticking back and forth between Charlotte and me.

"I—I did. Charlotte—"

"It was super metaphorical. And as you can see, we pretty much figured out what it meant. Also, no one's future can be that crazy ominous. But big thing here—we didn't die!" Charlotte said.

"I hope you're right," Augustine said. "Now, more than ever, we need fate to be in our favor."

———

Charlotte dressed us back up in cloaking spells to re-enter The House, which was thankfully a smooth process. At the early hour, The House was calm except for the band of agents still playing cards on the first floor. The sound drifted through the quiet areas of The House like white noise.

We reconvened in Charlotte's master suite, where she removed the charms and I put on my robe and slippers as part of my insomnia costume. In reality, I had never felt so exhausted before. Not even when I stayed up for two days straight to deal with an unexpected werewolf event caused by a solar eclipse.

On the walk back to my room, I passed by an agent who commented, "Early morning, huh Miss Prescott?"

"Something like that," I replied with a tired sigh.

Nearing my door, I heard Augustine call out my name behind me.

Just go to sleep, I urged myself to ignore him. I was too exhausted to muster the energy and straight face I needed with one-on-one interactions with him these days. And after the shit-show that was the night's events, what more was there to say?

"Zoey, wait." Augustine grabbed my hand.

My head spun. Memories of us exploded in my mind at his familiar touch. Strong, warm, and gentle. My hand fit perfectly in his palm, like a key made just for one lock. His fingers were thicker than I remembered. The calluses on his palms and knuckles, rougher with age. I didn't want to ever let go.

I whirled around to face him. He was looking down at our hands. My gaze followed.

"You're shaking," he said.

I hadn't stopped since I saw Theo come out from under the arbor's shadows.

Silence passed between us as we stood there, soaking up the moment. It seemed as if time itself had stopped.

"Forgive me," Augustine said, suddenly flustered, dropping my hand.

"It's—it's fine." Heat rushed to my cheeks. "It's been a long night. I should—" I stopped mid-sentence, not able to think of anything witty, profound, or otherwise useful.

Turning my back on him, I pulled out the tiny key to my room and opened the door. Much-needed solitude and sleep laid just beyond the threshold.

"You're wrong," Augustine said.

With my hand on the curved brass doorknob, I slowly turned to face him with a look I hoped only showed my shocked expression.

My role at RIDER was technical and academic, and with that, I was rarely—if ever—wrong. I didn't belong in anything more than that. Where the stakes were high and people could get hurt. Diana's warning about my mistakes having deadly consequences had haunted me since I stepped foot outside the Mercedes-Benz SUV and onto the stone driveway in the shape of a pentagram. Now, I knew she had been right all along.

But I didn't need someone—especially Augustine—to rub it in.

"When you blamed your curiosity for what happened tonight. Your curiosity, whether it be about some new species of demon, or finding which coffee house in the five boroughs makes the best Dirty London Fog, is what makes you, you, Zoey. It's what I've always admired about you," he said.

Shocked by his unexpected response, my eyes cast down to the floor, uneasy.

"But it's not worth it if someone gets hurt," I said, my tone tinged with disgust. "I mean, look at Charlotte—she's so young and has so much life ahead of her. If something—"

"But nothing happened," Augustine said calmly. "The same goes for you, too. Just because your lifespan differs from most, it doesn't mean you're constantly at the end."

I let out the deep breath I had been holding. The rush of it through my mouth and nose was cathartic. Augustine had always been the one person who could help me see the big picture when I only had tunnel vision.

When I lifted my gaze, Augustine's hazel eyes met me there, issuing a tranquil reassurance. Part of me wanted to stay locked there forever. I felt seen, when most times I was just background noise.

"And to be perfectly honest, I think you helped prevent anything worse from happening tonight."

"Ha, how do you figure that?" I asked dryly, seeing through the gaping holes in his white lies.

"When Theo saw you, it seemed to throw him off. Almost like he short-circuited and didn't know what to do. I think if it were only Charlotte and me, we wouldn't have been so lucky."

"Ugh, who knows?" I shrugged. Thinking about my problematic vampire brother was honestly causing me to short-circuit. "We have to find him. Before he hurts someone else."

"I've already set up a reconnaissance team to scour Dumbarton Oaks at first light. If there's anything there that can tell us where he went, we'll find it."

I instantly thought of the singed plants and broken crossbow arrows that littered the Arbor Terrace.

"How are you going to explain what happened there?" I asked in a hushed voice as an agent walked up the stairs to our floor before turning down the hallway that led to the south wing.

"Well, as you know, Tristan and I met with Mandrake. And yes, we should have taken backup, but given the informant's sensitive identity, we handled it, since we both have the proper clearances to do so," Augustine lied. I liked it. His story became more and more believable with each word. Tristan wouldn't need convincing to play along. He was always reliable in the moment. When he knew it counted.

I nodded, satisfied that we hopefully wouldn't be overrun with detailed questions of the in-person Theo sighting. That would only slow us down, and we were so close now.

Bidding Augustine good night, he inclined his head in a courteous bow like he had at my apartment before hurrying away in the direction of his own room.

Inside my room, I shed my clothes to put on oversized and

well-worn sleeping ones, and switched out my watch for the RIDER-preferred gadget. The overly floral bed somehow felt more comfortable with my exhaustion than it did the night before when I crawled under its cloud-like covers.

The sun still hadn't fully risen, and I was eager to get a few hours of rest before the day officially began. Daytime was critical when dealing with creatures of the night, and was always fleeting. It would render Theo virtually immobile from wherever he sought shelter until sundown. We couldn't miss the opportunity to find him.

I closed my eyes, hoping that sleep would come quickly to transport me away to happy, fantastic dreams. But on the underside of my eyelids, I could only see Theo's terrifying amber-colored irises glaring back at me. Angry and full of vengeance.

———

At 7:30 AM, my arm buzzed with its frantic morning call. I slapped and swatted at it until it silenced and took a long, full-body stretch. It felt good. My body ached from the stress of last night's encounter and practically running out of Dumbarton Oaks.

Rolling out of bed, I headed immediately into the bathroom for a much-needed shower. There, the steam enveloped me in a warm fog and I did my best to scrub away the night before, along with the campfire smell that lingered on my hair and skin from being too close to Charlotte's sparks for comfort.

Out of the shower, I was towel-drying my hair when a familiar cooing came from the window.

The mourning doves. My lips formed a small smile just thinking about them. I wondered how much nest-building progress they'd made from the day before and if they'd laid an egg yet. Hopefully, they'd been more productive than I had in the past day.

"Hello, my friends," I said in a soft, sing-song voice as I ambled to the window, careful not to scare them.

The two pinkish gray-colored mates were snug in a nest of twigs, pine needles and even something that looked like wadded up fishing wire. But something between the nest and the windowpane gave me pause. I cocked my head to the side, trying to understand what I was looking at. It definitely hadn't been there the previous day.

It was a small white square of folded paper. About two inches in both height and length. At first, I thought the birds had used it as improvised nesting material. But it wasn't in the nest, it had been thoughtfully slid between the nest and the window. So that it wouldn't blow away.

And so that I would see it.

"Sorry guys," I apologized to the doves as I slid the window open.

They cooed in unison, something in bird that no doubt translated to an agitated string of curse words before they flew off into the backyard.

The paper was stuck to the outside of the window from the morning's dew. I had to wedge my hand under the pane to pry it off before I could unfold it to see what was inside.

Volta Park. Midnight. Come alone.
- Theo

THIRTEEN

"So the Mandrake person is Theo?" Mirza asked, a little skeptical.

"I guess so. It still doesn't make much sense," I replied, equally uncertain.

I took a bite of toast smothered in lemon curd and dusted with cinnamon to mull over last night's disastrous encounter once more. As if I hadn't thought about it enough.

"Charlotte said everything Mandrake had told her: the victims, where the killer was headed next, all the details of the slayings—it all lined up to the same information on our end. She also mentioned that Mandrake sounded desperate to find the killer. Not like she was being lured into a trap."

Mirza twirled the pen in his hand, turning the facts over in his mind. Hearing his take on the whole thing would provide valuable insight. Mirza was a scientist, after all. He approached things from an analytical, fact-based point of view. I didn't want any rash decisions to be made because of my emotional connection to COI 86.

We were eating breakfast in the command center, not able to have the luxury of a leisurely one in the dining room with everything going on. I had alerted Augustine and Diana immediately about the note. That, combined with the white-lie-filled intel

126

Augustine had provided, had set off a domino effect of alarms, protocols, and overall sense of urgency.

Mirza and I had been busy the minute we sat down, sending off flurries of emails and chatting with the enforcement team leads on the conference phone in between carb-filled bites and sips of hot beverages.

"Maybe Theo ate Mandrake and now he's trying to play both sides," Mirza offered.

I hadn't thought of that.

"It's a possibility," I said, raising my brow at the idea before quickly scribbling it down as a note in my Moleskine. There was a reason Theo had lived this long, and it wasn't because he was stupid.

A pair of footsteps and voices traveled up the stairs outside and wafted in through the small slit in the command center's pocket doors. We had pulled them shut to privately discuss what had actually transpired over the past six hours.

Charlotte burst through the doors, rumbling them back into their respective pockets with two loud *thunks*. Thick, white gauze wrapped around both of her palms, but she managed to carry a large steaming blue and white toile print takeaway coffee cup in her hands. Despite the large bandages she wore, she looked glamorous as ever. A pair of oversized Chanel sunglasses covered most of her face, while the rest of her was clad in an olive maxi dress with a tie waist and thigh-high slit on one side, suede tan ankle boots, and lots of gold jewelry.

"Thank you for the escort, Damian. Much appreciated," she said airily to the enforcement agent behind her.

She set her coffee down in front of an empty chair at the table. "Not sure if it's the weather, or just waking up alive, but it is absolutely gorgeous out this morning," she added cheerfully.

"You know, in the group text we all agreed to meet here an hour ago," Mirza said, sending the witch a disapproving look.

"Okay, respectfully noted," she said, slowly removing her

sunglasses and closing them with two loud clicks. "But given last night's events, there was no way I could get through the day without a butterfly pea flower latte. And Café Georgetown down the street makes the best."

Mirza and I exchanged looks across the table. At least I wasn't alone in having no clue what she was talking about.

"Butterfly pea flower," she repeated in a deadpan tone, astonished we weren't familiar. "Well, aren't you a pair of Norms today? Us witches are much more sensitive to herbs and plants than humans. Butterfly pea flower does wonders for calming my nerves and helping me focus. Plus, the blue color matches my Instagram aesthetic." She lifted the lid just enough to show a cap of white foam in the shape of a heart with bright blue liquid that sloshed underneath.

"Is it supposed to look radioactive?" I asked, genuinely curious. It was an alarming shade of blue.

Charlotte shot me a dirty look and pulled out the chair in front of her to sit down. In mid-crouch, she paused and reached into one of the side pockets of her dress to pull out a slender but sharp wooden stake. On the handle, it had the initials *CAT* carved into it in between a design of pentagrams and crescent moons.

The sight surprised me. Despite most of my research being focused on vampires, even I didn't normally carry a stake. Let alone a personalized one.

"Oh, and Damian, would you mind dropping this in my room on the way down? Thanks," Charlotte said, handing the stake to the agent. The agent looked as if he was about to melt in Charlotte's presence and gladly accepted the weapon with a smile and a polite nod as he left the room.

"Considering what happened last night, you never can be too careful, you know," she added, slipping into her seat and taking a drink from her cup.

"You know sunlight is deadly to vampires, right? They can't

hurt us in the daytime. They tend to go 'poof,'" I said, opening and closing my hand in the gesture of something igniting.

"Humph!" Charlotte snorted. "I've caught enough snippets of Blade when it plays on TV to know better. And they can be so crafty when they want something. I should know. The only reason I have a stake is because I dated a vampire in college. Oof, what a mistake that was."

My mouth fell open.

Vampire relationships with creatures outside their own species —especially the warm-blooded types, did not end well for either party. Even humans who wanted to be turned by their partner risked not making it all the way through the resurrection process. Witches also favored keeping their powers over becoming a blood-sucking demon, even with the lure of immortality. Once the relationship moved past the infatuation stage, the differences often became too much.

Luckily, Mirza took the abridged version out of my mouth.

"Charlotte..." he said in a patronizing tone.

"I know, I know," she said, waving her hand as if to brush away Mirza's words and the condescending look he gave her. "I was going through my bad boy phase and he was a very hot and a very bad boy. We only dated for like a month before I broke it off to date my economics TA instead, who didn't have the problem of decapitating his food when he ate it." She grimaced. "Anyway, fangs-for-brains got super jealous and majorly stalker-y. That's how I got so good at ward casting and I never went anywhere without my stake. Took him a while, but he finally got the hint."

"I'm not surprised. Vampires are very emotional creatures. He couldn't help it if he tried; they're just wired like that," I said. Hers was not the first story like that I'd heard, nor would it be the last.

She smiled appreciatively, then glanced around the room at our setup of monitors, papers, charts, and raw data strewn about the room.

"Looks like you've been busy this morning. So, what are we doing about that creepy note and where's Auggs?"

"Augustine is meeting with the enforcement team's director," I replied. "The plan is to have several teams positioned around Volta Park so they'll be able to watch him enter. Then, when he gets into position, they'll close in and take him to a RIDER facility for intake and elimination."

"Elimination? Wow, you RIDER guys don't play around, do you?" Charlotte asked, a little taken aback.

"The facility on Massachusetts Avenue in Dupont that's a front for some quirky high-society club just got back to me. They confirmed that they have vampire-containment resources," Mirza said, looking up from his laptop.

"The Cosmos Club? Perfect," I said, pointing my pen in his direction before crossing it off the day's To-Do list in my Moleskine with a satisfying stroke.

"Hello team," Augustine greeted in sunny baritone. He entered the room and took a seat at the head of the table. His eyes settled on Charlotte as she sipped from her cup. "How are your hands, Charlotte?"

"Better than last night, that's for sure," she replied, looking at the bandages. "I put a healing salve on them. One of my grandmother's spells. She always had a knack for potions. It should heal up by next morning."

"Excellent. So it seems like everything happens for a reason, when it comes to what happened last night, huh? Without Zoey there, we wouldn't be able to lure Theo out of his hiding space tonight," Augustine said with a thoughtful nod in my direction.

"While I don't like the idea of being the bait, I do like the idea of ridding the world of one more diabolical vampire. From a safe distance, of course. I think Tristan said there might be some kind of red button I could push?" I joked.

"Well, if all goes well—and it should now that enforcement is involved, we can ideally pack up to head back to New York tomorrow. Poor Matt Riley. He's probably going to miss the entire show, being tied up in Salem," Augustine said.

"Well, he's not totally off the hook. I'll need him to help me write the press briefing on how our collective powers of collaboration helped apprehend the vampire responsible for seven witch murders. But before that, I'll need to put together a little goodbye soiree. I'll rummage in the basement for the good vintage stuff."

Mirza and I nodded. Charlotte had a knack for hosting that rivaled RIDER's resident event planner.

"It seems a little weird, though," the witch added, gently tapping on her top lip with a forefinger. "Theo last night. He seemed almost... I don't know, confused? Unsure? But you keep telling me he's a slippery son of a bitch, so I guess it was all just some kind of act."

Charlotte shrugged, then stood, grabbing her coffee.

"Well, I should check on the enforcement teams. Make sure The House gives them some peace before it's go-time." With a quick bandaged-hand wave goodbye, she whirled around and left the room.

Turning my attention back to my laptop, an instant message had popped up on the screen.

ElliePhilips: Diana just emailed me a signed copy of the protocol approval to file—you're nabbing Theo tonight??

ZoeyPrescott: Yes! Only a matter of hours now. Aiming to head back tomorrow. Kind of sad I haven't been able to see much of DC. :(

ElliePhilips: Well, you've definitely been missed. The whole DIDs department is going bananas over everything. Keep me posted with live updates. I know how much this means to you!

I smiled.

ZoeyPrescott: Will do! :)

FOURTEEN

We were killing time around the table on the back veranda, the three of us: Mirza, Charlotte, and I. It was nearly 11:00 PM, and the real show on the large monitor in the command center was about to begin.

My whole body felt jittery. Butterflies flapped endlessly in my gut in anticipation that tonight justice (and vengeance) would be duly served. I couldn't help but to think what it was going to be like. Theo had always been stubborn, even with the most inconsequential things. So rather than going easily, accepting his fate, he'd most likely fight to the end, even as his body self-incinerated.

The rest of the day had been spent finalizing all the details. At my recommendation, which Diana approved without so much as a second thought, was that a stake through the heart was the most efficient and humane method of disposal.

The RIDER facility on Massachusetts Avenue was equipped with what Mirza had coined as 'The Stakemaster 5000,' a piece of automated machinery that could target the center of a vampire's unbeating heart and puncture it with a tool the size of a scalpel with a wooden spade on the tip. All in less than five seconds. Then, depending on how much fight he had left in him, he would turn to ash in another one to three seconds.

Part of me wanted to be creative. He upended my entire life and I wanted him to suffer for all the pain he'd caused.

Even if it was just for a millisecond.

Asking his opinion of the sunrise while strapped to a lethal injection table strategically positioned underneath a skylight was how I envisioned he would go. Death by sunlight was by far the most painful way for a vampire to die, according to my extensive research on the topic. It took a while before their body stopped trying to rapidly repair itself and finally burn all the way through. The entire process took minutes, but to them it felt like an eternity.

Unfortunately, this method often resulted in not just the vampire being burned but also the restraints and cushioned table itself. Which would cost money to replace that would then be charged to my department's budget. I could already see the disapproving look Diana would give me for such a selfish indulgence. Also, the smell of charred vampire was both a unique and difficult aroma to get out of walls and clothes. Almost as bad as ectoplasm.

So extermination by stake it was. Simple, effective, and slightly more hygienic.

But on the veranda, we weren't talking about Theo, the plan, or even the mission. We were talking about what would happen after all that. Once things had settled down a bit.

"You have to come visit us in New York City, Charlotte," Mirza said. "And wait till you see Zoey's apartment. It has the most stunning views. Oh, and her private chef makes the best canapés."

I nodded excitedly. Compared to RIDER HQ, The House was small and quaint, but I could easily see Charlotte loving the cosmopolitan ambiance of the Upper West Side building. Not to mention the proximity of the 5th Avenue shops.

Charlotte's eyes lit up. "Ooh, I can't wait. I haven't been to

New York in ages. But it'll have to be after Samhain. My parents want me to showcase my powers as a full-fledged witch during the ceremony. But as we saw from last night's firework show, I still have a lot of work to do." She looked down glumly and flexed her bandaged hands.

"About that," I said. "Have you thought about having Augustine tutor you even after we wrap-up the mission?"

I had been thinking about saying something about it all day. Although Augustine was a generalist, he spent his first few years at RIDER helping witches hone their powers when nothing else seemed to work. Even though he possessed none of his own, he offered a new perspective that worked well with his students. I had also noticed that Augustine had taken a paternal mentorship to Charlotte in just the few days we'd been at The House.

Charlotte and Mirza looked at each other and then back at me with the same sly look.

"It's just that he's worked with young witches in the past, and you two seem to get along well. I think he could really help. I could talk to him if you want," I added.

Talking to Augustine never got any easier, but if it would benefit Charlotte, I would do it.

"And is that all you want to talk to Augustine about?" Mirza asked, smirking and raising an accusatory eyebrow.

"What are you talking about?"

"Oh, come on, you don't need a witch's third eye to see that you're totally into him," Charlotte said.

I didn't know what to say, so I just sat there, speechless and trapped. Not to mention incredibly embarrassed.

"Zo, it's also like the worst-kept secret at RIDER. Spill, we're dying to know the deets," Mirza added.

I let out a defeated sigh and glanced around to make sure there was no way Augustine could be within earshot.

"I assure you, there are no 'deets.' It was simple. We were

MEMORIES, LIES, AND OTHER BINDS

together, and then we were not together. It was a long time ago, and we're completely different people now than we were back then," I lied coolly, putting on my best poker face.

"Uh-huh," Charlotte said, unconvinced. "Well, in that case, if talking to him about *moi* might rekindle that fire, then go ahead— talk all you want."

I rolled my eyes and opened up my Moleskine that had been resting in my lap, quickly scribbling in a note about it.

A nearby phone buzzed, and Mirza answered it.

"Astrid! How's—....oh no, Mango did what now?.... In the bathroom? Okay good. Well, not good, but manageable. You recited the incantation, right?... Oh damn. Okay, well here's what you do. Just close the bathroom door to contain it. Jason said he'll be back in the city in a few hours..."

Mirza moved to the edge of the veranda for more privacy to deal with what sounded like classic inter-dimensional gremlin issues.

"Also, there will be no rekindling of any kind," I stated, retracting my pen and closing my journal as if to say this was my last and final comment on the whole Augustine *thing*. "He is a happily married family man, and if there is one thing that hasn't changed about him, it's his faithfulness."

"If you say so. But I see the googly eyes you've been giving him in that makeshift command center." Charlotte placed her hand under her chin and dramatically batted her eyes at me.

Warmth rushed to my cheeks, and I sucked the inside of my lip, mortified. I had been so careful to practice restraint and keep my cool around him. Or so I thought.

Charlotte stood up from the table and stretched. "Well, anyway, we should probably get set up upstairs."

Mirza hurried over once he saw we were headed back into The House.

"Oh, and did you know Augustine's daughter is starting at

RIDER soon?" he said, pressing his mobile to his chest while he spoke before pressing it back to his ear.

Wow, gossip traveled fast at RIDER. I hadn't even said anything to Tristan about it yet, knowing I would need something stronger than rosé to process it all.

Charlotte recoiled. "For real? Yikes! That's not awkward," she said, throwing me a bewildered look as she opened the back door.

She had no idea.

It wasn't until we got to the first-floor staircase that I felt naked. Something was missing. I looked down at my empty hands.

"My journal, I left it out back. I'll catch up with you upstairs," I said as Charlotte and Mirza scaled the staircase.

Of course. There it was, right where I had left it. The Moleskine journal sat on top of the table with my pen clipped to its cover, waiting patiently for my return.

I shook my head and let out a light laugh. It rarely left my side. Lack of sleep and dealing with Theo must be taking its toll on me.

Picking up the journal and cradling it in my arm, I turned toward The House.

Something caught my eye, and I paused mid-step.

It was small. A flash of movement in the bushes before the dense tree line that marked the perimeter of the backyard. I turned back around and peered into the darkness.

The wind blew, gently rustling the leaves on the trees and hydrangea bushes. The one on the far right was still a sad, charred heap. In the otherwise perfect line of manicured topiary, it gave the impression of a mouth with a missing tooth. Other than that, everything was still.

The hair on the back of my neck tingled and stood straight.

"Hello?" I called out, thinking it was an agent returning from patrol.

I waited for them to reveal themselves so I could lightheartedly scold them about giving me a scare before we would both laugh it off and mention something about having nerves before a COI operation.

Silence.

I let out a staggered breath. I couldn't let it all get to me. It was just stress and my imagination. Gripping the journal tightly to my chest, I started back to The House again.

An icy hand from behind tightly covered my mouth.

I screamed, more surprised than scared, but it came out muffled in their palm. An arm wrapped around my waist. It was firm and very strong.

Before I could react further, my feet left the ground, and I felt myself moving through the air. The sensation made my stomach turn, and I felt the sudden urge to vomit.

Then, as quickly as it began, it stopped.

My feet settled back down, but this time on soft earth. My back pressed firmly against what felt like the rough, mottled bark of a tree trunk.

Someone was standing directly in front of me.

A man wearing a dark cotton shirt and a silver pendant in the shape of a crest that looked familiar, but I couldn't place. His hand still pressed firm against my mouth.

My eyes went wide, and I struggled against his grip when I saw it was Theo.

"Don't scream," he said evenly. His tone was stern.

Vampires required an invitation to enter homes, but backyards were fair game. And Charlotte's concealing wards were aimed at humans, not creatures, so Theo could see and move through them.

Cold dread poured through me and my stomach flopped over. But I dared not move or flinch.

Any sudden movements might trigger his prey drive. And there was no way I would be quick enough to dodge a bite or a swipe to rip my throat out.

The grip around my mouth softened, and he carefully took his hand away.

Only moving my eyes, I looked around to see where he had taken me. We were standing in the line of trees just beyond the sight line of the backyard.

If I hadn't been absolutely terrified, I would have been utterly disappointed in myself. The note about meeting in the park had been a trap for Theo to get me alone, and I walked right into it. My eagerness to catch him had completely blinded me to the obvious.

"I don't want to hurt you. I just want to talk," he said, staring me square in the eye.

The key word here was *want*. He didn't *want* to hurt me. But considering what he was and his track record, there was a good possibility he might not be able to stop himself from doing just that.

"So talk then," I replied tightly. It took all my focus to ground myself enough to speak.

I had to keep Theo talking and hoped he had a lot to say. At least long enough to catch the attention of an agent strolling by. Hopefully, not all of them had been re-stationed to Volta Park.

"Bess, it's really you, isn't it?" He sounded mystified.

I nodded, keeping my movements slow and steady. "I go by a different name now."

Theo's eyes drifted to the front of my journal that I still clutched in both arms, undoubtedly noticing the gold embossed monogram that spelled out 'ZP' on the cover. "Zoey?" he asked.

Biting my lower lip anxiously, I nodded again.

I tried to recall if Charlotte or Augustine had said my name in the garden last night or if Theo picked it up while he had been stalking The House. The image of him scaling the whitewashed brick walls, peering into its many windows from the shadows, or watching us track him during the late hours in the command center or, even worse—watching us sleep—it was all unsettling. Especially considering he left the note in my window...

He must have heard it last night in the garden. That's what I was going to tell myself.

"Zoey," he repeated, moving the sound of my name around in his mouth, trying it out. He shriveled his face in distaste. "I don't like it. It doesn't suit you. It's too modern. And Greek, I think."

Theo was the last person I needed approval for my alias that was supposed to conceal me from him and anyone else from my previous life as Bess Abbott. I had never been too wild about it myself, and pushed back on the original Byzantine spelling of Zoë because it was nearly impossible to type on a typewriter. But what did Theo have against the Greeks? I was pretty sure the name Theodore also had Greek origins.

Before I could correct him or even roll my eyes, his lips were moving.

"Your voice too. It's different."

"I've been in The States for a while now," I replied as coolly as my racing heart allowed. "Seems you have too."

"Hmm," Theo said with a quick snort. I took that as a yes.

He looked at me again, this time giving me a full scan up and down and flaring his nose to take in more of my scent. His gaze hovered over my bare neck before quickly darting away. Theo's movements had a predatory smoothness to them. Like a snake about to strike.

"You're human," he concluded, his voice touched with intrigue.

I swallowed hard. A difficult movement as my mouth had run dry.

"Yes, I am. Very much so, thank you."

Theo shook his head and looked skyward. "Out of all the people on Earth, my own sister is the Immortal."

The Immortal. It was the second time I had heard him say those words since he had first mentioned it at the Arbor Terrace. What gave me pause wasn't the 'immortal' part, but the 'the' before it.

The Immortal.

Not is *immortal*, or an *immortal*. But *The Immortal.*

It sounded fancy in its own way, like I was special. But that was ridiculous. I was just a researcher who didn't age.

Theo's face suddenly went blank. "You really have no idea what I'm talking about, do you?"

The House's back door opened, releasing a tired, rusted squeak into the air.

"Zoey? Zo, are you out here?" Charlotte called into the night.

My mind screamed to yell for help, but Theo glared at me in warning. If I so much as took my next breath too loudly, it could be my last.

Another set of footsteps clomped out onto the veranda. "Maybe she went to her room." Mirza's voice floated across the backyard. "Come on, let's check upstairs again."

The door let out another metallic cry as it closed and Theo's expression lightened, but only a little.

"I don't have much time. The organization you work for—RIDER. It's not what you think it is."

I frowned. He was gaslighting me now. Trying to make me second-guess everything.

"Is that your plan, Theo?" How daft did he think I was? "Make me paranoid about the organization I've served for over two centuries so you can keep murdering high-profile witches and stealing their magic? Is Daisy a part of this?" I asked, craning my neck around Theo's form to see if I could glimpse his partner's signature shock of copper hair behind him.

Theo gritted his teeth. The corner of his lip twitched.

"Daisy and I aren't together anymore. Haven't been for a while. I'm not how I used to be—the vampire I used to be. I'm sure you've noticed I've been keeping a low profile these days. And I'm trying—I've been trying to help the witch stop all this."

"You've been helping Charlotte? So you are Mandrake?"

"Yes. Charlotte. She might be next. I wanted to warn her in person last night, but then I saw you. It was... it was like seeing a ghost. It threw me off." He paused for a moment, seemingly lost in his thoughts. "Listen. You and Charlotte have to get as far away from RIDER as possible. You're both in danger."

He was becoming more erratic the longer we spoke. I stood with my back against the tree and my mouth open agape, unsure what to say and still too afraid to move. My muscles ached with exhaustion as the adrenaline left my body, and it was becoming harder to keep Theo pacified.

"If you don't believe me, find Summer Coogan. She'll tell you everything you need to know," he said, looking around as if he could hear something I couldn't.

A dog barked loudly in the distance, fierce and alarmed, followed by a high-pitched, anxious whine. Startled, my eyes flitted toward the direction of the noise.

By the time I looked back, I was staring into the empty thick brush where Theo had been seconds before.

Theo was gone. Without a sound or movement. As if he, too, had been a ghost.

Using the tree for support, I pushed off it and ran faster than any drill I had PR'd during the annual combat course. Gripping my journal tightly to my chest, I leapt up the steps to the veranda.

The House flew open its back door like an arm, ushering me into its comforting embrace. Dashing to cross the safety of the threshold, I fell to my knees on the polished hardwood, panting. I was drenched in a cold sweat that had soaked through both the front and back of my blouse.

The House slammed the backdoor shut behind me, engaging its three locks for good measure with satisfying dull *shinks* as the deadbolts fit through their latches.

With a trembling hand, I brushed the sweat and damp hair from my forehead. Above, I could hear a heavy thunder of footsteps race down the staircase. Charlotte and Mirza were calling my name.

I sat there, unable to shake what my brother had said. My mind was a foggy, clouded mix of emotions as I tried to piece together what had just happened. Through the haziness, one thought rang clear. With each labored exhale, it rolled off my lips in a whisper.

A question.

Who is Summer Coogan?

FIFTEEN

After catching Charlotte and Mirza up on what happened in the backyard—which required many minutes of heavy breathing into a brown paper bag to stop hyperventilating—Augustine also confirmed that Theo had been a no-show in the park. But he promised the agents wouldn't stop searching for him.

Unsure what to believe about Theo's cryptic message about RIDER, we decided to keep it only between the four of us, plus Astrid and Ellie, and Tristan (whenever he would decide to turn up at The House again). No use in sounding all the alarm bells again if it was just another trap.

The following two days were spent in full research mode locating anything and everything on Summer Coogan. A deceptively simple task considering social media, the internet, and other equally annoying and complex modern-day technologies. But the only trace of Summer Coogan anywhere was a Darien, Connecticut youth league soccer roster and accompanying team photo from 1991 that Astrid found on microfilm.

An impressive feat, considering we had no other leads than a name. There was a rumor that Astrid had received full-time offers from both RIDER and the FBI, and I was beginning to see the truth in that. Along with gratitude for her ultimate career decision.

The soccer photo identified Summer as the scrawny ten-year-old girl with straight chestnut brown hair pulled back into a ponytail, a splash of freckles across her nose, and a toothy grin so wide her eyes squinted into thin slits. From the roster, we knew that her middle name started with an 'E.'

But that was all we had. Nothing existed about her adult life, or any connection to RIDER, as Theo had suggested.

She would be forty years old now. And given RIDER's sizable resources and research team, I was sure there would be a utility bill, college paper, or even an app dating profile that would give us more insight into who she might be.

Perhaps she had become a vampire. That was our thesis at the end of day one.

But even vampires left behind some context clues on their whereabouts. Also, there was no obituary, death certificate, or even a missing person's file bearing her name. Luke and Olivia had come to the command center to help at one point, perusing through Reddit and Discord threads and other forums at the edge of 'The Dark Web' (Luke's exact words), both supernatural and mundane. But again, no matches.

We had nothing.

On the second day, Tristan joined us. I had missed his company. We were without our near daily routine of grabbing coffee in the lobby's café or a post-work drink in The Lounge. Tristan had also stopped coming to Charlotte's small evening gettogethers, even when I tried to entice him with the towers of charcuterie she'd ordered.

"The entire world might as well be on fire," he said, when I pressed him in the most cheeky way possible about where he'd been. "It was also a full moon this week. Humans and creatures have gone bonkers, and of course, I have to deal with the clean-up."

After dinner, Tristan went to his room, saying that he needed to read through new, 'fresh hot' protocol regulations from the Departed Human Entities department that could not be missed. Something about when a poltergeist was determined to actually be a non-corporeal demon.

Augustine also had many other responsibilities to attend to in the form of conference calls, emails, and checking in with his wife. He took those in a sitting room in the north wing for what I could assume was for some much-needed privacy. But the room felt vacant without the sound of him munching on handfuls of almonds.

And Charlotte had slunk off to the depths of The House after complaining that the command center had taken on a certain 'funk' from the many hours and bodies spent there in the past few days. She vowed not to come back until after the RIDER cleaning crew had given it a thorough refresh.

That left Mirza and me.

We sat across the table from one another in the makeshift conference room with an entire night ahead of us of dead leads about a potentially fake person my homicidal vampire brother gave us to spin our wheels.

Or so I thought.

The large monitor mounted on the wall in front of us flickered and Astrid Scott's circular photo avatar of her smiling face pulsed on the screen in tune to the incoming video call jingle we all knew too well.

Mirza eagerly reached across the table to accept the call and the monitor filled with a live video of Astrid. She was in one of the RIDER lab's glass conference rooms. Ellie leaned into frame from the right to give a small wave before sliding back out of view.

"Astrid, Ellie—tell me you've got something. Zo and I are about to lose our minds over here," Mirza pleaded.

Astrid smirked, an expression I recognized she made when she had found the jackpot. "Oh, we found something. I just hope you guys are ready."

"I'm strapping my titties in. Give it to me," Mirza said, flexing his fingers.

I snorted a much-needed laugh and turned to a fresh page in my journal. Pen in hand, I hovered over the blank space, ready as ever.

"Okay, so it looked like everything had been scrubbed on Summer Coogan. And when I say everything, I mean it. But when we tried putting just her initials through the database, we found a match for an S.E. Coogan," Astrid said. She split the monitor to share her screen.

It was a smeared photocopy, but I could decipher that the document was a patient intake record from 2013. AIRY VIEW MANOR blazed across the top, along with an address in Greenwich, Connecticut.

"Airy View Manor is a luxury assisted living facility in Connecticut. Heavy on the luxury and the private. Even with all of our data bells and whistles, it was hard to pull the records from their database. But not hard enough for us, of course," Astrid said with another self-satisfied look. "This patient is only referred to as S.E. Coogan. She was a thirty-two-year-old woman at the time of intake at Airy View Manor, which fits Summer's age. Also, the facility is only a twenty-minute drive from where she grew up."

"So, is she still there? Can we send someone to talk to her? It's not far from RIDER," I said, pulling up a map on my laptop. It was barely an hour's drive from Manhattan and still relatively early in the night. Theoretically, we could speak with her tonight.

Astrid's face soured. "So... that's kind of the issue." Scrolling down the patient intake document, she paused at the patient summary section. "It looks like Summer suffered a massive brain injury. She's at the assisted care facility because she's been in a coma for the past eight years."

My heart sank. With my elbows resting on the table, I held my head in my hands.

"Theo seemed so adamant that I speak with Summer. And he seemed scared himself. Like panicked. So why would he lead us to a woman in a coma?" I asked, raking my fingers through my hair, trying to rack my mind to find any sense in the situation.

"But that's not the strangest part," Astrid said hastily. "We looked into who was making the monthly care payments. Because the cost for a facility like Airy View Manor is not for the faint of wallet. The payments for Summer's care are pre-paid annually by a trust. When Ellie and I tried to track down who the trust belonged to, all we found was that it was owned by a holding company in Switzerland. But it was just a shell organization, and we hit a dead end there. With Swiss privacy laws, there is no way to track down the holding company's owners or originators."

"Okay, so we've got a woman who we think is Summer Coogan, who otherwise has zero information about her anywhere, and she's been in a coma for the past eight years. And some mysterious donor has been paying for her to live her very best Sleeping Beauty life. Anything else?" Mirza recapped, looking through his notes.

"Just one more thing. We pulled the visitor logs, and every month like clockwork, she's had the same visitor since she arrived." Astrid flicked to another screen on her computer and a visitation log appeared. Month after month, the same name repeated.

Nicole Wiles.

"Nicole, thankfully, has a pretty average internet presence."

A Facebook profile page came up on the screen. The most recently posted photo was a woman with shoulder-length dark brown hair standing next to a man with a graying beard. Below them, she and the man's arms draped around two small children, both boys who held pumpkins in their hands. All four wore the same flannel pattern in what was undeniably a fall family photo.

"She lives in White Plains and is a stay-at-home mom with two kids. Husband is a real estate lawyer in the city. She studied jour-nalism at the University of Connecticut, and apparently between 2010 and 2015, she had a somewhat successful food blog," Astrid said, impressed at the last fact.

"Okay, but what's her connection to Summer?" I asked, eager to find out how Summer might be associated with RIDER.

"We're still trying to figure that out. Ellie's been trying to reach out to her, but we haven't heard back yet."

I sat back in my chair with a sigh and tapped my pen on the table. We needed to figure this out before Charlotte, or another witch, ended up face down in a pool of their own blood.

"Keep trying. And let us know as soon as you find out more," Mirza said.

Astrid nodded. "We're on it. Keep you both posted."

The screen faded to black as the call ended. Mirza and I looked at each other with the same strained expression as we sat in silence. The only thing in the room that moved was the red RIDER calli-graphic 'R' screensaver that bounced aimlessly around the screen's black background.

———

RIDER's prestige for clockwork efficiency was something I always appreciated, because an hour later, we were speaking with Nicole Wiles.

Ellie patched in a brunette with shifty brown eyes who appeared on her mobile's camera in what looked to be a closed bathroom in her house. She had the shower running, which created a lot of background noise, but we could still hear her.

"Mrs. Wiles? Can you hear us?" Mirza asked, leaning into the conference microphone.

The woman nodded quickly. "Yes, yes, I can."

"My name is Mr. Ahmani and these are my colleagues, Ms. Prescott, Ms. Scott, and Ms. Philips. We're working on an investigation concerning Summer Coogan. We believe you know her?"

"I was told this was a secure line. Is that true?" Nicole asked. Her eyes darted around suspiciously, as if there might be someone else lurking in the bathroom.

"Yes. What can you tell us about Summer? We noticed you visit her at the Airy View Manor assisted living facility in Greenwich," Mirza pressed.

"I-I was given a lot of money. To forget about Summer. To not talk about her to anyone else. But, every time I see her lying in her bed there... I... I don't think I can do it anymore. I'm ready for someone else to know what happened."

Well, this was promising.

"It's okay, Mrs. Wiles, you can tell us what happened to her. Did she have an accident?" I asked, leaning toward the microphone.

Mirza was just as surprised as I was when I spoke up, considering I usually relegated myself to all things note-taking during these types of calls. But he smiled reassuringly and nodded, confirming that I was asking the right questions.

"Not so much an accident as someone she met. Summer and I met at UConn and we were still close, even after college. When we were in our late twenties, she started dating this guy. He was weird. Maybe weird's not the right word. He was just really arrogant, like he had this superiority complex. And he had the strangest eyes. We thought he was always wearing contacts, but he was adamant they were real."

"So what happened? Was he abusive to Summer?" Mirza asked as I quickly jotted down notes, not wanting to miss any details.

A shadow crossed Nicole's face, and she sucked the bottom of her lip. "Well, not at first. And um, this is where things kind of got really weird."

Mirza and I glanced at each other. We liked really weird.

"Okay, you guys are probably going to think this sounds nuts,"

Nicole said, taking in a big breath. "But Summer told me they liked to go into her mind together. She said it was fun, and special —at first. That it was really intimate and they would revisit all of her favorite memories. She described it as a big attic, like the one in her grandmother's house in the Berkshires that she visited every summer when she was a kid. And in the boxes and trunks were all of her memories."

Goosebumps rippled down my arms. Her story sounded eerily familiar.

"But then, after a while, Summer said he started getting really possessive. Well, we all thought he was like that when we first met him, but Summer said she liked that about him. She liked feeling wanted. But he started getting paranoid. Summer would call me crying late at night after they'd get into huge fights because he thought she was cheating on him—which she denied. And she said he started forcing himself into her mind to find the truth." Nicole's eyes glossed, and her voice cracked.

She paused, closing her eyes to steady herself. When she opened them, she had a new fierce determination when she gazed into the camera.

"A few weeks later, she ended up in the ER. They said she had a brain aneurysm. Which, for our age was rare, but it-it can happen sometimes, you know. When I visited her at the hospital, she seemed okay. Like she was awake and talking and the doctors were positive about her prognosis. When I left her that day, I passed her boyfriend in the hallway who was coming to see her and he seemed happy about her recovery. But the next day she slipped into a coma and hasn't been able to come out of it since. Everyone was shocked."

"Do you think the boyfriend had something to do with it?" I asked.

It sounded eerily close to my Memory Walks with Dr. Kelley. No doubt the doctor was unsettling, but I was optimistic that he wasn't actually insidious. Had to be a coincidence. Maybe the boyfriend was some kind of psychic succubus or other life-force siphoning demon.

"Absolutely," Nicole said. "I just don't know how. When Summer wasn't getting any better and was sent to Airy View Manor, I started looking into things and even hired a private investigator. But even the P.I. got spooked and dropped the case. And shortly after that, I got this weird letter from a lawyer saying that her family requested that I honor Summer's privacy. Then, everything about her just disappeared overnight. Every Facebook photo, email address, even her anonymous Twitter account that only our close friends knew about had been wiped clean.

"The worst part of all of this is that in exchange for my silence, they gave me a lot of money. Like a lot. I feel so guilty for taking it, but things were getting out of hand and it was an easy way out. Since then, they've seemed okay with me still visiting her, but sometimes I feel like someone's watching my family."

That explained Nicole's fearful anxiety and her need for background noise on the call.

"Do you remember his name—the boyfriend's?" Mirza asked.

"How could I not?" Nicole snorted. "His name was Jack. Jack Kelley. And that's Kelley with two 'e's."

My blood ran cold. Not a coincidence.

Mirza had a similar reaction. His mouth and eyes went wide in a silent gasp as he tried to maintain his professional composure.

This was the information my brother wanted me to find. Dr. Jack Kelley, my Gifted therapist who gave me the creeps when my entire career was based on creepy things, was as dangerous as I had feared.

Sixteen

I nearly flew down the staircase, searching for Charlotte. My first stop had been Tristan's room, but he refused to answer my panicked knocks. I envisioned him passed out on top of his overly yellow floral bed with a stack of papers spread out on his chest, snoring loudly with one hand still clutching his highlighter while his other held his mobile. Mirza had headed to the opposite wing to alert Augustine.

All of us agreed to keep what we had just learned about Dr. Jack Kelley between us until we had more information. RIDER practically invented the background check, making it all the more unsettling to think that they might have known what his Gift was capable of. And that he'd abused it in the past.

Were there other victims? Did Dr. Kelley have something to do with the witch murders? I tried to push the thoughts from my mind so I could focus. But as one horrific thought left, two more took its place. The academic side of my brain was wreaking all kinds of havoc, using Nicole's story to find patterns and draw dreadful conclusions about my experience with the doctor. The worsening scrambled, lobotomy-like feeling my mind had after each session. The way I got lost in the past, even outside of his office.

How many more sessions did I have until I ended up like Summer Coogan?

On the second floor's landing, I peered down the long hallway that connected the two wings for any sign of the witch.

It was empty.

Grabbing onto the staircase post, I rounded the corner and headed down the last flight that dumped me onto the first floor. It was also empty, save for a few lingering agents that patrolled The House. Most of them had left to survey the city for Theo and other COIs in the area. My list of potential vampire nests had become a proven heat map, and the teams had their hands full with exterminations.

I looked about the living room for any sign of Charlotte or where she might have gone off to. Then, right in front of me, a Gifted enforcement agent walked through the connecting wall of the kitchen eating from a bag of potato chips.

He popped another chip in his mouth and froze with a mild look of panic when we locked eyes. As if I knew or cared that he wasn't supposed to be on a break.

"Do you know where Charlotte is?" I asked, breathless.

The agent shook his head. "Sorry," he replied through a mouthful of chips.

I grunted, frustrated. She wouldn't have left The House. We (or more so Augustine) talked about that earlier. At night, she was even more vulnerable to a vampire like Theo or one of his hench-creatures, no matter how Gifted the agent escorting her might be.

Of course, that was before we knew Theo was telling the truth. Or a partial truth.

There was one last person who might help me. Well, not technically a person, but definitely a personality. And a big one at that.

"House!" I shouted, tilting my head back. I looked upward to address it as Charlotte did when they were at odds with one another. "I need your help—where is she?"

The agent in front of me, still frozen in place, continued to feed himself chip after chip from the bag at a cautious pace. He looked at me like I had lost my last marble. Which was fair—I was attempting to have a full-on conversation with an inanimate object.

Nothing moved. Everything was still and silent between me, the agent, and the living room.

I cursed under my breath. My mind began reeling again, thinking about what Dr. Kelley's ulterior motives might be. My heart beat loudly in my chest and I felt the anxiety rise toward my throat.

A warm gust of air blew in front of me and the feeling of a disembodied hand gently touched my face and tucked my hair behind my left ear. It caressed my left cheek and the bottom of my jaw. With the slightest pressure, it turned my head to the right, so that I faced the back of The House.

Come.

The word breathed in my ear. It was soft, barely above a whisper, but undeniably clear. The House talks, and it spoke to me.

Not skipping a beat, I started toward the back of the first floor, heading for the door that led out to the veranda. The wind whipped up again, urging me to turn right down the long back hallway. Hurrying down it, The House suddenly tugged on my blouse and pushed me from the side.

It wasn't violent, but forceful, and I stumbled slightly, using the door it had blown me against to catch myself. When I stepped back to see where The House had directed me, my mouth opened in shock.

I was standing in front of the basement door.

"She's in here?" It was strange. Since I had first arrived, both Charlotte and The House seemed to keep me away from this very door.

Warm wind whirled around me like a playful dust devil before it took off floating down the hall.

I guess that was a yes.

I opened the door and jogged down the steep unfinished staircase inside. One step away from the polished cement floor, I froze mid-step, and blinked several times to confirm the scene that was unfolding in the basement.

Like most half-finished, subterranean basements, part of the space had been partitioned off as a small lounge area. A modular 'L' shaped blue sectional, coffee table, and flat screen TV mounted on the wall made the area perfect for watching those university football games that took up so much of Luke and Olivia's time. Opposite the sitting area were a series of metal shelves lined with Miracle Grow potting soil, unused terracotta planter pots, rakes, and a couple of mismatched toolboxes.

But it was a pair of person-sized cages against the adjacent cinderblock wall that gave me pause.

The twin prison cells were constructed of thick metal bars and sizable key latch locks. A pair of surveillance cameras anchored on the wall a few feet away were positioned directly at the enclosures. Interestingly enough, the cells also appeared to have a superb view of the TV.

Luke, clad in a welding helmet and work gloves that reached down to his elbows, stood on top of a ladder nestled in the back left corner of one cell. A welding torch in his hand, bright blue and orange flame erupted from it as he held it in the corner of the metal structure.

Charlotte stood below him with her arms crossed, monitoring Luke's progress with a scrutinizing gaze.

Meanwhile, Olivia was standing in the lounge area. Playing with her necklace of gold circles and slivers with one hand, she held her mobile sideways in her other that was projected onto the TV in front of her. With gentle swipes of her thumb, she rewound and played the video on her phone.

The video was footage from the security camera fixed on the cell Luke and Charlotte were working on. It showed a small, wolflike creature with black fur pacing back and forth on two legs. Its pointed ears were flat against its head, and it swished its tail back and forth, agitated. Snarling to show a muzzle filled with long pointed teeth, the creature suddenly jumped up to the back left corner of the cage, latching onto one of the metal poles. It thrashed violently back and forth, until the pole loosened from its weld and bent back, creating a small opening.

Content with the destruction it had created, it leapt back down, growled, then began to pace again. On the far right edge of the frame was another creature. This one was larger, with light brown fur that matched Luke's beard. It laid on the ground on its side as if trying to sleep, but its head was still raised as it watched its neighbor with a forlorn look on its canine face.

Werewolves. North American Bi-Pedal Lycanthropes, to be exact.

"I think you need to weld it flatter and wider, so it doesn't stick out as much," Olivia suggested, rewinding and playing back the video once more.

Luke flipped up his welding helmet. "The corner's really tight. I think that's the best I can do."

Olivia frowned, and Luke smirked.

"Leave it to Liv to rip apart the werewolf-proof cage." He laughed.

"What can I say? I'm a formidable she-wolf—especially when I'm annoyed. And my wolf cannot stand the cage," Olivia said coolly, flicking her pink hair over her shoulder with the back of her hand.

"Here, let me try," Charlotte offered, gazing up at the weld job.

Rolling up the sleeves of her sweater, she flexed her freshly healed palms, igniting one of her signature white flames in her right. Raising her arm up, the flame extended from her hand until it met its target at the top of the cell. With the flick of her wrist, she increased the pressure, melting and molding the metal into place. Luke quickly snapped his helmet down to avoid the heat and stray sparks.

"There. Much better, huh?" Charlotte said proudly, extinguishing the fire and wiping her hands together.

Luke descended the ladder. "Should have spoken up sooner, Char. Could have saved us an expensive trip to the hardware store."

Olivia and Luke were werewolves. Who stayed in cages in the basement of The House during the three nights of the full moon.

Which had taken place earlier in the week.

While I was sleeping in my room, only a few floors up.

I shivered, thinking back to the other night when Charlotte gave me the Tarot card reading. Everything clicked into place. It would have been their second night of turning, so when I approached the basement door, The House distracted me by throwing Charlotte's mobile off the table. Charlotte had probably just secured the wolves, which is why she had been close to the door.

Olivia's necklace too—it was so painfully obvious that I wanted to kick myself. Each graduated sliver depicted the lunar phases. I had been so focused on my own personal drama that I had missed all the signs to make the connection.

Olivia was the first to notice my presence on the staircase. Her head snapped in my direction and her expression immediately fell into a wryly smirk. With the smoke and fire from welding along with the noise, it likely clouded both my scent and sound from her preternatural senses.

"Great, now we've got RIDER suits to deal with," she said, more annoyed than fearful or surprised.

Charlotte hurried out of the cage to stand in front of me. "Okay, so I know what this might look like, but there's no reason to freak. It's not what you think."

"So, you haven't been harboring werewolves and keeping them

in the basement during the three nights of the full moon?" I asked. It seemed pretty straightforward to me.

The witch cast a nervous glance at both lycanthropes, as if hoping some kind of miracle explanation to the contrary would come. Despite Charlotte's plea that it wasn't, it was a very big and dangerous deal. And although I'd defied many of the rules RIDER had given me during the mission, I couldn't help but to default to protocol.

"Are they even registered? Is Luke even your cousin?" I asked, my voice raising another octave. RIDER HQ was about to have a field day with the infractions that were piling up.

Charlotte's mouth hung open for several seconds. Of course they weren't. That explained the odd introduction during our arrival and the fabricated 'Luke-is-my-cousin' story.

Olivia marched toward the staircase with a determined gait.

"No, we're not. Luke and I refuse to be just a number to your organization. We're real people. Not animals to be tracked."

I put a hand to my forehead. Undocumented werewolves. My therapist was trying to put me in a permanent coma. My evil vampire brother perhaps was not as evil as we thought. I wasn't sure if I could take any more mind-bending revelations.

Steadying myself on the unfinished wooden railing beside me, I took a much-needed moment to collect myself before I spoke.

"Olivia. Lycanthrope Registration exists to help you. We have programs and support groups, and regional packs that you can join to help you adjust to your new lifestyle," I explained.

It was a proven system. I mean, I was part of the original team who helped create it over fifty years ago. Weres thrived in pack-like groups and a community environment, and I had the decades of data to prove it.

Olivia crossed her arms. "Luke and I don't need a pack. We have each other. We were bitten together and went through our First Moon together. We can handle things on our own."

Luke walked out of the cage, leaving his welding gear behind to stand next to Olivia.

"What I think Liv is trying to say is that the RIDER program doesn't work with our lifestyle. We've talked to others through the supernatural grapevine. Being shuffled by those National Guard-looking agents to some place in the middle of bumblefuck for an entire week—not just three days—where we're basically forced into a pack with other Weres we don't know doesn't work for us.

"We live in a city and have school and friends who don't know about our condition. We can't put our lives on pause for that long each month. Charlotte's solution keeps us safe from hurting ourselves or anyone else and lets us live our lives. Also, I'll take a cage for the night than having to deal with the tracking collars and being micro-chipped," he said, placing a broad-shouldered arm around Olivia in a show of solidarity.

Luke's fear of RIDER as a new creature was to be expected. Werewolves were naturally cautious and suspicious in their human form. To overcome that hesitation, RIDER's Lycanthrope Program was designed to resemble a luxurious wilderness retreat rather than a containment operation. All to entice members to stay.

The week of the full moon, black car service chauffeured members to a remote site based on their region. Isolated areas on federal protected land that people in Tristan's department had secured in some kind of leaseback deal. During the day, members were free to do as they pleased within the pack housing; luxury cabins outfitted with hot water, high-speed Wi-Fi, and cable TV. On nights before, during, and after the full moon, the packs were released into heavily wooded areas to do all things wolf, while RIDER analysts watched from secured data centers. Expandable tracking harnesses adorned just before their transformation allowed us to collect data on their behavior, whereabouts, and any pack stragglers who had wandered away at sunrise.

It was a very controlled, safe, and systematic program.

But clearly, not every wolf could be convinced.

I let out an agitated sigh and gave Charlotte a scolding look as I tried to channel Diana when she was at her most disappointed. "Well, the Lycanthrope Program is a hell of a lot safer than having a pair of bi-pedals in the basement of a house filled with sleeping humans. Charlotte, do you know how dangerous this is? You put everyone here at risk of infection. It just takes one bite—if they survive it—for transmission. Regardless of wolf or human form."

"The Werewolf Airbnb *is* safe. The cages are pretty much werewolf-proof, unless Liv gnaws on the same metal bar night after night. And, as you can see, we fixed it! I also always cast a containment ward and silencing spell on the basement, so they don't bother anyone. Even The House has approved of the situation. It keeps people away from the basement and I'm sure it would help in the event of a breakout. Which, by the way, hasn't happened. Ever."

The Werewolf Airbnb. I couldn't believe it. Leave it to Charlotte to make werewolf transformations, as terrifying and daunting as they were, into something that sounded trendy.

"How..." I paused, running a stressed hand through my hair.

There would be other opportunities to explain the importance of joining the program. The foremost being that werewolves not in the program were at the risk of immediate onsite extermination if caught too close to human civilization in wolf form without proper containment.

"How long has this been going on? What were the dates and location of your transmission?"

Changing the subject to gather more information seemed like the best option at this point. But when Luke and Olivia stared back, blank and slightly confused, I realized that defaulting to RIDER formality was too technical for my current audience.

"Bitten. When and where were you bitten?"

"A little over a year ago, last August," Luke replied.

"It happened during the camping trip in Yellowstone, where

we met. We didn't know what had happened—we just thought a bear attacked our tent one night. But, a month later, after we both moved to DC, we found out it gave us the gift that keeps on giving. Luckily, we were at my family's cabin in Shenandoah for our First Moon. It was supposed to be a romantic getaway. But let's just say, the romance fades when the hand you're holding your champagne flute with turns into a paw." Olivia grimaced.

"Have you knowingly infected—I mean, do you know if you've bitten anyone else?" I asked, nervous of the answer, but I had to know.

Luke and Olivia looked at each other.

"No. We don't think so," Luke replied evenly.

I felt myself deflate. Well, that was a relief. Kind of.

"Look, we don't take this whole wolf-thing lightly. We knew we were in over our heads. So I started looking on message boards and forums, hoping to find other wolves. Instead, we found Charlotte's coven. And Charlotte's been helping us ever since with this setup. Now we can transform safely without having to put our lives on hold for days," Luke added appreciatively.

Charlotte smiled. "Aw, thanks, Luke. The cages were actually here before I moved in. I try not to think what they might have been used for before, because ew. But it just made sense, you know? I've also been working on a potion to ease the soreness that comes the day after a transformation."

"That part's still a work in progress," Olivia said with a frown.

Charlotte shrugged nonchalantly. "I'll add more moonflower next time."

I could only imagine how painful the breaking and re-molding of bones, muscles, and internal organs was for Weres during their transformation. In an interview I had with one Were, he said the experience left him feeling the next day as though he'd run a marathon and attended a bachelor party in the same day that even strong opioids could barely penetrate. For that reason, addiction was unfortunately common amongst their species.

Charlotte's passion for helping others—especially creatures, impressed me. But the whole 'werewolves in the basement' thing would need to take a back seat. At least for now. Or until after we figured out why Dr. Kelley was at RIDER.

"That all sounds wonderful. But I came down here because we have bigger issues to deal with at the moment," I said, folding my arms to show I was all business.

"Oh, my goddess. Did you find Summer Coogan?" Charlotte asked, enthused.

"Yeah. We found her alright."

"Well, out with it—what did she say?"

"That's the problem."

———

Out on the veranda, I reluctantly looked back at Charlotte, who stood a few feet behind me. She steadied herself, holding her hands out, palms up, to brace herself for a fight if one broke out. A single nod told me she was ready.

I swallowed hard and turned to look out into the darkened backyard.

This was Charlotte's idea. Once I caught her up on the nefarious therapist, she suggested we try to make direct contact with my brother, noting that it was the best way, albeit the only way (as a frequent user of burner phones and fake emails), we were going to find more information.

That didn't make my palms any less sweaty or throat any less dry.

"Theo!" I called into the night. It came out as a harsh whisper that quickly faded away once it caught in the wind.

"Louder!" Charlotte hissed, encouraging from behind.

I rolled my eyes. "He's a vampire. If he's close, he can hear me just fine."

My gaze swept over the yard, searching its dark, shadowed

foliage and around The House for any signs of a human-sized creature lurking around with a cat-like prowess.

Nothing.

Of course, the one time I expected to talk with Theo, he was nowhere to be found. That was so like him. He pulled this kind of shit when he was human all the time.

Clearing my throat, I took Charlotte's advice and spoke louder. "Theo! I found what you wanted me to find. I—I believe you!"

"And I've believed you from the beginning!" Charlotte added proudly.

Shooting her a pained look, she returned it with a smug one.

"I told you my witch's sense is never wrong. This is just one more example that proves it."

I was still unconvinced of Theo's perceived new innocence. Charlotte hadn't seen his entire file, and for her sake, I hoped she never would.

For another few minutes, we took turns calling the vampire before taking a seat at the table.

In silence, we searched the dark, looking for signs that he might answer.

The backyard's plain of grass rippled, the thin tree branches just beginning to brittle for winter gently waved back and forth. An owl hooted in the distance.

But Theo did not come.

Seventeen

"Well team, I'm afraid we've overstayed our welcome," Augustine announced in the command center. He stood at the head of the conference table with both palms firmly planted down on the cherry wood, clearly agitated.

"We'll be departing at 7:00 AM sharp tomorrow, so please make sure you put your bags on the first floor before breakfast so one of the agents can attend to them."

Grabbing his steaming mug of coffee, he turned and faced out one of the turret's windows as if to take in Georgetown's golden domed view one last time.

This had not been Augustine's decision, but Diana's.

My director sent the email early in the morning, when I was naively buzzing through my inbox queue of unreads before breakfast. Marked with the ever-annoying High Priority red exclamation point, it contained instructions for my immediate return to RIDER New York HQ by tomorrow morning. And as if her word wasn't enough, attached to the email was the official Notice of Recall, complete with the RIDER seal and signed by Diana and ten others of senior leadership.

I wanted to toss my laptop out the window.

But when I remembered it contained draft articles that hadn't yet been backed up to the central server, I thought better of it.

"We can't go back now," I said, exasperated. I looked around the table for support. "Especially with what we know about Dr. Kelley. RIDER leadership already wants me to have another session with him as a debrief. And we still haven't found out who the witch murderer is—Charlotte could still be in danger!"

To my right, a speechless Mirza tightened his lips to complete the solemn look on his face. Charlotte, directly across the table, silently sipped from another butterfly pea flower latte. And Tristan, (present for once in what seemed like years) sat diagonally across from me, enthralled in his laptop.

I couldn't blame them. RIDER was an impenetrable force of red tape bureaucracy, if the overly official Notice of Recall wasn't proof of that enough.

Moaning loudly, I crossed my arms over the table and put my head down. With no good ideas or ways to prolong our stay at The House, or how to rid myself of Dr. Kelley, it seemed like the most logical thing to do.

"Zoey, I'll do everything in my power to delay any more sessions with Kelley. Or make sure that someone trustworthy stays with you in the room the entire time. At least until I can find out if he is the one responsible for Summer's coma," Augustine said firmly.

"And Charlotte shouldn't have anything to worry about," Tristan said, finally looking up from his computer. "Theo doesn't seem to have an interest in her, and Matt Riley is coming down tomorrow anyway for whatever witch stuff you guys do. You'll still have RIDER protection."

"And what about Theo? He's still out there, regardless of which side he's on. We haven't completed the mission yet," I said, vengeance was still at the forefront of my mind.

"Honestly, Diana probably thinks this is all taking too long for a simple bag-and-tag operation. It wouldn't be the first time

Theo's slipped through RIDER's hands. He's still on the Big Bad list, so it's not like we're ever going to stop searching for him," Tristan offered. He curled his lips into a smirk. "Plus, I have a feeling that Diana misses her favorite researcher."

"Ha, I doubt that." I snorted, folding my arms.

What Diana probably missed was a clean inquiry queue. I had been so focused on Theo and Dr. Kelley that I was days behind in demonic infectious disease consultation requests. Not to mention the monthly reports. I was still debating whether to add two new known werewolf infections to the East Coast map.

Augustine sat down in his chair with a sigh.

"We will figure this out." His tone was unyielding, but his eyes held a wavering uncertainty in them. "Anyway, I don't know about you all, but I'm very much looking forward to a stiff drink at The Lounge when we get back."

"Only if it's on Augustine's tab," Mirza replied.

"And only if it's top shelf," Tristan said.

Meanwhile, the only thing I could think about was how many drinks it would take me to forget that I worked and lived in the same building as a mind-melting lunatic.

———

That evening, I was upstairs in my room, packing away the last of my things in the weekender. Leaving out my pajamas, and the outfit and shoes I'd wear the next day, I satisfyingly set the bag aside and plopped on the bed, tired and frustrated.

Sweeping a gaze around the guest room, I took in the excessive floral decor one last time. I was going to miss this little room, with its cloud-like duvet and nesting bird friends. But part of me looked forward to being in the familiar space of my apartment again.

With the mourning doves in mind, I started toward the window to see if I could still see them in the dark, nestled down for the night.

Ding-Dooong. The doorbell rang out below on the first floor.

It was a loud, irritating two-toned sound where the second tone pitched lower than the first. It made a long, droning noise before it ended.

It was odd. The doorbell had only been rung a few times as most personnel and catering were intercepted first by an agent guarding the perimeter of The House. Also, the wards were impenetrable to the average human passerby.

Ding-Dooong.

I paused expectantly, waiting to hear the indiscernible movement and chatter of an agent answering the door.

Ding-Dooong, Ding-Dooong, Ding-Ding-Ding Dooong.

The sound was giving me a headache.

Taking matters into my own hands, I was halfway down the last flight of stairs when I saw Charlotte in the vestibule at the front door. I stopped a few feet behind, peering curiously around her.

When she opened the door, Theo stood on the front steps just outside the star-and-moon-patterned tile. A pained, pale look written on his already pallid face. Was it possible for a dead person to look more dead?

He anxiously wrung his hands together, and for a split second, he glanced at me in a quick gesture of acknowledgment.

Despite the tip-off on Dr. Kelley, and not yet making a meal out of me, his presence still made my blood run cold. I wrapped my arms tightly around my chest.

"Freaking finally," Charlotte said. "You know, we've been trying to get a hold of your dead ass."

Having come to know the witch fairly well over the past week and her desire to be the perfect host, I knew what she was about to offer next. I wanted to shout for her not to, but I was paralyzed in place with fear.

Thankfully, Augustine came to the rescue.

"Charlotte! Do not invite him in!" he shouted, passing by me as he bounded down the stairs. He stood behind Charlotte in the vestibule and folded his arms, eyeing Theo up and down. "What is it you want? And why aren't there any agents around?"

Augustine looked back into The House, as did I from my view. Other than us four, the first floor was vacant. At this hour, it should have been crawling with at least half a dozen agents.

"Someone might have phoned in a tip about a certain high-ish profile vampire seen feeding on a civilian on the docks in Navy Yard. Conveniently, during the time the shifts switch out. Two of them are patrolling the backyard now, but the next shift will be here in about five minutes," Theo explained with a shrug.

I couldn't see Charlotte or Augustine's faces, but I'm sure they held the same look of panic. Not only because of Theo's faked self-sighting, but because he confirmed he had been watching The House. Closely.

"Look, I found something. Someone, actually. I found someone who I think is going to be the next target. Hopefully, we can get to them now before the killer does, so we can figure out why this is happening and finally stop it," Theo continued.

"Why?" I finally asked.

A simple word, but it had so many meanings when I said it to my brother. Why did you kill all those people? Why our family? Why have you been dormant for so long?

Putting the past aside, I reminded myself why we were here in the first place and settled on the one question that stood out from all the others.

"Why are you helping us?"

With a shifty gaze, Theo tipped his head to the right as if he heard something.

"There have been whispers. Rumors," he replied in a low voice. "Amongst the supernatural community. Of something big coming. World-changing. And bad. And it has something to do with whoever has been murdering these witches."

"Okay, so who's this next target, Fangs Bond? Hopefully not me," Charlotte asked, sounding a little giddy.

"No, it's not you. He doesn't live too far from here. I can text you the address and meet you there." There was a vulnerable look in Theo's eyes I hadn't seen in centuries.

"And why would we trust you?" Augustine asked skeptically. Another good 'why' question.

"You don't," the vampire said simply. "But you should."

Before any of us could say another word, Theo vanished from the front stoop in the blink of an eye.

While characteristically vampire, I was growing tired of his frequent disappearing act.

A buzzing sound came from Charlotte. She pulled out her rhinestone-encrusted phone from the back pocket of her jeans and glanced at the screen before turning it around to show us.

Without reading it, I knew it was a text from an unknown number with an address.

"So, who's up for another adventure?" Charlotte's lips broke out into a wide smile, and her eyes glistened with excitement. "This time, I promise I won't spark. At least not on purpose."

EIGHTEEN

Tristan had taken the SUV out to a fancy dinner with some kind of dignitary. Creature, human—or possibly both—I had not been privy to the details. So we took Charlotte's car instead.

It was a small, sleek, silver Audi hatchback sedan that she proudly announced was one hundred percent electric because, "As witches, we always have to acknowledge balance with the elements."

We found the car waiting patiently for its next trip in The House's garage with a vanity plate that read BROOM2.

Expecting the last night in The House to have been a relatively quiet one, I was dressed in a white T-shirt, charcoal grey leggings, and white sneakers—underdressed for any occasion other than the gym or lounging in my room. But Charlotte had balked at switching into something more professional since the more time we wasted, the greater the chance Theo might ghost us again. Augustine agreed. So I threw on my cardigan and off we went.

Heading north, at a somewhat alarming speed, Charlotte drove toward the Woodley Park neighborhood. A quiet, suburban-looking residential area near the National Zoo, at least according to

Augustine, who spouted random bits of DC knowledge from the front seat.

"Is the car also bewitched like The House?" Mirza asked anxiously next to me in the back after the car careened into a sharp left through a yellow stoplight.

"Nope, this is all me and my years of learning to weave through LA traffic!" Charlotte replied with a laugh.

I exchanged a nervous glance with the lab tech, and we both gripped the inside door handles for leverage. Thank god for seatbelts.

Eventually, the car slowed as it entered a small street lined with boxy, three-story row homes on each side. Much different from the large brownstones of New York, these houses were smaller, but still stately in their own way. And unlike row homes in Georgetown, most had covered front porches and large front lawns.

Augustine noted that these were 'Wardman Houses,' named after an influential architect in the area during the early 1900s.

Finding a parking space on the street with relative ease, Charlotte held her car keys over her shoulder as she walked away and the Audi sedan issued a friendly beep goodbye.

She pointed to the house. It was small and charming, with a brown brick facade that covered the front and long arched windows on the first and second floors. Two nautical-looking circular windows jutted out under its dark, shingled roof. Like a pair of eyes peering out of the top attic space.

"Oh my goddess, I know this house," Charlotte said, awestruck, as we neared.

Theo silently walked out of the shadows of the neighbor's overgrown hedge to join us in scaling the long stoop to the front door. I made a mental note that he seemed deliberate in the timing of his entry. Not wanting to be seen by outsiders, but ensuring to make his presence known within enough pacing so as not to startle us.

"My coven celebrated Litha here a few months ago. There's a

good-sized fire pit in the back. Nothing like the beach bonfires we'd light when I was growing up, but we made it work. And if I remember correctly, an old witch lives here. I didn't get so much of an evil 'I want to take over the world' vibe from him. More like grandpa vibes."

Thinking back to a wheel-like diagram of significant witch holidays Matt Riley had shown me, Litha was the celebration of the Summer Solstice. A bonfire was traditionally lit to ward away evil spirits.

Summiting the stoop, Charlotte took the lead and rang the doorbell. Meanwhile, I kept a watchful eye on Theo. Hands in the pockets of my cardigan, I gripped the stake concealed in the right one tightly.

The door swung open to reveal a short man in his sixties. His features were mouselike, with a mop of greying, slightly curly brown hair on his head, small inset eyes of the same color, large ears, and a slender nose that pointed slightly upward at the tip.

Despite the evening hour, he wore a navy suit with a white button down underneath and a richly detailed purple paisley scarf over his neck.

"Charlie!" Charlotte squealed, raising her arms with excitement.

"Lottie!" the witch replied with an enthusiasm of his own. His eyes were warm, and a white toothed smile stretched across his face.

But the elder witch's excitement faded to confusion when he looked beyond Charlotte at our small group huddled behind.

"I wasn't expecting to see you so soon. Who—who are your friends, dear?"

"Oh, they're just friends from work. Sorry to drop in on you like this, but there's something we need to discuss with you. It's important."

From my view, I couldn't see Charlotte's face but I knew she had given him some sort of look because Charlie's smile dropped and his expression changed to one of concern. Gazing at the rest of us, he smiled again (this one more pained than genuine) and waved.

"Well, hello there! I'm Charlie Dunn."

Suddenly, Charlie doubled over in a coughing fit that lasted several seconds. The coughs started out hoarse, but took on a wetness as they continued. I'd lived long enough to know that sound was never good.

"Please, do come in." He beckoned with a hand once he collected himself.

After the others had filtered in, I passed by Theo. Just the sight of him standing next to my colleagues and me without a muzzle and an enforcement agent restraining him while another pointed a stake at his chest was absolutely infuriating. All the frustration and anger I felt toward him bubbled up, and the fact that he was a dangerous vampire suddenly became the farthest thing from my mind.

I whirled around on the stoop and leaned in close toward him.

"Don't you think for one second that I haven't forgotten what you are or what you've done. You might have them all fooled with this 'good vampire' act, but I know better. And I've been waiting a *very* long time to make sure justice is served for not just our family, but for everyone else you've maimed, killed, or tortured." I hissed in a low voice, giving him the coldest glare I could muster.

Theo's eyes went wide and he opened his mouth to speak, but nothing came out.

"Zo, are you coming?" Charlotte said from inside the house.

I gave him another deadly look, then glanced at the threshold —daring him to cross it—before turning back to head into the house. Whatever he was going to say to me, I didn't want to hear it. It wouldn't matter, anyway.

My intimidation tactic seemed to work. Because when I glanced over my shoulder, Theo was still paused there hesitantly, standing on the tattered and faded welcome mat that now just read 'com'.

"You too, vampire!" Charlie called from inside the house. "You know, I always thought RIDER had some kind of rule against working with vampires, but any vampire that's associated with RIDER and a friend of Lottie's is welcome in my house. Just keep those fangs to yourself, young man, or I'll be forced to use these bad boys." He laughed, jokingly motioning to his hands.

Theo smiled sheepishly and entered the house, closing the door behind him.

Wonderful. I now shared a small, contained space with my vampire brother.

Walking a few hurried paces to catch up with Charlotte, I touched her arm and gave her an inquisitive look. How did Charlie know Theo was a vampire?

'*Witch's sense,*' she mouthed to me matter-of-factly.

Ah yes, how could I forget?

Inside Charlie's house, there were dark hardwood floors throughout, and an entryway with a tall, cathedral-like ceiling that led to a modern marble kitchen with high-end stainless steel appliances. To the right of a kitchen island where we assembled, there was a sophisticated dining room with two large glass bell jar chandeliers suspended over a wooden table and cream-colored upholstered dining chairs. Beyond the kitchen and dining area were floor-to-ceiling windows that looked out onto the backyard. And as Charlotte had mentioned, a large stone fire pit adorned the center, surrounded by Adirondack chairs.

It was unexpected, in a way. I assumed there would be some kind of kitschy sign or a decorative pentagram that otherwise proclaimed a witch lived there. Charlotte seemed to be into that stuff, anyway. But to anyone none the wiser, it looked like the home of a retired lobbyist. Refined and comfortable and definitely not anything to do with the supernatural.

Taking a seat in a chair at the far end of the kitchen island,

Mirza sat down next to me and Augustine stood at my other side. Theo took his place a few feet away, against a wall. While quiet, his eyes darted back and forth in calculated observation. Like a hawk surveying an open field.

On the island in front of me was a stack of mail. Mostly nondescript white envelopes, but many had bright red ink stamped on the front with PAST DUE and FINAL NOTICE.

Charlie swooped over from behind and snatched up the stack of mail, shoving it into a nearby kitchen drawer while flashing a smile.

"I was just about to brew some mugwort tea. I grow it here in the back garden myself. I've just been having the worst indigestion for the past few days. Would anyone else like a cup?" Charlie spoke in a rapid but friendly cadence. Like he'd had a lot to say and no one to say it to in a long time.

"I'll take one! Cups are in here, right?" Charlotte asked, joining Charlie in the kitchen.

Charlie nodded, placing a well-loved copper kettle, cloudy and discolored with age, on the range and igniting the gas.

"The coven and I were so excited to hear that Lottie had been selected as the witchcraft liaison to RIDER," Charlie said, returning to the island to face us with a cheerful expression. "Not unexpected, though. I've known Lottie and her family for a long time. She's got a lot of potential. Lottie—are you ready for Samhain? I'm sure your presentation will be the best in decades." He added emphasis to the word 'best,' spreading his hands out in front of him.

Charlotte's mouth opened, but her face went blank as she searched for the best words. "Um, it's still a work in progress. But… I'm getting there. It's one of those things where it just all comes together in the eleventh hour."

From her tone, it sounded like she was trying to convince herself more than anyone else in the room.

"You know, I've been working with RIDER as a consultant for

a special project. Such a great feeling to be collaborating with such a prestigious institution," the elder witch boasted with a bit of playful smugness.

It made me wonder just how many special projects RIDER had going on. The more time I spent with colleagues outside of my DIDs bubble, the more the organization seemed to grow.

But there was something else about this specific 'special project' of Charlie's that perked my ears. And not just mine. Around the kitchen, we all shared the same curious look.

Charlie bent over in another lengthy coughing fit. Like the one before, it started out dry but became more wet with each heave. It reminded me of the sound a cat made before hacking up a hairball.

Charlotte rushed to his side with a glass of water when he stood up, seemingly recovered.

"Charlie, are you okay? You didn't have that cough at Litha," she asked, concerned.

"Thanks, but I'm fine," Charlie replied, accepting the glass and taking a long drink. "Must be the changing seasons. Mold in the leaves and such. Happens every year."

Charlotte flashed our side of the island a grimace before hopping up to take a seat on the kitchen counter.

Meanwhile, I watched Charlie anxiously play with his silk scarf with one hand as he poured hot water from the kettle into two cups with the other. It seemed as though he were thinking through a complicated puzzle. Placing the empty kettle on the range with intention, he slipped a sachet into each cup and handed one to Charlotte. When he returned to the island, he draped his forearms across the marble.

"I have to be honest with you. I didn't think you'd expect me to finish the project by now. I'm not sure if I have it all nailed down. It's a very ancient and complex spell. These things take time. They can't be hurried. And have you even located the resources for extraction? I made it very clear in our agreement that I wanted nothing to do with finding the offerings." Charlie's composure had changed instantly to one of grave seriousness as his gaze ticked from me to Augustine.

Goosebumps broke out over my arms. Whatever Charlie was working on, it didn't sound good.

"What exactly is the nature of this project?" Augustine asked, just as confused as I.

Then it was Charlie's turn to look confused. His brow knitted, and he tilted his head to look me in the eye.

"That's why you've come, isn't it? To check on my progress to reverse engineer the immortality spell? I have to say, it is really an honor to meet you. The spell caster who cast it on you was very talented or just lucky. The incantation inflection alone is the most complicated I've ever seen. And the notes I've gotten from what you remember are good, but there are still some holes to fill."

It was true. I was the Immortal, just like Theo had said.

Was this why Dr. Kelley was so intent on recalling the accident in the prison from over two hundred years ago in such detail? He wanted to recreate the immortality spell? That would definitely be something big and world-changing.

Suddenly feeling exposed, I felt the urge to grab Augustine's hand. It was just inches away from me at his side. I wanted to grab it and feel its warmth and reassuring squeeze so I didn't feel so alone.

But it was Mirza who placed a comforting hand on my arm and offered a half-smile, as if to say, *'Well, shit.'*

Well, shit. Indeed.

Charlotte spit out her tea, spewing the hardwood with her projectile spray. "Charlie, no!"

She leapt off the counter, blue eyes wild with shock and something else. Hurt, disgust? It was hard to tell, but she was visibly upset.

"The immortality spell? Are you insane? You know that's considered black magic—which, hello—is strictly forbidden if you've forgotten! And we both know there's a damn good reason why that incantation has been lost in the first place and why the Collective Coven has agreed to keep it that way."

From what Matt had briefed me, The Collective Coven was a sort of global board of witches that governed the smaller, local covens. They had the final say on rules and regulations.

Charlie was speechless as he looked down at the floor, ashamed. Like a child being reprimanded. Charlotte's gaze swept over to our side of the island and likely saw the lost look we shared.

"Witchcraft is all about balance," she explained. "An equal exchange of elements to cause a specific reaction. When I conjure flame, I'm channeling my energy and the energy of the surrounding elements. The key to open the gate at Dumbarton Oaks? Channeled energy that became dust that went back into the earth to cultivate plants to create future energy. The immortality spell grants one person infinite life, but where do you think that life-force comes from?"

I knew the answer. A weight fell in the pit of my stomach because of it.

"Life for life," Augustine replied in a low voice. "To give multiple lives to one person, multiple lives must be taken in return."

Charlotte nodded and caught my gaze with a solemn look. "Do you remember where you were when the spell was cast?"

"It was a prison," I replied slowly. "With at least a hundred inmates, if not more, when the spell was performed."

"And after the spell was cast, how many survived?"

Charlotte knew my answer. It reflected there in the gloss of her unblinking stare. She wanted me to say it out loud.

"No one," I said grimly, biting my lip when I recalled the nightmarish scene. "I woke up the next day and everyone... everyone was dead. I was the only survivor."

I closed my eyes. The cries of agony and smell of burning brimstone from that night never really went away, with or without Dr. Kelley's sessions.

Mirza cursed, and this time Augustine placed a comforting hand on my shoulder. It was warm and soothing. I resisted the urge to lean my head against it.

"Exactly my point," Charlotte said, her voice rising. "What were you thinking, trying to perfect this heinous spell? I'm feeling all kinds of dark energy just thinking about it. This entire house is probably seeped in it too. Yuck!"

"Lottie, I know, I know. I'm sorry," Charlie said. "But when Madeline passed away a few years ago, I was so lost without her. And you know how much I love going to the casino... I started to love it even more when she wasn't around. And then everything just spiraled out of control. Bills kept stacking up, and I was about to lose the house—*our* house. And I didn't want to bother any of our kids about it.

"But then these guys at RIDER reached out to me, looking for a witch to help piece back the immortality spell. They said we'd make a fortune selling the charm to whoever could afford it. At first I didn't believe them. But they said there was an immortal —not someone Gifted, but who had the spell performed on them. And they were trying to piece back what they could remember."

When Charlie made eye contact with me, I wanted to throw up. I was being used by the same organization I had devoted centuries of my life to. It was my home. It was all that I knew. But I knew nothing.

Augustine stood up straight.

"Names. We need them. Now. Who at RIDER are you working with on this?" he demanded, pulling out his mobile. Augustine was going into full senior leadership mode and we certainly needed someone like him to swashbuckle through whatever red tape there might be to stop it.

Charlie put a hand to his head and closed his eyes. "Ah, I apologize. I'm terrible with names. There's two of them. One gentleman—he's younger than I expected when he mentioned he was a director. Talks fast, always on his cell phone. I think his name starts with a 'T'. Um, maybe it's Tyler, Trevor?"

"Tristan," I answered, barely above a whisper. I was surprised I didn't vomit right there and then on the kitchen island. We had told Tristan everything. Theo, Summer Coogan, all of it.

Charlie snapped his fingers together. "Tristan! Yes, that's it! And the other guy. Oof, he gives me the heebie jeebies, if I'm being perfectly honest. He's Gifted—can go into people's minds and such. He's also got these very alarming-looking eyes. Grey and orange. He should really think about wearing sunglasses around humans. They're very noticeable. And humans can sense that sort of thing—the supernatural—even if they don't know what it means."

"Jack Kelley," Augustine confirmed.

We were officially fucked.

"Who else?"

"Those are the only contacts I've been working with, just the three of us."

"How deep into RIDER do you think this goes?" Theo asked Augustine.

"I'm not sure. Part of me doesn't want to know," Augustine replied, browsing through his mobile's contact list. I could tell choosing the best person to call was like playing a game of chess, except all the pieces were the same color. Nothing to differentiate the opposing team.

"What about Diana?" I ventured with hope in my voice.

An oxymoron if I ever had one. If the topic were any lighter, I would have laughed. Gazing out the windows to the backyard, I half expected to see a flying pig glide by.

"I've known Diana for a long time. I'd like to think that she would not involve herself in something like this. But with conspiracies, you never know how deep or wide it may be."

"Wait, let's back up for a moment to make sure I've got this straight. Because my head is spinning," Mirza said. It was good to know mine wasn't the only one. "As far as we know, Tristan and Dr. Kelley are trying to use Zoey's memories to find the spell that caused her immortality, so they can sell immortality to the highest bidder. And they've been working with witches—like Charlie—to help complete the incantation. But who's been murdering the other witches? Do you think it's connected?"

"That's a good point," Augustine said.

"Murdered witches?" Charlie looked stunned, with wide eyes and a slacked expression. As if realizing for the first time that he had gotten himself way in over his head.

"That's why we came over. We received some... information." Charlotte's eyes flitted toward Theo for a moment. "That you might be in danger to who—or what—is behind the killings. I have a feeling you're not the first witch to have been working with Tristan and Kelley."

The elder witch paled. Then, as if something clicked in his mind, straightened and smoothed down his silk scarf.

"Well, whoever that might be is in for a surprise. The wards on this house are impenetrable. If someone with ill intentions even steps one foot on my property, this place'll lock up tighter than Fort Knox and the alarm bells will start screaming. And I might not be as spry as I used to be, but I can still conjure fire in a jiff."

He snapped his fingers together and opened his hand to reveal a palm-sized flickering blue flame.

"Well, that's a relief," Charlotte said. "Do you have what you've been able to decipher from the immortality spell? We should tell the coven so they can properly dispose of it."

Charlie looked pained, but ultimately gave in. "Yes, it's upstairs. I'll go grab it now."

"Great. And bring a pair of gloves too. I don't even want to touch it with my bare hands," Charlotte added with a visible shiver.

Charlie made it halfway down the hallway before he bent over in yet another coughing fit.

But this time it was different.

The wet sound that slapped around his throat grew louder and thicker. Like something was lodged deep inside. With each hack, whatever it was sounded like it was about to breach his mouth.

Charlie fell to his hands and knees, mouth open and heaving. His eyes teared from the effort, causing small streams to run down the sides of his face.

"Charlie?" Charlotte asked, cautiously moving toward him.

Theo, who had otherwise been statuesque, reached out and grabbed her arm as she passed.

"Be careful," he warned.

Charlotte ripped her arm from his grip and looked offended. But before she could reach Charlie, we all saw what had been stuck in his chest.

It came out slowly. A single, black piece of wet, sticky tar-like saliva flew out of his mouth and onto the hardwood. The next few coughs flew more pieces of black from his mouth. Then a much thicker strand came out, landing on the floor with a loud, disgusting slop. It stuck there, both on the floor and attached to whatever was in his throat, like an anchor. I recoiled in my chair.

Another thick anchor joined the first, and Charlie looked to be in visible pain as he tried to expel what was inside of him. His jaw extended far wider than I thought was humanly or witchly possible. Then, a spherical ball of white light, wrapped in black tar, emerged from his mouth. It popped out and rode the length of his tongue until it hit the floor with a damp smack.

The bright light within its stringy cage was nothing like I had seen before, and it pulsed irregularly to a rhythm of its own. It was beautiful.

Then, as quickly as it had come out of Charlie, it faded. The ball dimmed until it completely dissipated and the black tar that remained seeped into the hardwood, leaving nothing behind but a dark stain where it was before.

The air in the house went still, suddenly feeling vacant and cold.

"No." Charlotte breathed. She backed up and grabbed Theo, ducking behind him like a makeshift shield.

Charlie, breathing hard, had managed to sit upright against a nearby wall. He was covered in sweat and tears, completely exhausted. A small smidge of black saliva hung on the corner of his lips.

"What just happened?" I asked, not sure how to piece together what I had seen.

"Charlie, are you okay?" Augustine asked.

The witch nodded slowly. "I—I think so," he croaked.

Charlotte looked skeptical. "Charlie, I want you to conjure flame again." Her voice held an uneasy calm.

With a few forced breaths, Charlie seemed to gather himself enough to raise his dominant hand. He snapped his fingers and opened his palm.

It was empty.

He tried again and again, becoming more frantic with each snap. He even tried to verbally incite the incantation to ignite fire. But the fire refused to appear.

"No, no, no. This can't be happening," Charlie moaned, catching his face in his hands.

"Um, can someone please catch the humans in the room up to speed?" Mirza asked, looking from Charlotte and Theo to the exhausted man on the floor, and finally to the black splotchy stains on the hardwood.

"His magic's been taken. That's why it feels, you know... *weird* in here. The wards are down," Charlotte said, fearful. She continued to back away from Charlie as if he were a leper. "He's been deemed unworthy. The Honored Gods and Goddesses who first gave us witches power have taken his away as punishment for using black magic. I didn't think this could actually happen. I always thought it was just a myth. Stories my parents told me when

I was a kid. You know, be good or the bogeyman will take away your powers."

Charlotte sent a scolding look toward Charlie. "This probably isn't your first time using black magic, is it?"

"No, it's not," he cried, still collapsed on the floor.

"Well, as unfortunate as this is, we need to track down Tristan as quickly as possible before he can find a replacement," Augustine said.

Charlie moaned again, but this time, he sounded surprised. When I turned to look at him, he had his hand held in front of his face. His fingers were red. Tears continued to stream down his face, but they had turned a dark crimson. He opened his mouth in a confused, devoid-of-thought stare and a stream of blood leaked out of his nose and onto his lap.

I jumped out of my chair and backed away. The sight of blood always made me queasy, and I held a hand to my mouth, trying not to gag. I wasn't sure if I should look away or run to offer him aid. Instead, we all stood still, watching as rivers of blood poured out of him.

Charlie looked around the room with pitiful, red-stained eyes. He suddenly stiffened as if lightning had struck him, and his head snapped back to stare at the ceiling.

A single raspy "Ah" escaped his lips. A sound that was relief, terror, and wonder all wrapped in one as it released into the air. Then he tipped over like a felled tree, slowly at first, then faster as gravity took hold. Blood poured out onto the floor and pooled around him. His eyes were wide, staring straight in our direction. They were vacant and unseeing.

Charlie was as dead as a doornail.

I screamed. As did Mirza, who backed out of his chair and ran over to where the rest of us huddled in the back of the room. He gripped onto my shoulder for comfort.

"Well, I think we just solved how they were murdered. But I'm still not entirely sure what I just saw," Theo said, attempting to find any silver lining in the grotesque scene we just witnessed.

"Black magic. If you haven't gotten the memo by now, it's... dangerous," Charlotte said with a gulp. "If performed improperly, it eats away at you from the inside out. Like a poison. Since he was trying to perform a forbidden spell without all the pieces, it was probably slowly eating away at him for weeks. The Honored Gods and Goddesses took his magic right before it killed him to make it as painful of a punishment as possible. To tip the scale back into balance."

Theo pressed his lips in a tight line and grimly nodded. "He smelled... off. Even his blood doesn't smell right. It smells... rotten. The witch in Philly smelled like that too."

A shiver ran down my spine at the thought that black magic could rot someone from the inside out in ways I couldn't comprehend.

"Let me get ahold of Matt Riley, get his team involved right away. They can also handle the cleanup," Augustine said tiredly, punching numbers into his mobile.

Rapid knocking at the front door reverberated through the still room. Theo started toward it, but Augustine motioned to him to stay in place and approached the door himself. Before he could reach it, the door handle turned and opened.

Tristan stood in the entryway, looking frantic with his face covered in a glistening sheen of perspiration. But his expression turned to one of exhausted frustration when his eyes settled on the dead witch in the hallway.

"God dammit," he spat out, annoyed. "Not again."

NINETEEN

Tristan looked up from Charlie's body on the floor, his gaze roving around us on the opposite end of the hallway as if noticing us for the first time. I tensed when our eyes locked for a beat. I had known Tristan for years, but now all I saw was a stranger.

"So I take it Charlie squawked and croaked, huh?" he asked.

"Tristan, we can stop this all right now with little repercussion on your part. It's not too late," Augustine said.

Tristan smiled. One of his wide, toothy, ones that made the first-year girls (and some boys) melt. But his usual friendly and energetic exterior had changed to one more sinister.

"Augustine, are you kidding me?" he laughed. The sound was slightly manic and unhinged. "I have the world's billionaires kissing my feet, waiting for us to finish perfecting the immortality spell. There's something about remaining human that they find really alluring about it. You know, none of the pesky side effects that come with vampirism. This is going to change the world, and I'll be at the top, controlling all of it. Why would I want to stop that?"

"Because your witch is dead and RIDER will come down hard

on you for what you've done. You're high-level enough now to know the... creativity our organization can have."

I didn't like the way Augustine said the word 'creativity,' and I definitely didn't want to think what he meant by it.

"I already have another one lined up. I came here because I had a feeling Charlie might get cold feet or was just screwing around. When it's the latter, they tend to end up like that." Tristan motioned to Charlie's body and rolled his eyes.

"And RIDER doesn't concern me. The whole place is so archaic and naïve. They only focus on the academic side of the supernatural. But once we start selectively choosing people in influential positions to become immortal, they'll have no choice but to support us. You know, it's not too late if you want in. We're offering quite a deal on founding member rates."

"You're psycho," Charlotte said. She stepped forward and held her arms out to conjure flame.

Tristan pulled out a small handgun from the pocket of his overcoat and pointed it at the witch before she could finish.

"Don't even think about it." Flicking off the safety with his thumb, he kept the firearm fixed on Charlotte, but his gaze slid toward me. "Zoey, you're coming with me."

Mirza moved in front of me, reaching out an arm in a protective block.

"Nope, nope, we're not doing that. Back where you were. No hero bullshit or you'll end up like Charlie," Tristan warned, waving the gun at the lab tech.

Mirza threw his hands up and complied, slowly stepping away. For a moment, he and Theo exchanged glances and the slightest of nods in aligned agreement.

Theo took a defiant step forward, entering Tristan's trajectory.

"She's not going anywhere with you," he growled.

Tristan snorted. "Zo, that is so like you. Always having others fight your battles. Have you ever done anything yourself other than sit in the library? It's such a shame to see how the gift of immortality has been wasted on you." He pointed the gun at Theo. "And you—the only reason she's here in the first place was to hunt you down. You were getting too close for comfort, digging around the other witches, playing vampire detective. Kelley and I could never figure out why a bloodsucker would involve themselves in the affairs of witches. But, whatever—having Zoey come on her *exciting little mission* to take you out and distract the RIDER higher-ups was a win-win. But then you had to let the Kelley stuff out of the bag."

Tristan paused but kept the gun fixed on Theo.

"It's funny. For as long as I've known your sister, all she ever seems to talk about is killing you. I bet she has a wooden stake in her back pocket right now with every intention of burying it in your heart if you so much as flinch the wrong way."

A wave of anxiety washed over me, tightening the knot in my throat. But my fingers gripped the stake in my pocket tighter.

"She'd be stupid if she didn't," Theo replied coolly.

For a moment I wondered if that was a vampire thing, or just a Theo thing. To automatically assume that everyone you encountered was prepared to stake or decapitate you at any moment. What a stressful way to live. Then again, vampires weren't technically alive in the first place.

"Whatever. It's getting late, and we need to meet with Kelley and the new witch. Zo, come on." Tristan kept the gun steady and beckoned me with his other hand as if I were a trained dog.

I scowled, having heard enough of his patronizing monologue. "I'm not going anywhere with you, Tristan."

Tristan sighed, hesitating for a moment. Then, in the next instant, he straightened and promptly fired the gun.

A loud, reverberating bang echoed through the house. The shot hit Theo in his right upper arm. He grunted and shifted to his Other Face, wincing in pain and clutching his arm as he slumped against the wall for support. Not a lethal shot, but a painful one that would slow him down.

"Theo!" Charlotte cried out, starting toward him.

"Don't—I'm fine. Just stay where you are," he said, breathing hard through clenched fangs.

Tristan aimed the gun directly at Charlotte. "Next one is for the witch. Whether or not you try any magic shit. I'm not playing around here."

Unlike Theo, who was probably already healing, Charlotte would be significantly less likely to survive a gunshot. Everyone stayed silent and motionless for a few seconds. It seemed like hours.

"Is this what you want?" Tristan asked, looking me in the eye. For the first time since I'd known him, the warmth had drained out, leaving only two cold shells staring back at me. "For me to have to kill everyone in this room until it's just you and I left? Would you really be that selfish to let them sacrifice themselves for you?"

"No." I choked on the word as it came out in a painful whisper. My eyes stung and became glossy as I tried to hold back tears.

It seemed a bit ironic. That with all the supernatural cases, creatures, and magic we dealt with, it was a very non-magical gun that held power over all of us.

They didn't deserve that. And with Theo injured, I wasn't sure how well he could fend off Tristan by himself. There was only one solution that kept everyone alive.

In the best-case scenario, maybe Dr. Kelley would scramble my mind into oblivion before he could finish deciphering my memory.

I slowly shuffled one step forward. My feet were heavy, like weights had been attached to them.

Then all hell broke loose.

Augustine rushed Tristan and plowed into his side. The arm Tristan held the gun with flew sideways, away from Charlotte, and fired another shot. Augustine wrestled the director of External Affairs to the floor, kicking the firearm out of his grasp with his foot. It skittered across the floor and Theo picked it up in the blink of an eye. He quickly emptied the remaining magazine, then clamped the gun shut and flicked on the safety.

"Is everyone alright?" Augustine shouted toward the kitchen.

Tristan tried to sputter something under his grip, but Augustine shifted his weight to cover his mouth with a hand to silence him.

"I'm fine," said Charlotte.

"Good, here," Mirza said.

I looked around at the floor and the windows behind me. The shot sounded so close that I was sure it was going to hit and shatter the glass. But the glass remained intact and nothing else looked out of place.

There was something wet on my lower abdomen. It was soaking through my T-shirt.

"Zoey..." Charlotte's tone was a mix of panic and surprise.

The witch's gaze was fixed on my torso. Peering down, a dark red stain bled through the white fabric. It grew larger at an alarming pace.

It seemed unreal at first, like an out-of-body experience. What I saw wasn't happening. It couldn't be. With two fingers, I reached down and touched the stain. More red seeped out. It dripped over my leggings and onto the hardwood floor, feet away from Charlie's own pool of red. Holding my fingers up where I could see them, they were tipped in shiny bright red blood. My blood.

Out of the corner of my eye, Theo was staring at me. He hungrily licked his lips before glancing away.

"W-what?" I stuttered in shock, realization dawning on me. The bullet didn't shatter the glass, because it had hit me.

And I had definitely been in shock for the past few minutes because the adrenaline that had been keeping the pain of the gunshot at bay receded and I cried out, doubling over in agony. It was a pain that I'd never experienced before. Hot, like a blister, and it burned so intensely that I wanted to pass out.

"Zoey? Oh, my god." Forgetting about Tristan, Augustine leapt from the floor and rushed over.

Tristan scrambled to his hands and knees. He took one frightened look at me and froze. Theo started toward him, his shoulder slumping to the side as he moved.

"Theo!" Augustine said before he could reach him. "We'll deal with him later. I need you here now."

My brother paused, visibly annoyed. He gave Tristan a disgusted look that promised revenge before leaving him in the hallway. When Theo reached the kitchen, his face had changed back to its human-looking form.

Charlotte held out a hand toward the kitchen stove as if she were asking someone to dance. The tea towel that hung on the oven's handle flew across the room and landed gently in her grasp, accepting her offer.

"Compress—good thinking, Charlotte," Augustine said, going into full triage mode. "Mirza, call the RIDER field emergency line. Tell them we have a human agent down and in need of an ambulance and the closest RIDER surgical suite a-sap. We're also going to need a clean-up crew."

"On it," Mirza said, pulling out his mobile.

When Charlotte came toward me with the compress, my whole body shook and I reached out to hold onto the kitchen island for support.

"Hey girl, you're going to be fine. I'm super not like a doctor, but I've binge watched all the medical dramas to know this is nothing," she said in a strangely calm voice. I prayed she was right.

She lifted my shirt up enough to press the tea towel tightly against the wound. I didn't expect the amount of pressure that came from her delicate hands. The force against the tender tissue sent a shock of pain rippling through me. I gasped, buckling to my knees.

Augustine's face suddenly took up my entire view as he crouched down next to me and draped a supporting hand across my back.

"Hey Zoey, look at me. I want you to focus on me right here."

I blinked. My vision blurred at the peripheral, so Augustine's face was all that I could see. His warm brown eyes remained the same as he spoke, but the older man that had been there moments before morphed into the young man I knew decades ago. As if he hadn't changed at all, either.

"Auggie..." I smiled. My voice was wistful.

"That's it, just focus on me, keep those eyes open."

It was getting harder. My eyelids were so heavy. Maybe they would feel lighter if I closed them for just a second.

Augustine shook me and held my face closer. "Zoey, come on —look at me. Do you remember when we used to watch the boats in the pond at Central Park?"

A memory blossomed in my mind of our walks through the city when we were together. When that sort of thing was allowed instead of the full SWAT team of enforcement agents that tailed me whenever I wanted to leave campus. I thought of the glittering water in the pond and the juxtaposition of the modern skyscrapers against the park's lush greenery.

"Mmhm." I nodded.

"Tell me again, which ones were your favorite?"

There were the rowboats, which seemed untouched by time, looking the same as when I had first come to New York. And the gondolas too. But there was one that always stuck out in my mind.

"The little sailboats," I replied, nostalgic.

My tongue was suddenly thicker, like a dead fish in my mouth. It was becoming difficult to speak without slurring.

Augustine smiled and nodded encouragingly. "Yes, the little remote-controlled sailboats. You were always too scared to use the controller to drive them yourself, but you loved to watch them for hours."

I did. I loved how they zipped along the water as if it were a vast ocean, their miniature sails flapping in the wind. Augustine had been into photography at the time and he'd bring his fancy camera and large telescopic lenses. My favorite photos of his were forced perspective ones, where at just the right angle, the toy sailboats looked life-sized against the New York City backdrop.

"Augustine!" Charlotte said with rising alarm. "We need more towels. This one's not holding up."

Blinking slowly, I looked at my side and saw blood covered Charlotte's hands. The tea towel she held was a soggy mess.

Without warning, Theo was at my other side. He handed her a fresh towel, and she quickly swapped it out, pressing it harder against the wound. I winced and cried out as pain shot through me.

"She's losing too much blood. Lie her down on her back," Augustine instructed.

Shockingly cold hands touched me, and I recoiled away from them.

"It's okay, he's here to help," Augustine whispered to me.

Theo reached out to touch my arm and back again, and this time, I allowed it. Together, he and Augustine carefully laid me down on the hardwood floor.

Something was wrong.

Although I remained conscious, my vision tunneled until all I could see was darkness. A comforting warmness spread over me and the pain receded. Thinking about the Central Park boats brought on all the other memories of all the decades I had lived. The good, the bad, the mundane, the magical. The time before Theo was turned, and we were just an ordinary family and all the events after that, including tonight. It all played like a movie set on fast-forward.

I knew what was happening. I had studied the topic to an exhausted state. My body was shutting down, preparing to die.

But I wasn't ready.

I wanted to be like the immortals in the movies and on TV who were brave when death came. But I'd grown to fear the finality of death. The absolute of non-existence. The thought terrified me more than the most ferocious hellbeast.

"I'm scared," I said to Augustine. "I-I'm not ready. Please, do something. I don't want to—" I was too exhausted to finish.

Augustine grasped my hands and held them tightly against my chest. "It's okay, you're going to be fine," he said. Lifting his head up, he shouted across the room, "Mirza, time check?"

"The ambulance is twelve minutes out!"

"Is that enough time?" Augustine asked Theo.

"She's lost too much blood, her heart is slowing." I could still feel his icy presence beside me, but his voice was distant and muffled.

I closed my eyes and breathed in deeply. When I exhaled, the air left my chest in a ragged sigh. I wanted to cry, but I didn't have the energy. I was too tired. And a deep, warm sleep called out louder. Death was inevitable. It was waiting for me. And there was nothing I could do to avoid it. Charlotte's cards had been right all along.

There was indiscernible murmuring above me. Then Augustine's voice bled into clarity again.

"Are you sure?" he asked.

"No," came Theo's solemn response. It sounded dreamlike, and the word echoed around me.

Unnaturally cold fingertips touched my chin, propping open my mouth.

Then I felt them. Tiny, cold droplets rained down, pelting my lips and tongue. I thought it was water at first, but the taste was metallic and a little salty. Repulsed, I cringed, wanting to spit it out. But I was too weak, so I forced myself to swallow it to get the taste out of my mouth. The drops kept coming.

And then I was floating. Away in a sea of darkness. Away from the chaos in the kitchen. Away from the quaint house in Woodley Park. Away from everything.

Until there was nothing except the expanse, and in it I grew colder and colder.

TWENTY

I opened my eyes slowly and cautiously, blinking several times until my vision became clear again. I was lying on my back on a freezing hard surface, staring at a solid iron roof that hovered above me.

Sitting up, my organs sloshed around my gut. For a moment, I thought I was going to be sick, but after a brief pause, the nausea subsided. Scanning my surroundings, I noticed two things that made me crave the blissful ignorance of the previous ten seconds.

One: the thick perpendicular iron bars surrounding me suggested I was sitting in a large, person-sized cage. I would have thought it was a jail cell, but it had neither a bench nor a toilet.

And two: Charlotte was screaming.

"You vampires are all the same!" she shouted at Theo. The two were outside the cage. She marched toward him, light flying from her palms in his direction. "You only think with your teeth!"

Theo backed away from her with his hands up to block the shower of sparks. Most extinguished themselves on the cement floor, but a stray bolt whizzed by him, shattering a terracotta planter into shards and red dust on the shelf behind him.

Slowly rising to my feet, I stumbled. It took a few seconds before I could get my bearings. Everything felt fuzzy and numb, like a dream. Most likely the effects of the drugs the RIDER surgeons pumped me with during emergency surgery. But that still didn't explain why I was in the cage.

I looked downward and saw I had been changed out of the leggings and blood-soaked T-shirt for the sweater and trousers I had set out in my room when I was packing to return to New York.

"She's awake," Theo said to Charlotte.

Charlotte shook her hands to snuff out the sparks and gently massaged her red, blistering palms. She and Theo exchanged an anxious look before cautiously approaching me. What the hell was going on?

I took a clumsy step toward them and held a hand to my head. It was swimming, like I had been hit by a bus.

"Careful," Theo said. "Just go slow, don't rush it."

"What's going on? Where am I?" I asked, confused.

It suddenly dawned on me. Just beyond Theo and Charlotte was the small sitting area with a blue sectional, the unfinished wooden staircase to my left.

I was in the basement of The House in one of the werewolf cages. What a wonderful place to wake up.

The fuzzy, slow, dreamlike fog suddenly dissolved, and everything felt like it was rushing toward me. My senses overloaded all at once.

Colors brightened until my eyes hurt so much that I had to close them. The cage suddenly smelled intensely of wet dog. I could also smell the wet, earthy dirt outside, the water from a small leak on the far side of the basement, even the dust on the ground.

But sound was the worst. I could hear the small squeaks and footsteps of a mouse that lived in the wall on the floor above me, the folding leather-on-leather sound of Theo's jacket when he made the slightest movement. And a pounding—like the beating of a drum—reverberated in my ears. It sounded like it came from Charlotte.

I clapped my hands over my ears and crouched low over my knees. "Make it stop!" I cried.

It was like being caught in a stampede—so unrelenting that I didn't know how much more of it I could take.

A few harrowing beats later, the smells and sounds dissipated like a passing train. I opened my eyes to see that while colors still appeared brighter than they should be; they were no longer painful to look at.

I inhaled and exhaled deeply to ground myself, then stood and looked at Charlotte and Theo again. This time, more than desperate for answers.

"She's settling. Talk low like this," Theo said to Charlotte. I didn't get it. He sounded normal to me.

"Hey girl, how are you feeling?" Charlotte asked cheerfully.

Her voice was shrill and loud, like fingernails dragging across a chalkboard. My face twitched into a grimace and I covered my ears again at the unpleasant noise. Ouch.

"Sorry, is this better?" she asked sheepishly, her voice now leveled out.

Still reeling, I nodded and lowered my hands. What was happening?

"So, as you can see, you've been staying in the Garden View Room of the Werewolf Airbnb," she announced proudly.

I looked at her, still confused. Charlotte turned to the side and motioned to the shelving behind her and Theo that was in my direct line of sight. It was filled with gardening supplies and large bags of Miracle Grow. The planter on the bottom shelf remained a broken heap.

I returned her forced, sunny expression with a suspicious glare. Charlotte was a terrible liar.

"What happened? Why am I in the cage?" I asked again, my tone stern. I was over being handled with kid gloves. I wanted the truth.

"What do you remember last?" Theo asked. His eyes were cautiously fixed on me, waiting for my response.

I thought back; the events rewinding in my mind. "I remember being at Charlie's house. And then Tristan showed up. He wanted me to go back with him and Dr. Kelley. Then he shot you in the arm. How—"

"It's healed. What else do you remember?"

Oh right. Theo wasn't the only person who had been shot. Lifting my sweater, I inspected my lower right torso where I had been hit. It had fully healed and was nothing but a light pink scar. I touched the area with my finger. It wasn't even bruised, and there were no signs of stitches. The results surprised me, but RIDER had access to resources I couldn't even begin to comprehend.

"Wow," I snorted, impressed. "I really thought I wasn't going to make it there for a moment."

My smiling face froze when I met Theo and Charlotte's matching grim expressions.

"Well, that's the thing," Charlotte said slowly, shooting a quick glance at Theo. "You kind of... didn't. And for the record, I was against this whole thing. But what's happened has happened and we all just need to accept it and move on," she said tartly, glaring at Theo, who suddenly found the ground to be the most interesting thing in the room.

What the hell was that supposed to mean? If I died, this definitely didn't seem like Heaven. A bit more like Hell, but even then I would have expected it to feel warmer than the cold basement and there to be at least one person prancing around with a pitchfork.

"If I died," I said, still unconvinced. "Then how am I here?"

"I—I gave you some of my blood," Theo said quietly, still looking at the ground. His shoulders hunched forward and his body fell inward in an undeniable gesture of guilt.

My blood ran cold. And it was when I expected to feel my heart race with panic. There was... nothing. My chest was still.

While there were many ways to kill a vampire, there was only one way to make them. A human had to have ingested vampire blood to become infected and then die when it was still in their system. Traditionally, vampires drained their victims of blood, then exchanged some of their own right before they died. But humans could become vampires at the result of any fatal injury, so as long as they had vampire blood in their system. Including a lethal gunshot to the abdomen.

"Theo?"

Theo looked up to meet my gaze with a sad knowing in his eyes.

He took a deep breath. Then, like ripping off a band-aid, said, "You lost too much blood. I gave you mine, and you died. But it brought you back... as a vampire."

"No," I said weakly, feeling like someone had punched me in the gut.

But I would rather take a million gut punches than have to live the rest of eternity as a vile, bloodthirsty monster. A vampire. I didn't even want to think what my Other Face might look like. The thought alone made me want to scream and vomit at the same time.

"I think I'm going to be sick."

"See, Theo?" Charlotte sighed. "I told you she'd be seriously freaked."

"You asked us to help you. To do something. So I... helped," Theo explained. He seemed to talk a bit easier, like a weight had been lifted after dropping the 'V' word.

"I meant like take me to a hospital!" I shouted, flailing my arms. A pang of anger sparked in my gut and it spread throughout my body and limbs like a wildfire.

I ran up to the bars and grabbed them tightly with both hands. "Charlotte, there must be some kind of spell you can do. To bring me back to life." I said, sending a pleading look to the witch. I wasn't sure what I would be if she brought me back to life, but I'd never heard of a vampire that had a beating heart.

Charlotte shook her head. "I'm sorry. Those kinds of enchantments are considered necromancy. Which is strictly—"

"Forbidden. Because it's Black Magic," I said rhetorically. The sobering look on her face confirmed my assumption.

I whipped my head toward Theo. Rage continued to swirl within me, picking up speed.

"You." The word dripped with fury when it left my mouth.

The bars were werewolf-proof, which also meant that they were vampire-proof. But if they were any less, I wanted nothing more than to pry them open with whatever supernatural strength I had just inherited and rip Theo's face off.

"This was your plan all along, wasn't it? After two hundred years, you couldn't just kill me. No, you have to make me suffer," I snarled, gripping the bars until my knuckles turned an even paler shade of white than I thought possible.

Theo's body snapped back, and he looked hurt, as if my words had actually punched him. Then his brow furrowed and his face hardened. "Let's make one thing clear, I did not spite-sire you. I know this isn't what you expected, but vampirism is a gift or an accident. Spite-siring is barbaric—performed only by the most uncivilized and callow of vampires."

I blinked, trying to process how I had offended the seventh most heinous vampire in North America by assuming he was a vindictive asshole. His track record was as long as the scrolls of CVS receipts Ellie often earthed from her work tote, but integrity and any shred of morality were most definitely not on there.

"So which was it? A gift or an accident?" I asked, pursing my lips in a scowl. It didn't feel like anything other than a curse to me.

"A necessity," he replied evenly. "You lost too much blood—it was too late to take you anywhere for help. And we need you just as much as you need us if we're going to stop Tristan and Kelley. No one knows Tristan better than you. And even if you didn't come back, they would find another way to complete the immortality spell. Also, I saved your life."

Saved my life. So Theo did think of it as a gift. But living as a disgusting vampire was not a life. That I knew for sure. I hated how he acted, like it was some act of chivalry. That after everything he'd done, that I should be thankful for waking up as an undead anomaly.

The thought enraged me.

My hands flew down at my sides and balled into fists, nails burrowing so deep into my palms that I thought the skin might break. I screamed.

Charlotte's eyes widened and she looked at Theo. "Theo, I think she's about to do that thing where vampires go all bat-shit crazy," Charlotte said uneasy, quickly becoming panicked.

There it was, the answer to why I was in the werewolf cage. In case I flipped. And for good reason. Even I wasn't sure if a centuries-old vampire, a witch, and a handful of Gifted enforcement agents would be enough to stop a newly turned vampire from causing significant carnage.

"Zoey, I know how you feel. I've been there. Just try to calm down," Theo said. His tone was deliberately pitched to be reassuring, but it still felt condescending.

"Fuck you," I spat. My words were venom.

I paced the width of the cell like a caged predator, opening and closing my fists, trying to work out the anger that kept rising.

"She's right," Charlotte said to Theo, folding her arms. "If you want to live another two hundred-and-whatever years, *never* tell a woman to calm down."

I stopped mid-pace and closed my eyes, recentering myself. I was determined to not become the monster I could already feel manifesting within me.

"I'm not going to flip," I said, mostly trying to convince myself. "I just... I need a minute."

I whirled around to stare at the craggy cinderblock wall behind me. The anger was addicting. Part of me wanted to just give up and let it consume me. That would be so much easier than using all of my will to fight it off.

Warm wind drifted into the cell and wound itself around me before two arm-like gusts extended in a comforting embrace. While previous encounters with The House had startled me, this time I welcomed it. Melting into its presence, a ripple of serenity passed through me, stamping out the anger as it went.

Friend, The House breathed.

"See? I told you The House likes you," Charlotte said when my temper had evened out enough to turn around, somewhat confident that I wasn't about to tear everything—or everyone, to shreds.

"You can hear it too?" Of all the things I'd encountered, a talking house was still a little hard to wrap my mind around.

"Duh," Charlotte said. "Sometimes I can't get it to shut up."

Heavy boots charged overhead in a thundering rumble, and all three of us looked toward the ceiling.

"Start in the basement and work your way up through the house!" a voice barked above. Enforcement agents. A lot of them.

"We need to get her out of here. Can you take her to a safe place?" Charlotte asked Theo. Her tone held an unsettling urgency.

Theo frowned, and his gaze ticked between me and the witch. "She can't stay with you?"

"No, she can't stay with me," Charlotte replied tartly. "In case you didn't realize, my house is currently being ransacked. And I can barely look after my baby cousins, let alone a baby vampire. Don't you vamps have like *rules* or whatever about taking responsibility for the people you turn?"

Theo's gaze swept the ground, and he let out an agitated sigh. "I have a place. We can regroup later."

I was also not thrilled at the idea of being alone with Theo at some covert site that only he knew the location of, but it was a slightly better alternative than sitting in a cage waiting to be discovered by my vampire hunting colleagues.

Charlotte pulled out a set of keys from her jeans pocket and headed toward the cage's iron door.

"Does RIDER know? About what happened to me or Tristan?" I asked wearily.

Even I wasn't sure of the exact protocol, but I imagined my undead existence wouldn't receive a warm welcome. And what would Augustine think of me now? Could he even stand to look at me like this?

"Well, considering Tristan saw everything before high-tailing it out of Charlie's house, I would say RIDER most definitely knows you're now part of the living dead," Charlotte said. "We were going to go after him, but Augustine reminded us that we have no hard evidence tying the conspiracy to Tristan or Dr. Kelley. Just Charlie, who can't talk for obvious reasons, and his messy notes on the immortality spell."

Charlotte unlocked the door and swung it open. The hinges creaked so loudly that I thought my eardrums were going to burst.

I looked out uneasily at the open space beyond the cell. Could I trust myself to be on the other side without the barred walls and massive lock? The last thing I wanted to do was to hurt Charlotte. Theo, on the other hand, I wanted to turn into a pile of fertilizer on the unfinished basement floor.

"Everything will be okay. Come on, we need to go," he said with a nod toward the back door.

I took two steps out of the cage and glared at him again. My face twitched—a strange sensation from sets of muscles I'd never felt before.

But as much as I wanted to end Theo while he was right in front of me, I had to stay focused. Stay in control. If I wanted to stay alive—whatever that meant now—I'd have to leave with him. Even if it was begrudgingly.

I closed my eyes and took in a deep breath. The House's presence rubbed my shoulders encouragingly. Breathing out slowly through my mouth, I opened my eyes. It was now or never.

I bid goodbye to Charlotte, who responded with a lighthearted half-smile and wave, and followed Theo to the rear door that led to the backyard. He took a step outside and looked around.

"Stay close to me and don't say a word," he said before disappearing into the night.

I followed swiftly behind him through the backyard, sticking close to the hedges as we worked our way toward the tree line at the end of the property.

When I looked over my shoulder, The House was dark inside, but through the windows I could see it was swarming with dozens of RIDER agents. Outfitted in their black fatigues and small white LED flashlights, the lights bounced around The House as they moved, roaming floor to floor and room to room with systematic finesse.

A shiver ran down my spine when I remembered their flashlights had multiple light settings. Including an ultraviolet light emitting one that mimicked the sun.

"Don't get distracted. We're almost there," Theo called back at me.

Breaking through a line of brush, my skin tingled, and I suddenly felt the urge to sneeze when we emerged through Charlotte's wards. We were out on a lamppost-dotted sidewalk in the neighborhood, surrounded by the quiet night.

Theo grabbed my forearm and held it tightly. Startled by the motion and that his touch still felt icy cold on my skin, I looked up to meet his dark gaze. He wasn't wearing his Other Face, but he was just as terrifying as if he were.

"I'm helping you because this immortality spell thing is bigger than the both of us. The human world isn't ready to find out about the supernatural, and it may never be. But I'm less than enthused about having to watch over the person who's leveraged RIDER to hunt me for the better part of the past two centuries."

"The feeling is mutual," I replied, jerking my arm out of his frosty grip. His demeanor was meant to intimidate—and it was working—but my tone held firm. "But I think you're forgetting that *you're* the one that's evil and—"

"*Was* evil—and the terms good and evil are such stupid constructs, anyway." He waved his hand as if to shoo away an annoying fly. "Reality is more complicated than that. I told you, I'm not like that—*evil*—in your sense of the word, anymore. Not that you RIDER people even stop to think for a moment to take notice. I haven't killed a human for decades and yet you're still after me. I've had to live in the shadows and on the run for over a century. Do you have any idea what that's like?"

I did. My shadows were from the shade of RIDER's towering perimeter walls. But I wasn't ready to allude to Theo that we shared anything more in common other than DNA.

"It doesn't make up for what you did. All the people you hurt, the destruction you caused. RIDER keeps the supernatural world accountable. Without it, the human world would be overrun with magical and demonic chaos."

"I'm trying to make amends for my past, but it's not something that happens overnight." Theo paused and inhaled deeply. "And if I'm going to watch over you, you need to do exactly what I tell you—no getting distracted. Now come on, we need to keep moving before someone sees us."

Theo turned and moved down the sidewalk, but I folded my arms and stood my ground. He was treating me like some errant child and it unnerved me to my core. I wasn't the one who'd ruthlessly murdered our family and ravaged the better part of the Western Hemisphere—I was always cleaning up his aftermath. Just like I had to even before he became a vampire.

Halfway down the block, Theo turned and gave me another piercing look over his shoulder.

"No getting distracted," he repeated icily.

I swore, but trotted ahead to follow at his side.

After a couple of blocks, we had seen little of anyone else around, but both noticed a man walking his German Shepard down the street to our left. Well, more so Theo took notice, and I was watching Theo, wondering what he found so interesting about it.

"Wait here," he said. And before I could react, Theo ripped my smart watch off my wrist and headed down the sidewalk.

The dog reacted as most animals did in the presence of an approaching vampire. Snarling, barking, and sending the owner in a frantic dance of reining in his dog without losing balance, calling out apologies of "He never does this!" to Theo.

Using the chaos to his advantage, Theo slipped the watch onto the underside of the dog's harness before the owner could notice.

"That should send Tristan and RIDER on a nice little goose-chase if they try to look for you," Theo said with a small laugh when he caught up with me, his dark mood from minutes earlier lifting.

Another block and Theo led me to a late 1970s black Aston Martin Vantage parallel parked between two later model Mercedes sedans. The coupe was in perfect condition, with a freshly polished sloping back and long curved hood.

"I thought you said you were trying to keep a low profile?" I asked suspiciously.

The Georgetown neighborhood was an affluent one, so vintage collectible cars and their modern luxury counterparts were not uncommon. Among them, the Aston Martin didn't look completely out of place, but it certainly wasn't as inconspicuous as a Honda.

"I am," Theo replied confidently. "But I need to have a little fun every once in a while," he smirked as he popped open the driver's side door.

I rolled my eyes. Lame excuse for a vampire on the run.

With one hand on the car's door handle, my gaze drifted down the dark, empty street ahead. With everything that had happened, my legs itched to sprint down it and through the trees at the far end with no destination in mind. Just to run away. From The House, from Georgetown, from the demon inside me.

"Don't even think about it," Theo said in a low voice. "I'm a lot older than you in vampire years, and I made you. You wouldn't even make it ten feet."

Ugh, thanks for the reminder.

With a sigh, I opened the passenger side door, slipped into the seat's smooth tan leather upholstery, and stared blankly through the front dashboard window.

"I want to go home," I said weakly.

The thrill of adventure had long worn off. I yearned for the comfort of my cozy apartment and one of Marcy's croque monsieurs. Even if it tasted like sawdust to my undead tastebuds now.

"You know you can't go back," Theo said, starting the car. "But I can take you to *a* home."

And for now, that would have to be good enough.

TWENTY-ONE

Turning off the main road, Theo drove the car down a side street and into a small alley. We passed by an abandoned brick-covered apartment building under construction, and the car ambled forward until we came to a small gravel parking lot in the rear. A large blue tarp and a skeleton of vacant scaffolding braced the backside of the building.

Theo cut the ignition and juggled the keys in his hand for a moment. I winced. The sound made a loud, irritating clanging noise in my ears. I didn't like these new sensations. At all.

As much as I knew what changes were happening to my body —enhanced hearing, sight, smell, strength, and eventually a craving for blood—I was doing my best to ignore all of it. Denial? Absolutely. But it was the only coping mechanism I had left to keep me from going off the deep end that would most likely end in some mass-casualty rampage. I clung to it.

"Home, sweet home," Theo said, popping open the door and exiting the car.

No way. What happened to the vampire I read about who only liked to stay in high-end hotels and mansions? Or at least a place where the roof wasn't about to cave in.

I sat firmly in the car and stared straight ahead, unmoving.

Waking up undead was bad enough, but staying in a gross and dirty—not to mention probably roach-infested building—was something I was not prepared for.

"Come on, we don't have all night," Theo coaxed. He was by the passenger side door and opened it, revealing the weed-riddled gravel outside.

I grumbled something under my breath in protest, but there was an odd sensation in my throat and it ended up coming out as a low, throaty growl.

A heavy weight dropped in my stomach. It was a disgusting, animal-like sound.

"I heard that," Theo said, slightly amused.

He extended his hand toward me. It hung in the air for a few uncomfortable moments before I reluctantly unfastened my seat-belt and accepted it, climbing out of the car.

Theo led the way through the makeshift parking lot to the building. When we reached the blue tarp, he pushed it aside, uncovering a set of cement steps that led down to a door with a heavy padlock. He pulled out his keys again and unlocked the door.

"So, you really live here?" I asked, failing to mask the disgust in my voice.

"For now. It's safe. Humans won't bother us here," he replied casually.

Humans won't bother us here.

His words were just another haunting reminder that I was no longer part of that group anymore. The human group. I was now squarely in the creature group. The demonic infectious disease creature group, to be exact.

He held the door open and ushered me inside the basement.

While it was pitch dark, with no lights to guide the way, I could still see remarkably well. But on my first step inside, my heel landed in a puddle of something wet and slimy. It splashed on my bare ankles. Ew, so gross. I frowned and fought the urge to cry.

We continued down the lengthy basement corridor. A series of pipes ran above us, and their clanging and gurgling echoed loudly around the cement walls. The smell was overwhelming—fetid and stale. I held a hand over my nose.

"It stinks in here," I complained, making a face.

Theo's eyes flickered toward me for a moment before he rolled them. "You'll get used to it."

I hoped not.

Theo paused when we came to a large, hulking metal door. Palm-sized rivets dotted the perimeter. At one point, it had been painted green, but it had mostly chipped away. A faded yellow sign of a circle with three downward pointing black triangles was fixed on the wall to the right. A mid-century bomb shelter.

Producing another key for this door, Theo unlocked it and used what seemed to be all of his strength to push the door open. To say I was not excited to see what type of offsite shithole he was taking me to would be a wild understatement. Maybe I should have just stayed in the Werewolf Airbnb cage at Charlotte's house. At least The House's basement smelled less rank.

I reluctantly peered inside and my mouth hung open. "Oh," I said, not able to conceal the astonishment in my voice.

Behind the door was a, dare I say—trendy, loft-style apartment.

I mean, yes, it was still in the basement. And yes, the flooring was polished concrete with many dark, questionable stains. But it also had a grand open concept floor plan and was well-furnished.

The entrance opened into the foyer, and beyond that was a large, grey tufted sectional and sling back leather chair with a cozy-looking rug. A wooden, six-person dining room table and chairs completed the living and dining area. Straight and to the left appeared to be an alcove for the kitchen, separated by an exposed brick wall. The space to the right hinted at where the bedroom and bathroom might be. Long, heavy blackout curtains hung floor to ceiling above tiny high-placed windows in the back. It made the space appear much larger than it actually was.

"So, what's the deal with this place?" I asked, walking around the apartment and carefully scanning its contents for more clues. Pausing at the mirror in the foyer, I waved and saw that it reflected the space behind me and nothing else. Yet another thing to get used to.

"Um, it's kind of a safe house for demons and creatures, but mostly demons. You'll understand when you're... older. It's temporary. Come here," Theo vaguely explained, heading into the kitchen.

I followed him to a narrow, but functional, galley-styled kitchen. On the opposite side, against an exposed brick wall, was a petite, four-seater metal table with a particle board top in a shade of dark gray. I half expected to see some kind of artwork or decorations. Maybe even a needlepoint emblazoned with "Home Sweet Hell" to represent its guest clientele.

Instead, the walls were bachelor pad-esque. Barren and cold except for an industrial-sized clock that ticked noisily on the wall in the back of the kitchen.

"Take a seat." Theo acknowledged me with a quick glance, motioning toward the table.

"No, I'm okay. I still feel too wired to sit still. I'll stand," I said, leaning against the framed entrance.

Theo looked me in the eye. "Sit."

That was it. One word. Three letters. That's all it took. Suddenly and without thought, my body walked a few steps to the table, pulled out the nearest chair, and obediently took a seat.

He was using the sire-child bond to his advantage, and it was humiliating. Researching vampire phenomena was one thing, but being subjected to it was utterly demeaning.

I huffed and pouted, crossing my arms as I stared at the wall ahead and definitely not in Theo's direction.

Theo appeared oblivious to my displeasure. He opened the fridge and pulled out an industrial-looking gallon-sized container. Grabbing a mug from the cabinet above, he poured in the container's red, viscous contents before zapping the liquid in the microwave overhead.

My nose flared when the scent reached me. Blood.

There was no question about it. The sight of blood twenty-four hours ago made me feel faint. Now the smell was undeniably metallic and sweet. My mouth watered.

Theo set the mug on the table in front of me. "Drink this," he said.

It was one of those mugs you find in tourist shops with a picture of the White House and above it the words 'I love DC', with a bright red heart in place of the word 'love.'

My eyes widened into the crimson void of its steaming contents. Between the sight and the smell, it was oddly hypnotic. I wasn't sure if that frightened or disgusted me more.

I blinked and turned to give Theo a dirty look. "Or what? You gonna make me drink it?"

The thought of him being able to constantly command me to do something against my will was making my room-temperature blood boil.

Theo took a seat at the table across from me and clasped his hands on the tabletop.

"No." He sighed heavily, with sadness in his tone. "I'm not going to make you do that. That's something you have to do all on your own. But you're moody because you're hungry. You'll feel much better after you feed. And I suggest you do it soon. It tastes better when it's warm."

Feed. I never had an issue with it before to describe the vampire diet (in great detail, no less). But now, the word grated on me. It felt gross and more appropriate in describing how some slimy, slithery hellbeast with ten tentacled arms and five mouths ate. Not me.

I looked from the mug to Theo's weary brown eyes and then back to the mug.

This was it.

This little mug with twelve ounces of blood is what stood between me and absolutely accepting the fact that I was now undead.

I didn't need to drink blood after being sired to become a vampire. That damage had already been done. But drinking blood was the last stop between being human and accepting this new life. Or death. Or afterlife. Depending how you looked at it.

Until now, the heightened senses, the way breathing felt more like forced habit, even the growling—all of that could be explained away as some form of black spellbinding. A practical joke, even. But once I drank from that mug, that was it. The joke would officially become my reality. There was nothing that could be done to undo it.

"I'm not drinking that," I declared, crossing my arms and leaning back in the chair.

"Fine. I'll wait here until you do," Theo replied. "It's not like either of us is getting any older."

———

Several hours passed. At least according to the annoying constant ticking of the kitchen clock overhead. Theo and I remained dead-locked in a silent standoff at the table, with the untouched mug between us.

All the while, my body puzzle-pieced its way into its new form. I felt considerably colder, the result of my human body dying off. My attention span had also dissipated. To keep from going completely berserk, I busied myself by counting the dots on the popcorn concrete ceiling above. Of which there were exactly four thousand sixty-two.

I shifted in the chair, stretching my legs. Though restless, I was determined to not give Theo the satisfaction of giving in. I mean, he's the one who did this to me. I'm allowed to be upset for the next one hundred years. At least.

Looking at the mug, the blood it contained was as still as a placid lake. It was cold now, but the scent that emanated from it was intoxicating. It called out to me: *Drink! Drink! Drink!*

I gulped.

It took every fiber of my focus to not drink from it. I looked to the right and busied myself following the road map of gray veins in the stone kitchen counter.

Theo sighed loudly. The unexpected sound startled me, but I tried to not let it show.

"I'm going to make some tea," he announced, standing and walking to the stove.

Filling the kettle that had been idling patiently on the rear hot plate, he set it back down in its place and ignited the burner.

Then it happened.

The moment I didn't even know I had been waiting for. With his back to me, I sprung forward, grabbed the mug, and drank from it. Heavily, and without care.

My face shifted. Muscle and bone crawled into new arrangements beneath my skin. And something sharp protruded from my gums as I guzzled the mug's contents. It hurt, but only for a second.

The blood was both unlike and like everything I had ever tasted. Sweet and savory, rich and comforting. It tasted like Christmas dinner, that feta honey pastry thing from Charlotte's—even traces of the Cronut. It was all there. Everything good and delicious I had ever eaten, or was ever going to eat, was in that liquid.

I gulped it down until there was nothing left. Then, using my fingers, I scraped down the sides before sticking them in my mouth to suck the liquid off.

I touched the sharp edges of my teeth. My fangs.

Setting the mug down, I shoved two exploratory fingers into my mouth, feeling their sharp points and uneven edges. The upper canines, of course, were the longest.

My stomach dropped, and cold tingles of dread washed over me.

Then, out of my mouth, my hands moved upward to my face. My lips and below the cheek area were smooth, but the skin under my eyes and my nose felt misshapen. Covered in the telltale skin folds and muscle mapping of a vampire.

And my hands, specifically my fingers, also felt strange. When I held them in front of me, my fingernails had elongated by a solid inch. They had hardened, becoming slightly curved and pointed at the tip. Just by looking at them, I knew they were razor-sharp.

This was not happening.

It was rare, but not unheard of for new vampires to have 'claws.' But it was a feature typically reserved for Old Ones.

And I had them. Lucky me.

Old Ones were ancient vampires who were bat-like in appearance, with bald heads, pointed ears, claws, and fangs that could no longer retract as the demon underneath their human-looking skin became more pronounced over time.

Theo, having heard the mug clank noisily on the table, cautiously approached me.

"Don't look at me!" I shouted, turning away from him.

Eventually, he would see what my Other Face looked like. But I wasn't ready for that. Not just yet.

"Okay, okay," he said defensively. There was silence between us for a few tense moments. "I'm just going to take the mug away."

When he reached for the mug, his eyes glanced over at my hands, and I quickly crossed my arms to hide them.

"Let me see."

I sat and scowled, sucking on the inside of my lip. Silent and unmoving.

"Hands. Show 'em. Now."

That tone again, stern and steady. I couldn't fight it even if I wanted to.

My arms unfolded and my vampy hands dutifully rested themselves on the table. The mere sight of my nails, with their unnaturally long shape and sharpened tips, was absolutely revolting.

Theo silently inspected them with careful, analytical precision. Then, turning them over, he lightly tapped the end of my left forefinger.

A metallic tang released in the air.

The nail had broken through his skin, drawing a small bead of red blood on the pad of his finger.

"Hmm," he mused, letting go of my hands. Then he reached up toward my face and I recoiled. With a gentle but firm grip, Theo held my face in the yoke of his hand. "Hold still."

I was suddenly a statue. Even my chest stopped heaving. No longer needing to breathe to survive was such a strange sensation. It was like constantly being underwater without the panic of needing to return to the surface.

Theo brushed the hair from my face so he could look at me. Still able to narrow my eyes at him, I did so in the most smoldering way possible to show my resentment.

But Theo wasn't looking into my eyes. He searched my features with a curious expression before lifting my hair to look at the sides of my head. Satisfied with his analysis, he picked up the blood-smeared mug from the table and returned to the kitchen sink.

As soon as Theo's attention turned back to tea making, his command broke, and I began breathing again. Habitually speaking.

With both hands, I touched my ears, careful not to scratch them. I sighed relief, when I felt they were rounded and more or less the same as they were before. Looking like the female version of Nosferatu was not the look I was going for.

I took another look at my hands. Accustomed to keeping my

nails short, the new length felt foreign. How do I even type or hold a pencil with these things?

"I don't think I can live like this," I mumbled.

Concentrating on my nails, I watched them recede back into their nail beds. Simultaneously, my face smoothed itself out. Running my tongue across my teeth confirmed they had returned to their more blunt and human-looking forms.

Shifting between forms was like flexing a new limb. As simple and complex as making a fist or raising a leg to walk.

"You can, and you will," Theo answered with his back to me. "Your hands. It's a sign of progressed aging. But only your hands seem affected and they're still mostly human-passing, from what I've seen of trends lately. You'll otherwise remain the same until you become an Old One. But I've only seen this happen with two other young vampires in my time. It's—"

"Rare. I know," I said dryly, staring intensely at his back.

For a moment, I hoped that my transformation had somehow also gifted me with the ability to shoot lasers from my eyes to burn holes in his back. As if becoming a creature wasn't bad enough, I had my (apparently) ex-homicidal brother mansplaining my life's research to me. The night just kept getting better and better.

Unbothered, Theo continued to dunk the tea bag in his mug until he became pleased with the brew and placed the bag in the sink. Returning to his seat at the table, he took a long drink.

Alas, no eye-lasers. At least for now.

"We need to go over some ground rules," he said, looking me square in the eye.

As my liquid dinner had been working its way through my system, I felt more at ease and no longer had the overwhelming urge to rip Theo's head off. But given the opportunity, general maiming was not off the table.

I rolled my eyes and slumped back into my chair. "Fine, let's hear it."

"Number one: Until this mess with RIDER blows over, you

are to stick with me. I'm your safest bet from that doctor with the creepy eyes boiling your brain or becoming some kind of taxidermied trophy on RIDER's walls."

I fought back a chuckle. Aside from the ridiculous notion that RIDER proudly displayed creatures in hunting lodge fashion (except for the Yeti in the first-floor study), it was only now that I realized RIDER was as much the bogeyman to the dangerous creatures we studied as they were to us.

"Number two: While you're with me, you'll be on an animal blood only diet. Human blood can be problematic. If human blood is food, then the humans we surround ourselves with also start to smell like food. It clouds the mind and can make you do cruel and irrational things if you rely on it as a food source. You just fed on some pig, which is the closest I've found to human. It's also easier to find. Usually in butcher shops, if you find the right ones. The only exception to this rule is if you are injured and weakened to the point of almost catatonic stasis. Only then does the nutritional value of human blood outweigh the danger."

Since vampires could only be killed by fire, decapitation, a stake through the heart, or exposure to sunlight, the term 'catatonic stasis' referred to a state of suspended animation. When vampires became too weak for their supernatural bodies to heal themselves. A vampire could remain locked in that comatose state for centuries—millennia, even. I shuddered.

"And along with that, you must always feed before interacting with humans. It's safer that way."

Feed. That word again.

He then described the more general rules of being a vampire. At this point, his voice sounded like endless monotone droning.

"No Other Face in public. Aside from the obvious, it's just rude. No disrespecting older vampires. And if I hadn't made myself abundantly clear: No hunting. Not even animal game. It's too dangerous."

No, no, no. That's all I heard.

After living over two centuries with the mountains of rules at RIDER, the only silver lining in any of this hot mess was to be free from that. But these rules—they were too much! Too constricting. They were piled up high, like a giant tsunami about to crash on top of me, smothering me into the ground.

I couldn't let that happen again.

"No! No more rules!" I shouted. I stood and slammed both hands down on the table. The particle board crunched within its metal rim.

"What's the point of being a... being like this if I have to follow all these rules? I'm a creature of the night now. I can do whatever I want."

I still couldn't say the 'V' word aloud when describing myself.

"Listen, I know—well, I've *heard* that at RIDER you haven't had the liberty to do much of... anything. But you have a new responsibility now," Theo said calmly. I looked at him, confused, so he clarified. "To your own kind."

That was the last straw.

I didn't choose this—this undead life. The fangs, the claws, the gross permanent liquid diet. Any of it.

I tried to scream, or attempted to. Instead, an animalistic growl escaped my mouth. The sound infuriated me even more. I suddenly felt the violent urge to kill... something. Anything.

I settled for the table.

Gripping the table with both hands, I moved to throw it across the kitchen. I wanted to hear it crash and break apart into a bunch of little pieces.

But I didn't move.

A wave of exhaustion had rushed through me, filling every vein and ounce of my body with heavy sand. Instead of throwing the table across the room, I stumbled and held onto it for support.

Theo was suddenly at my side, holding me upright. He hadn't given a verbal command. Did he put something in the blood?

"What's happening?" I slurred, eyes wide and tone filled with panic.

Theo glanced at the clock. "The sun's rising. You'll feel it more intensely at first, but it will lessen as you get older. You won't be able to rise on your own during daylight hours for a while. Come on, let's get you to bed. It's been a long night."

Obviously vampires slept during the day, but I had no idea that the pull was this strong. I had actually always wondered if vampires suffered from insomnia.

Theo led me out of the kitchen and through the living and dining rooms. Feeling like I had overdosed on NyQuil, I staggered the entire way. We headed toward the area sectioned off with a curtain for a bedroom, but Theo banked right and into the bathroom.

"Theo, what are we doing? I just want to sleep," I whined as he sat me down on top of the toilet.

I wavered for a moment, about to fall over. Theo shifted my weight until I could sit upright on my own. As he did, the small silver pendant on the necklace he wore dangled in front of my face. It looked so familiar, but I still couldn't place it. Fixated on it with eyes I could barely keep open, it swung back and forth and I reached up with a hand to grasp it for a better look. But I was only able to raise my hand an inch before it collapsed back in my lap.

Theo left the bathroom and returned with a few blankets, a long gray rectangle I recognized as the living room's couch cushion, and a handful of clothes. He thrust the clothes in my face.

"Here. Whatever creature was here before left these. And you'll sleep here," he said simply, gesturing to the bathtub.

I blinked hard. "You have got to be kidding me."

Accepting the clothes, an oversized and tattered Warped Tour t-shirt and a pair of grey sweatpants, they smelled funny. Musty mixed with something acidic, like vinegar. But clean enough, I guess.

"Zoey, I've been doing this vampire thing a lot longer than you have. Trust me. For thousands of years, bitten humans who died have been buried in their coffins, only to rise as vampires. It's in your DNA now. And I'm going to assume that the idea of actually being buried in the ground outside sounds less appealing to you. This is the next best option. The coolness of the tub mimics the temperature of the earth, and the cushion on top acts as the coffin lid. I think you'll actually find it quite cozy," Theo said, laying the blankets on the bottom of the tub and resting the cushion on top. Lifting the cushion as if it were on a hinge, he motioned for me to get in.

"Why are you being nice to me?" I asked, trying to keep my eyes focused on him after I had pulled the clothing over my wet noodle limbs. They were warm and soft and my body screamed for sleep. "I thought you said you hated me for working at RIDER and for coming here to drive a stake through your heart."

Teetering on the toilet, I fumbled in making my best staking myself in the chest motion with my hands.

"I never used the word 'hate'," Theo replied hastily. He then paused, and looked down at the beige bathroom tile. "I... I think I'm now realizing how much I missed having a family—a real family. Being part of a vampire pack isn't the same. The familial ties aren't there. It's all just lust and carnage and the hunt. The time when I had just turned, it's still foggy. I don't remember much, but I know I did a lot of bad things and I thought you had died along with everyone else. I guess what I'm trying to say is that I know the transformation you're going through is tough. And with RIDER at our backs, it'll only be tougher. We need to trust each other if we're going to make it through this."

I wanted to punch Theo. He couldn't just appear out of nowhere, claim to be good, turn me into a vampire, and then get to be my brother again. That's not how vengeance worked.

But instead of fighting him, at least for now, I closed my eyes and nodded, knowing that in reality it relayed as jerky, drunken movements. As a vampire, I would never be allowed back in my position at RIDER, or be invited inside the New York office. As much as I hated to admit, Theo was one of the few allies I had left. And somehow, I was more helpless now as a newly sired vampire than I ever was human. I needed Theo if I was going to survive.

With a reluctant sigh, I crawled inside the bathtub and laid down.

"Sweet dreams," Theo said, hovering over me with a smirk.

I said nothing but rolled my eyes. I bet he found this whole night of me stumbling around, trying to navigate all things vampire just absolutely hilarious in his whole big brother way.

Oddly enough, once I pulled the blankets over me, the space became cozy and comfortable. The makeshift coffin wrapped me in a cool, calming embrace.

I closed my eyes.

Sleep came quickly to rejuvenate my mind and body for another night. As it would sunrise after sunrise, forever and always. Until the end of time.

Or until a wooden stake had been driven through my heart.

Whichever would come first.

TWENTY-TWO

That night I dreamt of a glorious full moon in a shade of amber, like a vampire's iris. It shone brightly above as Augustine and I danced below in RIDER's courtyard. He held me close, with one firm hand on the small of my back and the other clasping my hand to guide our steps. Just like he did when we were together.

We were smiling and laughing. And when he twirled me with one hand, the long skirt of my white silk and tulle dress flared out; dramatic and graceful.

Augustine leaned in close and whispered in my ear, "I've been waiting a long time for this night."

The clouds moved in to cover the moon, and when they passed, the moon had changed. It was grey with an orange sunflower pattern and a black dot in the center, just like Dr. Kelley's eyes.

The moon blinked, and it began to rain. Thick, viscous, dark red drops fell from the sky. They splattered on my dress and face and when I opened my mouth surprised, a drop landed on my tongue. It was coppery and sweet.

I looked at Augustine, confused, as the crimson rain patted down. He pulled me closer, cradling me in his arms.

The rain suddenly began to monsoon and the ground shook. The blood rain drenched our hair and ran down our faces. I gasped for air as I choked on it.

The ground cracked open between our feet, and Augustine's hold faltered. I fell to one side of the crack and watched as it widened between us.

I screamed Augustine's name and reached a hand toward him. He did the same. Leaning over, our fingers grasped to touch, but the crevice was too wide. The side Augustine was on tipped backward and fell inward, engulfing him.

I cried out to him, searching for him below the cliff edge where I stood. What was left of the courtyard filled with burgundy. It quickly covered my shoes, my knees, then my waist. I was chest-deep and struggling to stay afloat in an angry, sanguine ocean.

I screamed for help, but the rain fell harder until my head finally went under and the blood consumed me.

———

My eyes shot open, awake and alert. When I gasped, the noise bounced around the enamel confines of the tub, reminding me where I was. The makeshift tub coffin in the bathroom of my brother's temporary apartment.

It was hard to tell which nightmare was worse: the one with Dr. Kelley's watchful eye drowning me in blood, or that I was actually a vampire. Somehow, drowning seemed much less daunting. I had a full night of Theo's teachings on bullshit vampire culture ahead of me.

Pushing the couch cushion to the side, I crawled out of the tub. Before bed, I had shed my clothes into a pile on the floor. Now they appeared neatly folded on top of the toilet.

I grabbed my sweater and tweed trousers and changed back into them. But as I zipped up the side of the trousers, I paused.

There was a familiar scent in the air. Tangy and sweet.

It came from a stainless-steel travel mug that sat innocently on the bathroom sink's counter. A small tendril of steam wafted continuously from the overflow hole.

My body reacted before my mind could catch up, and it contorted in anticipation. Snatching up the cup with two clawed hands, I flicked open the lid and took a long, satisfying gulp.

Mmm. It tasted so much better warm, and its warmth filled my cold body, making it feel more alive and ready for the night. I closed my eyes, feeling content.

Outside, Theo was talking on his mobile. Charlotte was on the other end, who I could hear with crystal clarity even though she wasn't on speaker.

"When do you think you guys can get here?" Charlotte asked.

"As soon as Zoey rises and feeds. I think I hear her now, which... yes, 7:11 PM, right on schedule. Newborns are wonderfully predictable like that."

Ugh, that word again. *Feed.* It made my skin crawl. I also didn't like the term 'Newborn,' or really any of the terminology Theo used.

"How... How is she doing?" Charlotte's voice wavered, as if she wasn't sure she wanted to know the answer. I certainly did.

"She's... adapting. More defiant than I would have expected, but nothing that's required a vampire timeout. It's funny, I've sired more than a handful of children in my time, but I always seem to forget how both willful and helpless they can be in their first few days," Theo said with a laugh.

I rolled my eyes and took another drink.

"What's a vampire timeout?" Charlotte asked.

"You don't want to know," Theo said quickly. "Oh, and can you do me a favor? If she shifts in front of you, just don't call attention to her hands. She's... a little sensitive about them right now."

"Oh. What's wrong with—"

"Just don't. We'll head over soon. Is anyone else there yet?"

"Mirza's here. I just got off the phone with Matt, and Luke and Liv are coming as soon as they finish their lab at school."

Bidding their goodbyes, a dull beep confirmed the mobile had disconnected.

I gazed into the bathroom mirror, imagining what kind of courage it could give despite that I could no longer, you know, reflect in it.

Shifting back to my human form, I exited the bathroom to find Theo standing in the living room. He looked at me with soft eyes and a friendly smile.

"Good eveni—"

I strode across the room. "I don't like that word: *feed*. Why can't we just say, 'eat' or 'we'll leave once Zoey's had breakfast'?" I asked, shoving the empty travel mug in his face.

"Well, sis, I think the vernacular comes from the fact that we're vampires whose very nature is to *feed* on blood. But fine. How was your *breakfast?*" he asked in a mocking tone.

"Delicious," I replied, shaking the cup in front of him for him to take.

Theo crossed his arms. "Zo, I'm not one of your RIDER housemaids. You can put that in the kitchen yourself."

Fine. I stomped into the kitchen, all the while glaring at Theo, and dramatically slammed the mug in the sink. Steel met steel in a loud *clank* that reverberated through the apartment. I looked down to see a small dent below.

Theo sighed. "So, another long night for the both of us, then?"

TWENTY-THREE

The car ride back to Georgetown was mostly silent, except for the sound of the radio.

Theo had turned it down low when I clamped my hands over my ears in pain. Sound was still something to get used to, but my other senses had settled from the previous night. No longer overwhelming, I could analyze scents and sights with laser-like precision.

Theo, for example. He had a distinct scent of moss, cedar, and allspice. I could even smell the combination of blood and coffee that rolled off his lips.

Although, when I had asked where the pods to the Nespresso machine were in the apartment, he had replied with a stern, "Your body's still settling. It's too early to reintroduce human foods." And mentioned something about me literally bouncing off the walls with the tiniest bit of caffeine at this stage of vampirism.

Whatever. As if I hadn't been through enough, I now had to suffer through the next few days, or perhaps weeks, in an uncaffeinated state of being. I might as well be dead-dead, not just undead.

Through Theo's shirt, I could see an indentation on his back right shoulder where it looked like he had been shot and it had scarred over. But with what; a bullet, musket ball, or even a crossbow, was still left to be told. The other night hadn't been the first time he'd been shot, and I doubted it would be the last.

He kept looking over at me when I stared ahead or out the side window. His stare felt like cold nudges across my back. Despite centuries of dedicated research, nothing could have prepared me for the crash course that came with becoming a creature overnight.

"Why does it feel like that?" I asked, moving uncomfortably in my seat as I tried to brush his gaze off my back. "When you look at me, I can feel it. It feels cold."

"We have the same vampire blood running through us. We'll always feel it when we're close. You'll feel the presence of other creatures, too. Soon enough."

I didn't like it. It felt like someone was incessantly tapping on my shoulder. So what fantastic news to know that I would always feel the agitating sensation given the large number of creatures I encountered on a day-to-day basis.

Letting out a long sigh, I tapped at the prong of the inside car lock with a fingernail to pass the time.

We zoomed past Twenty-Ninth Street without turning northward toward Charlotte's house on O Street.

I looked at Theo quizzically. "I thought we were going to Charlotte's?"

I was actually looking forward to being in the presence of The House again. It provided a sense of comfort and belonging when I was there. The two things I wanted most right now. Aside from more blood. Something I seemed to crave constantly, even just after eating.

"It's not safe to go to The House right now. It's still crawling with RIDER agents looking for you. Charlotte said she had to cast a cloaking spell just to leave. We're heading to her condo. It's not far."

Theo shifted the car into another gear, zipping past a few more intersections and crossing through M Street, Georgetown's main thoroughfare.

The evening was warm, and the sidewalks were thronged with crowds shopping and dining. They seemed oblivious to the fact that the vintage Aston Martin that passed by was filled with two blood-guzzling vampires bent on stopping a plan to commercialize immortality.

Another few turns off the main streets and we entered an alley lined with tall brick buildings and paved lots. Theo made a left, where we met a gated parking lot secured with a keypad. He rolled down the driver's side window and punched in a code. After a moment of hesitation, the gate shuddered to life and rose.

"Remember, if you feel overwhelmed at any moment, just let me know," Theo said, searching for a spot in the lot. There were a few other parked cars, but the space was otherwise deserted except for the handful of lamp posts splashing their yellow light on the dark pavement.

"Got it," I replied tiredly. More rules. Fantastic.

"And if you get hungry, just let me know. I packed some blood in the cooler in the back."

"Got. It."

The car slowed as we pulled into a spot on the left.

"And if you feel like you might lose control—"

I couldn't wait for Theo to kill the engine.

"I got it! I got it! I got it!" I shouted, opening the door and leaping out of the car.

When I slammed the door behind me, it was with enough force that the car lurched woefully on its side. The passenger-side tires even lifted off the ground before settling back down.

Stomping toward the rear of the car, Theo met me there in a flash, blocking my path. He towered over me in his typical Frankenstein stance, and the mere sight of his stupid face made me livid. My entire body bristled with anger and my face shifted to match my mood.

"Let's get one thing straight, Theodore Thomas Abbott," I said, poking him in the chest with a clawed finger. "You may be my brother, and by some sick joke of the universe, you may be my sire, but you are not my parent. I had parents. Two of them. And you took them away from me."

Theo remained calm, but I knew I had struck a chord with him. Good. I wanted him to show me his Other Face, too. To show that I could make him as angry as he made me.

Instead, his brow furrowed and he narrowed his eyes. "How quickly you forget when enough time passes, sis." His voice was fluid, like a snake. "Do you remember what great parents we had when Father beat us with the belt at the smallest disappointment or inconvenience to him? Or how I was there for you when he whipped you so badly you needed me to help dress the wounds properly to stop the bleeding because our mother was too drunk to be there for us? That's why I spent every moment I could away from them when I got older. And when I was turned, the anger and resentment they made me feel fueled my rampage for decades."

Cold tears burst from my eyes and rained down my face. I pushed Theo in the chest with both hands, and to both of our surprise, he stumbled back a few steps.

"No, Theo—it's you! I had a life then and a future and you ruined it! And now that you're back in my life, it's happening all over again. Just look at me! I look hideous! You ruin everything!" I seethed through my fangs. They still felt strange in my mouth. Unnatural.

"A future?" Theo rolled his eyes. "With who? That loser who our parents arranged for you to marry? Please. You were looking for an escape as much as I was. I just found mine first."

"You're lying."

"Am I? Or are you just choosing to forget parts of the past?"

"I don't know what you're talking about," I said, angrily wiping the tears from my face.

Theo snorted and shook his head in a gesture that I couldn't discern as disbelief or pity. He licked his lips. "Maybe that doctor burned off all your memories except for the ones he wants."

That was it. The rage I had bottled up since I stepped outside the werewolf cage suddenly exploded. It raced through me until all I could feel was pain and anger.

I lunged at Theo, claws out. Slamming into him, I tackled him to the ground on his back where he let out an audible 'Oof' as I knocked the air from his lungs.

"Take it back!" I screamed in his face before promptly punching him in it. After waiting over two hundred years to do just that, it felt *so* good.

His head rocked back from the force of my fist, but he otherwise remained motionless. He didn't even try to toss me off his chest or command me to stop. So I kept going.

"Take it back! Take it all—take everything back! Your vampire blood, your help—all of it! I don't want it! I want to be human again and I just want you to be evil so I can kill you and go back to my life!"

It took two more punches in the face for him to finally shift to his Other Face. But even then, he still wouldn't fight me. He only looked at me with sympathetic amber eyes when he realized I wasn't only talking about his Dr. Kelley comment.

And I definitely didn't want his compassion, either. I tore at his face with my claws, slicing thin marks across his skin. Bright red quickly seeped out and onto his face. I hoped he would open his mouth to cry out so I could rip his tongue out while I was at it. He wouldn't be able to spout any more annoying sire commands if he couldn't talk.

But Theo refused to move. He just stared at me patiently, only to wince every time I brought my hands down to slash him. This was going nowhere.

I stopped, panting over him as my body heaved with a noxious mix of anger, frustration, and grief. With a deep inhale, I screamed those feelings out and into the empty parking lot, not caring if anyone heard me. They'd probably just think it was some rabid animal, anyway.

I looked around the lot and at the surrounding unfamiliar buildings and streets. Nothing felt like home here.

My eyes settled on Theo's car to the right. The perfectly restored and spotless Aston Martin Vantage that looked like it received weekly detailed cleanings.

Pushing off Theo and onto my feet, I stared at the car. My lips curled into a mischievous smile. Being on the run for decades meant Theo didn't have many friends or possessions. But he had this car.

I shifted my weight to one leg and raised the knee of my other to my chest.

This car, that he drove with care and whose pristine interior didn't have so much as a loose receipt, let alone a crumb littering the floor. Theo loved this car.

I couldn't wait to hear the metallic crunching sound it would make when I kicked it with all my supernatural strength.

A powerful force knocked into me from the side, throwing me to the pavement.

Theo grabbed both my arms and rolled me over onto my back, pinning me to the ground. I squirmed under his grip. But he was centuries older than me in vampire years and therefore infinitely stronger. Without many options left, I curled my lips back to let out a fang-filled snarl, thrashing from side to side to break his hold. When I failed, my body, covered in cold sweat, finally went limp from exhaustion.

"You'll find that the world outside of RIDER isn't as black and white as you'd like it to be. And believe me, neither of us want me to be like how I was before," Theo said evenly. The cuts on his face had already clotted and begun to heal, but he still looked like he had tripped and fallen face-first into a garbage disposal.

"Yeah, well, it would be a hell of a lot easier if it were," I replied tightly.

"Are you done?" he asked, still hovering over me. His voice was calm and measured now, but his tone was filled with authority.

I pushed against his vice-like grip once more, but ended up flopping around like a fish. Defeated, I pouted and turned my head to the side, not wanting to look at him.

"Maybe," I muttered.

"Do you feel better now?"

"Maybe."

"Okay," Theo said, letting out a long sigh.

The truth was that I felt a lot better. Accustomed to controlling my emotions until I was alone in my apartment where I could cry it all out, purging it all in one messy, ugly, violent stream was more cleansing than anything. But Theo didn't need to know that.

He carefully eased his hold on me and when I didn't make a move, he released his hands and stood up. I rose to my feet and brushed away the dirt and gravel from my trousers and top.

"New ground rule: You can be as mad as you want with me, but leave the Vantage out of it. Deal?" Theo's eyes were deadlocked onto mine. Unlike his other rules, this one required confirmation.

"Fine," I said airily, trying to conceal the satisfaction of finally landing a meaningful punch. Even if it wasn't a physical one.

"Okay, we need to get going. This way," he said, moving toward the parking lot exit.

"Theo?" I called to him before he got too far. He stopped mid-stride and looked back. "I think I'm getting hungry again."

───────

Lunch was another twelve ounces of pig's blood, as likely every meal would be for the foreseeable future. The satiating fullness was enough to calm my nerves so I could finally shift to my human form. That, and Theo threatened he would command me to stay in the car by myself until I did. I wasn't sure if his sire commands were powerful enough to last that long, but I also didn't want to find out.

The two of us headed down an alley, approaching a large building that sat a block from the Potomac River's edge. Balconies covered the structure, jutting out on all sides. It had to be Charlotte's condo building.

Theo stopped alongside the building and looked up.

"Okay, this is it," he said.

"What's wrong with the front entrance?" I asked. For once desperate for the tiniest bit of normalcy.

"The fact that it's also probably crawling with RIDER agents. Come on, follow my lead."

He gracefully leapt on top of a nearby dumpster and then onto a pipe that he used to nimbly crawl up toward the roof.

I looked down at my feet. "But, I'm wearing heels!"

"You'll be fine!" Theo called down, now three quarters up the building.

Staring at the tall dumpster, I sucked on the inside of my lip, unsure if I possessed the same supernatural athleticism. I thought back to how sparring with Tristan a few weeks ago had left me flat on my back.

A quick glance up and down the alley to confirm it was still clear, then I jumped.

To my surprise, I landed soundlessly on top of the dumpster. I grinned. It was as easy as walking up a flight of stairs.

Eyeing the pole, I bounded off the dumpster and onto it a few feet up. My body was light and agile as I scaled the side of the building. When I looked below at the alley that grew more minuscule the higher I climbed, I realized I had no fear of the height or falling.

Okay, so maybe this part of being a vampire wasn't so bad.

My brother was waiting for me at the top with a smug grin that I remembered from our childhood.

"See? I knew you could do it," he said before breaking into a run across the roof.

For the first time, the predator within me sparked to life, eager to give chase. I ran after him, trying my best to catch up.

But halfway across the roof, I skidded to a stop.

The moon was high overhead, a waning gibbous. She shone proudly, illuminating the roof, the river, and even the twinkling city on the adjacent bank in white light.

It was one of the most amazing sights I had ever seen.

Even more, I could *feel* her. She let out pulsating, energetic vibrations that fell all over me. I no longer had a beating heart, thumping and pumping blood through my body, and the absence had left me with a hollow stillness. A constant reminder that my human body had died and was now puppeted by demonic means.

But the moon showered me in a comforting rhythm that made me feel alive again. She left me in complete awe.

"What is it?" Theo asked with a little alarm. He had stopped ahead, once realizing I was no longer right behind.

"The moon!" I exclaimed, not able to break my gaze. "She's so beautiful! And I can feel her. It's like vibrations. It feels incredible!"

It was equivalent to the most perfect sunny day at the beach. Whatever Theo had agreed to with Charlotte would need to be rescheduled. Because for the rest of the night, I could think of nothing better to do than lounging on the condo building's rooftop, bathing in the moon's rays.

"Newborns," Theo muttered. He grabbed my hand, dragging me forward. "Yes, yes, the moon. She's exquisite. And on any other night, you'll be able to enjoy her moonshine for an eternity. But tonight we're running late and people are waiting for us."

Reluctantly breaking from the sight, I continued to dash across the roof after my brother. Our movements were swift, barely touching the ground or making a sound as we ran. But keeping up with Theo was difficult. No matter how hard I tried to match his pace, he was always three strides ahead of me.

Theo slowed to a stop and peered over the edge. Then, in one swift motion, he stepped off the ledge and onto the side of the building. I followed, mimicking his path. We crawled past three balconies before I dropped to join him on the fourth.

The balcony was of an impressive size, almost like an entire room itself. It was filled with high-end modern furniture I had only seen in magazines in RIDER's cocktail lounge.

Through the glass was the condo's kitchen and living room. It was mostly white with light wood finishes, decorated here and there with bohemian floral wall art and decor. The direct opposite of The House's traditional Victorian aesthetic.

Charlotte stood behind a white stone kitchen island, talking to Mirza and Matt in the living room.

"Is it true? What they're saying? Prescott's a vampire now?" I heard Matt ask through the glass.

I looked at the balcony door and saw it was unlocked, yet Theo continued to wait patiently next to me.

"What are you waiting for?" I asked him. My entire body vibrated with energy from the exhilarating run across the rooftop. The thought of standing still for another moment was excruciating.

I couldn't wait for him to respond. Swinging open the balcony door, I stepped inside.

"Ouch!" I exclaimed, putting a hand to my stinging nose.

I had hit an invisible wall, face first.

Inside, Matt's eyes widened, and he ran a hand through his hair. "Oh no. This is bad. This is really bad."

"Come in, come in!" Charlotte beckoned with a friendly wave, but I stayed put, having learned my lesson.

Theo brushed past me and hurried into the condo. "That's what I was waiting for," he answered with a smirk.

I followed cautiously behind, first testing the threshold with my foot before fully entering.

Inside, Charlotte was the first thing that caught my attention.

Mirza and Matt seemed muted compared to the crackling energy that radiated from her. Like static before lightning struck. I could even feel it in my mouth.

A voice bubbled up in the back of my mind. The same voice that screamed at me to drink blood the night before. My vampire instincts. This time, it rose from my subconscious to issue a stern warning.

Be careful, this is a powerful creature.

"Oh my goddess, Theo—your face!" Charlotte shrieked, covering her mouth with a hand.

"It's fine. It'll heal completely in an hour," Theo replied, gingerly touching the scabbed marks on his face and slipping me a sly look. I looked at the floor.

When I glanced back up, I noticed someone was missing.

"Where's Augustine?" I had expected him, of all people, to be here. I wanted him to hold me and tell me everything was going to be okay, but part of me was afraid of what he might think of me now.

"When the news broke out about your... situation, he was immediately recalled back to New York. But he left this for you," Matt said. He brandished a small white envelope and passed it to me.

The envelope had a 'Z' written on the front in a familiar flourish of black ink.

I always liked how he crossed the 'Z' through the middle. Brushing my thumb on the indentation, I retraced his pen stroke. The last touches of his hands on the note.

A musty scent of rose water and almonds emanated from the envelope. It became stronger as I fished out the small card inside.

It matters not what you are, but who you are.

Stay true.
- A.H.

Oh, Auggie. He always knew what to say, even when he wasn't physically there.

Biting my lip to hold back a tear, I slipped the card back into its envelope and into my trouser pocket.

"You look good, Zoey," Mirza offered brightly, breaking the silence in the room. "A lot of people can't pull off a pale complexion, but I think it really works for you."

Charlotte flashed a wide smile and nodded her head enthusiastically.

Matt, however, continued to look pained and distraught.

"As her sire, I assume you've got her under control?" he asked, anxiously eyeing Theo. "She's not going to flip at the drop of a hat and try to bite one of us, right?"

I shriveled my nose, disgusted.

Matt smelled of cheap cologne, menthol cigarettes, and remnants of the Victoria Secret Love Spell perfume from the woman he was with last night. I did not want to touch him with a ten-foot pole, let alone bite him. I mean, ew.

Charlotte's mouth hung open as if someone had slapped her.

"Zoey, I'm so sorry you had to hear that. I'm also sorry that I have to apologize for Matt's idiotic and bigoted comments," she said, shooting Matt a glare so cold I was surprised it didn't literally freeze the blood in his veins.

Matt held his hands up. "Hey, listen—I could lose my job just for being here. And I'm not the one who came up with that narrative."

The director of Witchcraft Relations pulled out a folded piece of paper and passed it around the group. First to Mirza, who gaped at it, then to Charlotte, who rolled her eyes and spouted, "Whatever." and finally onto Theo, who studied it with a grim, furrowed brow.

I held my hand out, ready to intercept the sheet, when Mirza spoke up. "Z, I don't think you want to see that."

Now I definitely wanted to see what all the fuss was about. Snatching the sheet from my brother's hands, I gave it a quick scan.

If my heart still beat, I think it would have stopped entirely. My legs became weak, and I collapsed, sitting on the couch next to me, staring at the paper in my hands.

It was a new Vampire Top Ten Chart, and I was at the top, in the number one slot.

ZOEY PRESCOTT FKA ELIZABETH ABBOTT, was in large bold letters next to a photo pulled from my work badge. To the right of that was a sketch of what was assumed to be my Other Face. It looked more monstrous and deformed than any vampire I had ever seen.

"I gotta give you props, sis. You've been a vampire for less than forty-eight hours and you've already made the number one spot on the Big Bad list. Even I could never break past number four," Theo said, impressed.

"Tristan said you attacked him back at The House the other night. He claims you were feral beyond reason. I came here tonight because after speaking with Charlotte, I wasn't sure what to believe myself," Matt explained.

"I just knew that guy was a total douche when I met him," Charlotte said with a soured look.

"Do I really look like that?" I asked Theo, pointing to the vicious-looking vampire next to my name.

"No," he dismissed quickly, shaking his head. He took the paper from my hands and folded it back up, as if to erase its existence.

But I knew what this meant. Using his connections, influential position within RIDER, and bullshitting mastery, Tristan lobbied for an emergency update to the list. And with my location narrowed down to a single city, RIDER would spare no expense in tracking me down.

"I don't understand," I said to Matt. "If Augustine is back at HQ, why hasn't he called this off? He knows Tristan and Dr. Kelley are the real threat."

"You know Augustine," Matt said tiredly. "He won't get other senior leaders involved until he's absolutely sure he has all the legitimate proof he needs to get proper backing. Last time I talked to him, he was still working on it. We also have no idea who else at RIDER might be involved. He just needs time."

"Well, time is something we don't have. We have to leave. Tonight. I can get in touch with the local area covens and see what they can do. They won't be ecstatic about helping a couple of vampires, but I do have some favors to call in," Charlotte suggested with hope in her voice.

"There's no point," Matt said, folding his arms and placing a hand on his forehead. "With RIDER resources under Tristan's direction, they're probably already working with local law enforcement and mystical groups to secure the city's borders. We're sitting ducks."

Other potential solutions were tossed back and forth around the room. Each one was knocked down based on hedging our bets against RIDER's operational strategy and our very limited resources.

But I wasn't listening. I had become distracted, continually shifting positions on the couch, not able to find one that was comfortable.

Charlotte's head snapped in my direction. "What's wrong?"

"My clothes," I replied, frustrated. "They feel really itchy and scratchy, for some reason." Not to mention they were also covered in gross pavement grime from my scuffle with Theo.

"Our skin is much more sensitive," Theo spoke up. "Think about it. Aside from my sister, have you ever seen a vampire in tweed?"

KATY FORAKER

My brother's dry attempt at humor earned a snicker from Mirza, who halfheartedly apologized when all eyes looked at him.

"Okay, now that's a problem I actually have a solution for," Charlotte said. "Follow me. We can leave the boys here to figure out what we're supposed to do next. Hopefully, something that won't get us all killed before morning."

TWENTY-FOUR

Charlotte's "closet" was not a closet by any ordinary definition of the word. Rather, it was a large, expansive room. The second den in the east wing of her condo, to be exact. It was, however, the textbook definition of a fashionista's dreamland.

Floor to ceiling shelves and racks flanked the walls, neatly stacked with shoes and clothing of every color and texture imaginable. Every item was arranged by color, and then by type for what seemed like every occasion. There were sections for contemporary workwear, party dresses, garments with feathers and sequins, to thick-knit wool sweaters and classic felted winter coats. I half expected to see space suits for walking on the moon next to the selection of ball gowns.

A waist-tall white dresser stood in the middle of the room with a glass top that displayed Charlotte's extensive jewelry collection. Peering over the showcase, many of the baubles and trinkets were pentagram-shaped stars and moon slivers. One advantage of being in a Pagan witch's house was that there weren't any crucifixes that needed dodging.

Charlotte strode around the room, grandly gesturing to the racks with both hands.

"So, what are we feeling?" she asked, twirling around to face me. "You strike me as a Ralph Lauren girl, so Americana chic? Or do you want to try something more glam? I have a couple of Hervé Leger bandage dresses in here somewhere. Everyone says they're due for another revival."

"Um, I'm not really sure," I replied, looking around the room in awe. "There's so many..."

I trailed off when I locked eyes with a cluster of black and darkly muted colors on the racks to the right. They seemed calming compared to the brash harshness of their more brightly pigmented counterparts.

With a burst of supernatural speed, I beelined across the room and started sifting through the racks.

"Show off." Charlotte snorted as she walked over with what seemed like a tortoise's pace to join me.

Rifling through the hangers, we both scrutinized each piece before moving on to the next.

Every few moments, the silence between us was filled with "This?" or "How about this one?" As she fished out items for my approval. I shook my head to dismiss them all.

"So," Charlotte finally said. "Do you want to talk about it?"

I froze. And when I noticed that the metallic clanging on my end of the rack had suspiciously stopped, I started mindlessly rifling through them again.

"Talk about what?" I replied coolly, trying to brush off the fact that my life was a raging dumpster fire.

"Zo, I don't need my witch's sense to tell me you're upset. I mean, obviously rightfully so. And you and Augustine always say that vampires are super emotional. I can only imagine—"

I turned to give Charlotte a death glare that made her stop speaking and nervously suck on the bottom of her lip.

I was wrong earlier. This had to be Hell, I was sure of it. I had died and been sent to Hell. That was the only plausible explanation for the irony of my life's work constantly slapping me in my Other Face.

"Anyway, that's why I thought it might be good to have some girl time, you know? Plus, overly sensitive vampire skin or not, putting together a fab outfit always helps to clear my head," she added, sliding through more hangers.

"Thanks. I could definitely use some clarity with everything going on. This whole vampire transition thing is... a lot," I said, pulling out and inspecting a black sweater before placing it back on the rack.

"Speaking of which, did you drink blood yet?"

The clanging and sliding on Charlotte's side stopped abruptly, and I knew her attention was fixed on me.

Before I could respond, the hairs on the back of my neck bristled and the yeasty scent of dog wafted into the room.

"Oh, hey girl!" Charlotte said in a friendly greeting.

When I looked up, Olivia had entered the room. Her bubblegum pink hair was braided into a crown on her head and she was wearing a black bustier top with ripped, loose fitting blue jeans over what I now recognized as her characteristic fishnets and combat boots. I paused there, with my hands on the hangers, and gave her a curious glance. My senses received information in a constant stream, wondering what to make of her. Honestly, the overload was becoming exhausting.

Olivia tilted her head, giving me a full look up and down with unblinking eyes. Her gaze was not aggressive, but predatory, as she took in my sight. Her nose flared. I wondered what I smelled like to her. How different I appeared to her than before. But something about her demeanor didn't make me want to speak first.

After another few tense moments, Olivia's brow lifted as if to shrug, disinterested, and she walked to the back of the room where she casually flopped on a mauve settee that could seat a crowd.

I suddenly realized that I no longer had the privilege of

walking through the world with human rose-colored glasses. Each encounter with another creature carried a sense of formality. A combination of sizing up and measuring the level of civility the other had. And tonight, the werewolf and the vampire had both silently agreed, in so many ways, to be respectful and courteous. And basically not rip each other to shreds inside the confines of Charlotte's walk-in closet.

I mean, there was a lot of vintage Fendi around us.

And although a witch, Charlotte appeared oblivious to the intense encounter between two supernatural predators in front of her.

"Playing dress-up in Charlotte's closet? Maybe someone should turn me into a vamp so I can get those privileges, too. Seems like my wolf ones have run out," Olivia said dryly.

"Oh come on Liv, you know you're welcome to borrow anything you like, anytime you'd like. All you have to do is ask," Charlotte replied.

I turned my attention back to the rack, rifling through the hangers once more.

Then I saw it.

A long-sleeved, black pleather jumpsuit with pockets on the outer thighs. The material was soft in my hands and I imagined that the form-fitting cut would keep my cold body warm and comfortable. Next to the jumpsuit was a matching pleather trench coat. I briefly fantasized about wearing it as I ran back across the condo's roof. The coat flaring out dramatically behind me in the wind.

"What do you think of this?" I asked enthusiastically, pulling both pieces off the rack and showing them to Charlotte and Olivia.

There was silence in the closet between the three of us. When I looked at Charlotte, her mouth was open in a small 'O' as her mind seemed to search for words that evaded her. Olivia put a hand to cover her mouth, stifling a laugh.

"What? What's wrong? It's soft, I can move in it. And it has pockets. I like it," I said, not understanding their reactions. What was I missing?

"That," Charlotte finally said. "Was my Halloween costume from last year. I was Selene from Underworld."

"Oh," was all I could say as I stared at the costume, crestfallen and embarrassed. A vampire Halloween costume? What was this transformation doing to me?

"If you want to look like a stereotypical vampire, I mean go for it. Who am I to stop you?" Charlotte said slowly, throwing glances at Olivia for back up. The pink-haired wolf pursed her lips, not offering much in return.

Charlotte snatched the costume from my hands and placed it back on the rack.

"Who am I kidding? I can't let you dress like someone permanently going to Comic-Con. Not on my watch."

Diving into the rack next to her, the witch pulled out a black pair of leggings and an oversized gray cotton t-shirt.

"Here. The dark colors, I can respect. But being a vampire does not give you a license to lose all sense of style and, you know, go camp. Camp was the theme of the Met Gala in 2019, which is neither here nor now. And we are trying to lie low, right? Nothing screams 'I'm one of the undead' more than an all-black pleather jumpsuit and matching trench coat. Sheesh," she said, exasperated, handing the new pieces to me. They were buttery soft in my hands.

As I put them on, Charlotte came back with a pair of black ankle boots and a black jacket to complete the look. The boots had shiny, gold buckles on the side. For a moment, I became transfixed on their sheen and had to blink to clear my focus. The jacket had a drape front and was mostly knit except for a leather-like material on the sleeves.

I felt instant relief once I shed my old clothes and put on the softer ones.

"How do I look?" I asked Charlotte and Olivia. I glanced toward the tri-fold mirror behind me out of habit, but it proved to be completely useless.

Charlotte squinted her eyes, carefully scanning the outfit. Then, grabbing the bottom of the shirt, she tied the tail end into a small knot before stepping back to survey it again.

"Looks great," she said. "Charlotte-Tennet-approved."

Olivia jutted out her lip and nodded.

There was one thing I didn't want to forget. Fishing out Augustine's note from my trousers, I placed it in my jacket pocket. I wanted it to stay close to me.

As I folded my old clothes, about to place them out of the way, Charlotte's electric gaze bored into my skin.

"What?" I asked without looking up, finally getting used to interpreting the new preternatural sensations.

Charlotte didn't answer, so I turned my total attention to her once I finished setting the clothes aside. She was staring at me with a curious, almost mischievous, sparkle in her eyes.

"Okay, out with it. I can tell you're super self-conscious about the whole vampire thing. So come on, go all 'grrr,'" she said, making an angry face and shaping her hand into a claw. "Let's see what the big deal is."

"You want to see my Other Face?" I repeated slowly. She had to be joking.

"I mean, we're all going to see it, right? Eventually. Why not just get it out of the way?"

Oh god, she was serious.

My stomach tied into knots. I was barely comfortable with my brother seeing that side of me—and he's another vampire. And after seeing the sketch of my Other Face on the Top Ten Chart, I didn't want to confirm any likeness it might have.

I looked over at Olivia for reassurance. She shrugged and leaned back on the settee.

"Charlotte's just curious. She can't help herself. She'll keep asking until you show her. For three months straight, she begged to watch Luke and I transform in front of her before I let her. At least you're not butt-ass naked in a cage," she said.

Right. She had a point.

Taking in a deep inhale, I exhaled, closed my eyes, and shifted. When I opened them, I looked at the witch through amber-colored irises.

Shifting was becoming more comfortable each time I did it. The feeling of my fangs bursting through my gums didn't hurt as much as it had the first time. In fact, now it was invigorating.

I stared at Charlotte, fiddling with my clawed fingers, waiting for any subtle movement, expression, or scent. The anticipation was near torturous.

Was she able to see the scared girl behind feral eyes? Or did she just see a monster like in the sketch? I didn't know what fear smelled like yet, but I kept an eye—er, nostril—out for it. I imagined it smelled pungent. Like bad, stagnant, oniony B.O.

Charlotte appeared to have one of the best poker faces I'd ever seen, stoic and calm, as she looked at me.

"Happy?" I asked in an annoyed tone, rolling my eyes. I didn't like the feeling of being on display—being exposed. Like I was some sideshow attraction or an animal in a zoo.

"Zoey, it's not that big of a deal," Olivia said lazily. "We were human. Something happened to us, and now we're like this. We learn to live with it."

"Well, technically I'm dead."

"Potato, potahto." Olivia dismissed with a wave of her hand. "You're pretty chatty and corporeal for a dead person."

Again, she had a point. But her tone was downright irritating.

Looking back at Charlotte, I noticed her gaze had become transfixed on my hands. Exactly what Theo had told her not to do. Awesome. I quickly folded my arms to conceal them.

Charlotte stepped forward and grabbed one of my hands. Her

touch was warm and I could feel the blood pulsing through her veins. It was a shock against my cold flesh. I didn't like it.

I tried to pull away from her without hurting her, but her grip was strong as she held my clawed hand up for all three of us to see.

"This?! You're self-conscious about this?" she asked, her eyes wide with disbelief.

I wrestled my hand out of her grasp and held it protectively against my body.

"Yes," I sounded harassed. "The face and the fangs are bad enough. But I actually have to look at these. They're a constant reminder that I'm not human anymore. And also... different. Even by vampire standards."

"And the whole drinking blood, not reflecting in mirrors, and aversion to daylight thing isn't an indicator enough?" Olivia paused, noticing the unenthused look on my monstrous face. "Don't get it twisted, Fangs. What happened to you sucks. But shit happens. You just need to get over it and stop being so insecure."

But it was a big deal. It was a big deal because it was happening to me. I was on day two of being a creature and of having a global supernatural organization after me, and it sucked. A lot.

The corner of my lip twitched. Olivia was seriously pissing me off with her annoying 'cool girl' attitude. My vampire mind urged to snarl at her. Sure, werewolves could take down a vampire during the three nights of the full moon, but I could easily take her any other night of the month. Including tonight.

Charlotte distracted me before I could react.

"You're crazy. A lot of people would pay good money for nails like those. And yours are real," she said.

"They're just... They're just not me. It's all a lot to get used to," I said sadly, shaking off my Other Face.

Charlotte tilted her head and gave me an empathetic half-smile. I knew she was coming from a good place, but I wasn't ready for Theo's sympathy or hers.

"I think I hear my brother calling me," I lied. I needed some fresh air, or at least a room that didn't smell of pungent dog.

Olivia rolled her eyes, her preternatural ears catching my fib.

"What? What did I miss?" Charlotte asked, confused, looking from me to Olivia as I headed out of the closet.

"Nothing," Olivia replied with a sigh.

TWENTY-FIVE

Out in the main room, the boys circled around a map laid out over the dining table, immersed in conversation with something about a boat. Theo crouched over the map, tracing his finger down the Potomac River and indicating his thoughts on the best route.

Their expressions were grim, and the air was dense with worry. It whirled around the room and did actually smell like bad B.O., but a little sweeter.

The moment I entered the room, their roving glances darted toward me like a hundred hot breaths all over my flesh. Questioning, prying, smothering.

Despite not needing to breathe anymore, the sensation was suffocating. I could feel it down in my bones. That, combined with the myriad of creature and human scents circulating the room, the scene was becoming very overwhelming, very fast.

I couldn't take it anymore.

Marching past the group, I turned to face them and shifted just long enough to issue the most menacing hiss I could muster before continuing forward and out onto the balcony.

If they wanted something to look at, so be it. Who was I to disappoint?

Outside, the air was cool and refreshing. But most importantly, it was quiet.

Placing my hands on the railing, my chest rose with a deep inhalation and I closed my eyes to gently blow the air through my nose to ground myself from the dizzying smells and emotions in the condo. When I opened them, I glanced down to survey the park below. It was empty aside from an old man who shuffled along a path with his tiny white dog. Beyond the park, the water of the Potomac ebbed and flowed in a soothing tempo, only broken up by the wake of a small water taxi that churned southward.

I looked to the sky and asked the moon for higher guidance as she showered me with her comforting rays. It was strange to feel so much power from something that seemed so ordinary when I was human. But the moon and her stars now governed when I woke and rested, so maybe they could help answer the existential questions I had about my prolonged life.

Everything was still raw with newness. Yes, I was alive... ish. But at what cost? Losing everything I had known for decades? All I wanted to do was crawl into my bed in New York and wake up as if none of this had happened.

I heard the balcony door open, and cold daggers stabbed at my back. My brother had come outside, and he was very upset with me.

"Zoey, what the fuck was that?" Theo demanded.

"Go away, Theo. I don't want to talk to you right now," I replied dryly. The last thing I needed was to be reprimanded on bogus vampire etiquette.

"Oh, we're going to talk. Right now. You can scream at me, push me, punch me. Hell, you can even bite me. Fine. I can take it. But now you're acting like a—"

"Vampire?" I interjected. It was the truth, wasn't it?

"I was going to say brat. I don't think you understand that we —vampires—have a bad enough reputation as it is. No thanks to places like RIDER. You can't throw the spectacle like you just did in front of other creatures. Especially humans. We're better than that."

Spreading my hands outward along the balcony railing, I made one last silent plea to the celestial elements to give me just one freaking break.

No response.

I sighed. Fuck me.

"Everyone keeps looking at me. I don't like it," I spat out, eyes still fixed on the park below.

My tone was terse and childish, but I couldn't help it. Being angry was easier than allowing myself to be vulnerable to the sadness and longing I felt. It made sense, I guess, from an evolutionary standpoint. My instincts were trying to protect me from being self-destructive.

"So what? You're just going to go around snarling and baring your fangs at anyone who pisses you off? To humans on the street who might catcall you?" Theo asked.

The answer was yes. That was exactly what I would do. Maybe even pluck out their eyeballs with my bare clawed hands if I were feeling particularly spicy.

In lieu of a response, I gripped the balcony railing tightly and quietly seethed. Silence was the better alternative than being subjected to any more of Theo's commands. Or finding out the details behind the ominous sounding 'Vampire Time Out.' The thought of being muzzled, shackled, or caged was enraging. I had been sheltered enough. Right now, I just wanted to be mad.

"You're going to end up in a mental hospital, or police custody, or worse, if you keep acting like this. And I think we both know that our kind does not do well in human captivity," Theo continued.

This was something we could both agree on. Even RIDER had been unsuccessful in keeping vampires against their will. It only took a few days before they went completely insane and feral to where they had to be put out of their misery.

"Shit. I knew two days was too young to leave the apartment," Theo mumbled to himself. Then louder to me, "Zoey, whether or not you want it, we're trying to help you. This is just an adjustment. For everyone. Char—"

"Charlotte acts like I'm her new pet vampire," I snapped, cutting him off.

Whirling around, I folded my arms and leaned against the railing, making sure to give him an extra dose of stink eye.

Theo glared back at me with an intense gaze of his own, and I noticed that the scratches on his face had completely healed, not even leaving a light scar behind. He looked to the side and ran a hand through his hair.

"She's just trying to be supportive in the best way she knows how," he said, his tone cooling down a notch.

"No. They look at me now like I'm just some demon. A monster. But, I mean, can I blame them?" I replied. My words dripped with disgust.

"Is that what you think of yourself now? That you're just 'some demon'?" Theo shoved his hands into his jacket pockets and looked me square in the eye.

Charged with emotion, I opened my mouth, but nothing actually came out. His question was so straightforward, but it caught me off guard.

Thinking for a moment, I chose my words carefully, trying to find clarity in my emotions.

"I don't even know what to think anymore. I have been studying vampires and the supernatural for over two hundred years. I thought I had it all figured out. I was so sure of it. But now that I'm like this... I—I just don't even know anymore."

"How so?" Theo asked, cocking his head to the side, intrigued.

"Everything pointed to the fact that vampires are pure evil. That the human that was there before was gone and never coming back. But I... I still feel like myself. But also different. I don't want to hurt anyone. Yet, I guess." I paused and sucked on the bottom of my lip. "Aside from when I tried to rip your face off earlier. But honestly, I just don't know what I am, or who I am, or where I even belong right now."

Theo smirked and snorted a puff of laughter. "Well, I'll take you trying to rip my face off as an improvement from trying to stake me. Less lethal, anyway. Listen, I get it. You're scared and angry. But we have a choice. You have a choice. You know there are more vampires in this world than just the ones you hear about at RIDER. Why do you think that is? If you think of yourself as just a demon, then that's what you'll be: a monster who spends their nights causing pain and suffering in the world. But if you believe you're still you—the woman who is smart and curious, and has seen the world in lifetimes instead of years, then you are. You're still Bess, still Zoey. You're still my sister."

I remained silent, letting his words sink in. Moments passed between us as we both looked down at our feet until those moments grew into an awkward silence.

"I think you need to give your speech to whoever's taken over the Big Bad list," I finally said. It was only a matter of time now before RIDER caught up with us.

"We'll figure it out. We have a plan," Theo said, gesturing with a hand in his jacket pocket to the group huddled in discussion on the other side of the glass. Charlotte and Olivia had joined them and were nodding their heads, listening to the details.

"Luke has access to the University Boathouse. We can take a boat from there and sail south to where they won't be looking for us. Matt suggested Tangier Island."

"Tangier Island?" I had never heard of it before.

Theo nodded. "Yeah, Matt said it's the last place someone would look for two vampires on the run. Apparently, it's a small, religious island community. We can get there before sunrise. It'll give us some breathing room to think about our next move."

I nodded. Not like I had a better idea, or really any say in the matter.

Looking past my brother at the creatures and humans inside, I sucked on the inside of my cheek, suddenly feeling embarrassed for my outburst minutes before.

"How do I even go back in there now?" I asked, not able to conceal the anxiety in my tone.

"Well, you can always start with an apology," Theo replied with a knowing look.

Staking myself with a toothpick sounded more appealing.

I scowled and opened my mouth to protest, but Theo kept talking.

"Come on, it can't be any harder than drinking blood for the first time," he said, turning to head back inside.

My proud vampire ego prayed he was right.

"Everything okay?" Luke asked apprehensively, eyes shifting between Theo and me as we approached the huddle.

In a movement too fast for the human eye, Theo jabbed me in the side with his elbow. I flashed him another dirty look before reluctantly addressing the group.

"Yes. Everything is fine. Being like this is still new, and I got a little... overwhelmed." My teeth gritted on the word as Theo's cautionary warning from earlier haunted me. "I'll try, but I can't guarantee that it won't—"

Theo cleared his throat loudly. His obsession with having perfect manners in front of humans and other creatures was becoming less of an amusing quirk by the minute.

"—I mean, it won't happen again. Sorry." I forced the words from my mouth in a single stream.

When I was human, the tiniest bit of unpleasantry (regardless of fault) was always met with a handwritten apology note and the largest bouquet of fresh flowers RIDER could buy. Now humility was agonizing. Like getting my fingernails ripped out one by one.

"Awesome. Good to hear. Now we can move on to our next order of business—getting to the boathouse before RIDER finds us. Which is what we should be doing now," Luke said without skipping a beat.

The huddle broke off as coats and bags were retrieved, but I could still sense Luke's gaze on me.

"Hey, if it makes you feel any better, Liv took down an entire deer when we were still getting used to everything," he said to me, sliding his arms through the sleeves of his jacket. "In human form."

My eyes widened, and a surprised, "Oh." was all I could say. It sounded unreal, but I wouldn't put it past her.

Olivia, visibly recalling the memory, smirked and lifted her shoulders for a moment, as if to say '*Meh*'.

Theo was in the kitchen, and I joined him there, trying to rid myself of the mental imagery of Olivia with the unfortunate deer. Standing at Charlotte's knife block, he inspected the knives. Pulling each one out, he held the handle close to his face, peering down the length of the blade before flipping it around in his hand to feel the weight.

Passing on a rectangular Santoku knife and a small, but sharp, paring knife, he settled on the large chef's knife and slipped it into the inner pocket of his jacket.

"Good thinking," I said, reaching over to pull out a thin, but deadly looking boning knife. It wasn't much, especially compared to what RIDER might have, but it was something.

A weary look crossed his face.

"Um, maybe next time. Once you've fully settled," he said, carefully plucking the knife from my hand and placing it back into the block.

I frowned. I knew what he was thinking. They were all thinking it. *Don't give the unhinged newbie vampire any sharp objects.*

Theo was right. This was going to be a long night.

TWENTY-SIX

Our supernatural caravan made its way toward the Georgetown University Boathouse, using the well-marked walking trail along the Chesapeake and Ohio Canal to avoid the more crowded, and likely monitored, main streets. Wolves led the pack, as was their nature, with Charlotte behind them chatting animatedly to Matt about the impact of the last few night's events on witch affairs and how Matt had delayed the agents from searching the condo by telling them Charlotte had booked a private jet to escape to her family's place in Montauk. Mirza followed close behind them, and finally, Theo and I brought up the rear, thinking it was best to have supernatural predators at both ends. I was just glad to be as far away from the stench of werewolf as possible.

After a short walk, the dirt towpath gave way to a paved biking and walking trail that cut through a wooded area with a marker, declaring we had entered the Capital Crescent Trail. Luke noted the boathouse wasn't too far up ahead, and that we were making good time in reaching Tangier Island well before sunrise.

I wished that was all I was able to hear.

When Matt asked Luke how he became an assistant coach to

the university undergrad crew team, Olivia, of all people, would not shut up about it.

"It's so crazy, right?" she said enthused. "In high school and undergrad, I would only date guys in bands who had at least two tattoos. The last person I would expect to be with would be a preppy, former high-school-quarterback-turned-crew-assistant-coach. Not to mention nerd." She glowed, giving Luke a quick peck on the cheek.

I found Olivia's entire essence to be irritating to an antagonizing level. It wasn't just one thing. It was everything about her. The way she moved and smelled and talked. Even the way she breathed—so unnecessarily loud and deep. Luke was a bit more palatable, but not by much. I didn't remember feeling so repulsed by them at The House.

"Ugh, does she ever shut up?" I whispered to Theo. "I swear it's like she's become so annoying overnight."

Theo looked at me, puzzled. "Of course you do. It'd be strange if you didn't."

I was so shocked by his reply that I stopped walking. When everyone continued to move ahead, I had to jog a few paces to catch back up.

"What are you talking about?" I asked him, confused.

"Wait, you're telling me you don't know?" He laughed, a bit amused at my ignorance. I didn't see what was so funny. "All your fancy data, and maps and charts, and you still weren't able to make the connection?"

"If you're just going to patronize me—" I scowled. But through my newly acquired fangs and claws, I was still an academic at heart and was dying (again) to understand what he was getting at.

"Okay, okay," he conceded. "So, you know that witches and vampires rarely interact with one another, right?"

"Yeah. It's because vampires fear witches. Of what they can do to them—I mean—us. I felt Charlotte's power earlier at her condo. It was... intense."

"Mhmm, sort of. Charlotte is more powerful than she realizes. But I'd say it goes a bit both ways. Overall, yes, throughout the evolution of all creatures, we've learned it is best to keep to ourselves. The same goes for werewolves and vampires. Tell me, did any of our territories overlap on your population charts?"

"Cluster maps," I corrected. Taking a moment to mull over his question, I shook my head. "No. But in general, werewolves stick to rural areas where they can hunt larger animal game without human interference. Vampires, on the other hand, position themselves near large human populations. For obvious reasons."

"But you've seen it yourself. You don't need human blood to survive," he countered.

Good point. I crossed my arms, still not able to figure it out. Even after walking a few more paces in silence.

"Alright," I said, exasperated. "What am I missing?"

"There are stories. From the Old Ones, of the times before the great civilizations of humans. Creatures lived closer together then and, like with most cultures with differing ideologies and people, there were wars between our kind and others. And as human populations grew around the world, we became more vulnerable to them. Humans fear what they don't understand, and destroy what they fear. We learned it's safer for creatures to isolate ourselves from each other and our instincts have adapted to that. That's why you sensed warning around Charlotte and an aversion to Olivia and Luke."

"Oh," I replied with a hollowness in my voice as I looked down at the paved walking path we continued along. It was like I was on my first day at RIDER learning the basics.

"Don't worry," Theo said encouragingly. "It's a very old way of thinking. And the more time you spend around other creatures, the more your instincts will lighten. Hell, I even dated a werewolf a few years ago."

"You did what?"

The entire group came to an abrupt halt, and I almost ran into Mirza's backside.

"Hey vamps! You smell that back there?" Luke called from the front.

Ugh, how could I not? It was a revolting, sulfurous, thousand-decaying-carcasses kind of smell. So gross. I envied the humans in our group who looked confused, fortunate enough to have mundane olfactory senses.

I gagged a bit, and when I glanced at my brother, he was looking a tinge green himself.

To my right was the sound of something in the thick brush. Bipedal feet crunching through leaves and sticks at an increasing pace.

I watched as it came into view. Slowly at first, as a dark movement bounding through the foliage. As it neared, I saw it more clearly. A towering green frog-like creature with long, curved claws, and oversized fangs jutting out over its lips. It roared a loud, throaty bellow as it neared.

I tilted my head, analyzing it in more detail. There was a subtle familiarity to it.

I knew this creature.

It was a Buskar demon. The Demonic Entities Department had profiled them in a Lunch-and-Learn a few months ago. They were the mercenaries of the demon world. With their aggressiveness, low intelligence, and formidable strength, the department had proposed employing them as bounty hunters for especially difficult COIs. With many safety protocols in place, of course—to prevent them from accidentally eating RIDER personnel. They also had a unique, sulfurous scent that came from a thick layer of mucus excreted on their backs.

A Buskar demon was the type of creature that could subdue a vampire long enough for capture.

RIDER had sent it for me.

If its beady, red eyes deadlocked onto me weren't convincing of that enough, it raised and pointed a clawed finger in my direction as it galloped closer.

Theo protectively stepped in front of me, but I moved around him.

"I have to lead it away. I've seen these in action. It'll rip everyone else apart just to get to me. Stay here with the group in case there's more," I said.

"Zo, don't! You shouldn't go alone," Theo said, panic rising in his voice.

But it was too late. In a movement so quick that it appeared to surprise Theo, I reached into his jacket pocket, pulled out the knife he had been hiding there, and slipped it under the right leg of my leggings. Then I broke into a run down the path.

When I looked behind me, the Buskar had blown by our group with little regard and bounded after me. Its grotesque lips pulled upwards at the sides into an insidious smile as it picked up speed in pursuit.

It was exhilarating. Wind in my hair, feet barely touching the ground as I raced down the paved trail. It felt so good. So natural to be running free through the night.

Forking right, I crossed over a wooden bridge above a small rushing stream that glittered in the moonlight and then through a curved stone tunnel, hoping it was too shallow and narrow for the tall, lumbering demon to follow.

The tunnel emptied into an open park and I paused, listening to cars that zoomed by on a nearby road. Just when I thought the Buskar had given up, my gut plunged at the smell of bad eggs and trash before it bounded out of the tunnel with a thundering growl. Shit.

I darted deeper into the park, passing through trees and sprawling open patches of grass. The demon followed closely behind, making a wet, raspy chuckling noise.

Was it laughing at me? Now, I was certain it was going to die. If it didn't kill me first.

Despite supernatural speed and senses, I was quickly becoming tired. I paused when I came upon a deserted, overgrown field with the rusted, metal skeletal remains of a trolley trestle cutting through it.

I stopped and whirled around, waiting for the demon to follow. Covered in sweat, I was breathing hard from a combination of adrenaline and habit. And it was from that adrenaline that I shifted, flexing my clawed hands in anticipation. It wasn't just that my face and hands that changed when I shifted. All my muscles tightened. I still wasn't sure exactly what I could do, but I was stronger in this form. And I was ready.

Seeing that I had stopped, the Buskar bored toward me like a linebacker through the field. I jumped to the side, and it ran past me.

Positioning myself behind it, I jumped up, attempting to take it down from its backside.

It was a decision I instantly regretted.

The demon was so slimy that I couldn't get a good hold on any part of it and instead slid back to the ground. My front was completely covered in its sticky, smelly ooze. So gross.

The demon roared. A high-pitched shrieking noise to let me know it was angry. It turned to face me and rushed forward, slicing at the air with its enormous claws. Dodging its blows, it pushed me backward until I backed up against the trestle's concrete foundation.

I turned around and jumped up onto the metal structure, scrambling up the side, knowing the Buskar's wide stature and small brain wouldn't follow my climb. When I reached the splintered, rickety wooden track on top, I peered down.

Sure enough, the demon was prowling around beneath me, growling and snapping its jaws upward in frustration.

Using the trestle as leverage, I sprung off it and onto the

Buskar's leathery shoulders. It screeched angrily and blindly clawed at me as I squeezed my legs around its neck, trying to bring it down.

It didn't work.

New abilities aside, with my small frame, I was minuscule compared to the eight-foot-tall creature.

Then, with a powerful jerk, it was suddenly on the move.

It ran in circles and then in zigzags through the field as I dodged its claws and held on tight from being bucked off. I noticed Theo had caught up to us and was surprised he didn't burst out laughing from the sight: a small vampire riding on top of a towering, smelly green demon in a city park, holding on for dear life as if it were a runaway bull.

I grabbed at the creature's head with both hands and tried my hardest to snap its neck, hoping that the technique I had learned in the combat training course and newfound strength would make it easy.

That didn't work either.

Running out of options, I briefly thought about sinking my fangs into the side of its neck. But the mere thought of having to pick Buskar hide out of my teeth over the next several days was nauseating. No thanks.

Then I remembered the knife.

Bending backward, I removed the knife from under the bottom of my leggings. I held it above the demon's head with both hands before plunging the blade into the back of its neck.

The creature screeched, wailing in pain. Then, I too, felt pain. I had been holding the knife in both hands, wrenching it deeper into its neck that I didn't notice when it grabbed my shoulder.

I yelped—a wild, animal-like sound as its claws sunk deep into my muscles before tossing me off its shoulders like a rag doll.

I let out a whimper when I hit the grass with a solid thud.

Rolling onto my back, I saw Theo a few feet away, also wearing his game face, glancing nervously from me to the creature. Taking note that I was still conscious, he gave me a quick nod of reassurance. Then, turning his attention to the creature, he rushed and leapt onto it, grabbing the knife and wrenching it out. Using his foot for leverage, he gracefully bounded off of its back, to the ground.

The Buskar held its neck, moaning and snarling as blue blood poured out of the wound I had created. It hunched over—and that's when Theo struck. He plunged the knife deep into its chest cavity, the location of its heart-like organ. The demon stumbled backward before tripping over itself and falling motionless to the ground.

"Don't forget—the head! You have to—" I winced, sitting up as shocks of pain rippled through my shoulder and down my back. More blood poured out all over my shirt as I inspected the wounds. Great. Charlotte was definitely going to revoke clothes-sharing privileges if she didn't stake me first.

Theo grabbed the end of the knife and pulled it out of the creature's chest. It made a sickening, wet sound when it released. He walked up toward its head and held the knife high above it with two hands. Moonlight glinted off the blade before he powerfully brought it down on the demon's neck.

I could feel the Buskar's energy snuff out of existence before it rapidly decomposed into nothing but a small pile of sticky slime. By dawn, the residue would evaporate, leaving no trace of it behind.

"Decapitate it before it can regenerate. I know," Theo panted through his fangs.

I shifted to my human face and stood up; a slow and painful process. My clothes were saturated and heavy with both mine and the creature's bodily fluids that it made a gross purple color when smeared together.

"Let me see the damage." Theo was by my side, looking at my wounds through brown eyes.

"I'm fine," I lied, feeling a little lightheaded. "I heal fast now, anyway."

Mirza and Charlotte jogged into the field, with Matt, Luke, and Olivia following close behind.

Charlotte gasped when she saw me, but I was thankful when she mentioned nothing about her clothes that likely needed an incinerator to be properly disposed of.

"Zo, you look weak. Do you need blood?" Mirza asked. He rolled his sleeve up as he waded toward me through the tall grass.

My eyes narrowed to his wrist, transfixed by the large blue vein there that quivered in tune to his pulse. I could smell the sweetness that laid within it, and I wanted to taste it. Badly.

Licking my lips, I reached out with both hands to accept his offer, eager to find out if human blood tasted any different from pig's.

Theo was between us in an instant, one powerful hand clenched around Mirza's wrist.

"*Never* offer your blood to a vampire," he warned, staring him square in his green eyes. "Ever. You don't know what you're agreeing to. My sister can wait until we reach the island."

"Sorry. I was just trying to help," Mirza replied, sufficiently spooked and massaging his wrist when Theo, satisfied that his message had been received, had shoved it back to him.

"It's better if you don't. Come on, RIDER and Tristan are probably close by and will be here soon looking for their demon. We need to keep moving before sunrise."

Theo started back toward the paved trail, and Charlotte trotted after him.

"You didn't have to be so harsh," she said to him in a hushed voice. My brother was silent.

Theo's grave demeanor had frightened me too, but I tried not to let it show. Instead, I bit my lower lip and passed a comforting glance toward Mirza.

"Leave it to me to be turned by the world's only vegan vampire," I said, trying to lighten the mood.

"If anything, we're closer to vegetarian. And we're not the only ones," Theo called back.

The lab tech and I exchanged surprised looks before treading back through the grass.

Vegetarian vampires. The world was still full of surprises.

TWENTY-SEVEN

Locating the boathouse and the motorboat docked in the marina behind it was remarkably easy when you didn't have a large, ravenous, slime-covered demon on your tail. And with each step in our journey there, I could feel myself healing and growing stronger again. Even the gashes in my shoulder itched as muscle and skin mended themselves back together.

To everyone's pleasant surprise, the boat was larger than expected. A twenty-six-foot bay boat, as Luke had called it. It had light grey upholstered seating throughout and two well-cushioned captain's chairs under a small overhang in the middle, where the navigation system was stationed.

The university's new toy, Luke and the other coaches used it to zoom around the Potomac River to check water conditions, monitor competitions, and pick up unfortunate capsized rowers. And now it was being used to smuggle a vampire wanted for her memories out of Washington, DC.

Setting sail, the boat sliced through the Potomac's waters at a healthy speed, heading south. Theo was optimistic that we'd still reach Tangier Island a few hours before sunrise, double-checking the map and coordinates with Luke. But despite his optimism, we also confirmed that the boat's windowless, interior bathroom could fit us both from the sun's harmful rays. But only if we crammed our bodies in there in a way-too-close-for-comfort formation. I prayed we wouldn't have to use it.

The wind whipped my hair around wildly as I stood at the bow, gazing at the inky, dark water below.

There was a myth that vampires could not cross running water. And that's exactly what it was—a myth, with no hard fact behind it. But as I stared out and across the choppy river, I understood where the aversion came from. My mind and senses were in a constant state of analysis. Always taking in new information to determine size, depth, density, body language, what was spoken, what was not spoken, and everything in between. All to decide how best to react in order to stay alive.

Open water was different. It clung to its secrets. I couldn't tell how deep it was, the salinity, how fast the current cut through it, or what creatures lurked below its surface.

If I fell in, would a massive sturgeon waiting at the bottom nibble on my undead flesh, thinking I was food? Or would they stay away as most animals did when there was a vampire nearby?

Pushing the thoughts from my mind, I collapsed on the cushioned seat beside me, stretching my legs out in front. I was beyond exhausted, and while the sun was still many hours away, I craved the cool comfort and rest of the makeshift coffin tub in Theo's apartment. Hopefully, there would be something similar wherever we were going.

Theo walked over and sat in the seat across from me, having handed off his co-captain duties to Olivia. She stood excitedly at the helm, wisps of pink hair flying backward, watching intently as Luke pointed out the navigation instruments.

"You were good back there. Leading the demon away from everyone like that. It was brave," he said with a small smile. Pausing for a moment, his eyes flitted skyward in thought. "Also a little impulsive and reckless. And a bit stupid, too. But brave."

Was that a compliment? I smiled. As much as I didn't want or need it, having my big brother's approval felt good. It also felt good to be seen as good, despite what I was now. I held onto that.

Sweeping my gaze beyond him and across the water, I noticed we were now miles from shore. The bright city lights and imposing Washington monuments illuminated in their ghostly white-light glow had faded from view as we moved south, away from the city.

All I could see now was dark choppy water and a dense line of forest in the distance with a dot of dim light every mile or so. The only sounds were the droning buzz of the engine, the rhythmic slap of waves against the boat's hull, and the sound of Mirza retching over the toilet in the bathroom, as he had been most of the journey. Aside from that last bit, it was all eerily peaceful.

I cocked my head to look at Theo. There was a question I had been wanting to ask him since first seeing him at the Arbor Terrace. But only now did I feel comfortable, and willing to accept his answer, whatever it might be.

"Theo, what happened? What made you want to...stop? It was like you were a Big Bad the second you were turned. Vampires rarely change from that." I asked, avoiding the word 'good' because there was no such thing as the cliche'd 'good vampire.' Only a vampire who tried to be good until they ate the wrong person.

"Well... " Theo took in a deep breath and clasped his hands in his lap. While we no longer needed to breathe, we still needed to take air into our lungs to talk. And my brother was preparing to do a lot of just that.

"In the late-1800s, Daisy and I were traveling through the Blue Ridge Mountains. Somewhere between North Carolina and Tennessee. News traveled a lot slower in those areas, so we could move around easily without drawing attention to ourselves until we left. Daisy said the people there still listened to the land. They believed deeply in the ancient lore that had been passed down by the natives. She said it made them easier to terrify. Made their blood sweeter when we fed on them. She was actually right about that. City folk act like they've seen it all.

"We were in one of those little villages in the dead of winter. It snowed constantly and snow drifts several feet high were all around us. Daisy and I got into a fight. It was over something stupid—I think I accused her of flirting with a man when she was just playing with her food. Like I said, human blood makes you irrational. And when I got drunk and tried to make her jealous, doing the same with the barmaids at the local tavern, she left me. Didn't even tell me where she was going. She just left. I was so drunk on bloodlust and whiskey that I flipped. And for that night and the next, I rampaged through the town, feeding on everyone. Or just killing them when I was too full—even the horses. Until there was no one left."

My eyes widened, hanging onto every word of his story. He was describing the Theo that I knew at RIDER. Wicked, ferocious, unrelenting.

"I was stuck there, in the tiny hill town that I had single-handedly turned into a ghost town. Being alone was far worse than jealousy or rage. And when I got hungry again, I moved on. But towns back then were farther apart and travel was difficult in the winter. Even with our speed and strength, hunting animal game in three feet of snow was impossible. I was lost in the wilderness for weeks."

"What happened? How did you make it back? And how did you survive during the daylight?" I asked, leaning forward in my seat, intrigued.

"I found caves and sometimes had to bury myself in the snow and the ground. Eventually, I found a cabin. A young widow lived there—a real spitfire of a woman. She threatened to blow my head off with her shotgun when she found me in her chicken coop feeding on her prize rooster." Theo laughed, nostalgic. "It's strange how the world sometimes seems to align everything perfectly. She wasn't scared of me. Not one bit. But we were both lonely creatures and neither of us really wanted to off the other because of it.

"Vampire nests are built on lust and greed. She helped me learn how to control myself. Of course, it still took decades to figure out what worked best to prevent a relapse."

A million more questions rose to my lips, but I settled on two to escape them. "What was her name—the widow? Did you love her?"

Theo looked upward again. It seemed like no one had asked him before. Finally, he said, "Her name was Winnie. And I did, for many reasons. During our time together that winter, I realized there was more to being what we are than indulgence without consequence. Things like purpose, trust, and family. And speaking of that last one—I thought I had killed all of mine. But look, here you are," Theo mused, nudging my leg with his foot.

"Here I am," I repeated quietly, casting my eyes downward. It was far from the family reunion I expected, but somehow more in other ways.

I reached out and grasped the pendant that hung on the necklace over his chest. I had been trying to figure out what it was for days, but hadn't been able to get a good look at it.

"What's this?" I asked, turning it over in my hand. It was a small silver crest with three pears in the formation of an upside-down triangle with a single chevron stripe through the middle. It looked so familiar.

"You don't recognize it?" Theo replied, surprised.

"No," I said flatly, turning it over again for another look.

"It's the Abbott family crest."

"Oh." I dropped the pendant as if it had burned me and leaned back in my seat like I'd had the wind knocked out. "I guess I've been Zoey Prescott for so long that I... I forgot."

"Well, I haven't," he said matter-of-factly, holding up the pendant to look at it. "This is a reminder for me. Of what I did, and of what I lost. Of who I am. "

Forgetting what the family crest looked like made me realize that RIDER had provided everything and nothing at the same time. I only knew what RIDER told me, from the data they provided to my new alias. I ate it up blindly with all my prepared meals and washed it down with the daily afternoon tea. Without those things, I had no idea who I was.

"After centuries of living in the box RIDER made for me, I don't think I know where it begins and where it ends anymore," I said wearily, collapsing my hands in my lap.

"Well, sometimes you need to take a leap to step out of the box in order to see the box."

Was that some kind of insightful ancient vampire proverb? I snorted a puff of laughter. Unbelievable. Not at the advice, but that over a week ago, Theo would have been the last person I'd expected to provide introspective guidance.

The boat crested off a series of choppy waves, bouncing us in our seats. I heard Charlotte shriek and then laugh at the sudden movement at the far end of the boat. A thought crossed my mind, and I suddenly became excited to solve another of my brother's mysteries.

"Who's your sire?" I asked eagerly.

The boat settled back down to a smooth cruise, and Theo stood up and stretched.

"That's a story for another time, sis. I should check in with Luke to see where we are."

I also got up to have a look around. Charlotte and Matt were chatting at the stern of the boat, and I headed there in the hopes that they were talking about something more uplifting than centuries old carnage and familial remorse.

Padding down the side of the boat, I was thankful that my newfound agility allowed me to walk around the swaying vessel with graceful ease. We had been clipping through the water at such a high speed that those with less than preternatural abilities were left clinging to the railings for dear life as they moved about.

"Whoa, whoa, whoa—what is that?" Luke shouted as I walked

by. He pulled on one of the control panel's many levers and the boat's engine quieted as it slowed.

"What's going on?" Charlotte asked, curious. She staggered toward the helm, still yet to find her sea legs. Earlier, she had been very firm that she was a 'Champagne-All-Day, Sunday-Funday, Yacht Girl' and not an 'Any Other Kind of Boat' person.

Up ahead, three sizable boats blocked our path, flashing their blue police lights in the night. This was not good. At all.

"Fangs, please tell me that stereotype about vampires being able to hypnotize humans is true. I have a feeling we're going to need it unless we all want to go to jail," Olivia said to me.

"Unfortunately, that's just a myth." I frowned. "But Theo and I can definitely threaten to eat them if that helps."

"We'll be doing nothing of the sort," Theo chimed in tartly. He and Luke were hurriedly flipping through papers they'd found in the ship's console, searching for the permits and licenses the Coast Guard was about to request.

A loud thundering chopping sound cut through the air, and I covered my ears in pain. Strong winds blew from the backside of the boat and a helicopter swung into view. The sides of the aircraft were open, showing that it was filled with tactical agents in their black fatigues with a signature red serif 'R' on their chest.

The high-pitched sound of aerosol released overhead and a blanket of mist settled over us. It burned and stung, and I could feel the skin on my hands and face blister.

I screamed and crouched down, shutting my eyes to avoid the mist. It was like raining acid. By the sound and the pain, I knew they were the weaponized canisters of holy water I had ordered for the mission.

"We have to jump!" Theo screamed at me, grabbing my arm.

"I'm scared!" I shouted, stumbling after him, holding my face. The pain and noise were unbearable, as was the thought of swimming in the murky waters of the Potomac.

"It's okay, just follow me!"

We peered over the boat's edge. My vampire mind screamed not to jump, and I hesitated.

Something whizzed through the air close to me and I felt a sharp sting on my right hip. My hand instantly went to the pain, and I grabbed onto something hard and metal. Wrenching it out of my side, I squinted just enough to see a small, red tufted dart in my hand.

I cursed under my breath and then cried out for Theo. But when I checked to see if he was still next to me, everything started to blur and slow down.

I tried to jump out of the boat, but stumbled. I was suddenly on my hands and knees, disoriented.

Mirza and Charlotte were calling out to me, but they sounded far away. The boat tipped and jolted as more bodies boarded the vessel. Luke and Olivia were shouting at them.

"We have COI 6765 in sight, ready for extraction," an unfamiliar voice said over me.

The last thing I remembered before the dark were black-gloved hands reaching toward me.

TWENTY-EIGHT

I awoke, curled up in the back of a van—alone and with my hands chained to one of two steel benches lining the interior. Feeling weak and dazed from whatever tranquilizing cocktail I'd been struck with, the chains felt so heavy that I could barely lift them, let alone break out of them.

The van was still, but outside muffled voices shouted orders and discussed next steps. I caught mention of a witch and immediately thought of Charlotte. I hoped she was okay.

The back doors opened. It was still night, so I couldn't have been out for long. Beyond the van's bumper, I saw the pointed arms of a pentagram in mosaic tile. We were parked in The House's driveway.

"Yes, I can take it from here. She's a newly turned, drugged-up vampire. Believe me, I deal with far worse creatures between meetings on a Monday. Tell the teams no one goes in or out of the basement without my say," Tristan said, dismissing the RIDER agent next to him.

The agent nodded obediently and took one disgusted look at me before leaving. A few days earlier, I probably would have acted the same.

"Stay away from me!" I growled, backing away from him as much as the chains allowed.

"Or what, you're going to bite me? Yeah, that's not going to happen." Tristan laughed, climbing into the van.

I tried to shift to prove him wrong, but found that I couldn't. Although conscious, my muscles were still too relaxed to move into the form of my Other Face.

"How did you find us?" I asked as Tristan pulled out a key to unlock the heavy padlock that tied me to the van. He kept my hands chained together.

Matt Riley popped into my mind. Although he'd been at RIDER for a while, I didn't know him very well. Did he sell us out? Or had he been part of the conspiracy all along?

"It wasn't that hard," Tristan replied, dragging me out of the van and across the backyard. My legs were jelly, not able to find stable footing, and I stumbled the entire way. "We put out an alert across all law enforcement in DC, Maryland, and Virginia. But a boat going fifty-five knots in the middle of the night when the speed limit is thirty-five was pretty obvious."

Well, at least Matt could still be trusted. For now.

"I thought we were friends," I said as Tristan pushed me down the cement stairs that led to the back entrance of the basement. I knew we weren't anymore, but trying to talk him out of it was literally all I had left until Dr. Kelley would inevitably melt my mind into soup. "Remember—Remember the time the Gifted woman sneezed behind me in the library and caught my hair on fire? And after you put it out, I had to get that horrible pixie cut—I was so upset. But then the next day you brought me a Dirty London Fog from Starbucks and told me it made me look like one of the cool girls from the LES?"

"Don't flatter yourself," Tristan replied, pulling me through the basement door. "I spent my entire career learning about you. Getting to know every little detail about you, trying to figure out why a shy, insignificant girl like yourself got to be young forever when so many other people are more deserving. And yet, somehow you still surprise me. Because never would I have thought that you'd choose to be a disgusting, bloodsucking, half-breed demon over death."

Tristan pulled me into one of the werewolf cages and threw me into an armchair that had been placed there. When he untied my hands, I realized I was too slow to move out of his grasp when he retied them to the chair's arms, making sure my hands hung over the edge.

"It wasn't exactly my choice," I said. "And when Charlotte's family finds out what you've done to her—"

"I haven't done anything to Charlotte, or to anyone else that was on that boat. Not even your brother. We're still operating under RIDER. For now. And as you know, there are protocols we have to follow. I put all of RIDER's resources into tracking you down that we even put the mission to eliminate your brother on hold. I mean, there's nothing more dangerous than RIDER's resident vampire expert becoming a mindless, feral, vampire themselves. I'm sure the irony isn't lost on you," Tristan said, crouching down so he was eye level with me.

I flexed my hands and fingers in their binds, wanting to rip out his eyes and the smug look off his face.

"Believe me, I'm well aware," I said as evenly as my temper allowed.

"Another word about Charlotte and consider me out," a female voice called from the far side of the basement.

With my dulled senses focused on Tristan, I hadn't even noticed her.

She looked to be in her late twenties, with similar physical features to Charlotte. Olive skin, high cheekbones, and almond-shaped eyes, but her build was more petite. She also had straight dark hair like Charlotte's, but without the expensive highlights.

When I focused on her, she gave off the same static energy as

Charlotte, but not as bright. There was also a sourness in her scent. Pungent and bitter. I shriveled my nose.

The witch had been carefully laying out salt on the basement floor in a large circle. Goosebumps broke out on my arms at the familiar sight. She was preparing to cast the immortality spell.

"A bit of family rivalry, I suppose," Tristan said to me, lifting his brow. Then to the witch, "Don't worry, Paige. After tonight, no one is going to give a second glance to your cousin. It's going to be all you. All the recognition you deserve."

"You were right about one thing, Zoey," Tristan continued. "Your brother is pretty smart as vampires go. Not that that's a high bar to begin with. Charlotte was going to be our original backup witch for Charlie. But after spending a few days with her, it was clear she was too principled to help us. Willingly, anyway. There's also that whole sparking problem of hers."

"Does Paige know what happened to Charlie?" I said, raising my voice so she would hear.

Paige's head snapped toward me, and she narrowed her eyes.

"Charlie was reckless and didn't respect the dark arts. He got what he deserved." She curled her lips into a cruel smile. "Tristan, the vampire's a little too chatty for comfort. I think it needs another dose of sedative."

"No. Kelley made it clear—he needs her weak, but still lucid," Tristan said.

The door at the top of the unfinished stairs opened, spilling the interior lights of The House around the figure of a man. Over the past couple of days, I had learned that the musky scent that rolled off him told me he was human. But there was something more there, too. The unfamiliar smell tingled in my nose.

"Ah, finally. The man of the hour," Tristan announced.

Panic spiked through me, and I wrestled even harder against the restraints. But I wasn't even strong enough to tip the chair over.

Dr. Kelley descended the staircase with a confident grace. Just like he did before every session, he rolled up his sleeves and shook his left hand to settle his watch. He came into the cage and peered down at me in the chair with his unnatural grey and orange eyes.

"Ah, Miss Prescott," he said smoothly. "It's really wonderful to spend another session with you without the thirty-day wait. Given your....altered state, I'll admit that I've never worked on a creature of your kind. But I always welcome a new challenge."

"No, no, no," I whimpered, squirming in the chair against the restraints.

Thinking of my dream with Dr. Kelley's ever-watchful eyes suffocating me, my own eyes suddenly stung as tears cascaded down my face.

"Interesting. I don't think I've ever seen a vampire cry. I thought bloodlust was the only emotion your kind were capable of. But then again, you were always a meek sort of girl. I guess that trait carried over when you were turned," the doctor mused.

I was still me. Just... with retractable fangs and claws, and a near-constant hunger for blood. I wanted to scream that at him, but found myself shaking instead.

"In a way, we're lucky that you didn't die. In the finality sense of the word," Tristan said. "Although, because you did, the spell technically doesn't grant immortality. More of an anti-aging and longevity charm, I guess. We'll need to update the marketing brochures. Anyway, your blood is tainted now, which is a shame. I had been testing a prototype of a serum extracted from it. It seemed to stop my hair from greying, but that's about it. But in your current state, we can still use your memories to decipher the incantation for the motherlode."

"You don't even know what you're doing. You're just going to get yourselves killed," I spat. They had no idea of the level of destruction the immortality spell would cause. Let alone exposing humans to the supernatural world.

Tristan's face twisted into a mocking grin and he slipped out of the cage, locking it with Dr. Kelley and me inside.

"See, that's the kind of vampire bull-headedness I was expecting. Look around you. The House is a conduit. And Paige is powerful enough to harness and amplify its energy to your memories once Kelley ties into it. Whatever happens in your mind will project itself here, in the real world. Specifically onto me when it comes to your immortality memory. And I know you're probably wondering where the 'balance' is going to be since we're not in an eighteenth century prison. There's a reason why I requested several teams of agents to protect The House while we have an 'extremely dangerous and deranged' vampire in custody," he explained, making air quotes with his fingers to let me know that was the exact verbiage he had used in the official procurement request.

"The House won't let you do it," I replied, a bit surprised it hadn't already been slapping Tristan around or pelting him with potting soil from the bag on the shelf behind him.

Paige snorted loudly. "I can feel that The House has a soft spot for you, but it's under my control now, and it does exactly what I want it to. Charlotte lives in a fantasy world where all creatures live in harmony with all that free will bullshit. She can't assert her power like I can. Even when she needs to."

What a bitch. It was clear why Charlotte had been the one to inherit The House. If anyone in the basement was 'extremely dangerous and deranged,' it was Paige.

"Oh, Kelley, I almost forgot. Here's the muzzle in case the drugs wear off early and she becomes a little too feisty."

Tristan pulled out a thick piece of cloth with chain straps and my stomach plummeted.

It was the very effective vampire muzzle I helped design years ago when RIDER agents needed to interrogate COIs before their elimination. Constructed of a thick burlap material on the outside, it had a chain-mail-like interior that made it vampire-bite proof. The material also dulled their fangs if they tried.

"No need, Tris." Dr. Kelley waved it away, and for a moment, I felt relief. Then the doctor settled his gaze on me. "I know how to control my patient."

Without warning, Dr. Kelley reached out his hands and grabbed onto my exposed palms. This time, there was no meditative ease as my consciousness shifted. My body rocked with a powerful jolt and I was falling.

In the next moment, I was running. Boots pounding on the bright red plush carpet, rows of towering books on either side flashed by as Dr. Kelley pulled me forward by my hand, deeper into the stacks of my Mind Warehouse.

"Let go of me!" I shouted, skidding to a stop and jerking my hand out of his grasp.

"No," Dr. Kelley replied. There was an unsettling decisiveness in his tone. He took a step closer. "You don't even understand the full extent of my abilities. I let you go through these motions as a courtesy. To make you feel like you're in control. But in reality, I'm in control. I always have been."

The sensation of a searing hot needle pierced my forehead. I cried out in pain and fell to my knees. When the pain subsided, Dr. Kelley was standing over me.

"The next time will be more painful," he promised. "And if you don't want to play nice, then I won't indulge you in your charming little library simulation. I know exactly where I want to go, anyway."

Dr. Kelley grabbed both of my hands. Then, slowly at first, but rapidly gaining speed, everything around us spun. When it stopped, I lost my balance and fell to the floor, feeling cold stone. The soiled stench and deafening noise of close-quarter living filled my senses.

We were back in the prison with Bess and Anne. They were placing the final materials around the salted barriers that mimicked what I had just seen in the basement.

I tried to stand, but was too weak. Instead, I watched helplessly from the floor as the memory unfolded. Mr. Sims, crystal in hand, started chanting from the text. Wind whipped around the room, blowing the candles out.

When Anne tackled Mr. Sims, pushing Bess out of the salt circle, I realized something was wrong. In prior Memory Walks, I remembered the sensation of emotions and actions, but it was always from the perspective of the outside looking in.

This time, static filled the air, thick and suffocating. Energy rushed over me and there was a draining sensation, like being siphoned. My vampire mind shot up from my subconscious and screamed at me to move, to fight, to make it stop. But I was too tired to do any of that.

This must be it. What boiling my brain into catatonic stasis was like. I honestly thought it would be more painful. But it really just felt more like dying again. A slow sense of being carried away as what remained of my energy was drawn off.

When I fully went into stasis, would they revive me with blood until I was coherent? Only to replicate the process over and over again like I was some kind of rechargeable battery? Or would they just leave me there, in suspended animation? Would I still have thoughts?

I would have shivered, thinking about the potential scenarios of my fate—all of them terrible. But that took too much effort, and I was so, so, tired. A dense fog fell around me.

I let my mind wander instead.

I could still feel the gray t-shirt on my body. The disgusting mix of mucus, demon blood, and my own had dried, forming a thick, shell-like crust. It was scratchy and stuck to my skin in places.

I sighed, realizing I'd be stuck in these gross, dirty clothes for the next century. Out of everything, that was the most depressing.

My mind drifted out further, and I thought of Augustine. His kind eyes and warm touch. Thinking of my dream, where we were dancing in the courtyard, I wondered if we'd ever be able to do that again. I reimagined the silk dress I wore, flaring out as he twirled me under the moonlight. The dress made me feel beautiful and free. The silk and tulle, smooth and comfortable on my pale, sensitive skin.

A ripple washed over me, feeling like I had emerged from water. Looking down, I was no longer wearing Charlotte's ruined clothes, but the dress from my dream. Except instead of white, it was a deep, crimson red color. As if I had emerged from the courtyard's sea of blood.

Well, this was nice. At least when I became a vegetable, I'd be a fashionable one.

I looked over at Dr. Kelley. His focus was transfixed on the memory that played out before him with a satisfied look on his face. He seemed oblivious to my wardrobe change.

Rage and disgust ignited within me as I stared at him.

For years, I'd gotten so comfortable being complacent in allowing others to decide my future for me, that I couldn't even stand up for myself. I just let things happen, leaving my fate up to everyone else but me.

No more.

Sometimes you need to take a leap to step out of the box in order to see the box. My brother's voice sounded around me.

Concentrating, I focused on the last bit of strength I had. It was enough to allow me to shift to my Other Face.

Then I took that leap out of the box.

And onto Dr. Kelley.

His hands flew up defensively, and I pushed them down and out of the way, burying my fangs into the side of his neck.

His warm blood exploded in my mouth. The taste was beyond delicious. Coppery, with a delicate, honey-like sweetness and umami. In comparison, pig's blood suddenly tasted like dishwater. Watery and bland.

Dr. Kelley screamed and swatted at me. But I stayed latched onto him. As I drank, the fog receded around me.

I was so hungry and tired that all I wanted to do was to drink him dry. But I had to stay focused—this was far from over. With all of my will, I took two more gulps before I pushed him away. He staggered back a few steps, cradling his neck as blood dripped through his fingers. I had avoided the larger arteries, not wanting to kill him. Yet. I just wanted to get away from him.

Wiping his blood off my lips with the back of my hand, I shifted back to watch the shocked look on his face when he held his blood covered hands in front of him. Then I turned and ran as fast as I could toward the prison's front entrance.

"Fucking bitch!" Dr. Kelley screamed behind me, irate.

When I reached the large wooden door, I threw it open to see my mind library on the other side. Without hesitation, I dashed into it, and slammed the door shut behind me.

But I wasn't ready to go back to the real world. There was something I had to find first.

TWENTY-NINE

I sprinted down the arched hallway, heading deeper into the stacks. The skirt of my dress whipped wildly behind me as I ran past rows containing centuries of memories, encouraging me ahead. Back to the beginning.

"He's hurt. We have to go in and get him!"

"Don't interfere—just let it play out!"

The disembodied voices of Tristan and Paige boomed overhead, but I couldn't let it distract me.

I made a hard right at the dimly lit, claustrophobic row in the back. Slowing, I stopped to acknowledge the shelf Dr. Kelley and I usually visited—the one covered in dark, muted book spines. I brushed past them, moving further ahead. To the memories before RIDER. Before Theo had even become a vampire.

I reached out and grabbed the first text I saw—a chartreuse colored one—and flipped it open. The library faded, and I stood in the back of my father's study in the English manor house where I grew up.

Mahogany bookshelves lined the walls, and a desk on the left side of the room was covered in a heap of papers and quills. I smiled, thinking of the dining table in my apartment that routinely was under a similar, but more modern siege of a laptop and legal pads. It was one habit I had inherited from him.

My father sat at a small table on the right, playing chess with a man I recognized as one of his business partners. My five-year-old self peered through a crack in the study's door, spying on the room's occupants.

"Hmm, I think you finally have me beat this time," my father said, massaging the stubble on his face. Not wearing one of his wigs, he scratched his dark brunette hair and took a sip from the fluted gin glass in front of him, still not having yet made his move.

"Papa!" Bess exclaimed, bursting out of hiding and into the study. Running toward him, she slapped a large globe that sat near the entrance, sending the textured map into a dizzying spin within its wooden axis.

"Well, if it isn't Good Queen Bess!" my father said, lifting Bess into his lap. A nostalgic scent of tobacco and musk filled my nose.

"What's that?" Bess asked, meaning the game, but her finger pointed toward one specific chess piece.

"This," my father replied in a low voice, picking up the piece made of boxwood and lacquer. "Is the queen—just like you. She's the most powerful piece in the game."

He set the queen back on the board and leaned forward, whispering into Bess's ear. Bess excitedly grabbed the queen piece, moved it up the board, and took away the opponent's pawn, dutifully dropping it into Father's waiting palm.

"Check!" she shouted with glee.

My father's business partner did not look amused. But he was also a man I never recalled smiling, with a permanent scowl etched deep in his face underneath his expertly combed and curled wig. Leaning back in his chair, he thumbed at his bulbous, blush-tinged nose.

"We'll see about that," he scoffed. Returning to the board, he made a move that captured the queen with a pawn.

"Now watch this," my father whispered to Bess. He moved a

bishop up the board to capture the pawn, blocking in his opponent's king. "I believe that's mate, mate."

The business partner rolled his eyes and mumbled something under his breath before taking a long drink from his gin glass.

My father let loose one of his deep, rolling belly laughs as he bounced Bess on his knee, who squealed with delight.

I frowned and hurriedly flipped through more pages in the book. Brief scenes flew by of my mother teaching me how to braid my hair for the first time, laughing at a dumb joke my father said, to singing hymns with them at church.

Closing the book with a thud, I placed it back on the shelf with a disheartened sigh.

This wasn't what I was looking for. These memories were exactly how I remembered our family. Not at all like Theo had suggested to the contrary. Maybe he had been lying. And just when I had started to trust him again. Shit.

Then, out of the corner of my eye, I saw them.

They sat there expectantly, covered in cobwebs to my right. A small collection of books at the bottom of the shelf. Batting away the dust and frail webs, I tipped the edge of a deep red text out of its place and opened it, eager to see what was inside.

The library melted, and my childhood bedroom came into view. It was well-sized for the time, and larger than my brother's, which had always been a point of sibling contention between us growing up.

Floral chintz wallpaper climbed the walls, and tall wardrobes and a luxurious vanity covered in delicate glass-blown perfume bottles and make-up containers lined the walls. A plush, black-and-white striped upholstered stool sat tucked neatly underneath it.

But the main fixture in the room was the bed. A fourposter with a canopy constructed out of jewel-toned silks and finished in long, neat rows of hanging tassels.

While I expected to see Bess in the bed reading, or at the vanity brushing and pinning her hair, I found her on the floor instead. She looked older. This memory must have taken place only months before Theo was turned. Dressed in her bedgown, Bess was sobbing and furiously scrubbing at her face with a cloth that she rinsed in a bowl of red tinged water.

There was a knock at the bedroom door.

"I've retired for the night!" Bess called out.

"Bess, it's Theo. Amelia said you had an argument with Father... are you all right?"

Bess paused, cursing our servant's name under her breath. Coming to her feet, she opened the door a crack, gripping the cloth to one side of her face. With one eye, she looked Theo up and down. Despite the late evening hour, he was well dressed in his best clothes. A white ruffled shirt with gold cuff buttons, and matching linen breeches and waistcoat. He hadn't yet put on his jacket or wig.

"I thought you'd be at the public house by now," she said. Her tone was spiteful.

"I was on my way there... but Amelia said it was bad this time. I thought you might need this."

He held up a small glass jar with a lump of gray paste that had settled on the bottom, and a roll of cloth bandages.

Bess reached out to grab the medical supplies, but Theo pulled them away, just out of her reach. He wanted to talk.

"Fine." Bess sighed, rolling her eyes. She opened the door to let her brother slip in.

Bess sat on her vanity's stool as Theo pulled up another chair that had been against the wall. He meticulously set out the salve and bandages, and Bess lowered the cloth.

"It won't stop bleeding," she said, frustrated.

The entire left side of her face was swollen. Especially around her eye that was quickly closing shut and turning purple around the edges. A deep cut along her cheek brimmed with blood the moment she took the cloth away.

"You need to apply more pressure," Theo said calmly, taking the cloth and firmly pressing it against her face. "What happened?"

Bess looked down at the floor, but didn't say anything.

"He got upset, didn't he?" Theo finished. Bess closed her eyes and nodded. "Belt?"

She shook her head. "Boot. The buckle cut me."

"Ah," Theo said knowingly. "He's getting worse. Now not even the golden girl can escape his fits."

Bess slipped him an annoyed look. "I don't like it when you call me that. It's not true."

"What else would you call Mother and Father's favorite? The prized Abbott sibling who can do no wrong?" Theo glanced away. "But I guess that title goes to neither of us now."

Carefully removing the cloth, the gash had stopped bleeding. Theo got to work applying the salve and, finally, the bandage.

"Tomorrow it will look its worst. But it should start healing after that," he said when his work was finished.

"I hate it here," Bess said, gazing into the mirror beside her. She dabbed at the bandage with her fingers. "Mother said Jonathon Patton plans to court me at the Portsmouth Assembly next week. You know, the son of Thomas Patton, who runs the Patton Textile Supply Company? If that goes well—which it should—we'll be engaged soon. And when we're finally married, I'll get to leave this place. And Father's temper."

When she inspected the area around her eye, she winced. "I just hope I have enough powder to cover the dark mark I'll have on my face."

"Jonathon Patton?" Theo's face twisted, and he opened his mouth as if he were gagging. "Did Mother decide that before or after drinking her daily bottle of port?"

Bess, unperturbed, was busy brushing her hair in the mirror. "While his appearance and brilliance of mind is something...to be desired, being his wife has got to be better than living here." Her eyes flitted toward Theo. "It's not like you're doing anything to help."

If Theo had taken a wife by now and started his own household, I could have persuaded our parents to move in with them. With the notion that his wife could help prepare me to run a household of my own, while also providing a proper introduction to a new onslaught of eligible bachelors from her own family's connections. Bachelors that wouldn't include Jonathon Patton.

"I find it easier to avoid Father and his belt if I sleep in my room all day and move about at night," Theo replied stubbornly.

Bess put down her brush and looked at Theo empathetically. "Thank you. For the bandages and ointment."

"You're welcome. It won't be like this forever, I promise," he offered with a small smile.

My eyes filled, and when I blinked, cool liquid collected at the corners. Theo had been right about that.

In fact, Theo had been right all along. The realization hit me like a five-ton wrecking ball.

That in all of my two hundred and sixty-two years, I only looked at the *how*—but never the *why* to understand why Theo had been driven to do the things he did. It not only made me a bad family member.

It made me a bad academic.

Theo flipped as soon as he was turned because he was a ticking time bomb of resentment and anger. The fuse was lit the night Theo ingested vampire blood and died, and the rest was history.

Theo had been telling the truth. Whether it be by choice or from pain, I had just... forgotten.

The memory shivered. It was subtle, like a tiny earthquake, before it went still again. I looked around to see what caused it.

A firm hand grabbed my hair and pulled me backward.

I screamed as I fell out of the memory and onto the library's red carpet in an indignant heap of limbs and red silk.

And then I was moving.

Sliding across the carpet, the hand pulled me by my arm. I reached out desperately with the other, trying to grasp onto the wooden shelves as I passed by, but the hand jerked me away each time. When we reached the main hallway, two hands roughly grabbed my torso and lifted me to standing.

I was staring at Dr. Kelley. The wound on his neck had clotted, but he was looking a little worse for wear. His hair was flat and out of place in sections. Blood smeared down the side of his white collared shirt and his breathing was shallow and haggard.

"You must think you're something now, huh?" he sneered between gasps. "That you're special now because you're a vampire. Well, Miss Prescott, no one has been powerful enough to fight off my abilities. Most certainly not some half-breed excuse for a demon. Actually, that makes it easier. You don't need oxygen or food. Tristan came up with it first, but I'm really liking the idea of putting you in a box with a tiny window on the front—like a coffin—which seems appropriate. And whenever we need your memories, we'll drip just enough blood in there to awaken your mind, but that's it."

My lip twitched. But before I could move, Dr. Kelley's hot needle buried itself into my forehead. I screamed and fell to my knees, cradling my head in my hands. The pain was sharp and white-hot.

I had to focus.

I thought of Summer Coogan, laying in her bed—like a modern Sleeping Beauty as Mirza had said—with tubes going in and out of her body to keep her 'alive.' But there would be no prince to wake her up.

I thought of all the other Summer Coogans that Dr. Kelley might have wormed his way into like a cancer, destroying everything until there was nothing left but the husk of a body. And people thought vampires were leeches.

No more. This was all an illusion in *my* mind.

My mind. My rules. I was finally ready to take control for myself.

Concentrating on the pain, I pushed the needle-like feeling out of my mind. With a deep inhale, I shifted and gazed up at the doctor through amber eyes.

"No more pain and no more boxes," I growled, coming to my feet.

Dr. Kelley frowned, and the sharp tip of the needle bored into my head again.

Not this time. I rushed toward him, pulled back my arm and punched him square in the face. The pain in my head subsided in an instant. When his head snapped back, I grabbed onto the hair on the back of his head and swiveled it in front of my monstrous face. In that moment, I hoped I looked just like the drawing on the Top Ten Chart. I wanted his full attention.

His eyes rolled backward, and I shook his head until he focused on me again. A pang of fear released from his body. I liked the smell. Pungent and slightly saccharine.

"This is for Summer—I hope this hurts all the way to Hell!" I screamed in his face.

My vampire mind rose to the surface. Furious and hungry. I had been keeping her at bay, scared of what she represented within me. But this time, I stepped away and let her take control.

Wrenching his head to the side, I bit down into his neck again. This time aiming straight for the carotid artery. The feeling of biting into the soft flesh of his neck was absolutely euphoric, and Dr. Kelley's blood erupted into my mouth with shocking force. Like drinking from a fire hose.

As I drank from him, my large, towering library faded and the werewolf cage in the basement of a bewitched house in Georgetown solidified around me. Back in reality, I had broken free from the chair and was fangs-deep in Dr. Kelley's neck. And somehow, through it all, I still wore the crimson dress.

The doctor was dying now, cradled in my grasp as I remained

crouched over him. I could hear his heart beat slowing as I drank the last dregs of blood left in him.

Out of the corner of my eye, Charlotte and Theo were outside the cage. Charlotte grabbed the cage's lock, and with a single jolt of electricity from her palms, the locking mechanism snapped open. She swung open the gate and they both rushed in.

With a loud gasp, I detached from Dr. Kelley's neck and dropped his body. It collapsed to the floor in an unnatural position.

I ran to Theo and wrapped my arms around him.

"It's okay, it's over now. He can't hurt you ever again," he said, his lips moving over my shoulder.

I sobbed over him in big, uncontrollable gasps. Not just from guilt, or relief, or fear (I mean, I just ate someone), but something in between.

"Theo, I saw it," I whispered to him. "I went back and saw what happened before. You were right." I wanted to apologize for so many things in that moment—for being a terrible sister, for blaming him for everything for so long. But my mind was still reeling, and Dr. Kelley's warm blood was pumping through my veins like adrenaline. All I managed to get out was, "I'm sorry I didn't believe you—I'm sorry I didn't remember."

"It's okay," Theo said back. "I know why you didn't."

"Theo," I said between a fit of sobs. "I—I forgive you."

The destruction he wrought as a vampire was not justified, but I understood it now. I also understood that he was no longer the vampire whose picture graced the Top Ten Charts with cold, malicious eyes. He was kind, and patient, and disciplined. He was my brother.

At my last three words, Theo squeezed me tighter. "Thank you," he breathed, relieved.

It felt strange. We had never been the touchy-feely kind of family in our human lives. And cold vampire hugs didn't feel the same as warm human ones. But it was undeniably cathartic.

Breaking from our embrace, I wiped my eyes and looked around the basement, a little confused. "How did you guys get in here?"

Across the basement, Tristan moaned, slowly getting to his hands and knees. He was a few feet away from Paige, who was sitting on the blue couch with her hands and mouth bound with bands of electricity.

I looked at Charlotte, who smiled and waved her many-ringed fingers. "Apparently, I'm able to channel all the clarity I need when my friends are in danger. Oh, and you should have *seen* Tristan's face when Theo went after him. When you bit that Kelley guy and Tristan grabbed a stake and came toward you, Theo got this crazy look in his eyes and just picked him up and tossed him across the room. It was *great*."

Theo pulled out what I assumed was Tristan's stake out of his back pocket and twirled it in his fingers with a smirk.

I would have laughed, but a loud click echoed through the basement. I turned around to see Tristan pointing a crossbow loaded with a wooden arrow at my chest.

"Shut up!" He snapped at Charlotte before narrowing his eyes at me. "Kelley always seemed a little overzealous with his powers. But at RIDER, there's more than one way to get what we need from you. The only way you're getting out of here is with me, or as a pile of ash in a dustpan."

It had been a very, very long night and Tristan's fervent need for control was becoming annoying and tiresome at this point.

I took two slow paces toward him as his shaking hand tried to steady the crossbow. The smell of fear billowed off of him in large, rolling waves. It made my mouth water. Then, before he could even blink, I rushed toward him, swatted the weapon out of his hand and lifted him up by his throat with a clawed hand. The tips of his expensive leather shoes dangled above the concrete floor.

"Zoey, put him down. We can leave without needing to harm him," Theo said behind me.

Why would I want to do that? For years, I had trusted Tristan and he used that trust to exploit me. I was never a person in his eyes, just a means to an end. The demon in me wanted him to suffer for that, and I couldn't have agreed more.

"I wish you could see yourself now. The monster you've become, just like your disgusting brother. Your human self would be so disappointed." Tristan choked out stringy bits of spittle as his head bobbed over my grasp.

Blood and fury! Blood and fury! Blood and fury! My mind chanted. I snarled.

"Drop him. Now!" Theo ordered, his voice stern and steady.

My body ached to comply. The hand I held him with twitched, but I refused to let go. My sire's command wound itself through me, like an invisible hand closing around my spine. It screamed in my ear for obedience until I became nauseous.

But I stood my ground, resisting the urge to give in. After a few moments, it subsided to just barely a whisper that I could shake off.

"No," I said defiant, my gaze unmoving from Tristan's wide eyes. I hoped it wouldn't be long before he pissed himself.

"Your desire for vengeance is understandable," a baritone voice said to my right.

I froze. Augustine.

If my heart still beat, I imagined it would have skipped one at the sound of his voice. I wanted to turn and look at him, to have him help me figure out what to do, but I didn't want him to see my face. My Other Face, covered in tears and the blood of a dead man. The face of a vampire. A monster.

"He hurt you and betrayed you," Augustine continued. "Like I betrayed you."

I slowly turned to look at him, his confession had caught me off-guard. Augustine stood at the bottom of the stairs with a team of armored enforcement agents gathered behind him. The supposed cavalry, but I was not optimistic.

His gaze softened when our eyes met. Like he could see the small, uncertain girl hidden underneath the demonic exterior.

"I'm not proud of what happened back then. I was selfish and scared of the resentment that might have grown between us. I should have said this years ago: I'm sorry."

I opened my mouth to speak. Something elegant and sincere, but the only thing that squeaked out was, "Augustine, I..." Even as a vampire, he left me speechless.

"And you have every right to tear Mr. Campbell's throat out." Augustine continued. "He took advantage of your kindness and misused the organization's funds and resources for his own personal gain and at the expense of yours. And if you choose to tear him to pieces—I won't stop you. Honestly, I'd do the same in your position, even as a human."

"Augustine—what the fuck?" Tristan shouted in my grip.

"But doing so will only provide momentary justice. If you let us take him into custody, he'll go in front of the RIDER tribunal, where he'll be tried for his crimes and properly sentenced. And believe me when I say his punishment will be far worse than any you could inflict."

I tilted my head, mulling over Augustine's offer as he clasped his hands in front of him, awaiting my decision. A fate worse than death by a vampire was definitely intriguing.

But as I looked at Augustine, I realized that I finally saw him for who he was. A man. A man that at one time I loved and who had loved me. But he had changed, and for the first time, so had I. Call it my cold, unbeating heart at work, but I no longer felt a burning longing for what we had together.

In my hesitation, Tristan squirmed and fell out of my grasp. I reached out to grab at him, but missed. The fingertips on my right hand scratched the side of his face. He grunted in pain and stumbled toward the safety of Augustine and the RIDER agents, cradling his face in his hands.

When he drew his hands away, I saw I had etched four deep

claw marks on the left side of his face, barely missing his eye. Blood beaded to the surface, and he instinctively pressed the sleeve of his blazer to his face.

Augustine nodded to the agent next to him, who pulled out a pair of handcuffs and quickly cuffed Tristan's hands behind his back. Tristan scoffed and protested, but the agent's third arm reached out to restrain him so he could finish.

"Don't worry, Mr. Campbell, we have a first aid kit in the van to clean that up," the agent said amicably.

Augustine dismissed the agent, who walked Tristan up the stairs and into the main part of The House.

"I know it might not feel like it now, but you made the right choice, Zoey," Augustine said.

Eyeing the other agents, with their belts full of aerosol holy water and wooden stakes, I shifted to my human face. Not that I looked any less jarring, with blood smeared all over my mouth.

"What's going to happen to me? To us?" I asked, motioning to Theo.

Being what we were, we wouldn't last long in RIDER's custody. Physically or mentally.

"I think we both know you can't come back to RIDER now," Augustine replied with a pained sigh. "But I can do my best to get you off the Top Ten Chart. Theo too. Just don't give us a reason to put either of you back on there."

I bit my lip and nodded. I suddenly thought of my apartment, and who might inherit it. Hoping it would be someone like Ellie or Mirza and definitely not someone like Augustine's newly hired daughter, Daphne. For her own sake, in case someone Gifted could actually make the walls talk.

"I think it's time for us to go," Theo said to me as he moved toward the basement's back door.

With one last sweeping look, I bid goodbye to Augustine and my old life that he represented. Charlotte, still standing in the garden view Werewolf Airbnb, gestured and mouthed, "I'll call you."

"Where did you get that dress from?" my brother asked when I caught up to him.

"Long story. I'll tell you after I spend the next week sleeping in my makeshift coffin," I replied with a yawn, already feeling the sun's ascent.

"See? I knew you'd like the bathtub," Theo replied, sounding vindicated.

At the back of the basement, Theo opened the door, and we slipped out into the pre-dawn morning.

I didn't look back.

THIRTY

Three Months Later

"So sorry I'm late, Zo," Mirza said, hurriedly approaching the table I had saved for us. He slid into the chair across from me with a huff and ran a hand through his wild mop of dark wavy hair. Despite the sleek, all-black suit and shirt he wore, his hair refused to be tamed. "I'm still getting used to the LA traffic. Honestly, how is it worse than the R Train?"

"Oh, don't worry about it. At least your coffee's still cold," I said brightly, pushing forward the untouched iced coffee on the table. It had been a few weeks since we'd caught up, and I was excited to see his familiar face.

Mirza eyed the cup suspiciously. "Is it...?" he asked, as if afraid to touch it.

"Regular iced coffee with oat milk. Norm style."

He lifted the cup to his lips but paused reluctantly. Then, closing his eyes, he took a slow, cautious sip. His body instantly relaxed and his eyes snapped open, relieved.

"Thank god. I'm always afraid I'll accidentally pick up the wrong order here. But I know how much you love this place."

"I do," I said with a smile before taking a sip from my own cup, a lavender-infused rabbit's blood latte. Rabbit blood had quickly become my new favorite. The latte's lavender floral notes mixed with the subtle earthiness of the rabbit and added zing of espresso was absolute perfection.

"How are Mango and Salsa? Are they settling in okay after the move?" I asked. From what I'd heard, goblins often found conventional travel traumatizing.

Mirza groaned and sat back in his chair. "They definitely like the weather and the view of the park, but the two of them tried to conjure not one, but two portals in the living room when I was getting ready tonight. Thankfully, the sitter I found on that Familiar services app came and said they could handle it."

We were at Sanguine, Los Angeles's über trendy blood bar conveniently located under many of the city's Alfred Coffee cafes, where I was enjoying breakfast and Mirza was working on gaining his second wind. Coordinating with its upstairs neighbor, the cafe's windowless interior was decorated with subway tile, lots of plants, and a red neon sign on the back wall that spelled out, "*But First, Blood*" in cursive.

While the other patrons around us were mostly supernatural, I pointed out the couple of humans chatting to a group of faeries two tables away from us (much to Mirza's relief). Sanguine had a strict policy of animal-only sourced bloods and vegan milks. Apparently, in LA, drinking non-human blood was all the rage amongst fellow bloodsuckers. Go figure.

Suffice to say, much had happened since the events in the basement of The House.

First, there were the negotiations. Formal, diplomatic, and heavily documented. I signed the many paged documents that confirmed my departure from RIDER, where it explicitly stated that employment and any associated benefits had terminated at the time of my death and did not apply to my resurrection or current status as undead.

True to his word, Augustine removed Theo and me from both the North American and European Vampire Top Ten Charts. Under the strict stipulation that any human deaths resulting from blood loss that could be traced back to even a hair on either of our heads would result in immediate reinstatement on RIDER's Big Bad radar. But no matter how many times I asked, Augustine refused to tell me what fate the tribunal had decided for Tristan.

Charlotte did call. Theo, specifically, to announce that she'd resigned from her position as The House's resident and RIDER's witchcraft relations liaison, passing the position down to one of her many cousins. One her family assured didn't actively practice Black Magic or have grand delusions of controlling an immortal-run world.

She moved back to LA to be closer to her family and also to start her Werewolf Airbnb venture after securing a grant and (much needed) oversight from RIDER. And since I had instantly become homeless and Theo had been on the run for decades, she encouraged us to do the same. Moving as far west from RIDER as the country allowed for a fresh start seemed like the best option.

A month later, Mirza followed in our footsteps. The combination of saving the world from an internal work conspiracy and Jason ending their two-year relationship to 'find himself' by backpacking through Peru had been enough to throw him into a full-blown quarter-life crisis. One phone call half-suggesting he come out to California later, Mirza packed up both cat-goblins, boarded a plane, and found an apartment in Echo Park. He now worked as a technician at a very mundane, and not the least bit supernatural, gene-therapy start-up.

Luke and Olivia were still in DC finishing their programs, but promised to visit as early as the upcoming winter break. Charlotte had already committed me to three dinners and a few happy hours when that would happen, much to my concealed chagrin. And Matt Riley not only got to keep his job, but received a promotion for his cross-departmental collaboration during a crisis.

"So what's new with Miss Zoey Elizabeth Abbott these days?" Mirza teased through a grin.

The Prescott surname lost its luster after leaving RIDER. Also, the change back to my old one just seemed more fitting now.

As a creature, supernatural society was new and exciting—especially in a new city. It was a world of its own. Creatures no longer lived on the fringes, but were carefully tucked within it. Even Theo still had trouble adjusting, having lived on the outskirts for so long.

"Still trying to get used to everything. I mean, all this stuff is great," I said, gesturing around to the buzzing supernatural café. "But I still need to work on blending in amongst Normals. I thought I was pretty human-passing, but the witch who runs the occult bookstore in our neighborhood says I still move too quickly when I get excited, and I need to work on my eye contact. I've been trying to blink more often, but it's exhausting to remember *all* the time."

"Pssh. Don't worry about it, you look great and that stuff will come with time," Mirza dismissed with the wave of his hand. "Plus, most Normals are so oblivious these days. Myself included."

"Thanks," I said with a laugh. "So, are you excited for the Winter Solstice party tonight?"

"Um, I think that's more of a question for you since Charlotte said it's going to be *your* official debut to the LA supernatural society. Considering it's the—"

"'Longest and biggest night of the year for creatures,'" I finished in a mocking tone. For the past week, I had heard little other than that.

Naturally, Charlotte was hosting something at her new house for the holiday, but I still did not know what an 'official debut' entailed and was weary at the thought of anything that involved formal custom or being ogled at. As a vampire, I no longer had the patience for either.

"But that's not the entire reason for the party," I added. If it were, then I definitely wouldn't be going. All that attention on me? No, thank you.

"Well, whatever it turns out to be, I think it'd be good for you. I'm sure you'll meet tons of new creatures who can help you adjust to life here. It's definitely not New York or RID—" Mirza began to say, but with a burst of supernatural speed, I lurched forward and clapped my hand over his mouth before he could finish. His green eyes went wide.

"Don't say the 'R' word here!" I hissed in a low voice. I glanced around to see if anyone else had heard the faux pas. Only a minotaur in a dark grey business suit sipping from an espresso cup behind us quirked a suspicious eyebrow in our direction. But thankfully, no one else seemed to notice.

"My bad, I forgot. Totally different audience here than... before," Mirza apologized after I lowered myself back into my seat. He was right. RIDER always had its fair share of colorful creatures walking its halls, but those on the outside often viewed the organization's acronym as a dirty word.

"It's okay. It's just... I really want to try to make this whole undead thing work," I said. Tracing Sanguine's elaborate calligraphic 'S' logo embossed on the sleeve of my cup with a finger, I paused. "As best as it can. I just don't want the shadow of our former employer—or my brother's reputation—to make it any harder."

"Understandable," Mirza said, sloshing the ice around in his now half-empty cup. "Speaking of which, how is the vampire formerly known as Number Seven?"

I took another sip from my drink and shrugged. "Theo's Theo. Word has gotten around about his amateur detective skills, so he's started taking on some consulting jobs around town. He seems to like it, from what he's told me—says it gives him purpose. Apparently he's working on something for the Santa Monica mer-colony tonight before the party."

Mirza chuckled. "*If* he makes it to the party. You know how excited merfolk can be when there's a pair of legs around. They'll talk Theo's ears off, showing him all their trinkets for the next millennia if he's not careful."

I snorted a puff of laughter at the thought (merpeople were incredibly curious and loved collecting fallen items from the surface), then sat up straight as another popped into my mind. "Oh! I've been wanting to tell you—I'm officially going apartment hunting tomorrow!" I said, with a wide smile.

It was all I could think about now that the paperwork had cleared. A few weeks ago, I had received a letter in an envelope sealed with red wax and an imprint of the RIDER logo. Inside was a handwritten note—from Diana of all people—thanking me for my *countless years of distinguished service to studying life's mysteries.* And as if that hadn't been shocking enough, there was also a copy of a bank statement with a generous sum of money. My retirement.

"Moving already? Didn't you guys just move in a few months ago?"

It was Theo's idea to settle in Westwood, not mine. But until my retirement funds had cleared with the bank, my leverage on neighborhood preference was minimal, if not completely non-existent.

"Living with Theo is fine. But Westwood is so lame. The only reason Theo enjoys living there is because it's quiet and private. I want to be where the action is. Somewhere cool and exciting. I was thinking WeHo or maybe even near you in Silver Lake."

Despite my enthusiasm, Mirza looked unimpressed. "And living in a penthouse apartment in Los Angeles isn't exciting enough? I don't know, it just doesn't sound like the best idea."

My mouth opened to protest, but he calmly put a hand up to silence me. I allowed it, but not without shooting him an annoyed glare first.

"Listen, Zo, even though there are still times when Theo scares the piss out of me, he's a good man and a smart vampire. You should stick with him. He's your older brother, after all. And aren't you still too young to be out on your own?"

Unreal. I rolled my eyes. "Mirza, you're joking, right? Or at least know how ridiculous that sounds?"

"You know what I mean. By vampire standards. Don't young vampires need to hang out with their sires for a certain amount of time? You know, to learn all your secret handshakes or whatever?"

"Technically, yes, vampires are considered fledglings for the first five years. But for the record; there are no secret handshakes. And, as you can see, I'm on my own tonight. No security detail either. Plus, it's not like I'm moving halfway across the country. We'll still be in the same city."

No longer a floundering newbie, I thought I was adjusting well to both my new form and city. It still felt strange to leave the apartment on my own at times. The smallest things—like window shopping in a boutique or picking up our weekly order from the butcher—were thrilling new adventures. Not without a flurry of check-in texts from Theo, of course.

Mirza shook his head and smirked. "Well, consider me shook. You're becoming quite the modern, independent vampiress. Just don't get in over your head."

———

The car service ordered to Charlotte's house through the Familiar Services app was an uneventful ride. Driven by a selkie, his large, thick grey fur coat was carefully folded in the front passenger seat. It looked out of place, given the eighty-degree weather.

The car careened and swayed, its headlights cutting through the dark as we worked our way up through the winding Holly-wood Hills. Wedged in the middle of the backseat, I clung to Mirza and Theo, trying my best to maintain my balance as I bounced around. My preternatural stability and seatbelt were no match for the shifter's driving.

Eventually, we passed the wrought-iron gate, then down the long, curving driveway to the 1920s Spanish-styled house with a swimming pool in the backyard.

The front door was open, and a commotion of excited chatter and laughter wafted out of it and into the warm night. But Theo and I had to wait as Mirza wormed his way through the crowds to find Charlotte for an invitation inside.

"You know, we could have beaten the crowd if we'd left sooner," Theo said to me with a frown. In his black suit and crisp white shirt, he impatiently shifted his weight from foot to foot, looking chic but unamused.

I rolled my eyes and raked my fingers through my hair. "Is this about the iPad again?"

After the café, Mirza had come over to the apartment to pre-game. And even though Theo had made it back on time, despite LA traffic and the mer-colony's pleading that he stay longer to view their extensive fidget spinner collection, I had ultimately delayed everyone by taking longer than expected to get ready. But as everyone kept telling me, it was *my* debut, wasn't it?

"It's unnatural. Just because you found a loophole doesn't mean there isn't a good reason—probably a biological one—why we can't use mirrors," he replied, keeping his tone low and even.

I sighed, exhaling the air through my mouth in a wordless huff. Theo was definitely old school when it came to vampire living and did not like or approve of the digital workarounds that captured our image in ways traditional mirrors could not. The front-facing camera of the iPad I used to apply my make-up was public enemy number one.

But as much as it embarrassed me to admit, there was a thread of truth in his theory—one I'd been trying to ignore. Over the past few months, I had spent a significant amount of time alone in my room inspecting what my Other Face looked like. To the point where Theo had used the word 'unhealthy' and routinely banged on my bedroom door if he suspected I were spending countless hours in front of it. While my visage was undeniably vampire, it (thankfully) did not resemble the monstrous caricature sketch from the Top Ten Chart.

"Ah! You made it! Come in, come in!" Charlotte squealed when she saw us, ending the squabble on the subject, but not the war.

Charlotte wore a silver sequin jumpsuit that shimmered so brightly when she moved, it made me wonder if she had bewitched it.

Taking both of my hands into her warm ones, she gave me a full look up and down. I still didn't like the feeling of their warmth and her quick beating pulse within them. But I had learned to smile politely and suffer through, hoping the interaction would end quickly so I could have my cold hands back to myself.

"You look amazing. But of course you do—my witch's sense *knew* that dress was made for you," she said.

Earlier in the evening, Charlotte had sent over a large white box with an expertly tied red velvet bow. Inside was a long, sheer Gucci gown with delicate, billowy bishop's sleeves and high slits up the side of each leg. A separate black satin romper with a sweetheart neckline came with it to be worn underneath. It fit me perfectly and I turned from side to side to show it off.

"Thank you. I love it, especially the purse. But, it's just..." I couldn't conceal the sudden anxiety in my voice as I turned the crossbody clutch she had also sent over in my hands. It was a rhinestone mosaic of bright red lips with fangs and while I loved it, I was about to enter a party filled with other supernatural creatures, which I had never done before. "What if people think it's lame—or that I'm lame?"

"Um, no," Charlotte said, contorting her face as if she had tasted something bitter. "First of all, it's a *look*. And second, it's your debut—if anyone says anything to the contrary, I'll hex them with bad karma. They won't be able to get a table at Nobu for the next decade."

I smiled and laughed. Having a witch as a friend definitely had its perks.

"We brought you this," my brother said, holding out a bottle of red wine.

"Oh, thank you! I'm sure you've been around long enough to know all the best vintages." Accepting the bottle with both hands, she presented her cheek to Theo, who kissed it in greeting.

The two definitely had chemistry when they were together. But when I'd asked if they'd ever consider the other as more than just a friend, each one had scoffed at the idea, having sworn off relationships with the other's kind years ago. Time would tell. Mirza and I also had a running bet with fifty dollars on the line.

"Please, help yourselves!" Charlotte motioned to the counters and tables filled with food and drink as we passed through the kitchen toward the main living area.

The house was decorated in a coastal boho-chic; with cream-colored furniture, bold oriental rugs, and many a fiddle-leaf fig scattered throughout. The living room's arched doorways that led to the backyard were open, allowing the sea-scented breeze from the west to blow in. All kinds of creatures, and a few humans in formal attire crowded the space, and my senses instantly went into overdrive trying to take it all in.

An icy hand touched my shoulder.

"Don't worry, you'll be fine," Theo said to me in a voice low enough so that only we could hear. Rubbing my sweating palms together, I replied with a rueful half-smile, hoping he was right.

"There's no shortage of champagne," Charlotte continued on her mini tour. "Oh, and Ursula made some mulled blood." She pointed to a steaming crock pot in the kitchen, the source of the spiced, coppery sweet scent I noticed when we had first walked in. "I think she said it was duck."

A doe-eyed vampire with ice blonde hair styled in long, rolling curls underneath a beret, and for all intents and purposes looked to be in her early thirties, popped her head up from the group she was talking to at the mention of her name.

"It's venison, actually!" Ursula called out in a sing-song Brummie British accent.

"Mmm, deer blood. Yum!" Charlotte said to Theo and me, trying her best, but failing miserably, to mask the disgust in her voice.

"I'll catch you guys later," Mirza said, his eyes fixed on one area of the room. "I just spotted the incubus I've been Snapchatting with for the past week." He scurried into the immense crowd, grabbing two glasses of champagne and downing one of them in a gulp on his way.

A couple hours into the party, I sipped on mulled blood from a glass mug, trying to decide whether the decorative orange slice added to the flavor or not. My brother had abandoned me with three of Charlotte's gossipy witch friends who were talking endlessly about another friend's fiancé.

"Oh my goddess, and did you see who he follows on Instagram?" one gushed to the group.

"Yes!" hissed another. "Mostly models. And all part siren or nymph. Definitely a red flag."

"If I were her, I'd threaten to give back the ring if he didn't permanently delete the app," said the third. The other two nodded in agreement.

The catty chatter cycled its way through the three witches about all their mutual friends that were conveniently absent from the party. I remained silent, sipping and tapping on the mug's glass with a fingernail, and offering a friendly look when the witches took turns to regard me with an uneasy stare, followed by a forced, tight-lipped smile.

With blood in my mouth, resisting the urge to shift was difficult. But I willed myself not to so as to not fuel their fantasy that at any moment I was about to pounce on unsuspecting party guests in a bloodthirsty rage.

"There you are! Girl, it's showtime."

Saved by Charlotte. I sighed relief and bid goodbye to the trio who replied with the most disingenuous chorus of "It was so nice to meet you!"s I'd ever heard. The next twenty minutes of their conversation would undoubtedly be about me.

"Sorry you got stranded with Double, Toil, and Trouble," Charlotte said as we worked our way through the crowd. "My parents made me invite them. But now the fun can really begin." She smiled, wide and excited.

Wheeling me to the front of her living room, she plucked the mug from my grasp and thrust a glass of champagne in its place. Then, taking her place to stand next to me, she snapped her fingers overhead. The noise somehow sounded much louder than expected.

"Attention! Attention!" she announced over the crowd that quickly quieted. "First, thank you all for coming. As you know, December 21st is the longest and biggest night of celebration for us and I'm just so excited to spend it with all of you this year."

"We knew you wouldn't stay on the East Coast for long!" a werewolf shouted from the crowd.

"Facts! You know I've always been a Cali girl." Charlotte laughed and raised her glass. "Anyway, I also wanted to introduce you to someone who's become a dear friend of mine and has been through it all. I mean, she literally took a bullet. She's new in town and about to be the hottest thing with fangs LA has ever seen! Everyone give a warm welcome to Zoey Pres—I mean Zoey Abbott!"

As I stood in front of the crowd, I no longer had body heat to flush my cheeks with warmth, but I could still feel the stomach plunging rush of anxiety that usually came with it. And I waited in anticipation for the dreadful sensation to set in.

But this time it was different. I felt calm. Even a little excited when Charlotte raised her glass and I clinked mine against it. Instead of wanting to hide from the cheering, clapping crowd, I welcomed the attention, feeling confident as I allowed myself to enjoy the warmth and energy that radiated from it. I ignored the witch trio in the back, who collectively scowled through forced claps.

My eyes grazed the room until they landed on Mirza, who clapped and waved exuberantly to me next to a handsome incubus.

Theo was standing in the back. He smiled and gave me a single nod, tipping his champagne glass in my direction when our gaze met. He looked happy.

Showers of sparks suddenly rained from the air as spell casters in the crowd, led by Charlotte, created a miniature indoor fireworks display. I instinctively dodged them as they came down around me, the memory of singed hair and skin still fresh in my mind. But when one inadvertently landed on my arm, it was as cool as a snowflake.

I looked at Charlotte with shocked excitement, speechless at the whimsical (and non-combustible) sight.

"You can thank Augustine for teaching me that trick," she whispered to me. "So many Zoom sessions over the past few months, but they finally paid off."

Joy pushed my instincts aside and I wrapped my arms around her in a bear hug.

———

Several hours later, the party was still going strong, but I had migrated to the roof deck for a bit of social relief. Since Charlotte's announcement, it seemed like I met and shook hands, paws, and even hooves with every creature at the party. I was exhausted.

The roof was much more sparse, providing a relaxing reprieve with a small lounge area of furniture around a lit fireplace and soft music wafting through the outdoor speakers.

Sitting on the roof's edge, I dangled my legs below with the city of Los Angeles spread out before me. An expanse of shimmering lights in the darkness. What had Charlotte said? *Each light represents a person's dream of making it in this city.*

I leaned back, closed my eyes and made an audible sigh, drinking up the rays of the waxing half-moon overhead.

"Hey new vamp!"

My eyes snapped open to see that Ursula, and another female vampire—this one with raven-colored hair cropped short, had joined on the ledge a few yards down.

"Chloe, right?"

"It's Zoey."

"Zoey. Cool. I'm Ursula." She motioned to the vampire next to her. "This is Virginia. If you're interested, us and a few other vamps head out to Cabrillo Beach on nights of the full moon. Next one's in a few days. It's a really fun time. You should join us."

Moon bathing on the beach? Abso-fucking-lutely. Much better than lying out on my apartment's rooftop where my relaxation was constantly interrupted by drunk, obnoxious humans after a night out.

But I had to play it cool. I had been desperate to make friends with other vampires despite Theo's cautious reservations to keep to ourselves.

"Definitely. Count me in," I replied casually. Inside, I was bursting with excitement.

"Think you could convince your brother to come too?" Ursula smirked, and her gaze ticked behind me.

I followed it to see Theo deep in conversation with a wispy, fae-looking woman with sharp facial features and pointed ears that stuck out from her waist-long, wavy blonde hair.

"Oh, that won't be a problem," I said with a smile.

"Great Babes! We're going to go inside to grab another drink. See you soon then!"

And with the nimbleness of a cat and the fearlessness of an Olympic gymnast, Ursula and Virginia stepped off the edge of the roof. They landed on the grassy backyard below without a sound and walked back through one of the arched doorways into the living room.

"So you're the new dead thing in town that everyone's been talking about?" an unfamiliar male voice said behind me.

I sighed. I was so over small talk.

Making a pact with myself to give the conversation five minutes before ordering a ride home—with or without Theo and Mirza—I put on my best smile and turned around.

Behind me was a human-looking demon in his twenties. Roughly six-feet tall, he had muscular arms and shoulders that flowed down into a slender torso and then into toned legs beneath his dark suit. His brown wavy hair was cut short at the nape, but it flopped haphazardly in front of his face, just above his strong, rectangular-shaped jawline. His light brown eyes flitted around, looking me up and down with a curious expression.

Of course, what gave him away as a demon, and a Tealer one at that, were the red-tinted devil-like horns that protruded from his forehead and similarly colored spade-tipped tail that waved passively behind him from underneath the vent of his suit jacket.

He smiled. A warm, and almost nervous expression on his face. He was cute, actually. *Very* cute. And if I remembered correctly, Tealers were known for their slow aging. One year physically for every ten years. By the look of him, we were both eighteenth century babies. This suddenly made things very interesting.

I raised my brow in a nonverbal '*Yes?*'

His face twisted apologetically. "I'm sorry. Is that not a politically correct statement? On my way up here I was trying to think of something witty, but um... would you like another drink?"

His accent was distinctly American, but the way he drew out vowels and softened the consonants in his speech made him sound posh. Like he'd spent a lot of time in Europe.

There were two glasses of champagne in his hands. Freshly poured, they had twin lids of foam and hearty streams of bubbles flowing to the top.

"Thanks," I said, accepting a glass and taking a sip. "And no, it's not—at least I don't think it is. It's an accurate statement. But I'm still a little new to all of this. I would just stay away from words like 'bloodsucker' and 'leech.'"

I was rambling. Dammit. He meant it as a compliment. I should have just accepted it as that.

"Newly sired with all that vampire grace and charm? Could've fooled me. I'm Max, by the way." He extended his hand.

I knew it was impossible, but I swore my dead heart skipped a beat.

"Zoey," I replied, reaching out and shaking it.

"I know. One hell of an introduction earlier, too," Max said, taking a sip of champagne.

"Oh, that," I said. My eyes shot open wide, embarrassed. "That was all Charlotte's idea, not mine."

"Well, I'm glad she did. Do you also live out here in the hills?"

"No. My brother and I are renting an apartment in Westwood. It's temporary. I'm moving soon. Getting my own place in an area that's more my style. Westwood is not it." I didn't want him to think I was a complete loser.

"That's a shame," Max said, frowning. "We're practically neighbors. I live in Brentwood. I agree, it's not as trendy as other parts of LA. But both areas cater to the privacy of us supernatural types."

My mouth popped open, and I frantically began to backpedal.

"Oh, well. It's not like I'm moving tomorrow. With us vampires, when we say things like 'soon,' it can be a very vague sense of the word."

"Good to hear. I guess we'll be seeing more of each other around the neighborhood then." Max grinned and locked eyes with me. There was an energetic playfulness behind them and I became lost in his gaze, not able to break away.

His smile was cheerful. Infectious too, because in the next moment I was grinning from ear to ear. Maybe living with Theo for just a few more months wouldn't be the worst thing if it increased my chances of running into Max again.

"Would you like to dance?"

"Um, sure," I replied, reluctant. I didn't think I had ever actually danced with someone as a vampire, and I wasn't sure how different it would be than before. What if I tripped over my preternatural limbs and fell?

But setting down my glass on the roof's edge, I accepted his hand. Here goes nothing.

Max led me to the middle of the roof where a few other couples, including my brother and the fae woman, were dancing.

He gently wrapped an arm around my back and took my hand in his to lead. His body was warm, and I could hear his heartbeat. It beat much more slowly, and the sensation didn't make me recoil as I usually did around warm-blooded creatures.

He led me in a waltz and we strode across the roof as the music swelled. Twirling me, the bottom of my dress flared out, and for a split-second I became weightless and unsupported before he reined me back into his chest to safety. I smiled and laughed and Max looked at me as if I were the only other person on the roof.

It was just like my dream from when I first became a vampire, dancing under the night sky with Augustine. Except I was dancing with someone new now—and a demon at that. My human self could never.

With the moon and her stars shining their energizing light above, and the city of lights stretched out in the valley below, I felt a freeing sense of clarity, peace, and belonging. Though I had already lived an unnaturally long life and my heart no longer beat inside my chest, tonight was the first time, in a long time, that I felt alive.

I left a lifetime back at RIDER, but my story was far from over. In fact, something told me this was just the beginning.

GET FREE DELETED SCENES, AND EXCLUSIVE RIDER CONTENT

I love connecting with my readers and giving them free stuff! Occasionally, I also send newsletters with details on new releases, special offers, giveaways, and other bits related to the RIDER series.

Sign up now, and I'll send you this **free stuff**:

1. Alternative endings and bonus scenes with author's notes
2. RIDER-verse FAQ
3. *Memories, Lies, and Other Binds* Spotify playlist

All you have to do is sign up at:
https://katyforakerwrites.com/vip

Enjoy this book? You can make a big difference!

Reviews are so powerful when it comes to getting attention for my books.

If you've enjoyed this book, I would be very grateful (and Charlotte would charm you with 100 years of good luck) if you could spend a few minutes leaving an honest review on the book's sales page.

Thanks so much!

ACKNOWLEDGMENTS

Wow. The fact that this book is out of my head (where it lived for years) and in your hands is crazy. But like with most achievements, many hands helped to shape and support this story into what it has become.

First, many thanks to Matt Randle who is an amazing writing critique partner and indulged me in all my discussions of the supernatural, no matter how bonkers. And of course thanks to Lindsay Kuberka who supplied the L2 Pool Club for such a serendipitous meeting of two aspiring authors, when I hadn't yet told anyone I had started writing again (and apologies now for never shutting up about it).

Thanks to my sister, Mel Foraker, who encouraged me to start writing again in the depths of the pandemic because "what's the worst thing that can happen?" The best was obviously being able to release this story to all of you.

Thanks to the immensely talented and creative women I've met through The Wing and especially my bunkmates in Cabin 37 during Camp No Man's Land. Your passions for writing and creating stories full of fun and whimsy reminded me that it wasn't too late to write my own. I am forever grateful for your kindness and inspiration.

A huge thank you to my lovely global group of beta readers who helped cultivate this story from that first draft which only now somewhat resembles the final: Alaina Dimmig, Dan Overheim, Eric Poffenberger, Andrea Shedler, Emily Landis, Nicole Ciaravella, Amy Fredrickson, Jessica Netzke, Emilie, J. Flowers-Olnowich, Jared Silveira, Christina Calvano, Fay Collins,

Samantha Jordan, Lucy D., and Emily Wright. All of you helped bring this story to new heights. And of course, my editors: Erin Bledsoe, and Kristin McTiernan (aka The Nonsense-Free Editor) for their great ideas, helping me find the right words, and pushing me to be a better writer (even when it was really really hard sometimes).

ABOUT THE AUTHOR

Katy Foraker is an American author, and fashion-loving fan-girl, who works as a CPA when she's not writing. She loves morning walks to Georgetown, bingeing early 2000's supernatural shows, local cafes, and buttery croissants. She lives in Washington, DC with her Maine Coon-mix cat, Lola.

Find out more at: katyforakerwrites.com

CPSIA information can be obtained
at www.ICGtesting.com
Printed in the USA
BVHW040220051022
648716BV00005B/106

9 781088 028315